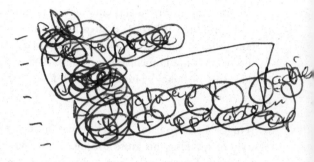

Acclaim for Kate Christensen's

THE EPICURE'S LAMENT

KATE CHRISTENSEN

THE EPICURE'S LAMENT

Kate Christensen is the author of the novels *In the Drink* and *Jeremy Thrane*. She lives in Brooklyn with her husband.

also by Kate Christensen

IN THE DRINK

JEREMY THRANE

the

EPICURE'S LAMENT

the

EPICURE'S LAMENT

A Novel

KATE CHRISTENSEN

Anchor Books
A Division of Random House, Inc.
New York

FIRST ANCHOR BOOKS EDITION, JANUARY 2005

All rights reserved under International and Pan-American Copyright Conventions.
Published in the United States by Anchor Books,
a division of Random House, Inc., New York, and simultaneously in Canada by
Random House of Canada Limited, Toronto.
Originally published in hardcover in the United States
by Doubleday, a division of Random House, Inc.,
New York, in 2004.

Anchor Books and colophon are registered trademarks
of Random House, Inc.

The Library of Congress has cataloged the Doubleday edition as follows:
Christensen, Kate.
The epicure's lament : a novel / Kate Christensen.—1st ed.
p. cm.
1. Hudson River Valley (N.Y. and N.J.)—Fiction.
2. Thromboangiitis obliterans—Patients—Fiction.
3. Suicidal behavior—Fiction. 4. Rich people—Fiction.
5. Recluses—Fiction. 6. Cookery—Fiction.
7. Smoking—Fiction. I. Title.
PS3553.H716O87   2004
813'.54—dc21
2003051503

Anchor ISBN: 978-0-385-72098-4

www.anchorbooks.com

Printed in the United States of America

for

⌒ **BEN LA FARGE** ⌒

"I shall see to it, if I can, that my death makes no statement that my life has not made already."

—MICHEL DE MONTAIGNE,
"THAT OUR ACTIONS SHOULD BE JUDGED BY OUR INTENTIONS"

FIRST NOTEBOOK

October 9, 2001—All the lonely people indeed. Whoever they are, I've never been one of them. The lack of other people is a balm. It's the absence of strain and stress. I understand monks and hermits, anyone who takes a vow of silence or lives in a far-flung cave. And I thought—hoped, rather—that I would live this way for the rest of my life, whatever time is left to me.

This morning I woke up, lit a cigarette as always. I remembered that Dennis was downstairs, and then instinctively I reached for my pen and rooted around for this old blank notebook, and here I still am, writing about myself with the date at the top of the page like a lovelorn teenage diarist with budding breasts and a zit she can't get rid of. Words stay neatly in the head during times of solitude, they don't jump out through the pen to land splat on the page. Knowing that Dennis is lurking down there makes me jumpy. I have a nasty feeling he's not leaving anytime soon. His presence has diverted my life from its natural course.

Here I am, a decaying forty-year-old man in his decaying childhood home at the ruined finale of a wasted life. My hand is stiff. My faculties are moribund. Outside, below my tower window, the Hudson River sparkles and glints with untoward goodwill, blue, placid, and untroubled today, but sure to change its mood. There it lies, and has lain all my life, always changing, always there, in all its mercurial quiddity.

The lascivious pleasure I derive from phrases such as "mercurial quiddity" might possibly be all that prevents me now from flinging myself downstairs to beat my brother about the face and neck with my bare hands, shouting invectives and heartfelt pleas to go away. I wish more than anything that Dennis had stayed where he belonged, across the river with his wife Marie and their spawn, the bony cantankerous second-grader Evie and the bubbly sexy kindergartner Isabelle. Girls: this generation of Whittier sperm seems to produce only girls. It's the end of our name and our line, unless they turn out to be lesbians who adopt children with their "wives" and call them Whittier. God fucking forbid.

It took me I don't know how long to write the above, and then I stared into space smoking and ruminating for half an hour at least. A shooting pain in my foot brought me back. Pain has become my chronic and intermittent link to the world, among other things—I refuse to take painkillers. The inherited puritan hidden deep inside my core is the only part of me that's satisfied at the retribution—I did the crime, I'll do the time—

maybe it's a Yankee diehard need to tough it out as long as I can. No parole, no halfway house. I'll eventually cave when it gets worse, in the months to come. Weeks to come.

Two nights ago, I was sitting on the large side veranda where I always sit, smoking and knocking back an occasional snort of whiskey and keeping my own counsel, when a car turned in at the driveway. I saw the headlights first and then the make: a Dodge Dart, which meant my brother. To the car was hitched a U-Haul trailer, which was clearly laden with belongings: the other prodigal son, returned to the roost.

He parked, turned off the engine, got out of the car, and stretched, one hand propping up the small of his back as if he'd driven hundreds of miles instead of just across the Hudson. Probably thinking himself unobserved, he let out a long, hard sigh.

"Well," I called. "If it isn't Dudley Doright."

His posture changed the instant he became aware that he was being watched: he stood erect, his long, handsome, abundantly haired head flung back. "Hugo!" he snapped manfully. "Hello!"

"I see you've brought gifts."

He came up to the porch and thumped me on the back in a sort of stilted hug. "Not gifts," he said. "My worldly possessions."

"She kicked you out?"

Something passed over his face, a weary premonition of the explaining he was going to have to do in the near future of his presumed marital failure, but he squelched it and said, "Marie has asked me to live elsewhere for a while, yes."

"You're joking."

Again I saw the effort it took for him to say in that bluff and seemingly easy way, "The truth is, it's about time. This has been a long time coming. It's sort of a relief, I have to admit. Is that whiskey you're drinking?"

I offered him the bottle, which he eyed without touching.

I'm sure he suspects that I only brush my teeth once or twice a year, which as a matter of fact is not the case.

"I'd better not just yet," he said.

"All righty then," I said. "Suit yourself." I tipped some more into my mouth.

"I'll carry some things inside first," he said. "Then I'll be very glad to join you in that drink. You're still in the tower room?"

"Still and forever."

"I'll take Grandma's old room then. At least it has its own bathroom. You have to go all the way through to the landing to get to the nearest one from the tower."

"I piss into a pitcher in cases of great urgency and dump it out on the lawn beneath my window," I remarked pleasantly, but he had already bounded down the steps. I watched my brother make several trips from U-Haul to house without offering to help him. Let him ask if he wanted help. *"Mi casa es su casa,"* I said to the empty veranda. "No matter how much I may wish otherwise."

He bounded back out to the veranda from the foyer with a glass in his hand. He extended it and said, "All right, that's that. All squared away. I assume the bed linens in the closet upstairs are clean?"

"Still clean," I said, "from the last time anybody washed them twenty years ago."

"I opened the windows up there; the room needs a good airing." He took a healthy gulp of whiskey. "The whole place needs an overhaul. It's falling down. You've let it go to seed, Hugo. You haven't done a thing to keep it up in all these years."

"This is true, as a matter of fact. But the process began long before I came back. No one's made any improvements in . . . how long since Dad died? Almost thirty-five years."

"I think it's time someone did. And I seem to be the only one willing."

I shifted in my chair and said through something like rising panic, "Dennis, you can't seriously be going to live here again."

"Why not?"

"Because you bought your house before you met Marie. It's your house. Let her move out. She ought to descend upon her elderly parents, brighten their dimming lives. Mellow their dotage. And make their hearts glad with the fluting cries of little children."

"First of all," Dennis said with a furrow in his brow, "the Dupins live in the city. Second, Marie has a private practice up here, she can't abandon her clients. Third, we agreed the girls would stay with her, and we don't want to uproot them. We'll figure it out eventually, but for now it makes the most sense for me to stay here."

"Sense to whom?" I muttered through the mouth of the bottle.

"Come again?" he said absently.

"Where will you do your . . . work? Don't you have a studio over there at your house? Won't you be a mollusk naked and quivering without a carapace here?"

"I'm taking a break for now. I just completed a new series and I'd like to clear my head before I start anything new. In fact, the more I think about it, the more I think I should try to fix up this place. Someone's got to save it from complete ruin."

"Why?"

"It's our heritage."

"Why does that matter?"

"It's who we are."

"This house may be who you are, but it's not who I am. I'm no mollusk and this is no carapace. More like a maggot feeding off a dying corpse, that's me, here."

"You think so?"

"I know so."

And so forth. Our conversational style hasn't changed in decades.

I stopped writing once again after that last sentence and stared into space for . . . a lacuna, a miasma, a hiatus, an unwieldy string of vowels' worth of time. I haven't written anything in years, and every word I write now feels false and stilted as the gestures of long-unused muscles. But still . . . all of a sudden I have to write again . . . a physical compulsion or necessary ablution, like shitting or shaving, or both. Michel de Montaigne, my primary bedfellow these days along with cigarettes and pain, would know what I mean by this.

Dennis has been back at Waverley only a day and a half, but already I see my old, solitary life as something lost, through a fog of mournful nostalgia. In that old, lost, former life, I took my breakfast out to the side porch on warm mornings with coffee cup, cigarettes, lighter, and ashtray, and sat for hours, with a book or without, watching the river in a completely solitary silence that is the closest thing to happiness I've ever known. In the winters, I sat at the kitchen table with the stove roaring, without any snot-nosed pestering local dependents or demanding chatty hangers-on to watch me, interrupt my thoughts, demand my attention. Not many people can say that. This is a freedom I'm convinced everyone dreams of, secretly. Sonia, my God, that *jolie-laide* bucktoothed Polish flat-chested bitch, she had me for a while, but since she left, I've been impervious, unfettered, and able to live exactly as I pleased. Almost ten years, it's been. . . . My days were full and productive. I slept, woke, drank coffee or whiskey, smoked, read books, sat in my chair looking out over the Hudson River as the light changed slowly and the air darkened as evening came. In the evenings, I cooked myself elaborate feasts and fancies in the kitchen, one lamp burning, my sleeves rolled up. Steam rose from the stove, the radio played, wind howled outside. When the meal was ready, I ate alone at the table, radio still on. A book was often propped against my whiskey bottle, but most nights I didn't read, I concentrated on tasting the food I'd made. This required all of my attention. I absorbed the story of the flavors, tracking the relationships between ingredients, one bite following another with anticipation, as if I were in the grip of some intricate and suspenseful prandial plot, a gustatory novel on a plate.

My rare visitors over the years have been women lured here every now and again for sexual purposes. Jennifer, the last, was the forty-two-year-old auburn-haired plumpish admissions administrator at the nearby liberal-arts college. For a number of months, she and I enjoyed a casual ongoing affair, which proceeded nicely enough and might have gone nowhere forever as far as I was concerned, but came to an abrupt halt about a year ago, when she reunited with and then precipitously married an old boyfriend I'd never heard of.

Since then I've been reluctantly celibate, but am always on the lookout.

Meanwhile, through the years I have not encouraged and in fact have scarcely tolerated Dennis's occasional casual drop-ins, with or without his offspring but never with his wife Marie, who has never liked me. He came ostensibly to touch base with the semi-estranged brother but really to make sure I wasn't burning all the fainting couches to keep warm, or giving away any heirloom silverware, or otherwise squandering his inheritance and history. He has always been suspicious of my caretaking abilities, and with very good reason.

It's breakfast time. Under normal circumstances—which is to say, if I were alone here—I would stroll by the options in my mental automat: omelet with leftover chunks of lamb, a daub of sour cream, some chopped parsley; or a fried jumble of eggs, onions, potatoes, and sausage, puddles of ketchup; or maybe a sandwich of smoked herring fillets on toasted rye with horse-radish and mustard; or a big chunk of extra-sharp cheddar, an apple cut into eighths, and a wad of sourdough bread ripped from a whole bakery loaf.

But Dennis is down there in the kitchen, all chipper and clean-shaven and wanting to talk to me. There's nothing I dread and resent more first thing in the morning than the double-headed monstrous hydra of obligatory pleasantries. It makes me want to bash his head in with a tire iron. As long as he's here, my life is ruined. Not to put too fine a point on it.

October 11—Good morning! I'm still alive, I see.

If I can hold on through the night, the morning is always better.

Here I am again, Dennis downstairs as usual in the kitchen with his wet-haired, soap-smelling self wedged in a chair, itch-ing for a little male bonding with the kid brother—Jesus, it's unbearable, but this is his house too.

Montaigne carved on the roof beams of his own hermit tower the following admirable thoughts:

> The plague of man is the opinion of knowledge.
> I establish nothing. I do not understand. I halt. I examine.
> Breath fills a goatskin as opinion fills a hollow head.
> Not more this than that—why this and not that? Have you
> seen a man that believes himself wise? Hope that he is a fool.
> Man, a vase of clay.
> I am human, let nothing human be foreign to me.
> What inanity is everything!

What inanity indeed. If I don't have a cup of coffee soon, my head will implode.

I'm smoking, as always, a long slow suicide that in recent years has got a fuck of a lot faster. Smoke, smoke. In draw, out blow, rush of nicotine. The first one of the day is the only one that matters to me, all the other ones are just habit. I wake up jonesing, shaken from the long night of pain. And the match, the dry sulfur hiss of promise, of comfort. And the first deep lungful of gray foul-fresh smoke. And then the finest moment of each day, the zing. I can never get it back all day long, no matter how much or little I smoke, no matter how carefully I space out the cigarettes, and I think I've tried everything, every trick of timing and dosage. Short of upgrading to heroin or crack, there's nothing left to do, it's just what it is now. And heroin or crack would eventually turn into the same drill.

Pain kept me awake all night; I'm saggy-faced and wrung out. Nerves, the electrical wiring of the body. Wish I could short-circuit myself. I seem to have suddenly entered a temporal waiting room I won't get out of until I'm alone again. Last night I read some of Montaigne's *Essais,* in French. My French isn't nearly good enough for this, so it helped me fall back to sleep, finally.

Maybe I'll take a bath soon. Now that I'm no longer alone here, I'm aware that I offend the nose with my unwashed person. Dennis's nose with my unwashed person.

What do I care what he thinks? What do I care if I offend him? Since he came home I've done everything to drive him away again.

Yesterday evening, as usual out on the veranda, I held my whiskey bottle as if its neck were Dennis's, twisting it with one hand while holding the body of the bottle with the other. I took a pull at its mouth as if I were sucking out its final breath. I hadn't offered him any and he hadn't asked.

"Autumnal gloaming," I intoned from the broad railing

where I was perched, looking down the lawn to the weeping willows at the edge of the dark river. "She creeps in on her velvet paws to curl around the windowpanes and swells my gourd with ripeness to the core."

"What's that?" asked Dennis from the other side of the veranda, where he was carving a pumpkin in the pool of overhead light.

"A pastiche," said I. "The conceit is that my girlfriend is the autumn evening, which I'm sure went right over your head like most of my inspired bloviating."

He didn't answer. He leaned back on his haunches and scraped some pumpkin pulp and seeds from the newspaper on the porch floor beside him. He lifted them absently to his nose and sniffed.

I know what they smell of, they smell of sex.

"Dennis," I said suddenly, and was gratified when he jumped a little. He had drifted far off into some reverie of his own, apparently. "Now that you've cast off your marital shackles . . ."

"What?" he asked, hacking industriously away at the pumpkin again. As a professional sculptor, my brother has achieved a certain amount of success, a Chelsea gallery, a couple of shows a year, work sold to serious collectors, articles about him in art magazines, the usual art-world hoo-hah. He's been called "versatile" and "inventive" by critics who presumably know what they're talking about, but not since we were lads have I seen him apply his so-called talents to the vegetable kingdom: he traffics mainly in heavy metals, as far as I know. So maybe he's come home to regress.

"You've got your mind on a woman, I can tell," I said, hazarding a guess. The night before, he'd gone on and on, after drinking quite a lot of wine. At first he was vague—he referred mysteriously to Another Woman—but it took very little prompting on my part to get the specifics out of him. He was obviously dying to talk about it.

"*Ça te regarde pas,*" he said with automatic absentness, sounding exactly like the ghost of our dead French mother, bless her needy, narcissistic bottomless pit of a soul; it was her stock response to anything we said that had nothing directly to do with her own thoughts, feelings, well-being, and opinions.

So I was right.

"I think I know who," I said sneakily. "Your friend Bun Fox's wife. In your cups last night, you mentioned that the lovely Stephanie Fox frequents Rex's Roadhouse alone after work sometimes. You intimated that she's unhappy with said friend Bun. You licked your chops, and I saw a plan afoot in your hothouse of a brainpan to rescue her and give her what you clearly believe she wants and needs."

"Back off," said Dennis in that tone of voice I know not to brook, if only for the sake of weaseling a discussion of the topic out of him later, after he's had a few. "I mean it, Hugo."

The subject of sex, once it rears its head, is not so easy to beat down again, like Lear's Fool's eels: Down, nuncle!

"Where the back door are my cigarettes?" I said, fumbling around in my pants pocket as if I fully expected to find them there.

"I don't know," Dennis said, gouging a tiny, shallow curlicue into the pumpkin's flesh. "Maybe you smoked them."

"Maybe I did." I got up and went inside for my wallet and keys.

"Watch out for Officer Friendly," Dennis called through the open window. "Actually, maybe I should drive you there."

"Oh, I'm all right," I said through gritted teeth, gimping across the weedy lawn to my truck. I sputtered off at a fuck-you stately pace up the long driveway to Route 23, and then to Stewart's, of course to buy cigarettes, but incidentally to chat up the cashier, a gormless, lumpen girl who has captured my heart with her idiot-savant–like chatter. We are both high-school dropouts, and, as such, are soulmates. I linger twice a

day, sometimes for as long as half an hour, tapping an unlit cigarette on the counter, talking nonstop to her, while customers
flow around me. The romance has, to my half-relieved dismay,
failed over the months to progress beyond these almost daily
manic, nonsensical, and yet strangely passionate colloquies. I'm
not sure whether Carla has yet reached the age of legal consent,
but even if she has there's sure to be an outcry of some kind if
I seduce her. Why, I don't know, but there ought to be.

Well, that's one thing you can say for those Ay-rab terrorists—at least, it's the one thing I myself will say here—they've
distracted a sovereign nation's collective mind from the goings-
on of other people's genitalia. But not our own—these have become even more urgent and paramount in our consciousness
since last month's attacks. I should say my own. To this end, I'm
tempted to make some degree of move on freckled, bony, big-
breasted, postpubescent Carla the same way Dennis is plotting
his own, equally inappropriate campaign to seduce his best
friend's wife. These are desperate times.

When I got back from Stewart's, my headlights picked out
the silhouette of Dennis, crouching down at the far edge of the
lawn on the bare earth in the near darkness under a weeping
willow, staring moodily across the Hudson, no doubt at staccato
bursts of streaming white light along some faraway road. He
used to spend a lot of time there as a kid, primarily alone, although sometimes he allowed me into his strategic paramilitary
games and spying missions. When he did, though, he'd make
me be his decoder or scout, in some unequivocally subordinate
position. Back then I was obedient, tractable, and eager to
please.

I turned five in 1966, a month before our father was killed
in Vietnam, a war he'd enlisted for, even though he was a
summa-cum-laude graduate of Harvard Law School and the father of two young sons. He enlisted as a matter of course; he'd

joined the Reserve Officer Training Corps at Harvard and graduated with a commission of second lieutenant, and so had already embarked on a military course of action. As an officer, he must have felt reasonably confident of returning home in one piece. Also, he must have wanted very badly to get far away from my mother, but this is only speculation. In any case, if he'd eschewed the college military rigmarole he would have been exempt from serving in Vietnam by virtue of being a father.

As it turned out, second lieutenants were required to serve on the front lines with their men. Being an officer was no guarantee of safety, no siree.

It was very hard for the family, to put it mildly, when Dad was blown to bits by a stray grenade. Maybe because I had nowhere else to put it, I somehow transferred all my shining adoration of Dad to the manifestly undeserving Dennis, who became my unchallenged leader for the remainder of my childhood. It wasn't until adolescence that I saw the light and started balking at Dennis, defying our mother, maybe because I was blindsided by a sudden surge of hormones and maybe because I woke up and saw them for who they were. At the time I was as perplexed by this as anyone else, although it was a relief to be wild and destructive, to turn it all outward.

The incident that ended forever my family life—and my youth too, for that matter—occurred during the autumn I turned seventeen and was a senior at Choate, when Dennis committed the fatal error of agreeing with our mother that I should finish high school in a military academy down south. I can fully understand that at that time this might have seemed the only solution to the parent-teacher conferences concerning my breaches of conduct, all the suspensions and inevitable expulsions, first from Winthrop Prep, a fine old school near Waverley where Dennis and I were day boys together, then Andover, my father's alma mater, and finally Choate, my grandfather's—none of their administrations or faculties much cared for my vandalism, my cheating on tests, my drinking during school hours. Finally, in my senior year, I got busted selling pot at the same time it emerged that I'd impregnated a Rosemary Hall freshman, a pathologically pissed-off candy heiress named Belinda Crake, the one other student there who actually gave me a run for my money in the juvenile-delinquent department, but no matter. Belinda received a voluntary legal abortion, and I got kicked out for good. Dennis drove our mother to Wallingford to collect me. I allowed myself to be collected, then festered in the back seat most of the way home, until she broke the news that I would have to undergo psychological testing and then go to military school. When Dennis seconded the motion and refused my appeals for brotherly solidarity, I called him a traitor, a spineless coward, a pussy, a mama's boy, all of which he arguably was. Then I lapsed into a ticking silence, slit-eyed, my knee jerking madly up and down. Several miles later, I announced I had to take a piss. I disappeared at the gas station. I went into the men's room, in other words, and didn't come back.

Dennis told me, long afterwards, that they'd put out a missing-persons report, had three different private detectives look for me at various times. They never found me. I lived for a while with a rich fat Jewish woman on the Upper East Side. Then I went to Europe and continued my life as a kept boy for a while, until I got bored with being a lapdog and turned to petty crime, mostly small drug deals, but a little bit of theft and whatnot. I eventually mooched my way back to the States, where I did a bit of this and that, including making several very lucrative drives from Canada to the U.S., big bags of marijuana taped to the underside of my wheel well. I was clean-shaven and polite, and never got any trouble from anyone.

I remember those seven or so years "on the run" chiefly as

being driven by rage and lust, equally. The law meant nothing
to me. Sex meant quite a lot, and still does. Money meant little
but was a necessity. I never had a steady girlfriend; I always kept
several girls going at once. I liked them all just fine, but I was
too pissed off to love anyone. This naturally made me unaccountably irresistible to many women. I suppose I broke some
hearts. I imagine I may have behaved like something of an asshole, but I moved around too frequently ever to fall into any
black holes of consequence. I lived here and there. I kept my
money in cash, and made sure never to have too much of it but
always to have enough. I made friends easily, automatically,
wherever I went, New York, France, Spain, California, Canada,
Long Island, Boston. I kept my emotional distance while being
as charming as I could. It was remarkable how popular this
made me with other men as well as with women. People on the
whole tend to be deeply intrigued by and gravitate toward anyone who is not insecure, vulnerable, or needy, who seems to be
comfortable in his own lonesome skin and in possession of the
secret of easy autonomy. I slithered around, as hungry and un-
obstructed as a snake in a nest of baby birds. People helped me,
looked the other way when I transgressed, offered a place to
stay or a loan, a ride somewhere, a meal.

Just after my twenty-fourth birthday, my mother died of
breast cancer. I read about it in the *New York Times* obituary
section, several paragraphs she'd earned by virtue of her marriage, having done nothing before or since to merit any notice.
I saw the obituary because someone pointed it out to me; I
wasn't in the habit of reading any newspapers then and am still
not. I was "house-sitting" in a Long Island beach house when
I heard—which is to say, I was squatting for several weeks with
nominal permission from the owners, an older couple I'd met
at a party, who had said I could crash there for a night or two
but had only the vaguest knowledge of how long I'd been there,

since they were there only rarely. . . . I showed up late with my rucksack for the funeral at the old family chapel and graveyard near Waverley, technically on our land. I was clean-shaven and wearing a suit of sorts, but I'm sure I looked scabrously pale and wild-eyed. I was tripping my brains out. Dennis has never been able (possibly because he has never really tried) to wrest from me the truth about where I was all those years. I've told him shadowy and deliberately vague stories about working my way around the world on freighters and as a courier on planes, feeding off the fat of the drug trade, being kept by rich older women, and so forth, but I've only alluded to all this in the course of discussing other things. He hasn't ever pressed me for dates or names or details.

There's a certain unspoken tradition in our family: every generation has its reclusive eccentric. I'm sure Dennis has consigned me in his own mind to their ranks as a rudimentary means of understanding me. Because, whatever my wanderings may or may not have actually entailed, they came to a complete end after my mother died, once the Waverley coast was clear. I've been here ever since, reading my way through the ancestral library, wearing the same clothes day after day until they fall apart.

Of course, given my animosity toward tradition of any sort, I have to flout it any way I can. How do I flout this one? By dying young, of course. All my hermit-monk forebears were gaunt nonagenarians when they kicked off. Me, I'll be less than half their average age.

Over the years, I find I've despised Dennis less and less vehemently, but without any increase of respect. I've never tried to hide my opinion that he's unoriginal and plodding. I let on to him, not that he asked me, that I found his years as a struggling bohemian artist in New York a tired cliché, and his purchase of that nice old solid-investment house in Stonekill the stodgily "smart" thing to do with his inheritance, and his marriage to Marie Dupin, a girl of recent French descent, an obvious imitation of Dad. When Evie was born, I wrote my newly hatched niece a letter in this same squat, crabbed handwriting, explaining that blood relations mean nothing in the grand scheme of things, and therefore she could expect to find me an unsatisfactory uncle throughout her life, but maybe one day she would understand my point of view. This, it developed after five pages or so, was my highest wish for her, although I didn't take the trouble to elaborate on what my philosophy involved. It would, I pompously maintained, speak for itself if she studied my actions and way of life, which I hoped for her own sake she would undertake to do throughout the years.

This was of course partially my own needling way of getting Dennis for having been born first, making me be the scout and the decoder, and finally having to be in the untenable position of being my would-be keeper at nineteen. But primarily it was how I felt, therefore genuine.

"You're spending quite a bit of time down there." My voice floated to him on fumes of exhaust. Dennis looked around and saw my truck, idling near the tree he was sitting under, and the night-splitting headlights. The taillights cast a red, wavering light on the indentations of the tires in the weeds behind the truck. "It might be time to set up camp. Bivouac."

"How was your date?" Dennis asked jocularly.

"She thinks Osama bin Laden is among us, here in this country; in fact, she's fairly sure of it. She says he could have sneaked in. All he had to do was shave off his beard and wear normal clothes and get a fake ID. How hard would that be for him? I told her she's wasting her talents at Stewart's. The CIA needs operatives." I turned off the engine and opened the door, put my good foot up on the dashboard, and sniffed loudly. "The air smells strangely like snow," I said. "I think I'll take the old iceboat out on the river this winter. Maybe I'll invite Carla. She can bring a thermos of Swiss Miss and a package of Lorna Doones."

"This sounds serious," Dennis said.

"You think I'm toying with her."

"Actually," said Dennis, "what I think is that I came down here for some peace and quiet and you've invaded my sanctuary."

"Tit for tat, brother mine," I rejoined meaningfully.

"Brother mine?" Dennis stretched his legs out and yawned, completely failing to catch my drift.

"It's all very nice to anticipate being together, you and I, day in, day out. But I wonder: do you plan at some point to rejoin your life as you knew it?"

"If you take it from Marie," said Dennis, "I'm not going back. She isn't wasting any time. Today she told me she's just hired an au-pair girl, sight unseen, someone her sister recommended—one of her former students, I think. And this girl came up immediately on the train."

"What sort of a girl?" I asked with a sidelong flick of my eyes.

"I don't know. A former student of Vero's. Whatever that means. Knowing Vero, it can't be good."

"A girl," I repeated, tasting the word on my lips. I like girls. I prefer women, but girls as long as they're plausibly over the age of eighteen are interesting too.

"Hugo," said Dennis. "Don't mess with the au pair who's looking after my children."

I said breezily, "Says who?"

There was another brief silence, this one tainted with my brother's disapproval. But what could he say? He has no jurisdiction over me, which he has always known, but it must have struck him in that moment that he has no more say over his wife's employee's private life than he has over mine. His distress over this knowledge was plainly visible.

"Do we have Caller ID block?" he asked abruptly. "On the phone, I mean the thing that prevents someone from dialing star-six-nine, or knowing who's calling?"

"You know how insufferably paranoid I am," I said. "I had them install every thwarting service that currently exists. Why do you ask?"

"I think I'll make some dinner," said Dennis, scrambling upright and brushing off his pants.

I fired up the truck engine. "Can I offer you a ride home?"

"Thanks," he said with the optimistic, daring tone that means he's about to make his idea of a joke. "I'll walk."

"You do that!" I rejoined hilariously.

In the cavernous, lamplit kitchen, I sat smoking at the table and fiddling with the radio, trying to find some big-band swing music, which is the cornerstone of my new War Effort aesthetic. Dennis opened a bottle of wine and poured himself a glass without offering me one, I suppose because I was already drinking whiskey. Bastard. He never shared as a kid either. He rummaged through the shopping bags he'd recently brought back from the grocery store and piled garlic, onions, canned tomatoes, frozen spinach, and an Italian sausage on the counter, got out a chopping block and butcher's knife, heated olive oil in a cast-iron skillet, filled a big pot with water for spaghetti, and turned the flame up high underneath it. He began chopping onions and garlic. He has made it known that he "likes to cook": he says, prosaically, that it soothes the troubled spirit, concentrates the ruffled mind. And Dennis's mind is nothing if not ruffled these days, his spirit so troubled it would look like a storm-tossed ocean if it looked like anything. At least, that's how I can see him explaining it to himself: I am convinced that Dennis narrates his own life to himself as if he were the hero of a Bildungsroman.

Well, as it happens, I like to cook too, but I'm a lot better at it than Dennis is. And I don't make a big deal about it, I don't pretend it's therapeutic, and I don't have an unforgivably heavy hand with the spices.

"All you get these days on the airwaves is anthrax," I said, snapping the radio off. "It sounds like a surgeon's instrument. Or a kind of super-durable plastic. Part of an ant. Carla thinks a pissed-off former lab employee is sending these envelopes. What are you making? Hash?"

"What did you eat before I moved in?" Dennis asked with his usual willful ignorance and disregard of whatever it is that I am.

"Dog food from the can," I snarled. "Rabbit-fetus fricassee. But at least I didn't have to answer any condescending questions. Ah, those were happy days."

Dennis scraped chopped onions and garlic into the skillet. "In answer to your question before," he said with maddening self-seriousness, "I'm not going back to my family. I will probably not move back to New York. I might stay here at Waverley a while. I don't know yet."

"Well, I make it a point never to interfere," I said. "But about that woman you married . . ."

"I already know what you think of her, so save your breath."

"Marie," I said with scorn, in hopes of provoking Dennis into defending his wife, and consequently missing her, and then, in a magical chain reaction, going back to her and leaving me alone. "In the thesaurus, next to 'virago,' 'shrew,' 'harridan,' 'fishwife,' 'alewife.'" I spat a fleck of tobacco off my tongue onto the floor. "The tyranny of domesticity, the cozy little horror-show of homey house arrest. And those little girls—"

"My little girls," said Dennis, who had heard all of this before and was both unimpressed and bored by it. "Don't forget."

"—embryonic proto-wives, lying in wait until they're big and breasty enough to lock some unsuspecting dupe of their own into the contractual shackles of mealtimes, don't do this, please close your mouth when you chew, and for God's sake take a shower. Wives in waiting, little emasculators-to-be." I smiled sinisterly at him; I've never shied away from trying to hit Dennis below the belt. He adores his daughters, and until now I believed he adored his wife as well. I still suspect he might harbor some vestige of this feeling for Marie, separation or no separation. "Misogyny, you think? Look to that human embodiment of ether, chloroform personified, my smother." I dropped my cigarette butt to the floor and crushed it with my heel. "Look to the source, Dr. Freud."

"Yeah, well," said Dennis sourly, shaking his head, "you should hear what Marie says about you."

"What does she say about me?"

"She calls you the troll under the bridge," Dennis said. "That, or Quasimodo."

"Whatever for?" I asked in wounded innocence.

October 13—Dennis announced yesterday evening that he was on his way to pick up the girls. He and Marie apparently arranged before he left that the kids would come to Waverley every Friday for the weekend and be home every Sunday in time for supper; it seemed that it was assumed by both of them that Dennis would do all the transporting and driving. This strikes me as another way in which he gets the raw end of the stick, and of course I told him so, but of course he ignored me.

With my vision of this new au-pair girl firmly in mind, I insisted on going with him at the last minute. Smelling aggressively of shampoo and aftershave, my wet hair plastered in comb-tooth furrows against my skull, I rode shotgun to Stonekill in Dennis's old rattletrap, thoughtfully blowing my cigarette smoke out his window. Dennis mused to his captive audience

on the way that maybe he'd drag them to the fair over in Columbia County, but he hated fairs and suspected they did too;
they would of course eat their cotton candy and suffer through
the indignity of all the dinky little rides without complaint, but
there would be something tawdry and manufactured about the
whole enterprise. He sounded nervous to see his own children,
apprehensive, as if he wouldn't be able to entertain them all of
a sudden, these small creatures he'd helped raise from birth who
presumably still adored him unthinkingly.

As we pulled up the driveway, I said in an unusually pleasant tone as Dennis set the emergency brake, "May I come in
with you?"

"Don't you want to avoid the tyranny of the emasculating
harridan?" he asked with a jocular tilt of the head that suggested
he considered this the height of witty repartee.

"Ha ha!" I said obligingly. He had clearly forgotten my interest in the new au-pair girl; I had only mentioned it once, of
course, and that a few days before, but this was the sort of
potential plot point I never would have forgotten even under
pain of torture or extreme duress. In all fairness, he has a lot on
his mind these days, and he's never paid any attention to my
plans and ideas before, so there was no reason to expect him to
start now.

I got out of the car and walked with my exaggeratedly stiff-
legged gait up the flagstone path. "I've forgotten how picturesque your house is," I called over my shoulder to Dennis. "It's
like an ivy-covered gingerbread cottage, size extra large."

"Well, it's what's left of the bulk of my inheritance," said
Dennis, "just about."

"Pshaw," I said, opening the front door, although in fact I
knew this to be true, "there's oodles left, you can't fool Uncle
Hugo. Hellooo," I trilled. "Anybody hooome?"

A red-haired girl looked up from the couch, where she was

reading to Isabelle. She looked like a lost lamb—or fatted calf, more like—far away from home and ready for slaughter. Her face showed everything she was thinking about me so clearly I could see myself through her eyes as if I were looking into a mirror. The man who'd just burst in had an old-fashioned hair-cut and a shambolic frame, slightly padded with the aftereffects of many good meals and little exercise but saved from any degree of overweight by a prodigiously fast metabolism. He was handsome in a rakishly dissolute way, I add without false modesty, because what would be the point?

I was not what she'd expected Marie's husband to be, and was not in fact Marie's husband at all, but I hoped I didn't displease her.

"Your father's here," she told Isabelle, who hadn't looked up from the book or even budged. "I'm Louisa," she told me. "The au pair."

"Louisa, what a gorgeous accent you have," I said. "Rich and pure, the song of my youth. Not that I grew up in Brooklyn, I just wish I had."

"Right, yeah," she said, to her credit straight-faced, although she clearly knew I was only spoofing: a lot of men my age hit on every woman they meet to prove they still have it, even when they don't. All the girls her age know that these days, which hampers my game but keeps me on my toes.

"Daddy!" yelled Isabelle as Dennis came in the door, her lips parted in breathy baby excitement. She twisted her curvy little body down from the couch and ran over to him just as he bent and opened his arms. Fatherly, quizzical, broad-shouldered, high-browed Dennis swept her up, and she buried her head in his shoulder, then twisted free, slid down to the floor to wrap her arms around his legs and butt her head against his hipbone. He cradled the crown of her head in his hands and smiled down at her.

"I'm actually not Daddy, I'm Uncle Hugo," I told Louisa as I came into the living room to sit about eight inches away from her on the couch, a little too close for her liking, but not so close that she could justifiably move away from me without being rude. "Lowest man on the family totem pole."

"Um," said Louisa, clearly at something of a loss as to how to take this sudden intimacy and proximity I was imposing on her. "Why lowest?"

I leaned back against the couch cushion, moving almost imperceptibly closer to her in the process. "You see how I was greeted by my younger niece. As the rest of the household reacts to my presence, you'll understand the general drift, if we agree that cries of gladness and affection are indications of a man's popularity in a female household, which I think we can."

I smiled disarmingly at her, crinkling my eyes around the edges on purpose. I can be very handsome when I put my mind to it, likewise smooth and charming. It's in my genes; I did nothing to earn it and rarely exploit it for this reason. She held my gaze. Her expression was noncommittal, unblinking. "Whatever," she said skeptically a beat later.

She was no beauty, she was a bit of a chubstein, she was all bottled up with nowhere to spritz, but she hadn't moved away from me; she wasn't fooled, intimidated, or put off. And right away I sensed something, a resilient, mature, knowing quality in her that belied her extreme youth. She might be a teenager technically, but I knew that in her soul she was my equal and my contemporary, and I could treat her as such. I may cross the line with her eventually, and in fact, given my itch to push buttons and test limits, it's fairly certain I will, but whatever line there is lies far back in the thickets of adult discourse and not on any shallow plain of teenagehood. Like Carla, she's someone I can talk to. Why I tend to meet my soulmates in the form of teenage girls does not bear examining, except insofar as teenage girls in many cultures are already considered fully grown. Those cultures may be on to something.

I said to her softly, "Louisa, this seems to be my lucky day."

She quirked her lips, looked away from me, her cheeks suddenly pink.

"You're a jewel," I said sincerely, "glowing in the dullness of my brother's house."

She laughed out loud and shook her head. "Come off it!" she said. Awf. "What are you talking about?" Tawking.

"An amazing discovery on an otherwise ordinary day," I insisted. I was pushing it, of course, but why not? I could tell it wouldn't do any harm, in fact the contrary. She obviously craves ridiculous, playful, even profane flattery, however she may try to deflect or minimize it.

"Hugo," came Marie's patently disapproving voice from the doorway, regretting my presence rather than greeting me.

I raised my eyebrows at Louisa as if to say, You see? But Louisa was looking anxiously at Marie, clearly dismayed to be caught in an attitude with the unpopular uncle that might be construed as collusion, even flirting. This was, after all, her first week on the job.

"Listen, Dennis," Marie went on, turning to her husband, "I think Isabelle's coming down with something. Can you make sure she gets to bed early and drinks plenty of fluids? And if she gets really sick will you call me?"

"Of course," said Dennis.

There were dark circles under Marie's eyes. Her hair was uncombed and flyaway, and she wore an old red sweater with pushed-up sleeves and baggy corduroy trousers. Marie is a beautiful woman, but right then she looked like a Modigliani gone to seed. The air between her and Dennis juddered with hurt feelings and molten rage.

Under cover of the family hubbub—girls gathering backpacks and bidding their mother goodbye, etc.—I asked Louisa if she'd like to go for a drive to Lovers' Lane later on tonight, after dark. She said no, of course. However, she laughed at my sleazy audacity, which is very promising.

I'll go back over there tonight and see what's what.

Forty minutes later, as we drove up the driveway to Waverley, Evie caught sight of the pumpkin man. "Daddy!" her imperious little dragon-lady voice issued from the back seat. "What's that?"

"His name is Don Luigi," I answered, even though she hadn't asked me. "He's a tenor, but don't cross him."

Evie and Isabelle tumbled out of the car and raced to inspect Don Luigi. The pumpkin gangster has slitty eyes, big ears stuck on with toothpicks, and a wide, thick-lipped, toothy grin. His head rides atop a two-inch-diameter, six-foot-tall dowel. He wears some dead ancestor's porkpie hat that Dennis nailed to his head, one of our father's suits stuffed with towels, and a pair of dapper old shoes. His left sleeve is attached to the trousers pocket to make it look as if he's got his hand in there; his right hand, carved out of a small butternut squash, rests on a second, hip-level dowel at the end of the right sleeve, its fingers spread as if he were beseeching everyone who passed by to give him a handout, or singing an aria, or introducing a special guest on a talk show.

"He needs a girlfriend," said Evie.

"Let's make one for him, then," Dennis said, his heart obviously singing. They had a project! I've always been able to read my brother's mind. The oppressed always know their oppressors, and conversely are not known by them at all. Now they wouldn't have to go to the fair; making a moll for Don Luigi would be a gas. There were all sorts of old dresses in the closets she could wear, and they could buy a blond wig and put lipstick on her.

"Hey," Evie said, "you made him, right, Daddy? Not Uncle Hugo."

"Uncle Hugo donated the hat," said Dennis dourly. This was a lie: he's always felt stodgily duty-bound to wage an ongoing, fruitless campaign to boost my acceptability with his daughters, although I myself have made no effort whatsoever on that score, and in fact have been hell-bent on being as offensive and weird as possible around them.

"The hat is icky," said Evie.

Isabelle was touching Don Luigi's hand; Evie stood on his other side, gazing up at his face. He looked like a lowlife with a creepy penchant for little girls. If I had been Dennis I would have yanked them away from him, especially Isabelle, who is an undeniable little sexpot-to-be and therefore a possible target for pedophiles. The very thought of any possible threat in that direction made me itch to thrust an umbrella between Don Luigi's nonexistent ribs.

October 14—I awoke just now, shattered from a pain-spiked dream, to a windy, leaf-blown, coruscating autumn day, sunlight embellishing charcoal clouds and glinting off the cold steel-dark river and the imported French tiles that were once on the roof of Waverley, those priceless two-hundred-year-old pieces of slate that have gradually, over the decades, lost their purchase and are now sliding one by one to plummet into the high, weedy lawn. They catch the sun down there beneath my tower window. The Hudson Valley quivers in this Sabbath-morning light; the sky is a blinding bowl of leaves and birds.

In the end, Dennis and his daughters didn't make a girlfriend for Don Luigi yesterday.

In the end, I did pay a visit to the new au-pair girl.

It was just after nine last night when I pulled up Marie's steep driveway. Evie had let slip that Marie was going out with "a friend" that night. "What friend?" Dennis had wondered wistfully aloud. "Stephanie Fox?"

"I think so," said Evie, oblivious to her father's yearning.

There was a light on in the kitchen of my brother's house. Aha! My quarry at her solitary supper. I idled there at the top of the driveway for a while, gunning the engine so Louisa would know I was there. Through the side window I watched her get up and leave the safe, well-lighted kitchen. She disappeared from view, then reappeared at the mudroom window, peering (she thought) surreptitiously through the curtains at the driveway, at my beat-up old pickup truck, sitting there with engine and headlights on. Then the driver, whoever he was, tapped the horn twice, beep beep, as if summoning her. But she stayed put: the house was nearly dark, and she must have thought it looked as if no one was home, and anyway, whoever it was could just wait there for a while and then drive away again, because no way was she going out there. She was a mouse cornered by a whisker-twitching alley tom sniffing at the entrance of her hidey-hole, although I have no whiskers and in any case was staying put in the cab of my truck, at least for now. But I sent out psychological antennae to tickle sneakily at her waist and throat, ascertaining by her fluttering pulse and the butterflies in her stomach her determination to wait me out.

She left her post by the door and made her way back through the dark house, sat down again at the table, and picked up her fork. The silhouetted, almost bare treetops shuddered overhead as a gust of wind moved through them. I turned off the engine and slid out of the truck, let the door fall quietly shut behind me. I let myself into the house with a key that has recently come into my possession by dint of rifling through Dennis's pockets and making myself a copy of his. Inside the house, I inhaled the smell of family life, the commingled sediment of hours-ago coffee, basement mold, musty books, and shampoo steam, the dust embedded in rugs that no vacuuming or broom-beating can ever completely remove, floor wax and laundry detergent and the earth and leaves of houseplants, years of sleep trapped in bedding. The smell gave me an almost metaphysical dread. I slunk through the living room, taking in as I did so the old dark rug, swaybacked armchairs and green sofa, fringed lamps, book-filled shelves, plants, old stone fireplace, scattered toys. Dennis has created a house and childhood for his own children as ordinary and commonplace as ours was extraordinary and bizarre.

At the back of the house I came to the small, cluttered kitchen. On a green-and-white patchwork linoleum floor are an old six-burner cast-iron range, a refrigerator festooned with crayoned artwork, built-in cupboards along the wall by the deep old double sink. Pots of herbs grow on the windowsill. A glass-paned door leads out to a walled-in porch lined with shelves of cans, boxes, jars, a mop in a bucket leaning against the doorway. In the wall to my right was the doorway that led to the spare bedroom, where I was certain Louisa had set up camp and was now, in fact, hiding, waiting to see what I would do next. I could almost hear her heart beating, her stilled breaths as I shambled over to the breakfast nook where she'd just been sitting, looking down at her plate. I ran my finger along her plate and then licked it. Shepherd's pie.

"A little too much salt," I said bossily. "For my tastes anyway. But my palate is highly developed, unlike those of certain people much younger than I am."

I heard a slight snort and turned to look at her darkened doorway. I pulled a cigarette pack from my jacket pocket, tapped one out, and lit it with the lighter I fished out of the other pocket. I stood smoking for a moment, inhaling, breathing the smoke out through my mouth toward her, as if I were trying to smoke her out. I saw the gleam of her eyes through the crack in the door. My smoke no doubt insinuated itself into her lungs, as intimately as the way I'd tasted her dinner.

I went into her room, a small, narrow space crowded with a bureau, desk, and chair, a nunlike single bed covered with a quilt. She was shielded by the half-open door, barely hidden from my view. I ran my finger along the top of her bureau, testing for dust.

"Hey!" she yelled.

I turned. The kitchen light was in my eyes; she brandished a thick book as if it were a brick. Her voice was high with fear, but somehow I knew it wasn't real fear; it was the explosively playful fear of a child playing hide-and-go-seek who can hardly contain a shriek before she's found.

"Get the fuck out of here!" she said.

"Louisa!" I said. "What joy. I hardly dared hope to find you here."

"You broke in," she said. "Get out."

"Broke in," I repeated sorrowfully. "My dear." I held up my ill-gotten key. "I'm family, Louisa, a member of the clan. I let myself in with my very own key, and I haven't touched a thing, I merely wanted to ascertain that all was well within. And seeing that the house's security is unbreached, I consider this a job well done."

"You ate my food," she shot back. "You smoked in the house. It's not allowed."

"Louisa, you're a fever dream come true!" I cried, my hand on my chest. "Look at you standing there, brandishing your weapon, all a-bristle with indignation, your hair aflame, you hotheaded Cerberus of my dreams! What book is it? I have to know."

"*Anna Karenina,*" she said, smiling in spite of herself.

"*Anna Karenina,*" I repeated in hushed, delighted tones. I held my hand out. . . . "May I take the book?"

She hesitated. "What for?" she asked.

"Because," I said with a kind of half-laughing, wheedling provocation, "I want to read part of it aloud to you. I think you'll find it interesting. Romantic, anyway. It's the passage about poor Kitty watching Anna and Vronsky dancing together at the first ball. I've always had a soft spot for that scene—something about Anna's powerful sexual triumph as seen through the eyes of a vulnerable young girl. I want to soften you up a little."

I took the book from her and fuddled around with it until I found the page. "Listen to this," I breathed. " 'Some supernatural force drew Kitty's eyes to Anna's face. She was enchanting in her simple black dress, enchanting were her full arms with the bracelets on them, enchanting her firm neck with its string of pearls, enchanting her curly hair in disarray, enchanting the graceful, light movements of her small feet and hands, enchanting the beautiful face in its animation; but there was something terrible and cruel in its enchantment.' "

Louisa, lulled into an enchantment of her own like a cat whose belly is scratched just right, was stilled in the doorway; her claws were retracted, eyes slitted shut, breathing slowed.

I flipped a page. "Here: 'She saw in her,' she being Kitty, her being Anna, 'a streak of the elation of success, which she knew so well herself. She could see that Anna was drunk with the wine of the rapture she inspired. She knew that feeling, knew the signs of it, and she saw them in Anna—saw the tremulous, flashing light in her eyes, the smile of happiness and excitement that involuntarily curved her lips, and the precise gracefulness, assurance, and lightness of her movements.' Here's Kitty's internal monologue, a little farther down: 'No, it's not the admiration of the crowd she's drunk with, but the rapture of one man.' "

When I paused to take a drag of my cigarette, the spell I'd cast on Louisa was suddenly lifted.

"Does Marie know you have a key?" she asked.

I gave one last suck to my cigarette, looked around for a place to crush it out, and dropped it into the near-empty water bottle on her desk, where it drowned with a hiss.

"That's my water!"

"So sorry," I said.

I as provocateur seemed to be in control, but that was only an illusion. It was really all up to her: she could either respond or walk away; my pitches would land on bare ground unless she caught them. Some change in her demeanor, a drawing-up of herself, told me she had just realized this.

"Okay, get out of my room," she said calmly, backing out of her room so I could pass through the door.

I leaned against her bureau and crossed my arms, waggling my good foot, humming to myself. "And if I don't?" I asked after a moment.

She rolled her eyes, evidently having realized how harmless I am. "I'm outta here," she said, and went off in the direction of the living room.

I nosed around in her bureau drawers for a moment, overtaken by the psychological equivalent of that powerful twitching in the nose before a sneeze.

A little while later, I slunk through the house holding a clean pair of her underpants pressed to my nose. I found her in the living room on the couch, pretending to read *Anna Karenina*.

"Oh, please," she burst out when she caught sight of me. "Oh my God. That's just, like, so weird. What are you *doing?*"

I grinned devilishly behind my makeshift burqa. "I think I'll keep them," I said.

"Go put them back."

I came to sit next to her, closer than I'd sat that morning, and leaned back against the cushions to gaze at her soulfully with the panties still pressed to the lower part of my face, inhaling with deep, ostentatious, connoisseurlike concentration. The air between us, the small space that separated us, felt charged with hostility, hilarity, and electricity.

"Louisa," I said, lowering the underwear, my tone all earnest and humble. "Please come out with me, just for a drink, or dessert. I'll have you home in an hour, I promise."

"A *drink?* I'm not of age, in case you've forgotten." She held out her hand. "Give those back."

I passed them to her silently, still watching her, leaning in as close to her as I could get without touching her, lips pursed with the force of my persuasion. The corner of her mouth twitched; she was trying not to smile.

"Come with me," I repeated. "For an hour. For dessert."

"One hour," she said. "Only because I need a hot-fudge sundae and Marie took the station wagon so I have no way to get there; otherwise I would tell you to go fuck yourself."

"But you won't," I said with joy, leaping to my feet and offering her a hand to help her up.

I took her to the appropriately named Friendly's, where we ordered an enormous oblong metal dish of ice cream heaped with nuts, whipped cream, and chocolate sauce for her, one vanilla scoop for me. The massive influx of sugar into her bloodstream seemed to relax her and loosen her tongue much the way alcohol affects others. She told me, unprompted except for unfeigned interest on my side of the booth, about the life in Greenpoint she'd so recently left behind. In short: her parents, Solly and Ruth Zimmerman, are a pair of basset hounds she mildly despises. She is under the spell of her older sister, Rachel, who is twenty-three but still lives at home, spending most of her time up in her room blasting techno music while she smokes joints or does her nails or tries on outfits to wear out with her friends. Rachel, being beautiful and spoiled, never helps their mother with the housework and contributes none of the money she makes selling clothes at a boutique in the East Village. Louisa has been helpless all her life against Rachel's charming cruelties and sense of entitlement; Rachel has always been able to provoke in Louisa a queasy desperation to prove her devotion. Although Louisa has always expected Rachel to do something big, to be a movie star or the president of her own company, it appears that her ambitions fall far short of her charisma.

Louisa has read enough novels, she says, to know her own place in the scheme of things: she's the plain younger daughter who goes to synagogue with her father on Friday evenings even though she's not religious and hates sitting upstairs in the balcony with all the other women because the whole arrangement is backward. She does the dishes, folds laundry, rubs Mommy's shoulders. Mommy teaches junior high. Daddy owns a small trucking company.

Apparently, Louisa has promised Marie that she'll stay until summer if things work out for everyone, but she'd envisioned her tenure here as a sort of dreamlike, transfiguring blur, seeing herself floating along through a time-warp tunnel, losing weight, making the children love her, severing the umbilicus that binds her so tortuously to Greenpoint. It's just beginning to hit her that her purpose here is to be completely involved in this family's daily life; this escape hatch is actually a job. She is panicking, a little.

"So what do *you* do all day?" she asked suddenly.

"I read, and I write a little," I said. "And until recently, I enjoyed unbroken solitude."

She had nothing to say to this, and I could understand why.

"To answer your question more directly," I said, "I have no truck with any so-called go-getter instinct. I came back to my childhood home to live because, to make a short story much shorter, there were people in New York a long time ago who wanted to do me harm, and I had no interest in being harmed. I thought it wise to get out of town. I stayed out of town, and found that there was nowhere else I wanted to go. When the time was right, I came back here, and am content to stay here for the rest of my life."

"I had to get out of town too," she said in a hushed voice. "That's why I took this job. People, someone, might have wanted to do me harm."

She didn't say why and neither did I, but there flashed between us a brief shared swagger, as if we were saying to each other, I did something bad and I can't tell you what it was but if I so much as show my face in Port Authority, if they so much as smell me on the breeze . . .

Her hair is copper red near her scalp and gold-shot toward the wavy ends. She has a *Fiddler on the Roof* quality that moves me, a humorously mournful Ashkenazi solidity. She eats like she means it.

"Anyway," she said, looking around to make sure no one was listening, lowering her voice, "I can't tell you any more than this, but I had to drop out of school and come up here. Someday I'll tell you why. It has to do with Sylvester." She looked over her shoulder and dropped her voice as she said his name.

I brought her home shortly after this, unscathed.

Sylvester. I look forward to learning about Sylvester.

Why is the pain worse at night? Sounds are louder too at night, magnified by the lack of ambient noise. I have nothing else to think about, that's the problem. I can't write any more, I have to put down my pen and howl like the beast I am. I could easily get a prescription for painkillers and sleeping pills from

Dr. Schuyler. I'm not sure why I don't. Maybe because that will mean I'm that much closer to the end. Maybe because it would feel like an internal admission that this disease is going to be allowed to go all the way to the end. But, still, I've decided to let it run its course. When I'm in the grip of this pain, I understand that death will be a release.

Dennis is right: Waverley is becoming as shabby and down-at-heels as I am, to my mind a natural and even proper devolution. The house was built in the early 1800s (on land given to the Irish and Italian Catholic servants of the old river families) by the descendants of one Chancellor Livingston, a signer of the Declaration of Independence. . . . Funny that he should be best known for scrawling his name, an act which took several seconds. Or so I was told as a child by my few surviving relatives, Fag Uncle Tommy and my now long-dead great-aunts Emily and Anne, the purveyors of all the family history and lore I'm in possession of. The original Livingston, possibly the chancellor's father, was given a land grant by one of the English kings; George I strikes me as a plausible suspect. This grant covered about fifty square miles and amounted to a medieval fiefdom, since the Livingston family was able to live off the rents paid by all their tenant farmers, the people living within the land grant. Early in the nineteenth century, the tenants rebelled by refusing to pay the rent, a famous uprising known as the Rent Wars. Learning about this as a child, and about the rest of my family history, I felt no small amount of disgust, guilt, and outrage— no pride, and no sense of loyalty or responsibility: why did these people feel so entitled to so much?

As for the name of the house, after the novel *Waverley,* Sir

Walter Scott was a Romantic, like his contemporaries Shelley and Byron. To some degree, his liberal ideals were a by-product of the French Revolution, which was why he was so admired by continental artists and middle-class rebels like Verdi, Schumann, Lizst, and Berlioz, who wanted their countries to become nations on the model of the new American Republic or the French Republic. The eponymous young hero of Scott's first novel, which was published around the time the house was built, is a passionate dilettante according to the Romantic model, a feckless scion who finds himself among the Jacobites on the Scottish Highlands during the rebellion of 1745. In the course of the book he experiences war, gets a load of the quirky Scottish Highland folk, and learns the invaluable lesson that life is not like Romantic literature. The book was a raging success, so much so that the newly rich, would-be patrician, staunchly American Standish-Parrish-Whittier clan was so enamored of it that they named their new estate after him.

The estate had its own train station until the 1950s. The railway company allowed this, even though there was already a law of eminent domain, because they'd built the train tracks along the river estates of the Livingston descendants, in return for which they granted each family the right to flag down a train for its own convenience. I can imagine some male forebear in a waistcoat and breeches flagging down a train, his lower lip thrust forward in a peremptory manner, his eyes glittering with imperious certainty that the train would stop. This image of his arm with its manicured hand commandeering all those tons of hot, pulsing steel-in-motion makes me want to throttle him and throw him under the wheels. . . .

It is because of this and other stories that I, as a laissez-faire, elitist man of no people, am of the (minority) opinion that the ludicrously named Waverley and the equally ludicrous life-style it was meant to support have reached a necessary end. This end should be honored, as all natural ends should be; I am against artificial life support. Accordingly, Waverley and I have moldered together in diplomatic mutual forbearance: I won't say anything about your wrinkles and wheezing if you don't mention mine. Plaster sags on the wall of the back staircase leading up to my tower bedroom. One night, if I brush against it, it will come cascading down on my head, and I don't care. The fussy imported French wallpaper, stretched on muslin, is peeling here, faded there, and the front-veranda fresco on the house's stucco face has faded; the faint fluffy blobs once were sheep, I think, but where oh where has their sylvan shepherdess gone? The field, which used to be a pruned green lawn, on which fine young aristocrats no doubt played croquet and drank lemon squash in the summertime in flannel trousers or seersucker suits or flapper dresses, is now returning to wilderness. Saplings are springing up in its expanse, and I let them thrive unmolested.

I've worn an invisible path through the years from the kitchen to the side veranda, up the back staircase to the tower, my bedroom and the library below, and in winter to the "home parlor," next to the dining room, the least cluttered and easiest to heat of all the downstairs rooms, the friendliest besides the kitchen. It contains, among other things, an original old chest-high Edison gramophone on whose turntable is a recording by Henri Gendron and his orchestra of a song called "Gigolette"; it's been there for as long as I can remember, and occasionally I play it. Who left it there? Maybe a dreamy young great-aunt. The gramophone works perfectly, even now, when the "modern" eight-track and cassette players of my youth long ago went belly-up. At the crank of the handle and touch of the needle the song warbles to life, slowing old-fashionedly as it progresses but almost free of crackles.

I tend to avoid the rest of the house and its teeming overcrowdedness. The accumulated strata of time and people and objects in parlor, sitting room, ballroom, and upstairs bedrooms make me slightly queasy, all the ornate marble fireplaces, beds with carved headboards, grand and lesser pianos with yellowed keys, probably out of tune, clarinets, flutes, autoharps lying still as dead animals . . . the blank-eyed marble busts . . . the pair of hand-painted screens, one with knock-kneed cranes in a stand of bamboo and the other depicting a black wolf passionately eviscerating a prim white stag. In these rooms I feel the intolerable pressure of too many things, all the historical significance of a family whose names are, in the end, more important and memorable than any of the individual souls who bore them—Livingston, Stuyvesant, Standish, Parrish, Whittier—it's like kicking around an archaeological site, walking through those rooms. I need a pickax and notebook and specimen bag, and an intern to carry my lunch.

I live in the octagonal tower on the river side of the house, a 1907 addition, the part of Waverley least burdened by ghosts and objects. On my tower's first floor is the octagonal library, whose upper walls and ceiling glow with intricate trompe-l'oeil faux-bois plaster, underneath which are walnut shelves that rise from floor to crown molding and hold crammed-together rows of priceless leather-bound books—such amazing books—ancient issues of *Cornhill* and *Blackwell's,* the *Encyclopædia Britannica* from the 1790s, with its fantastic illustrations, its contributions by Diderot and Rousseau. A treasure trove of eighteenth-century reference books, Dr. Johnson's *Dictionary,* all eleven volumes of Diderot's *Encyclopedia.* The room contains most of the great and minor classics of eighteenth- and nineteenth-century literature, tissue-thin ink-lined pages preserved in old leather.

I sleep in the former billiards room, one flight up from the library. Above my room, on the third floor, is an empty aerie that used to be a schoolroom, long ago. Now it contains only the spiral staircase to the circular widow's walk on the tower roof. When I was younger and in love, I brought my bride, Sonia, up there in warm weather with drinks and rattan chairs to watch the sunset turn the river all manner of lurid romantic colors. We slept together in my room. When Bellatrix was born (how long ago? almost eleven years?), we kept her in the old bassinet near our bed. When she cried, Sonia would leap naked and quivering with animal mother-love from our bed and snatch her up and suckle her, squawking what must have been Polish lullabies.

And now I sleep alone, in this same tower room . . . and eventually, maybe soon, I'll die here. My death isn't anything I fear or abhor. It's mine alone, and I'd like to be left in peace to get on with it.

This doesn't seem to be going to happen. Speaking of thriving unmolested.

In the five or six years since I retreated "for good" from the social hubbub and commerce of life, my so-called company has consisted until now primarily of canvas ghosts, the disembodied faces of ancestors in rooms I rarely enter. Every room of Waverley except my bedroom and the kitchen is roughly as crowded as a train station with mostly second-rate oil portraits of my line, a dark-haired race with veiled eyes, some dull and arrogant, a few others with a hint of wayward madness, rebellion, ironic mockery, which I seem to have inherited along with all the other remnants of my manifestly unwanted heritage. More of these portraits crowd the "new wing," built onto the main part of the house at the turn of the last century to accommodate my great-grandparents' crop of eight children. Upstairs are those children's old nurseries, bedrooms, and playrooms; the ballroom downstairs is where they "came out," got married, etc.

My grandmother Julia Standish's portraits hang in the parlor, on the second-floor landing, and upstairs in her old bedroom, all of them depicting at varying ages the same stubborn chin, mischievous eyes with a hint of meanness, and the mouth well shaped but not at all sensual. She was the firstborn and favorite, and as such inherited Waverley outright the day her parents' sailboat capsized in a sudden storm off the coast of Nantucket. Her seven younger siblings must have been distressed and outraged, but a will is a will. Grandma lived here for the rest of her life with my grandfather Henry Stuyvesant Whittier and their two sons and all the servants.

The Standish-Whittier line is dying out. . . . I have a number of scattered cousins around the area, but I don't know them well. There was some bad feeling in the family when my grandmother inherited Waverley. Her weak-minded spinster sisters, Emily and Anne, forgave her, and were eventually allowed to come back to live here until they died, but the rest of them stayed away from the place for the rest of their lives, as do their descendants. Not that I blame them. Or have any desire to know them.

When Grandma died, the place went to my father and Fag Uncle Tommy, now an ancient homo who lives in a West Village townhouse in the city and hasn't been back here since my mother's funeral sixteen years ago. Dennis and I inherited our father's half of Waverley along with his family money, which is for all practical purposes enough to support us and whatever dependents we amass, but not enough to do anything wild or extravagant, such as restoring and repairing this house or indulging whatever midlife crises we may fall prey to with Jaguars and starlets. We could of course have chosen to pursue legitimate careers, but that sort of thing doesn't suit me a bit, and Dennis would maintain that he has pursued a legitimate career despite the fact that he doesn't make much money at it.

Therefore, Waverley is falling down and Dennis and I are limited to well-built old American cars and ordinary women with pedestrian tastes, which seem to suit both of us equally well, one of the few things we have in common.

October 16—Was Sonia really everything I remember her as being? Nostalgia plays shadow-puppet tricks on the mind. She looked wan and tired in the winter. Her eyes had a beadiness in candlelight late at night over backgammon and grappa. Her voice squawked like a magpie's. She was a bit of a magpie, Sonia. Always looking for glittering objects and secreting them away. Sometimes I miss her in my bones. Knowing her is not the same as loving her. But people have layers like onions and planets, and Sonia's obdurate, complex, alien shell cracked to reveal something else entirely, like a crustacean smashed against a rock to free an ermine, something ineffably soft, rare, shy, and tender with a quivering little face. I knew that. I can't forget it. But I'm loath to believe it, nostalgia being the trickster god it is, the Loki of the emotions.

I must have been born under the sign of that trickster god, and have been ruled all my life by nothing more than his whims and illusions, his mischief. Maybe it's not only me. My generation is a sudden tail-end-of-the-Boom dip on the population-explosion graph, the unprepossessing trough characterized only by a shared generalized nostalgia for some America that almost but never quite existed—I envision us as a tiny tribe of isolates scattered around the coasts, clinging to the edges like aliens yearning for some golden, decadent, hot-browed era of martinis and Louis Prima and Harlem midnight suppers, apothecaries selling morphine-laced beverages, wooden dice rolling on deep-green baize, that zingy old New York pulse and fizzle, sad gas stations out west we drive up to in our roadsters and Thunderbird convertibles, to refill our tanks for fifteen cents a gallon and move on from, leave behind in red dust, Shell sign flapping in hot wind, on our way to Palm Springs to shack up in some turquoise geometric motel with intergalactic decor and a butterfly-shaped pool, drinking gin and fresh orange juice and smoking Luckys and solving murders and eating ham sandwiches at 3 a.m. . . . . We live in our own romance stories, detective novels, noir films, all that jazz.

It was another bad night. It's either generalize about my generation, or dwell self-pityingly on the electric demons in my leg. The instant I give in to self-pity, I'll shoot myself.

This is my garum mood. My rib cage is filled with a strong, caustic brew, and my bones are turning to jelly, my guts likewise liquefying, digesting themselves, giving rise to these thick, pungent, unspeakably reeking private thoughts.

Garum was the Roman delicacy that cost the earth and played a role in historical conquests and gourmandise alike, recipe as follows (I think, anyway, but am too lazy to get up and check my reference books): Take fish guts, add salt and water, let stand and rot in the sun. It will literally digest itself; rather, the intestinal bacteria will digest the intestines themselves. Strain the resulting effluvium, add fragrant dried herbs, let rot some more, put a cork in it, and use a few drops of this fish-gut liqueur (called alec, the animal equivalent of marc) to flavor everything from cereal to stew. The Romans used garum in almost all their recipes. No wonder they vomited so much. It's an ancient recipe; Greek colonists used it when Rome was still a caravansery, and it played a role in the conquest of Gaul, because of all the garum-prospering trading posts up and down the coasts of France and Spain. Add water to it and you have hydrogarum. Add oil: oleogarum. Vinegar: oxygarum. Sanguine garum: made with tuna guts and blood.

There's a modern dish, a descendant of garum, called pissaladière, a Provençal delicacy made of whole cheap strong-tasting oily fish like anchovies and mackerel, whatever is too tiny or bony or garbagey to eat on its own. Smash them all together in a big earthenware jar with coarse salt and herbs, in layers, finishing with a layer of herbs. Let it sit under a heavy flat stone in a cool place until all the salt dissolves. This takes a while, so be patient. Days, even weeks. Then strain it, purée it, and store it under a fresh layer of coarse salt. You can add onions and olives if you like it that way. Spread it on flatbread for Ligurian peasant pizza.

I tried to make it once. Sometimes I like to eat something for the idea, the romance of it. But this putrescence . . .

Was unforgivably distracted then by Dennis, who came a-knocking on my sanctuary door.

My leg pain would be alleviated if I quit smoking, but I'm uninterested in considering this because it's not a choice for me. To live without smoking is no life.

In another notebook, I recently tried to write down how I made some of the dishes I've cooked over the years. Recipes, all right, that's what they are. But the effort it took to reconstruct those meals I made and enjoyed a long time ago put me in a foul mood, this nostalgic Loki garum mood. Why do people write recipes?

A recipe is a cruel joke.

I'm conceiving a brutal, half-hateful crush on the late, great, much-lamented food-memoir author M.F.K. Fisher, that uppity little slyboots of a voluptuary autodidact, that fresh-faced Irish smartypants. I ask myself—as I set down measurements of this and that, tell my unknown galley slave to wait until the butter is foaming before adding minced shallots, conjure the giving, fleshy plumpness of dried cherries in stout sauce for holiday ham—where Mary Frances got the idea that her foodie musings would interest anyone. She wrote book after book about her own thoughts, experiences, and ideas concerning food. I lack that idea fundamentally. I can't expect anyone to look to me for any kitchenary authority. But . . . again, the futile urge to impart my deepest secrets before I go.

Montaigne, even in his original hard-to-follow old French, pleases me as much as Fisher these days. They were doing the same thing, really, hedging their bets against death, shoring the fragments of their ruins with words. That crazy old François Villon as well, who wrote, *"Qui meurt, a ses lois de tout dire."* The dying man has the right to say anything. And I suppose in my own way that's what I'm doing.

How to make holiday sauce for ham (not recommended for hermits, for obvious reasons): Whisk a couple of tablespoons of cornstarch into a cup of chicken stock or broth. Melt a wad of butter in a skillet till it foams, then sauté three minced shallots in it for a few minutes. Add a pinch of allspice; stir for half a minute. Add four cups of dark stout, a cup of tart dried cherries. Simmer this for ten minutes, until it thickens a little. Rewhisk the chicken broth and cornstarch to mix it again, and then stir it gradually into the stout mixture. Cook this until it thickens, remove from heat, add one and a half tablespoons balsamic vinegar, then salt and pepper to taste. Serve this smoky, fruity, blackish, bitter-at-the-end sauce with hot sliced hickory-smoked ham, in a pitcher on the side with a ladle.

I've left out an ingredient, the one that's supposed to go in with the stout and cherries. So whoever follows this recipe is guaranteed to fail, insofar as his or her sauce is guaranteed not to be the same as mine, the gold standard only because it's my recipe. I can't remember now what it was, but if I made it now in the kitchen, it would come to my hand at the right instant. It's not a malicious omission. . . . Maybe it's a drop of garum.

There is no better combination than that of velvety butter and fumey alcohol, and, later, fatty tender meat.

There is nothing less interesting to me than the idea of a hol-

iday meal with eight or ten or twenty people related to one another by blood or marriage; the thought of such a meal and its
proscriptions and protocols causes me to fall instantly asleep.

I'm boring myself so much I can hardly hold the pen.

After he barged into my chambers, Dennis parked his flat, entitled rear end on the seat of my favorite chair, the armchair facing the windows that look out over the river, and proceeded to
explain the end of his marriage to me while I sat on my bed in
my pajamas, squinting at him with all the hatred I bear him,
which is a heavy force, although he's as ignorant of that as he is
of everything else about me, including the fact that in a short
while I'll be dead. Dennis can be counted on to be a narcissist
in every particular until his own end, whenever that may be
slated to take place. My one regret in being terminal is that I
will never know this, or other things.

He told me much, much more than I wanted to know, and
now I feel unhealthily burdened and implicated. Nothing is
more revolting to me than other people's unasked-for, sweaty,
hot-breathed confidences, especially my brother's.

In that even, earnest, self-justifying voice I know as well as
the smell of my own shit, he announced that he had come back
to Waverley because Marie had asked him to leave.

She had forced him to admit that he had fallen out of love
with her, and then she kicked him out.

He didn't fight, which is typical of Dennis.

I'm sure she must have anticipated that, since she knows him
better than anyone else, even I.

She must also have known perfectly well that even though
the romantic part of their marriage was over, he would have

stayed anyway, for the kids' sake, for the sake of his vows, propriety, family honor, all the things he believes in most fervently, if she hadn't called his bluff.

"We never have sex any more," she'd apparently said the night before he left, in bed, just as they were falling asleep. The Bildungsroman narrator who channels himself through Dennis's vocal cords informed me that this statement came at my brother out of the depths of the darkness, trembling with outrage.

They'd both lost interest in sex in recent years, he replied, or so it seemed to him. But it was so like her to blame him for the whole problem.

"Well," she said harshly, "do you still want to?"

"Sometimes," he said. It was true, Dennis told me now, as always wide-eyed at his own forthright goodness, priggishly astonished at other people's raging passions, their needs. And sometimes he did still want her. But she'd made herself so remote and inaccessible, the effort it seemed it would take to arouse her seemed as if it wouldn't ultimately be worth the payoff, so he'd just given up altogether. He had been under the impression that it was she who was no longer interested, and so he had stopped trying, rather than suffer the indignity of rejection night after night.

I gazed up at my bedroom ceiling and followed with my eyes the long crack in the plaster that leads to nowhere.

They'd never had a great sex life, as far as Dennis was concerned, even during their courtship. Making love (of course he calls it that) with Marie had always been oddly unsatisfactory to him, even though he was attracted to her and loved her body and thought she was beautiful, because Dennis wanted to do everything, all the time, no holds barred, and she didn't. He'd respected Marie's cooler temperament and romantic notions of lovemaking, and maybe because of this, he'd always been hot for other women throughout their whole marriage, sometimes to the point of obsession, extreme temptation, but he'd never acted on his feelings. Though he could hardly admit this, he secretly felt that Marie should be grateful to him for overcoming his often intense yearning for other women. All right, for Stephanie Fox, she was the one he really wanted; he admitted it.

I perked up a little at the mention of Stephanie Fox. "Will you call her now and confess your ardor?" I asked with real interest.

"Other men would have cheated," said Dennis, oblivious, or pretending to be, and in any case not to be deterred from the narration of the story he'd set out to tell. "I didn't. Of course I know this is slightly disingenuous. Why should my wife be grateful to me for being faithful? Why didn't I just have an affair?"

"What I wonder," I said, "is this: why, given your history, did she bring up the topic of your sex life in that accusatory tone? She could have tried to seduce you if she'd really wanted the marriage to continue."

"Why do you think?" Dennis asked—rhetorically, no doubt.

"Obviously," I shot back, "she was trying to bring it all to a head so she could get it over and done with. She was looking for an out. She was sick of you."

"I think you're right," he said.

I sat up and lit a cigarette, then turned on my bedside radio and fiddled with the dial until I found Benny Goodman and his swingin' licorice stick.

"And then she told me to leave the next day," said Dennis. (I could easily imagine her half-hostile, wet-nosed voice.) "She said, 'I want you to move out tomorrow. It's over. I want a divorce.' "

At this point I had to point out, hypocritically, having driven my own once-beloved wife away, and having had plenty of time since then to mull it all over, that maybe he should have taken her into his arms, tried to win her back, smothered her with warmth; maybe he could have rekindled something.

"No," said Dennis. "I felt defeated by the hard, cold edge in her voice, even through her tears. It didn't invite reconciliation. She sounded almost relieved that I was finally going. I left the next night, after the girls were in bed, having spent the day loading my things into the U-Haul, and the evening reading stories to Evie and Isabelle. Marie said goodbye to me, then turned out the front-door light and closed the door before I'd even started the engine. So I drove away from the house we raised children in and lived in together, and now here I am. I always wondered how a marriage dissolved, what the straw was that would break the camel's back."

"You could have asked me," I said. "I could have given you a hint."

"And now I know. It's not so much a straw as a rising tide that finally overflows and drowns whatever goodwill and tenderness remain. Together we let the floodwaters rise between us, and together we sent me out to sea in a pea-green boat alone."

"Not literally to sea," I said glumly. "And not entirely alone."

"Well," said Dennis, "thanks for listening. I thought you should know the story."

He got up and went back downstairs.

October 17—A cup of hard-packed dark brown sugar. Just for the record.

October 18—The horse-chestnut tree that grows directly outside my window has a mottled pattern on its bark that looks like a smooth cellulose version of the fur of some great savanna cat. Most of the leaves are gone, but the few that remain are curled inward like reddish-dun claws, parchment-thin. Covering the tree like ornaments on a *Tannenbaum* are pairs of furry brown balls the size of walnuts. The birds who alight and roost in its branches are round, compact, having the meaty heft of small pheasants or doves and speckled black-and-white breasts and all-black overcoats; they are sociable and sharp-beaked, and seem to enjoy bouncing gently on the elastic smaller boughs. As the light changes throughout the day, the shades of bark and birds shift and change; the sun coats the leaves and testicle-balls with light that makes them seem to glow from the inside out.

It's beautiful, I say completely without irony.

Meanwhile, I have discovered another one of Dennis's secrets, this one completely by accident. It explains his question about the Caller ID block, which has been nagging at me.

He was dialing the phone in the front hall earlier, as I was coming downstairs. I paused to eavesdrop on his conversation. It was so quiet I could hear the purr of the line ringing faintly, and then a woman's voice, answering.

It was the oddest thing: Dennis didn't say a word. He waited, his back to me. I heard her sharp question, her rising indignation, and then the click as she broke the connection.

Who was she? I had to know, of course. I suspected strongly that he was telephoning Stephanie Fox to ask her to meet him at Rex's Roadhouse and then losing his nerve at the fatal last instant; this would have been all too typical of him. So, after he'd gone back outside, Encyclopedia Brown, boy detective, made his stealthy, sleuthy way down the stairs, took possession of the telephone, and cleverly hit the redial button.

"Hello?"

It was Marie's voice, unmistakably.

I didn't say a word.

"I'm calling the police," she said as I was hanging up.

So. Dennis has made a silent call to his own wife for reasons I can't even begin to guess at. At least one: who knows how many other times he's done it? And now I've done it too, after breaking into her house and making off with the au pair. What will we do next?

My old easy, habitual life of deception and crime seems to be smoldering to life again. Before I know it, I'll be running drugs or crashing uninvited in other people's houses once more.

No, I won't. Instead, I have a strong and not at all innocent desire to contact Louisa, to try to trick her into seeing me again. I could have asked whether she was home just then, instead of hanging up on Marie, and pleaded total ignorance of that other call and caller. But she would have suspected me, of course, and of course my entire life has been arranged to avoid getting in the middle of anything. Aha, she would have thought, Hugo—I knew it all along! I'm the natural enemy of my sister-in-law.

October 19—Last night, on my way across the river, the headlights cut through the darkness as if I could follow them and they'd take me wherever I wanted to go.

Rex's Roadhouse is an old shack on a small stream, set back from the road, lurking in the woods. Weekend people don't come here much, just locals—adulterers, drunks, college kids, and regulars. The back wall is almost all glass, so you sit at the dark bar and look out at the lit-from-below woods and stream. It's all very romantic, ramshackle, rough-hewn. The room is about the size of a basement rec room and holds an unassuming bar, some cracked red leatherette booths with scuffed tables, a dartboard, a cigarette-burned pool table, and a jukebox stocked with old country-and-Western legends' B-sides. The whole place smells of wet rags that have wiped used ashtrays and beer spills and then been left to molder in a wet heap in a bus tub.

I sat at the far end of the bar and ordered a shot of whiskey and a draft. While the droopy yokel behind the bar applied himself fervently to bottle and tap, I examined my hands, which I'd cleaned carefully that morning, along with every other inch of my visible self, in addition to trimming my nose hairs, cutting my toenails, and shaving twice. No more filth on my person, was the general idea I was suddenly espousing; Hugo goes a-hunting-oh in poontang season. But there was already a layer of dirt under my fingernails. And even as I write this, although I've cleaned my nails again in the interim, the grime has come seeping back, the exfoliated by-product of my unfulfilled yearnings.

That's a bunch of hogwash.

My yearnings have been fulfilled, every one of them: sex, revenge, trouble.

A woman came in when I was halfway through my second round. That made three of us here at Rex's: me, the yokel, and her. She stood in the doorway for a moment while her eyes got used to the murk, her face bright and anticipatory. She was older: no postpubescent girl, this was the real thing, established, professional, almost certainly married to a male counterpart, a matching duo of doctors or therapists or professors. She had a white-gold, wavy, but carefully managed mane, wore a low-cut white blouse and a form-fitting skirt that came to just above her shapely knees, and was an utterly acceptable variant of my librarian-taking-off-her-glasses fantasy except that she wore no glasses, and her hair, rather than being in some degree of bun, floated freely around her head and neck. She shimmered with the muscular vibrancy of someone focused, driven, healthy but very bored, that cerebral, pent-up lustiness that's always made my blood rise like a war cry from over the distant hills.

When she met my eyes, she headed straight toward me.

It occasionally happens that I meet people who become instant intimates. This happens more or less according to the period of my life I am in. This woman and I seemed to know something about each other right away, and dispensed accordingly with the usual sideways tactics.

Head-on, she slid onto the stool next to mine.

"Hi there," she said easily. I resisted a strong temptation to kiss her on the mouth. We had plenty of time, and our pick of five or six old motels within a mile of the place. "Been here long?"

"Feels like years," I said. "Where've you been?"

"Oh," she said with a half-smile, "you don't want to know."

"What are you drinking?"

"Hooch," she said to both me and the bartender. "Bombay-gin martini, very dry, shaken, and straight up with olives."

We sat elbow to elbow, looking out at the woods. She smelled lemony. I finished my whiskey and set the shot glass back down on the bar so it made a satisfying rap against the cheap wood.

"Who are you, anyway?" she asked.

"I'm Hugo."

"Are you sure?" she asked, puzzled. "You don't look like a Hugo."

"Oh, but I am," I said grandly.

"No, you look like a David," she said.

"Well, I'm not a David."

"Wait a minute. Hugo who?"

"Whittier," I told her, my pride suddenly all gone.

"Hugo Whittier," she said, snapping her fingers. "Not Dennis's brother?"

"Well, I'm a lot more than that," I said.

"I'm Stephanie Fox," she said. "Dennis and Marie are good friends of my husband's and mine."

"Dennis is not such a good friend to your husband, actually, Stephanie."

Her martini came. She lifted the big inverted pyramid in

both hands and took an oddly humble sip, as if she were a mendicant who'd been handed a charity soup bowl.

"Ah," she exhaled, licking her lips, then returned her attention to me. "Hugo, please tell me what you're talking about."

"I'd better not," I said, having used the interval of her tasting her drink to collect my wits, or as many of them as could be summoned, which had turned out to be just enough to realize that this line of inquiry was not in my own best interests.

She wasn't laughing, but her merriment was clearly visible, an effervescence around her head like tiny cartoon champagne bubbles rising from an uncorked bottle. "Fair enough," she said. "Although I hope you meant what I think you meant."

The bartender's pointy ears twitched with the effort to look as if he weren't listening.

"I'll have another whiskey," I said, and he leapt to the bottle and slung a good dose into my glass, hoping he wouldn't interrupt this conversation, which was the most entertaining thing to come down the pike in a while.

"So Dennis has moved back to his old house," she said.

"Pathetic, isn't it?" I said swiftly. "Running home to the roost."

"Well, he had to go somewhere," she said. "How is he these days?"

"Miserable," I said, baring my teeth at her in a smiling mammalian display of harmlessness, but inwardly violent.

"Poor thing," she said, her voice cracking with held-in laughter. "I'm laughing," she hastened to explain, possibly sensing my mood, "because he seemed like a fish out of water in that Stonekill house. Do you know what I mean? Wearing one of Marie's aprons in that kitchen, making chicken nuggets for the kiddies, watering the herbs on the windowsill, giving Marie a rundown of his day. Maybe because he strikes me as a born bachelor. Does it run in your family?"

"I have a wife, and her daughter bears my name," I said.

"At Waverley?"

"They chose to go elsewhere, oh, about ten years ago. But I am married, as is Dennis. Born bachelors don't tend to get themselves into such situations."

"They do if they're caught in them."

"Meanwhile, I came here to escape Dennis, and now you're insisting on talking about him."

"Well, frankly, I'm here to escape my husband. I'm a born bachelor too, you know. I can't believe I got caught, myself. To make everything worse, or at least more complicated, Bun wants to have a baby. Sorry, I know this is personal information. Whatever. I'm in a confidential mood. You can tell me to change the subject."

"And you don't?"

She glanced at me with appreciation for something: my willingness to pursue the topic, or my perspicacity at guessing her feelings? Maybe both. "I do not."

"What woman doesn't want a baby?" I asked with a roguish twinkle.

"This one," she said. "I don't want a baby, not now, not ever. I might have consented to breed one or two of them when I was twenty-five or thirty, but now we're just too old."

"How old are you?"

"Forty," she replied promptly.

I reassessed her openly. She didn't look it, but, then, who did these days, besides me?

"You look younger," I said. "What if it's still physically possible for you to have a baby?"

"We're still too old!" she said. "What is this new fad, elderly new parents? I was raised by young parents with a lot of energy to discipline us and take us places. I couldn't offer the same, I'm far too set in my ways and distracted and impatient. Of course,

Bun says we could offer wisdom and security instead of youthful energy."

"My wife gave birth to her daughter when she was twenty-seven and I was twenty-nine," I said proudly.

"Well, that's all very well," said Stephanie. "But, frankly, I don't think anyone over thirty, or thirty-two at the very latest, should have children. It doesn't seem right, either biologically or psychologically. Babies are boring, and you have to be young to put up with them. I'm just not in that mind-set any more. I like what I like, and I don't want to give any of it up for anyone."

She shook a cigarette from my pack, which was on the bar at her elbow, then offered the pack to me. I raised my eyebrows in ironic thanks, which she caught, and took one, then lit hers first.

"I'm not arguing," I said. "I agree with you."

"Look around the world. Are there too few people here, or too many? Are the billions of us worth replicating? Biology and hormones blind us to the fact that we've become indentured slaves to little egocentric tyrants."

"And why the fuss about DNA and genes and bloodlines?" I said innocently, conveniently not mentioning my own semi-quasi-obsession where my wife Sonia's daughter is concerned.

"Exactly," she said, visibly warming to me. As she resettled on her barstool, her shoulder brushed mine. The contact somehow released a cloud of lemony perfume from her hair. Then she steadied herself with a hand on my shoulder, as if she'd been about to tip over, and leaned into me; looking down, I caught a glimpse of the shapely tops of her breasts held in a bra under the slippery white blouse. This gave me an almost instant erection. "Children have no function any more," she went on as if she were unaware of her effect on me, which I would have bet any money she wasn't, "no social advantage. Almost no one questions the inevitability of parenthood; almost no one rebels against its tyranny. Well, here I am, Exhibit A: living proof that a life is not incomplete without children. I never have to forgo a dinner party, a movie, a walk, or any other civilized pleasure because of someone's naptime or feeding time or playdate or carpool or birthday party. The idea that a child-free life is empty is a myth perpetrated by proselytizing parents who can't remember what their lives were like before they had kids, or can't imagine what they'd do if they didn't have them. I think Bun is a deluded romantic."

I wanted to fuck her in the most biological, hormone-driven way. "Do you feel this way about marriage too?" I asked as if I were merely curious and had no agenda.

"Increasingly," she said. "But only because it has a way of softening otherwise interesting men. Bun used to be exciting. Now he's a big zero. Men are programmed to either please women or defy them; there doesn't seem to be any middle ground. If they defy their wives, we get angry. If they're too eager to please, we get bored. Men as a species need to evolve to the next level."

"My wife left me because I both defied and bored her," I said. "Maybe it's women's fault partially, for demanding this emasculating fealty from us. Maybe women could use a little evolving themselves."

"Touché," she said wearily. "But, really, what's the point? According to the rules, we all lose. We can't have anyone else, we have to train ourselves to act in ways that run completely counter to our natures, and financially, at least for me, there are no real advantages. Bun and I are both lawyers; we both make plenty of money. I get on his nerves as much as he gets on mine. I'm just not cut out for this."

"I see our time is up," I said. I didn't care for the topic of her husband; I would have been happy to discuss just about anything else under the sun with her.

"Oh, sorry," she blurted, and laughed again, but angrily this time. "Frankly, this isn't my first stop on my way home from work tonight. I put in some time earlier at a tavern near my office, but there was no one there to talk to."

"Ah," I said. I was doing my best impersonation of Hugo the Barfly, sweet-natured, passive drunk. Meanwhile, I itched to wrestle with her and slap her and bite her with heated blood-lust until she yelled and foamed at the mouth, then I wanted to slam every hard external appendage I owned into every wet warm receptor on her and repeatedly bash it all into her until we both went into frenzied spasms and collapsed.

I told her affably, "Stephanie, I'm dying. Dennis doesn't know. You're the only person I've told besides my doctor, who in fact told me."

She gave me a sidelong look. "You're dying of what, exactly?"

"Buerger's disease."

"Which is what?"

"Caused by smoking," I said. "Two packs a day, that's what did it. If I quit, I could beat it."

She looked intrigued. "Really? What are your symptoms? You look fine to me, quite frankly."

"Thank you," I said. "As it happens I have Buerger's disease, also known as thromboangiitis obliterans, which results when fatty deposits caused by bad health habits narrow the major arteries carrying blood to the legs and feet. The smaller, collateral vessels can't handle the load, and so any exertion, walking for a short distance or up several flights of stairs, causes muscle cramping and aches in the feet and calves. This is often the first symptom, which I first noticed last spring, and which has since worsened to the next level—namely, numbness, tingling, and, recently, often severe pain. Tra-la! And next will come vascular inflammation, ischemia, and claudication, and eventually ulceration, infection, gangrene, amputation, death. I can expect the pain to get much worse, spread to my other foot and both legs. I can expect my toes to blacken and have to be amputated, or an entire leg. I can expect hideous lesions on my limbs and face, chronic and intolerable pain, extreme sensitivity to heat and cold."

"My God," she said. "So quit smoking!"

"I won't quit smoking," I said, and lit another cigarette to prove it.

"You would rather die than quit?"

"Me and millions of other smokers," I said. "I'm just going to go faster and more honestly than some, that's all."

"Oh, come on," she said. "Are you serious?"

"About this," I said, "I couldn't be more serious. What's wrong with dying? Nothing, except most people are afraid of it. Well, I'm not afraid of it, and I see no reason to live if I can't smoke. Smoking," I added with a hint of laughter, "is the love of my life."

She encircled my wrist with her warm fingers and held my hand on the bar so I couldn't take another drag. "I'm in love with your brother," she said almost pleadingly, as if trading her darkest secret for my own. My cigarette fumed, stilled by her hand.

"Why?"

"Because he's exciting."

"Dennis? He was never exciting. He was born a stick and then he got married."

"He's an artist," she said with a sigh. "I wish I had become an artist. I didn't have the courage; I took the road most traveled. Law school? Any half-intelligent monkey can be a lawyer."

"Don't," I said with a grimace, "romanticize artists. Any brain-damaged monkey can be an artist. There's nothing ro-mantic about Dennis. He bangs big pieces of steel into unrecognizable but ostensibly interesting and oversized shapes and sells them at an upscale SoHo boutique. Actually, I believe it's in Chelsea now. The point is, the nobility of the artistic life is vastly overrated. Dennis has a trust fund. He didn't have to go to law school, although he could have gone to Harvard with no effort whatsoever because our father did. Being an artist is no more or less noble than being a lawyer. Please don't kid yourself. It's possibly the most selfish, childish, unjustifiable pursuit on the planet."

"We need art," said Stephanie. "It's the lungs of society the way religion is the immune system. Books and paintings and sculptures allow us hoi polloi to breathe."

"Artists have sold you so-called hoi polloi a bill of goods for centuries. They're just trying to justify the fact that all they have to do all day is drink too much and make mud pies and feel everything much too intensely because life just hurts too much. They're socially inept malcontents who can't hack working for anyone else. Take Dennis, for example."

"You only say that because you're his brother," she said.

"I say that because I'm myself," I said. "I don't base my opinions around what Dennis does or doesn't do."

She looked at her martini for a while. I waited for her to spit it out so we could move along to the next level of our budding friendship.

"I just wish I knew whether he feels the same way," she said finally, not quite meeting my eyes. "I think he does—in fact, I'm sure he does—but then I doubt myself. Do you know?"

"He doesn't," I lied smoothly and automatically, without batting an eye.

She flinched.

"Maybe it's better that you should know for sure than keep wondering and risk your marriage for him. Dennis is a stickler for propriety and commitment, no matter how much you wish he were a bachelor. He can't love you, it's not in his makeup. He loves his wife."

"Hugo," she said, "you're wrecking my day here."

"Sorry," I said with a purely manufactured but I hoped convincing sympathetic grimace, "but I happen to know that Dennis would eventually irritate and bore you as much as Bun does now, the minute that first flush of love wore off. It's the natural and inevitable progress of the disease of marriage: from cramps and fatigue to tingling and numbness to intolerable pain to amputation of major limbs. That's just the way it always goes, and nothing will ever change that. That's why God invented adultery and stuck it in the Bible as a big no-no, so we could sneak off and indulge ourselves in it with all the guilt in the world. The forbidden has always been the greatest aphrodisiac, and evermore shall be, amen."

I sat back and waited for Stephanie's pragmatic, lawyerlike internal calculus to unfold: she couldn't have Dennis, but here was his randy, available younger brother, all liquored up, with his bare wrist caught in her fist.

Shortly after this exchange, we checked into Betty Lou's Motor Court, a place of seedy perfection. We made the bedsprings squeak, banged our heads against the wall, made guttural noises, did everything according to the adultery script. She was technically cheating on Bun the same way I was cheating on Sonia, who despite everything is still my wife, and whom I've cheated on many times before, but, really, Dennis might as well have been watching from inside the particle-board half-closet or the cut-out eyes of the portrait of some long-ago hunter in a rococo frame on the wall above the bed, or huddled beneath the reeking flock flower-print bedspread we'd flung to the floor before boarding the bed itself. Stephanie's body consists of well-tended, exfoliated, barely aging flesh over gym-hard muscles. Her almost constant, extremely arousing moans and sighs were at once blindly selfish and heart-rendingly grateful. No one, it seemed, had touched this body in quite a while. Come to think of it, the same went for my own catastrophic and disreputable but still hydraulically sound person.

After I pounded all her orifices with all my limbs, we did indeed go into spasms and collapse. Then we stayed in that bed for a little while, lying on our backs, apart, not touching. For whole minutes, no one said anything. This in itself, this post-coital reticence on her part, was in its way as surprising and pleasurable to me as anything that had preceded it.

"Did you know," I said when the silence had become almost too pleasurable to bear, shattering it the way a little boy breaks apart a butterfly, tearing its flimsy shining wings off with a fiendish sadness, "speaking of adultery, how monks in the Middle Ages who were forbidden to eat meat got around the Vatican's proscription with an ingeniously sneaky and gluttonous loophole?"

"What a convoluted question," she answered. "You want me to guess what loophole they came up with, is that it?"

"Like a game," I said. "You can ask me ten yes or no questions, and if you figure it out, I owe you dinner. If not, you owe me. The intent being to coerce you into eating a meal with me at some point in the near future, of course."

"Does it have to do with disguising meat to look like something else?"

"No."

"Eggs?"

"No."

"Another species besides chicken?"

"Yes. Seven more."

"Meat in another form besides organs and muscles and fat?"

"Yes."

"Mammalian meat of a specific species?"

"Yes."

"Was it technically meat, meaning the flesh of that particular mammal?"

"Yes, counselor."

"Was it . . . some part of the animal the Vatican didn't think to specify as meat?"

"Technically . . . yes."

"Technically yes. So maybe it was the eyeballs—I'm not asking, just thinking out loud. Maybe it was the ground-up bones. Maybe they ate marrow? Is that it? Bone marrow?"

"No," I said gleefully; I love to win. "Two more."

There was a long silence. "I have to get home!" she cried suddenly, leaping out of bed. We showered together in the moldy, rickety little stall with its intermittent, spurting water pressure. She clutched the plastic curtain as the concave bones of my groin collided in deliberate syncopation with her soapy ass cheeks; she yelled out as I reached around and deftly manhandled her meaty goods.

"The genitals?" she asked, reaching for one of the hard, eroded towels that smelled of bleach.

"No. Last question."

"Okay," she said, drying off, "did they eat the unborn fetuses of rabbits, and keep a large number of rabbits for that very purpose in order to have a constant and unending supply, because of the fast turnover of their breeding cycles? Did they regularly make fricassees of dozens of these aborted whole hairless ravioli-sized bunnies with unopened slit eyes and still-liquid innards?"

I deflated—which is to say, every part of me did. "You knew all along?"

She held my gaze with her own in a way that made me lightheaded.

"Rumpelstiltskin is your name," she said mysteriously. "And now you owe me dinner, but not tonight."

Outside, in the parking lot, with the dark empty road gleam-

ing nearby, I took Stephanie into my arms and danced lightly
with her and crooned into her wet hair, "Goodbye, my friend,
it's hard to die, when all the birds are singing in the sky. Now
that the spring is in the air, pretty girls are everywhere—when
you see them I'll be there."

"Oh God," she said, laughing, pushing me away. " 'Seasons
in the Sun.' I haven't heard that song since junior high."

I chucked her under the chin. "It's Hugo's Theme."

And then, while she leaned against her car with her arms
folded, looking rosy and scrubbed clean and ten years younger
than she'd looked when she first walked into the roadhouse, I
recited in my facilely authentic French accent, the direct result
of my year or two as adolescent kept boy and later flaneur-
about-town in Paris:

> "C'est d'humaine beauté l'issue!
> Les bras courts et les mains contraites,
> Des épaules toutes bossues;
> Mamelles, quoi? toutes retraites;
> Telles les hanches que les tettes;
> Du sadinet, fi! Quand des cuisses,
> Cuisses ne sont plus, mais cuissettes
> Grivelées comme saucisses."

"What the fuck does that mean?" Stephanie asked lackadaisi-
cally, unlocking her door with a press of a button on her key
chain and a high beep in response from the car.

"It's medieval French," I said. "No wonder you didn't understand it."

"I don't speak a word of French," she shot back.

"Well, it's the final stanza of a Villon poem narrated by a
whore too old and withered to profit any longer by her trade.
She's describing her own decay, but naturally, this being my

man François, it's a meditation on the inescapable transience of all human beauty."

"Your man François," she said mockingly, and got into her car and drove off with a little spurt of gravel.

Smiling, beaming, floating like a fool on ice, I drove home. Dennis was sitting on the porch of Waverley, drinking a glass of wine, reading a book. I sat with him for a little while, brimming over with the memory of my delectable betrayal. The book he was reading, I couldn't help noticing, was *Anna Karenina*. Coincidence? Not at all: I stole Louisa's copy and then helpfully planted it on the kitchen table at the place Dennis has made his own with his typical domesticated-animal habitude. And, like an overly zealous lab rat, my brother walked with both eyes open right into the trap, because that's where he likes to be. I think it will be instructive, and certainly germane to his own current predicament, for him to read, or reread, the story of Anna and Vronsky and the train. For all I know, this was originally his copy.

Among the many things cluttering the top of the vast old desk in the library is a photograph in a silver frame of my grandfather Henry Whittier, taken on the front veranda with his English setter, Shad. Shad was deeply beloved by Grandpa, as hunting dogs traditionally were by those olden-days WASP men who hunted pheasant, grouse, and woodcock in full hunting regalia and fancied themselves country squires in the English manner, like Squire Allworthy in *Tom Jones*. A story I was told as a boy is the following: One day Grandpa was chopping wood for the fireplace, and Shad put his paw up on the block. Grandpa, not seeing it there, accidentally took it off, and then, as a result, had to have Shad put down. According to family lore, Grandpa thereafter referred to that day as the worst day of his life, this man who'd been through a terrible war, lost two sons barely out of their infancy, and watched his own father choke to death on a chicken bone at the dining-room table in this very house.

This story is, to me, deeply significant of the morbid patrician insanity of my ancestors. Dogs are, although insufferably needy and demanding, considered by some pleasant to have around; they're loyal and friendly and eager to please, and some of them even seem to have little personalities. But Grandpa's feelings for Shad were just unnatural.

Grandpa's first son, my uncle, was named Thomas, after Grandpa's father; his second and third were George and James. They both died of polio as toddlers. My father, his fourth and last son, was born when Tommy was twelve years old, named Henry after Grandpa and immediately given the inexplicable nickname of Bim, presumably to distinguish him from his father. Tommy was born a fag and remained a fag and is a fag to this day; Bim was born a robust red-blooded boy and grew into a Real American Man whose mettle was formed, tried, and proved at Andover, Harvard, Harvard Law, and a prestigious Manhattan law firm.

The girl Bim eventually married, my wretched mother, was the youngest of eight children and the only girl, and thus presumably intended to be a languorous lily-skinned ornament from birth. Her name, as long as Dennis and I knew her, was Mig Whittier, but despite the tennis-skirted, gin-scented alias she was as French as a baguette. She was born in 1937 outside of Paris, in the gatehouse of her land-poor family's Nazi-occupied château, and christened Marguerite Victoire Marie-France de Belloc, an oppressive mouthful that was truncated and Americanized to Mig at the time of her marriage to our father.

Her family had some nobility, a few titles scattered here and there, some money, some land. But, unlike Bim, Mig wasn't concerned with her lineage, and so we almost never heard about it. She rejected completely her family and her past. *"Collaborateurs,"* she would mutter when we asked about them, and leave it at that. Fair enough, I thought, not caring much about relatives. Dennis, on the other hand, naturally made an exploratory swashbuckling trip to France once, in his mid-twenties, in search of the de Bellocs. Whatever he found there caused him not to urge me to go after them in my turn; about them he said, "It was good to meet them, but I don't think I'll make the effort to see any of them again." By this, I assumed they were, despite their pretensions to class, neither interesting, colorful, well educated, nor worldly, all the qualities Dennis so dearly prizes in the mostly dead people on our father's side of things.

I suppose to her credit, Marguerite left her dull, provincially snooty family behind and sailed for America as soon as she was old enough. She taught French for a time at an upper-crust New York girls' school. She met my father, somehow. She married him; of course, she had to, or I wouldn't be here. But despite their matching-bookend names, Mig and Bim Whittier strike me now, in hindsight, as being as ill-matched as a pair could possibly have been without any miscegenation, sexual-identity confusion, or language barrier. As I vaguely but very fondly remember my father, Bim was tall and intelligent and kind and hearty and brimming with health and vigor; as I remember all too well about my mother, Mig was indolent, spoiled, sickly, manipulative, and completely out of her mind. After the wedding, she settled into Waverley and consigned herself to the housekeeper, a big mannish freak named Vivian Jones who ran the place single-handedly while my mother languished in her bedroom upstairs.

True to form, Bim impregnated Mig with his supercharged

sperm shortly after the wedding, and in due time out popped
Dennis. I can imagine, as this fine firstborn son graduated from
mini-tadpole to piscine lump to tailed mutant to arguably viable
fetus, Mig unpacking twee old prenatal fripperies, tiny spoons,
nightgowns, and rattles dragged from storage by Grandma (who
lived here with the young couple in what was after all her own
house, widowed and bossy as ever, until she died, when I was a
few months old) and laid it all carefully in "the nursery," the
huge cold room on the second floor which Dennis and I had to
share until he turned twelve and was sent to his own room to
jerk off alone so he wouldn't corrupt little Hughie, who had
been chafing his little stick raw under his blanket for years already. I had to stay warm somehow, after all.

Shortly after Dennis was born, Mig "took to spiritualism."
Her retroussé nose disappeared into the treatises of Rudolf
Steiner, Madame Blavatsky, and the like. The hive of her brain
amalgamated all this folderol into a proscriptive child-rearing
program that caused her to starve us when we were sick, keep
our bedrooms near freezing temperatures in the winter, and enforce a prisonlike diet, the regimen of camps and gulags. We
got no dairy, meat, fish, or fowl. We had oatmeal porridge for
breakfast with cut-up prunes in winter, and in summer a
gummy mess of raw oats and near-rotten fruit soaked overnight
in water. We had sandpapery brown bread for lunch along with
whatever Vivian hauled in from her truck garden, boiled, then
mashed with "health-giving" safflower oil. Supper was a plain
soup of garden vegetables, dried beans, rice or barley, and oil.
At bedtime came a tisane, boiled water poured over the
witches' wort du jour; it might be mint, which was acceptable
and even good, but could also be chamomile or melissa. The
word "tisane" gives me the dry heaves. The thought of boiled
zucchini or mashed turnips causes my stomach to cramp, as does
the memory of that brown bread, which Vivian baked herself

(I once caught her drooling into the dough as she kneaded, in a trance of some kind) and stored in a damp breadbox.

Our father wasn't home to provide any alleviation or protection from this regime. He was at work, and then he was at war. He commuted on the train; he died before I was in first grade.

Mig seemed to be made of brittle twigs and eyes, in the mold of so many Frenchwomen.

She liked me to wash her underwear by hand. I stood over the bathroom sink on a stool and scrubbed with a bar of Ivory soap at streaks of menstrual effluvia and whatnot. Her underthings were not the lacy and delicate "unmentionables" you'd expect. They were revolting cotton things as thick as washcloths. I had to get all the stains out. I couldn't use a scrub brush: it wasn't good for the cloth.

When she had migraines I was summoned to rub her neck and shoulders for what seemed like hours. "Yessss," she would hiss as if my massages were causing her to have some sort of extended pulmonary orgasm. She lay on her couch in her bedroom, a room that smelled of an elderly female invalid, sweaty flannel, camphor, and violets. Her neck and shoulders felt like vellum-covered straw. She was dry and frangible. I was her boy, Dennis was Bim's. When she turned to kiss me afterward and send me to bed, she might as well have devoured me alive and whole with her dry, pursed, weirdly sexy little mouth. She was a young, beautiful woman throughout my childhood, but I remember her as elderly. She was always sick, always dying, always reclusive, half bedridden. She believed in ghosts and elves and fairies. She droned on and on about the astral body, the choleric temperament, the forces of Ahriman and Lucifer in her hollow, French-accented voice. (She spoke French to us rarely, but somehow we learned it well enough.)

I am convinced that my father went to Vietnam to get away

from my mother, and that his death there was a welcome relief for him.

After he died it was just the four of us here at Waverley, Dennis, my mother, Vivian, and me.

October 21—Buerger's disease is almost certainly terminal in patients who keep smoking, but before it gets me, suicide will likely be necessary as the only way to escape what will one day be unbearable pain. I'm already planning for this. Mary Frances Kennedy Fisher lost the love of her life, Dillwyn Parrish, nick-named Timmy, to Buerger's. He shot himself when the pain got too bad to bear any more. He, like me, refused to quit smok-ing. The Parrishes and Whittiers are distant branches of the same family tree, going back two hundred years or more. This gives me a certain sense of kinship with Mary Frances inde-pendent of our shared foodie passions: this rare disease, most likely an autoimmune reaction to tobacco products, is limited almost exclusively to male smokers between the ages of twenty and forty and tends to run in families. I like to think I caught it from Timmy Parrish. He was a decent painter, but, most im-portant among all his achievements, he was so loved by his bril-liant, beautiful, robust, and original widow that she claimed that she had died along with him, although her husk lived on for decades, cooking and eating, bearing two daughters, marrying, divorcing, buying houses, traveling and telling the tale, etc.

My own feral, toxic, odd-duck widow very likely won't even know I'm gone, the way the trust is set up, and the way we haven't exchanged a word in a decade. If she did hear I'd died, she'd shrug with Slavic resignation. Not that this is a com-petitive issue between me and Eighth Cousin Timmy by any means.

Every book and ashtray in this room has its place. I know where everything goes: The bed must be aligned just so with the crack overhead, the windows. The edges of the books are lined up to be the right distance from the edge of the shelves. Likewise, every dish and piece of silverware in the kitchen downstairs used to have its place until Dennis came home. Sometimes of late I find myself sitting at the table hissing silently, "The fork goes there. Not there. The glass goes there. Not there." The beauty of human domestic existence is the control we exert over our surroundings. Nature is only attractive to me insofar as I can mow, cook, kill, or change its components to my liking. The tree outside my window is a microcosm of inhuman order. It's the house next door, filled with birds who know what to do there. If I sat in that tree I might gnash my teeth every time a bird flew onto the wrong nearby branch and disturbed my innate sense of what went where. But I could do nothing about it: they're the experts out there, I'm the expert in here. Do some birds resist chaos more stringently than others? Is there an obsessive-compulsive bird in that tree who knows how I feel in here?

Dennis has no idea where the clean dishes go, and for that I consider fratricide.

When did I develop this obsession with order? I can't remember. Maybe I always had it, but it didn't fully manifest itself until I settled into Waverley as a grown man to live amongst these old books and silent instruments, these paintings of ghosts.

Sonia left in part because she couldn't grasp the absolute necessity of placing each knife in the drawer with the blade facing the right way. She did fine with the glasses; she was always an artistic sort, and as such showed an elementary aesthetic appreciation for patterns. The old etched water glasses had to be aligned just so, right, until I broke them all, but that was after she left.

I have a slight fever. Caused by the fact that, just this morning, my own brother, flirting with death, jammed a handful of clean knives any old way into the drawer. I can't think straight, can hardly write. My eyes are burning as if they'd been scalded with acid. Sonia dried the glasses carefully, by hand, the right way, with the soft towels I asked her to use. Dennis takes the new glasses—the ones that replaced those old glasses after Sonia left and my compass went awry for a little while—he takes the new glasses from the drain and shoves them, whistling as if I weren't about to leap at his throat with my teeth bared, shoves them into the cupboard right side up. They go upside down. I wait until he leaves the kitchen to turn them. Meanwhile, as he "helpfully" putters, I sit at the table grinning derangedly—dangerously, if he only knew—not saying a word, tapping my painfully aching foot, inviting the pain as a distraction, almost exploding with the need to turn the glasses, turn the knives. There's a terrible jangling whoosh of disturbed blood and misaligned cells in my ears until he goes away and I fix everything.

There he is: I see him, *mon frère l'oiseau compulsif*. He's a scraggly, half-cracked, but obviously intelligent specimen like me. He watches the other birds, bouncing on his branch, eyes flicking desperately to and fro. He wants to kill them all. You land there, not here. Move. Not here. There. He's my soulmate in the bird kingdom.

His name is obviously Erasmus, after my old friend the medieval satirist and theologian who wrote the *Manual (or Dagger) of the Christian Gentleman,* published in 1503. The book's theme is sincerity. The chief evil of the day, according to Erasmus, was formalism, a respect for traditions, a regard for what other people thought essential, and never a thought of what the true teaching of Christ may have been. The remedy was for every man to ask himself at each point, What is the essential thing?, and to do this thing without fear. Forms were in themselves evil only when they hid or quenched the spirit. In this careful, rigorous, and thoroughly Dutch (which is to say, utterly assured of his own probity and correctness) examination of the special dangers of formalism, Erasmus paid due respects to monasticism, saint-worship, war, the spirit of class, the foibles of "society." I can get behind all that, at least in a secular sense, at least in a concrete, secular sense, the only sense I have. In all but the saint-worship, I applaud him, and I have a feeling his avian counterpart would too.

I know, despite those bouts of melancholy and nostalgia fueled by memories of her, that Sonia was diabolical and poisonous, a *jolie laide sans merci,* a black hole in the cosmos—and she didn't understand about the knives. My absolute, all-encompassing, nonnegotiable need to have the knives go the right way was what finally drove her from me forever. But she understood about the glasses, and for a little while, for the sake of the great love I bore her and the unfamiliar, uncharacteristic, and therefore interesting (to us both) tenderness I inspired in her cold black heart, she tried to understand about the knives. She was a black and shining pearl among women. Not once, ever, did I want to rip her jugular open with my incisors, at least not murderously. "It is for our daughter that I go," she spat from the taxi just before it spirited her to the train station and away. "She cannot grow up to learn such things."

"Whose daughter?" I asked futilely. She never admitted a thing. Until the end she kept up the pretense that the child was mine, likewise my wife.

We had just had a fight about the knives that wasn't really, of course, about the knives at all. It escalated until finally, in a speechless knot of fury, she cut me, not with one of the butter knives under dispute, but with the butcher's knife used to hack apart chicken carcasses. She sliced it across my forearm, then brandished the infant Bellatrix like a shield in her own defense as I advanced toward her blankly, a zombie in a horror flick, dripping blood as I went, my unharmed arm raised to—what? I would never hit a woman, never hurt one either, nor would I harm a baby—and meanwhile Sonia backed away from me, matching my speed and gait step for step, as if we were two-stepping, wide-eyed, gasping, into the hall away from me, and gabbled into the phone for a taxi, her monkey face white and red in equal parts. She must have been afraid of her own rage, not mine. I would never have hurt her and she knew that, if nothing else.

Birds mate, don't they? Erasmus has a wife, I'm sure; he's handsome enough, for a bird. Does Mrs. E. hide her head under her wing in despair as her implacable, hell-bent mate pulls apart the nest to rebuild it the right way, rearranges the eggs she sits on so they're right? Doesn't she know it's not his choice? Erasmus, old pal.

October 22—Speak of the she-devil.

I never should have mentioned her at all.

Yesterday I went into town to collect my mail at the post office. On my way there I stopped at Stewart's to replenish my dwindling supply of suicide tubes and to reassure the no-doubt heartsick Carla that I hadn't forsaken her. She wasn't there, though. Some big fat ox of a local cretin was behind the counter, trying to figure out how much change to give the *Hausfrau* in front of me for five dollars for a three-fifty pint of extra–milk-fat ice cream. He handed her two dollars and fifty cents after some deliberation, whereupon she Abe Lincoln–ly handed back the extra dollar, throwing him into a complete dither. His white-coated tongue was wedged between his front teeth. He breathed like a pregnant mastodon in the throes of labor.

"Keep it," she said frantically, and peeled off in her tank-sized hermetic Suburban, going home to her solitary narcotizing pleasures, pleasures I share and understand more fully than anything else.

I asked for a carton of cigarettes. "Where's Carla?" I asked, all innocence.

"Fired," the gentle giant replied without any visible emotion.

"Why?" I asked, piqued, nettled. "Wherefore?"

"Because," he answered. Now came a pause while he looked at the money I'd given him and calculated his most effective means of ascertaining the correct change without having to ask me straight out. I waited, then let him give me twenty cents too much without handing it back. I didn't want to upset or embarrass or humiliate him or, most important, distract him from the matter under discussion, which was only under discussion because I'd put it squarely there.

"Because," I prompted.

"Oh," he said, remembering. "She stole, I guess."

"She stole," I breathed. My little revolutionary. My miscreant, my rebel girl, my daredevil. "How do I get in touch with her?"

He looked at me, puzzling it out. Why would anyone want to get in touch with that stringy-haired, pug-nosed, knuckleheaded girl? I stared him down. "Carla?" he asked after a while, to make sure we were on the same page.

"Her telephone number," I said suavely, encouragingly, avuncularly, as if I had found the stack of library books or first-prize science-fair ribbon she'd accidentally left in church. "You don't happen to have it, do you? On an employee sheet somewhere?"

"She's my niece," he said, his eyes bulging with inbred and possibly incestuous and entirely understandable suspicion. "Her father is my brother."

I knew better than to press him. I'd be back; time enough to soften him up. I went on my merry way, which was a lot merrier now that I had some cigarettes to accompany me. Cigarettes are among those objects that have their absolute place in the world. I noticed a while ago that I smoke according to the internal directives of that very same internal demon who dictates my dish habits, my bedroom-accoutrement arrangements. Always hold the matchbook so the edge aligns with my thumbnail just so. Always strike the match toward the epicenter of the rising sun. Just kidding. The waiting cigarette must be wedged in at a particular spot along my lips, one cigarette's width away from the leftmost edge of my mouth, and inserted so the end grazes my dogtooth just so. I have to strike the match on a trajectory that runs exactly parallel to the ground. Always hold the lit match so the angle the match and flame create is a perfect square; otherwise I am required by these laws to start over. One suck only as I hold the flame to the tip, and if the cigarette isn't lit I have to douse the flame and start over. Hold the cigarette exactly between the second knuckles of first and second fingers. There's an indentation there now after all these years, a little slot where the cigarette automatically nestles. Tap the ash when it's that particular length I know but can't describe, squash the cigarette out when it's burned down exactly that far. Who set these parameters? I don't know and don't ask, I simply follow them. Is this proof of the existence of God? The intricacies of smoking confer upon my inutile life a gravity and passion it would otherwise lack.

Leviticus established the obsessive-compulsive dictates of the Judaic social fabric. He was the poster boy for obsessive-compulsives, our greatest success, our Olympic hero, our guide and paragon: he got millions of people through thousands of years to follow his hand-washing, counting, clothes-fondling, number-counting, ritualistic compulsions. Of course, Leviticus happened to be an infinitely more socially oriented creature than I and the rest of my kind. He cared deeply about human-ity and society and the well-being of an entire people, which I absolutely do not, and so his precepts held sway and established a foothold in the greatest religion in human history, whereas I couldn't even get my own wife to put the knives right in the drawer—Sonia the rabid anti-Semite—it all somehow stands to reason.

As I said, speak of the she-devil . . . I drove into town and parked. I gimped to the post office, past a row of stores set into the ground floors of shabby wood-frame houses, identified as such by old-fashioned hanging shingles or handmade signs: Grace's Beauty Shop; Groverton Hardware; Stern Paint; Pet-care Animal Hospital. Very depressing. In the road was a smat-tering of fallen chestnuts, green and bristling in their sci-fi space-pod casings; a big roadkilled crow, insides lurid and raw and edible-looking, in spite of everything. There's a roadkill cookbook somewhere: I will investigate. Out of the corner of my eye I thought I saw a pair of tied-together sneakers hanging from a power line, then looking up I saw a pair of large dingy-white birds perched there, watching me, heads cocked with the amused, sidelong disapproval of certain women I've known. I passed a red frame house with a row of carved pumpkins going up the porch steps, all of them having the features and expres-sions of those oversized, grinning, helmet-wearing children on the special short bus. Ah, the river town of my youth: as a gan-gly masturbating pubescent I rode into that very town on my Schwinn ten-speed, the road whirring by under my wheels like the ratcheting blank light-flecked film right before the start of a movie. I dismounted on Main Street at noon like the Lone-some Kid, swaggered along this same stretch of sidewalk, stared violently at all the girls and women, imagining them naked un-der me, pounding my chest with their fists, raking through my soon-to-be-copious chest hair with manicured dagger nails, crying out for more, more, more of the Lonesome Kid. In actuality I was getting no such lucky breaks, sexwise, and so instead I had a tendency to vandalize and steal. I seethed with energies I couldn't channel, as if I were a pastry bag of furtive, violent humors. I was on testosterone, more than THC or coke or Quaaludes or anything artificial or self-administered, testosterone, my first burst of it. It blindsided me with the heady sense that I could KILL, I could twist necks, punch lights out, gouge eyes, sock it to 'em and fuck 'em up bad.

How things have changed since then. I made my harmless old tomcat way into the clean, dim, creaky, linoleum-floored building, greeted Betsy Blackwell the postmistress in her wooden cage behind the screen, unlocked my box, and pulled forth the letters that had been accumulating there for a week or more. Bills, more bills. Why must there always be so many bills? A letter for Dennis from his daughter Evie. A letter to me from someone with handwriting exactly like Sonia's.

Who, of course, was Sonia, according to the name above the return address, a West 58th Street address in the city; immediately I envisioned a Hell's Kitchen walk-up, gentrified and respectable and appropriately expensive now, a former tenement dive with bad acoustics, a view of nothing, and cramped rooms that smelled of hundred-year-old cabbage steam.

I weighed the envelope on my outstretched palm for a moment, my scalp prickling unpleasantly, my already tingling nerves tingling even more, internally debating: if I ripped it up and threw it away unopened, I could walk out of here and, should anyone ever question me about it, simply claim it had never arrived. Nothing good could come of opening this envelope and reading the letter, whose very existence spelled trouble, or at least unpleasantness. . . .

Curiosity won out, as it always does. Slightly nauseated, I went back outside to the street and sat on the bench right outside the PO door. Old Glory writhed sinuously overhead. What a silly flag that is, especially these days, with all the enforced gung-ho rah-rah America the Beautiful wet-eyed jingo-patriotism, like a cross between a cartoon jailbird's uniform and a superhero's cape.

That dead crow inspires me to consider the historical propriety of eating the equivalent of roadkill. In the Middle Ages, the French aristocracy regularly consumed elderly birds in an advanced state of decay, which, in a fowl variant of garum, they inundated with and steeped in for lengthy periods of time spices and verjuice, an acidic liquor made of the juice of crab apples or green, unripe sour grapes. They didn't care for young creatures back then. Elderly game was left hanging until it had reached the state of putrefaction considered most tasty, which was known as "high." Grimod de la Reynière wrote that a pheasant killed on Ash Wednesday should not be eaten until Easter. Brillat-Savarin—Mary Frances's venerable mentor—thought the pheasant was most delicious in early decomposition. "At this time," he wrote, "its aroma is developing in association with its oil which requires slight fermentation to be given off." Small birds, such as woodcocks, were brought back from the hunt and hung up by the feet until their insides deliquesced and dripped out through the beak, and the feathers fell off. Only then were they prepared for the table.

But enough about that. I opened the letter. My long-estranged wife had covered the top third of one sheet of typing paper with her neat, black, deceptively innocent-looking handwriting.

"Dear Hugo," she began.

Dear Hugo!

I paused a moment to savor the rich layers of irony in this salutation, after ten years. . . . Dear Hugo, Dear Hugo. I breathed it in with my eyes as if it were an interesting smell I couldn't place, or get enough of, something unhealthy and complex and pungent, all at once. A low-tide mudflat smell. A diseased sexual organ. A drive-through whiff of the Fresh Kills Landfill. An old man's fungus-ridden foot newly freed from its tight leather shoe on a sweltering afternoon.

"Dear Hugo," she wrote. "I am well. Bellatrix has asked me to write to you. We are in NYC [NYC! How I savor this charming Americanism of an immigrant mother whose American-born child has taught her—not well, of course, because no immigrant mother ever fully learns her child's native tongue, but adequately enough to sling around a little slang] now, and will come up to see you next month. Maybe to live, if we stay. You are still my husband, and it has been a long time. I won't pretend. But our girl is getting older and should know her past. Time for her to know her father and her someday house. We will come on the train, and you can come and get us in your car. Please write to us at this address. Bellatrix sends you her fond regards. She is much older now, you won't know her at first, she is grown up and plays the violin. We will need to go to NYC on Saturdays on the train for her lessons. Your wife, Sonia."

That, in its entirety, is the first contact.

My vision began closing in from the top and sides like the walls and ceiling in that Sherlock Holmes story until I sat in a zooming tunnel, at the end of which were my faraway, vulnerable-looking feet in their old cracked-leather shoes. Women, women everywhere but not a drop to drink.

October 24—Dennis and I had another bedside chat this morning. My bedside, his chat. He came bustling in brandishing the newspaper as if it were a dirty diaper, a bad dog, a bundle of litter he'd found on a pristine highway. I gathered that he'd been reading it downstairs in the kitchen over his coffee, and, incensed by the news from the front and in the grip of an overdose of caffeine, was desperate for someone to vent to. Lucky me. I sat up in bed as he bristled in my doorway. I was shaking a little from the aftereffects of the pain in my foot all night, hoping he wouldn't choose my river-view chair, but knowing before he sat in it that he would, naturally, with his unerring instinct for pissing me off. He couldn't help himself, the same way I can't help needing those flower-patterned drinking glasses to go upside down and aligned in the cupboard. We all have our compulsions, our foibles. Pain has made me un-characteristically compassionate, or else weak in the head.

"Why," my distraught only sibling burst out, apropos of noth-ing, "must the media present men as stupid dolts? The humor, or sales pitch, of half the advertisements on TV now is: Men are like children, and women rule the world, so buy these sneak-ers, go to this superstore. We're like the village idiots all of a sudden. I don't see why we as an entire sex should be made into laughingstocks or scapegoats. We buy things too. Maybe they're trying to appeal to what they imagine is our guilt and self-loathing."

I lit another cigarette. "I don't have a TV. I have no idea what you're talking about. I couldn't care less about whatever humanity is up to these days."

"But that's just the least of it," he went on. "Those fucking little punks, those suicide terrorists. They're like cockroaches. I don't want to understand them, I just want them dead. I can't imagine what those knee-jerk lefty-liberal mealy-mouthed hypocrites are thinking, those idiots who claim to feel some-how implicated in these wholly unprovoked attacks just because they're privileged, educated, and white and therefore feel guilty for having what most of the rest of the world wants. Well, I may have my own issues with guilt, but I suffer from no such qualms about those terrorists: if those baby boomers really feel so guilty about having it all, they can give away their SUVs and satellite dishes to inner-city AIDS patients and move to third-world huts and die of dysentery or ebola or a machete in the head. If I were younger I would enlist and go over to Afghanistan. Our father died at war; we should all die at war. Meanwhile, what am I doing instead of risking my life like a real man? I'm wrecking it. I split up my family. I'm not getting any work done since I came back here. I'm shooting myself in the foot out of helpless frustration. Or so I tell myself, to convince myself that what I'm doing has some basis in logic and current events, when actually I'm beginning to believe that I'm just as crazy as you and it just took longer for my own self-destructive pathologies to emerge."

It amazes me how much time Dennis wants to spend with me, how he seeks me out whenever he can, as if he had a stored-up fount of things to tell me. It was this way when we were boys, only back then I was eager to please him and smaller than he and therefore under his rule.

"But," I said, making my face go all blank and inoffensive, "we aren't alike, you and I. I'm delighted with all of my so-called pathologies. You strike me, admittedly the layman but someone who has known you long and well, as clinically depressed. Maybe you need professional help. Maybe you need Zoloft or Prozac or Wellbutrin, but I wouldn't know a thing about that."

"Men in our family don't go to therapists."

"They marry them, apparently."

"And look where that got me," he shot back. "For all her clinical training, she doesn't have a clue about her own problems. That's her blind spot."

"Well, maybe you should move out of this old pile. Maybe you need a change of scene, Dennis."

"This old pile is my ancestral home," said Dennis. "I have as much reason to be here as anywhere. And you, Hugo, wing nut though you may be, are all the family I have."

"But why don't you move back down to the city if you're not getting any work done? Get yourself a cheap loft in TriBeCa—they're going for nothing these days, I hear, not to be morbid. What I'm trying to say is, why not make a fresh start down there? Don't all artists want to live in New York?"

He didn't say anything right away; I assumed he was mulling it all over.

"You know, Hugo, I've been wondering something," he said. "Why don't you live in New York?"

He asked this with what for Dennis was real curiosity. Usually I rely on his narcissism to keep the focus off myself, but my false sympathy, it seemed, had backfired. "I hope you're not really going," he added thoughtfully, "to spend the rest of your life moldering in this room."

"I'm a career hermit," I said equably. "Moldering is a valid life-style choice, as they say. The problem is that your being here is mucking up the whole deal, to put it mildly."

"How so?"

"Let's talk about those dishes," I snapped.

Our conversation went on from there. Violence was considered a few times by at least one of the parties involved, but I extracted a promise from Dennis to pay attention to the direction of the knife blades in the drawer. I am not holding my breath about this in any way.

October 25—I wrote back to Sonia, finally, to tell her that under no circumstances must she descend upon me and my life. Bad enough having Dennis here. "Dear Sonia," I wrote. "You signed the recent letter you wrote me 'your wife,' and legally you are. I have provided for you and will continue to do so but feel urgently that this must be the extent of our contact. The money will continue, and if you need more all you need to do is contact James Cahill. More than that I cannot offer. When you left me, we understood that it was forever. Your peremptory tone is unsettling to me, as there is no basis for it. Since Bellatrix has lived and from the sound of it even thrived for the past ten years without knowing me, I fail to comprehend even slightly how being uprooted from her present no-doubt full and happy life to become forcibly acquainted with a stranger, a man whose biological connection to her is shaky at best (you know what I mean by this) and whom she has every chance of disliking very much, can be considered a good thing for any of the parties involved in any way. In all sincerity, Hugo."

I mailed it yesterday, checked my mailbox and was delighted to find it empty except for a credit-card offer I disposed of at once, and then, reluctant to leave that sad little washed-up burg right away, I lunched at a diner. Here I was served rubbery bacon with a leaf of tough lettuce and a mealy tomato slice on stale rye with yellowish mayonnaise liberally applied to both slices, and a corrosively bubbly, refreshing glass of the world's most pervasive soft drink.

Then. Sitting in that grimy booth, breathing the tepid air, and wishing I could slap the fortyish, hard-faced waitress on her quivering mound of behind and rest my face between her smarting buttocks just for one brief delirious moment as the perfect coda to my seedy lunch, I saw a familiar face go by the window outside. It was a flash of recognition and then he was gone.

The knowledge of who it was came in a gradual development, first idle noticing, then puzzled consternation, then puzzled awareness, and finally panic.

I need to know what he's doing up here, whether it's a coincidence, and whether he's looking for me. . . .

How could I have thought I could escape? I wondered then,

and always wonder, about the fact that, no matter how hard one may try to live without the intolerable burden of society, the unwelcome recognition of a face, perfect solitude is always shown to be temporary, a phantasm, a dream. I envy the lonely. Loneliness, which is to say neediness, drives others away and keeps them at bay; the great irony is that the more those of us who desire only autonomy try to escape, the more we are pursued, whereas those who most long for companionship are most denied it, as if that pull of longing creates a force field around them that repels those they most want to attract. By those same laws of psychological physics, the attempt to escape creates an undertow in the social surf that pulls people along with you as you flee. True escape seems impossible for people who crave it like a drug. It seems that there can be no pure life, no essential aloneness.

It's slightly comforting to suspect that even monks of the most mute and reclusive orders, men who yearn so absolutely for perfect spiritual calm that they sacrifice sex for it, have to live cheek by jowl together in third-world–like close quarters. I would posit without doubt that the average monk becomes embroiled in petty power disputes over toothbrush slots, cringes at the eating noises of his brethren, chafes at interaction-fueled irritations, ferments with a barely restrained claustrophobia only hours of meditative prayer every day can begin to control.

A hermit in his cave must likewise, I'm sure, be driven to murderous frenzies by the banal and heedless shouts of hikers, smoke and guitar sounds from their campfires, the whine of big rigs all night long from a nearby freeway somewhere.

If I were deaf and blind, I sometimes think, I might be happy, but of course then there would be some maniacally well-intentioned Annie Sullivan pestering me day and night to re-join the world of language and communication, not resting until she succeeded in reattaching my hated umbilicus. Only in the caves, the cells, of night pain or this writing is there the letup for me now of this awful and debilitating human commerce. Death will of course bring it about in a final way, another reason I don't fear or fight this early stop for me. The carriage, though, had better hold just me alone, or I'll feel unforgivably gypped, and ask for my money back.

Sex, though. Sex, even though it necessarily involves another person, is a cave of its own. I never tire of it and would like to have it constantly. I've always been this way. As a wee lad I awaited its advent with breathless excitement, and since my hormonal spurt began, I have wanted nothing much more than to fuck and fuck and fuck, and never once have I felt hemmed in or impinged upon by any of my successes in doing so. A woman being penetrated doesn't say much, and if she does it's generally exciting and conducive. Afterward is another story. Stephanie Fox and I seem fundamentally alike in some way that's new to me with a woman. Sonia streamed with words, bled words, talked and talked and talked until I had to fuck her again to shut her up.

When we first met—my wife, Sonia, and I—I was a Writer with a capital double-you. Those were different days, and I was a different man. I had friends back then; I hadn't yet felt the desire to eschew human contact; in fact, in those young, far-off days, I think I actually enjoyed it. I drank and ate with my fellows, behaved well at parties, was altogether pleasant to have around, or so I seem to recall, if occasionally bellicose, self-indulgent, grandiose in my professed aims.

Throughout the end of my twenties, I lived at Waverley, but only as a stopgap. I planned to move on after I had finished what I intended to be the twin cornerstones on which I would build my literary career: two books, one of poetry, one of philosophical pensées, or maybe I called them essays, it depended on the time of day, the flavor of my mood. I had discovered reading years before, when I was sponging off various rich women, most of whom possessed the requisite rich person's good library, shelves of great and good books haphazardly collected, ostentatiously displayed, and for the most part largely ignored. I cultivated my reading habit as any secret vice, heady as opiates, clandestine as pornography. Although I can't prove this, I believe I had read more than the average English major by the time I was twenty. My reading was undertaken seriously, with an eye toward writing someday, when I felt I was ready. I was in no hurry. During those years as a kept boy in those several houses in New York and Europe, my so-called mistresses (well, what else were they? girlfriends? I think not) were society women whose romantic lives were split in two: their public escorts, the "bachelors" who chaperoned them to all the benefits, teas, auctions, and balls, and their pet boys, whom they ravished later, afterward, when the squire had handed them over to their doorman and gone off into the night in search of his own kind. Because of this, I had plenty of solitude, and little to do besides eat, walk around whatever city or seaside resort town I found myself in, and read.

Maybe because of my odd life-style, I gravitated at first to the most dreamy, dilatory, and passionate writers: my earliest influences were the English Romantic poets, the Russian novelists, the American Romantic mystics, and the German philosophers. I didn't remember much of what I'd read, an unfortunate but unavoidable by-product of all the actual drugs I indulged in, mainly champagne, cocaine, Benzedrine, and cognac, for some reason the universal drugs of choice of almost all my ladyloves. Still, the cadences, mannerisms, and modes of thinking of the likes of Coleridge, Dostoevski, Whitman, Emerson, and Kant were branded in my subconscious, and chunks of their intent somehow adhered to my cortical lobes as well. From there I branched out to the early moderns—Wharton and Forster, *The Waves,* Beckett, *Ulysses,* Ford Madox Ford, *Oblomov,* Kafka, Flannery O'Connor, Hemingway—then I was done for. This was my jumping-off point: once I'd sucked in the Romantics and digested the early moderns, I systematically gorged myself on everything I could find, early or late, lush or stark, nihilistic or overwrought, I didn't much care. Throughout my twenties I read and read, insatiable as a termite. When I came back to Waverley to live, I bored a steady hole through its library until I felt that I had traveled enough with my forebears, learned enough of their craft, to launch my own little bobbing flotilla in their wake.

I began to write; I disliked it very much and still do. However, it never seemed to be a matter of preference but absolute necessity. Naïvely, I made a solemn pact never to write a word I didn't mean, never to write an unnecessary word. I set out to revolutionize and awaken from its shallow slumber the moribund desert of contemporary literature. What young writer doesn't? I was on fire; I stayed up all night in the library with cigarettes burning through the predawn hours. I wrote thoughts and poems, dreams, reflections, all of it achingly candid, bright-eyed, blustering, hubristic. Utter shit. But I kept at it. I worked until my head ached, until I fell asleep in the lamplight with my head on the table. I thought I heard voices sometimes late at night, saw faces, heard scurryings in the walls. I forgot to piss. I awoke in the mornings sometimes stiff as a corpse from sleeping upright in my chair with the sun burning on my sweaty head.

One night I went to a party with my friend Fred and his girlfriend, Liza, a wicked brunette who always flirted hotly with me right under Fred's nose. This never seemed to bother him, which vaguely offended me: was I nothing, a fly, a harmless nonthreat in his eyes? I was always tempted to try to fuck her, but never did. That night we drank a lot, more even than usual, and decided to drive to a bar about half an hour north. We all, about six of us, piled into Fred's car and set off. It was one of those summer nights with a fine humid mist suspended uniformly in the air that makes everything seem mysterious and exciting and full of adventure, or did in those days anyway. Liza sat on my lap on the front seat; Fred drove. Everyone else was crammed into the back. We sang along with a song on the radio. Liza's shapely ass was pressed warmly into my crotch; her arm was slung around my shoulder. She leaned against the passenger-side door, her bare feet extended into Fred's lap, her head back against the window, half lolling against mine. I decided, determinedly, that tonight was the night. If Fred wasn't minding the store, it was going to get held up.

"What's that?" said Liza. "Look, there's someone in the road."

A girl was walking along facing the oncoming traffic with her arm thrust out, her thumb up. She looked young and slight, with pixie hair, white-faced in the headlights.

"Look at that," I said. "It's Peter Pan."

"She's in trouble," Liza said immediately. "Fred, stop the car, pick her up!"

"No room," said Fred through his cigarette.

"Fred, come on, don't be an asshole, stop the fucking car," Liza said evenly. "I'll sit in back."

She tossed herself casually over the back seat into the laps and elbows of everyone sitting back there. There was some jovial, drunken shouting and laughter as Fred slowed and then stopped and then reversed the car. I opened my door and the girl was on my lap like a shot. She was smaller and lighter than Liza. Her ass landed on what was left of my Liza-inflated pecker. "Thank you," she said in a hard, husky, accented voice that belonged to someone older, more world-weary, than this little elf. She smelled of the night air and cigarettes and something else, her own scent, a clean animal smell like the fur of a marmoset, not that I'd ever smelled one, but I was drunk and young and very horny and given to poetic associations. "You saved my life," she sighed dramatically.

"What do you mean, we saved your life?" Liza asked, leaning over the seat between Fred and me. "I'm Liza, by the way."

"I am Sonia," said the girl, turning to give Liza a wan smile, a fleeting acknowledgment.

"What happened?" asked Liza insistently.

"Oh," said Sonia, and sighed again. "I was out on this crazy date with someone, a man I know, and he tried to hurt me or something, I wasn't sure what he was going to do, but he threatened me. So I jumped out of the car while he was driving and rolled away and hid under some bushes, then I walked for a while, and you stopped and picked me up."

"What do you mean, he threatened you?"

"Sexually," she said, drawing the word out, scornfully. "Sexually, and possibly violently as well. He had a gun, he took it out and told me to . . ." Almost involuntarily, I held her close, as if she were a hurt child and I her affectionate uncle. Well, I'd been bewitched and bothered by Fred's cock-tease of a girlfriend and hadn't had much action in the past month or so. Sonia sighed and nestled into me, but even then I sensed there was nothing weak or defenseless about this little chick. Her sigh, her nestle, barely betrayed a withheld impatience, a kind of quivering expectation, a defiant insouciance, as if she had been through too much, had seen too much, to feel anything any more. She was merely the vessel for tragedy, not its victim in any way.

"You don't have to tell us if it's too painful to talk about," said Janey, the wife half of the couple whose party it had been, earlier that night. "But I think we should take you to the hospital so you can be looked at. Or, if you're not hurt, then the police, so you can have him caught."

"Press charges!" Sonia said. I'd always liked Janey, but now, in the cold blue light cast by Sonia's reaction to her, I felt irritated to have to be in the same car with her or to be associated with her in any way.

"Why not?" said Fred. "He deserves it."

"He is my boss," Sonia added patiently, "where I work. I want never to think of this again and never to say a word to anyone I know about this. I have to go to my job tomorrow. I work as a chambermaid at his motel and need this job because I am not a citizen. I am not hurt. In Poland we don't go to the police with such things."

Then I told her that what she needed was a drink, and she half smiled and agreed, and so we brought her along to the bar with us. She and I sat in a booth; somehow everyone understood that she was my charge. I had forgotten the treacherous, seductive Liza. Sonia was a street urchin straight out of a nineteenth-century novel, with her sharp, pale little face and short yellow hair. She and I were the same kind of thing, and I wanted her to know this. I wanted to impress on her the fact that I was nothing like these soft Americans. Over glasses of vodka, leaning into each other across the shitty old cigarette-burned table, I told her, as I had never told anyone, about all my years on the lam, starting with leaving my mother's car at the gas station, hitchhiking to New York, living in hotel lobbies pretending to be waiting for someone and dozing on couches and using the facilities (it helped to have that innate blue-blooded air of slouching entitlement, not to mention the prep-school haircut and outfit, which, even unwashed and rumpled, made me look altogether too purebred for a hotel doorman to question), until Tovah found me on her way to hear some homo jazz pianist at the Carlyle and rescued me and took me home. I told Sonia about escaping New York, crossing the Atlantic as crew on a freighter . . . and on and on, through Paris, the Riviera, the crazy countess in Aix-en-Provence who made her own goat cheese and liked to be taken from behind like a dog under the open-air baskets where the cheese aged, suspended from branches of the trees in her garden—her withered buttocks and her unfathomable tendresse, her generosity with me—and then the cold winter in Prague in the squat with the neo-Nazi and his feral pack of dogs, then picking olives in Greece before I ran into my old Parisian mistress's best friend, Marie-Chantal, at a discothèque and was taken by her to Paris again, then living in the States again, smuggling drugs between Boston and Canada, freeloading in houses in Los Angeles and on Long Island, hitchhiking aimlessly from coast to coast. . . . Sonia listened blank-faced, coldly rapt, as if she were taking in, along with my words, my gestures, point of view, manner of speaking and inflections, with a plan to impersonate me later, for her own profit.

"Are you an actress?" I asked her abruptly, on a hunch.

"Of course," she said. "I trained for it in Warsaw. I came to America to act. But so far"—she made a dismissive fricative noise—"only community theater, last summer, around here. Nothing! And I am twenty-five! Old."

"You're a baby," I crooned. I was twenty-seven.

"You're drunk," she shot back. She almost never smiled. Neither did I, for that matter. By the end of the night, she and I were in agreement that she would not go to work tomorrow, her boss be damned. She could find another job. She had to quit this one, and I would lend her—no, give her—money to tide her over.

Back at Waverley, we tumbled around my bed together. She was fierce and opaque, and not breakable. We got no sleep that night, no sleep for several nights to come. Sonia wanted to be abused. She wanted me to insult her, to treat her like a whore, to slap her ass and rough her up, force her to do whatever I wanted. It was the only way to reach her or arouse her or provoke a response in her. This was fine with me; I had had my share of being bossed around by many women, going all the way back to my mother. The tables were turned and there was, it seemed, no end to the indignities and humiliations I could subject another, willing person to. My appetite for this sort of thing felt bottomless. It seemed to be mutual. I forgot my work, forgot about food, forgot everything except this girl; she and I haunted Waverley together like gleaming white-fleshed young ghosts, naked in every room, night and day, sunlight or candle-light. I was sure my ancestors were watching in dismay and ab-horrence, which jacked up the pleasure. In her blank-shocked blue eyes I saw the disappointed, rotten, louche folk-soul of Europe itself. She was very bad news, which was all to the good; I had never been in love before, but it was high time. I was a romantic slob with her, a pushover. Sonia was my first and only free-fall swoon.

She confessed a week afterward, as we sat eating cold take-out sesame noodles on my bed, facing each other naked, listen-ing to Fauré's *Requiem* of all the preposterous things: it was all an act, that hitchhiking story, a bit of performance art. She was, in fact, a performance artist, and had never been a chamber-maid in a motel, or assaulted by her boss. Her cheeks flushed a little as she told me, and her eyes looked sharp and wary and filled with anticipation: here was fresh drama of her own making.

"No motel," I said. "No attempted attack. I don't see why you'd bother with that whole story, you scrawny teat-loose bitch. Why not just thumb a ride?"

She inhaled sharply through her nose and drew herself up. There had been a flick of pleasure in her eyes at the insult.

"It is my work," she said. "I consider what I am doing a form of storytelling and theater. I call this entire piece, this journey, my *Thousand and One Nights*. That is how long I will try to survive on the stories I tell, the roles I play. I am traveling around the U.S.A., seeing how far I can go with my art alone. My rule, though, is that after a week I must tell those I have interacted with, my fellow players, who do not yet realize they are in a piece of theater, a show. Hugo, you are my fellow actor. There are no rules, we can make this theater whatever we want. This has been my most successful piece so far. It alone of all my projects is engaged theater, as opposed to a piece in which I feel I've committed a wrong. People have been very angry at me, you know."

"I can easily imagine," I said, and slid my haunches under hers and pinioned her hips and went right up her ass without lubricant of any kind and began fucking her, slowly but hard and with intent to punish. There was silence for a while, and we both yelled from between our clenched teeth at the same instant. Then it was time to sit back and ponder this new development. I was besotted with this woman. I didn't care who she was or what she'd done; I didn't want her to leave again, I wanted her to stay here with me. All right, I knew all about her act, the young lost penniless waif of a foreigner in need of a warm bed and some sympathetic company. I had done it myself, many times, but it had never been done to me.

"Well, it's sort of brilliant," I said, almost laughing at my own cleverness, turning her own tables on her so slickly. "*A Thousand and One Nights*. Ironic and original."

"Yes," she said smugly, with her usual total lack of humor. "I am risking my life, I am putting myself at the mercy of strangers. I knew that you, out of everyone in that car, would understand. I felt that you and I were the same: we are both radicals, we write our own laws. I know this to be true after a week with you."

"You conned me, you bitch," I said, tugging at a piece of her short hair, hard enough to force her head down near my naked crotch, where a certain other show was taking place, one energetic puppet alone onstage, getting ready for its close-up. Ah, those were the days, of the eternally rising sap of youth. She did what she was meant to do down there, despite where my fellow had so recently been. Sonia was never squeamish about hygiene or bodily fluids or anything, really.

She sat up. "Give me some more champagne," she said. "I'm thirsty."

I handed her the champagne and she smiled. Seeing her smile was a rare and wondrous thing: she did it so seldom, and her smile was oddly and touchingly goofy. It also displayed her small brownish Eastern European teeth, which may be why she avoided it for the most part.

In due time, I married her; and in due time, she left me.

It pains me to admit this: I don't know, even now, whether her purported performance-art piece was yet another con, or whether she had actually embarked on such a project and been waylaid by me. I never knew anything about her for sure, how many other men she fucked while we were married, what her childhood had been like, who her family was. I was never sure what she wanted from me, if anything, besides my citizenship-conferring last name, my support, my adoration, my late-night cooking, my love of wine, my unending lust for her. It was a double-edged sword—I loved her because she had the power to fuck me up as much as my mother had, but she was as unlike my mother as any woman I'd ever dreamed of.

What a sap.

We went to Europe for our honeymoon after a quickie ceremony at City Hall that was attended by my friend Fred and his girlfriend, Liza, our witnesses and only guests. Sonia took me to Warsaw and showed me the dark, airless streets of her childhood, the house where her parents had lived before they'd died.

I took her to France and played the big man, the cosmopolitan epicure, the sugar daddy, the lovestruck young husband. I spent vast amounts of money on her. We ate every delicacy we could get our hungry little mitts on. In the Alps . . . Never mind, it was all a dream, and, like all dreams, it ended.

I struggled to keep writing after she moved in with me. I didn't see the point of my dogged, self-serving, old-fashioned endeavors in the face of her fresh understanding of art. She had breathed life into the rotten lungs, had reanimated the defunct veins and infused them with her mischief. She had electrified the old corpse. My books now seemed like pointless weights getting heavier with each page I scrawled. I read parts aloud to her, to prove to her that I was her equal, her fellow; but her dry, dismissive, even derisive comments ("The sorrows of young Hugo!" was one in particular that went right to the sticking-place; not to mention, "Hugo, you are such a child with your need for metaphor, metaphor, metaphor, everything compared to something else instead of just saying what it is. . . . What are you afraid of, saying what a thing is? In Poland we say straight what things are, we have not the luxury of your American ex-cess."). She was right about my writing's being callow and over-written; that was the thing that killed me. If I'd been able to muster any defense, I might have survived it, but I knew as soon as the words left her mouth that there was nothing I could say. And I had no such criticism of her to offer in return. I was too young to imagine that she might be manipulating me, keeping me in my place as a means of keeping me. I trusted her. . . .

Until I woke up one day to find myself divested of the illu-sion that she was in my thrall, an illusion I finally realized she had been in complete control of the entire time.

I became demented and justifiably suspicious of her long absences, her secretive airs, her unflappable attitude of superi-ority to me. She went out and slept with other men. I couldn't bear it. She was my wife, and I wanted her all to myself. Then she became pregnant, and I knew the baby wasn't mine; I don't know how I knew. Maybe I smelled on her the scent of another man's DNA, I don't know. After the baby was born, blond and round and looking nothing like me at all, I drove Sonia away, I guess is one way of looking at it, with my irrational jealousy and hotheaded accusations.

The fight about the knives was just an excuse.

Over the years I've come to see Sonia for what she was with a much more clear and cold understanding. I see what she did to me and how. And I want nothing more to do with her, beyond seeing that she's taken care of, she and that kid, whoever's spawn Bellatrix may be. Sonia doesn't deserve even this, but it's not in me to do otherwise. I do it for myself, as the saying goes. I will always have the moral upper hand with her, as long as she's dependent on me and beholden to me. Her own dreams for her work, assuming she wasn't lying when she told me she had had training to be an actress and was hoping to find success, ended exactly when mine did: she no more became an actress than I became a writer. The tumult of our marriage was no doubt drama enough for her while it lasted, and after she left me, my support of her from afar killed the fire in her belly, the burning need to claw her way up, killed the thing in her that I had loved, or so I comforted myself with thinking. She would never have to work as a waitress between auditions; she would never have to beg for a part, clutching her expensive headshots. She would never have to live in a cold-water walk-up with a bathtub in the kitchen, or strip, or go on welfare, or marry a man she didn't like, any of the single-mother would-be-actress escape valves. That was all right, I didn't mind rescuing her, because it also meant that she would never again be hungry enough to throw herself body and soul into her work; that was the punishment I set out for her.

Of course, she could have been lying about wanting to act—this could have been part of her con—in which case she succeeded as the only kind of artist she ever wanted to be, and got set up for life.

I was twenty-seven when I met her, twenty-eight when I married her, twenty-nine when Bellatrix was born, and thirty when she left me. When I met her I was filled with youthful life and inspiration, and when she left I was finished, washed up. She corroded me, is one way of looking at it. I allowed her to corrode me, is another way. A third: she was only the catalyst for what would have happened anyway, Sonia or no Sonia. Finally, after enduring her criticism of my writing, in the grip of an abject but defiant urge to show both of us that she was wrong, I went into town one day and had several expensive, dense Xeroxes made of each book-length manuscript I had written: poems about the metaphysics of sex, and philosophical essays about the ethics of living above or outside or "in spite of" the law. . . . Recalling these subjects, I cringe at my own audacity and sheer hubris: what, at twenty-eight, did I think I knew about anything? I had flouted the law, had slept with a lot of women, but those experiences were crude oil in my brain-pan still, the refinery of time hadn't even begun its processes yet. How could I have expected any editor to pony up an advance for this raw and undigested stuff? Nonetheless, I doggedly sent them out to agent after agent, editor after editor. For two years I kept at it, trundling back and forth between home and the post office, and for two years my manuscripts streamed back to me in stamped, self-addressed envelopes accompanied by rejection letters, many of them encouraging and respectful, or at least polite. At first egged on by some of the phrases they contained, I tried magazines, both glossy and literary. However, these efforts were likewise fruitless. A vanity press was out of the question: I would not pay to have my work published, because it would prove nothing to Sonia, or, for that matter, to me. It was bad enough to have to see those familiar envelopes waiting in my box, addressed to myself in my own handwriting. It felt like the most depressing sort of masturbation, the sort done only to relieve base need.

God, the past.

Finally, I had to admit to myself that Sonia was right and my work was crap. I tried to buck myself up, stay with it, keep writing, strike out in new directions. I started a few novels, several plays, new poems and essays. . . . I even tried a family history in my darkest night of the soul. I was desperately unable to make anything take off. I couldn't work up much interest in anything I wrote about; I suspected I had nothing of interest to say. So many before me had written so well. How could I ever have thought I could join their ranks? Instead of writing, I sat and berated myself for thinking I could write. I felt sick to my stomach at the sight of a blank sheet of paper. Phrases from rejection letters echoed in my head along with Sonia's derision. I knew everyone had to face rejection, and I knew that talent was cheap, and discipline and courage separated the men from the boys. But somehow I failed to overcome the loss of my faith in work and love. By my mid-thirties, wrung out and dried up, I stopped writing altogether, and stopped seeking out my fellows. Solitude was comforting. Other people made me weary. Conversations felt pointless and draining. A psychologist might have called what I was going through a breakdown of some kind; I called it a whole new way of life.

As my garum gloom deepened and intensified, my friends stopped trying to pull me back into their warm, happy circle. On our last outing together to a bar to get drunk amid noisy chaos, I told Fred I had decided to live as a hermit for a while because the end of my marriage had been too much for me to take. I didn't mention the rejection of my work—I was too proud. I needed to hole up alone for a while, I said, and nurse my wounds.

Fred said, shaking his head, "Well, some people find Jesus and convert to Christianity, you found Sonia and converted to Sonia, and she fucked you in the head. So now you're going to be a monk? That's fucked up, but I guess it's your decision." We toasted the dissolution of our friendship, and never saw each other again. From then on, no one needed or asked anything of me in my psychic demilitarized zone of near nonbeing. I found that this suited me; I became the inward leeward becalmed remote island I am today—or, rather, would still be if I could.

But I am forced now to admit, if only to myself, that I became a solitary do-nothing by attrition—not by philosophical choice, as Montaigne did, but because I had reached the end of my tenure in work and life and had become old at the arguably young age of thirty-five. It was around the same time that Dr. Schuyler told me in no uncertain terms that if I kept smoking I would eventually die of Buerger's disease, maybe within a few years. I decided that this wouldn't be the end of the world, only of me.

So here I am. For now, anyway.

Speaking of the past, there was that face earlier, going by the diner window. That face, flashing into view as I sat over the remains of my lunch, riding atop its body . . . that ratlike, intelligently citified face, a face from the distant past. His name escapes me but not for long. His pointy nose, bulging eyes, sinisterly transparent eyebrows, I know and fear that face. I know exactly who he is. He didn't see me. But if he can walk by me once, he can do it again, and next time I might not have the safety of glass between us. The world is a treeless backyard with a high fence around it, everyone milling around in stark sunlight, trapped. Dennis is at home. Sonia is coming back. That face.

I owe Stephanie a dinner. I want to plunder her rich, suave corpus, and I think I might be able to, if I break bread with her and go through the motions of listening to her not wholly uninteresting conclusions about marriage and procreation for an hour or two, if history is any indication.

So there's nothing for it but to telephone her and offer to pay my debt. No harm in trying, as they say.

I loathe myself, but am all I have.

October 30—Garum mood again.

November 1—Reeking stews of rotten fish entrails washing around skull and rib cage.

November 2—Drank all the whiskey I could hold last night, and it washed my head and chest clean of *poisson* poison. Feel like a new man, like Adam just made. It's healthy to have a good/bad hangover every now and then, the physiological equivalent of clear-burning forests or dousing a toilet with lye and ammonia, the aftermath of a noxious but beneficial procedure that leaves everything sparkling and black and dead, ready to rejuvenate. Like chemotherapy but a lot more fun.

Stephanie wasn't home tonight when I telephoned. Her husband, Bun, was. He was rather chatty; we had a long and amusing, for him anyway, discussion of my identity, relationship to Dennis, reason for calling, and interest in his wife. I thrust and parried like a real man, heave-ho. He was suspicious, as well he should have been. I meanwhile lied baldly and boldly, so as to give him the impression that I am in need of legal advice, which, now that I think of it, I might be: can Sonia come back to live here if she's still legally my wife? I have a grave fear that there's some obscure law on the books that entitles her to half of everything I own, which includes my half of this house. And my truck.

Which would lead the casual bystander to wonder why we never got divorced. Divorce is legal, easier than ever, expedient, and self-protective, a bulwark against potential calamities like the one I'm now facing. It was sheer laziness, of course. I always meant to get around to it. Sonia, of course, never would, being a Catholic and an evil conniver. Staying married meant she could always hedge her bets. She always meant to come back, I see that now. Now that she's ten years older, no doubt wrinkled and frumpy in the saddle, with a daughter who's old enough to crave things, to demand accountability and knowledge of her forebears . . . sure, it would be very nice for Sonia to come back here, to lounge about the house, Lady of the Manse, and turn Bellatrix over to me for the duration of her dependency on us, her mother having more than fulfilled her own parenting obligations, assuming they should be shared between mother and father, if I were in fact her father. In any case, legitimate or not, I prefer a parenting version of "I buy, you fly." This has worked beautifully for Sonia and me thus far, better than most parenting arrangements I've ever encountered, including Dennis and Marie's, which has always struck me as smarmily utopian and therefore suspect, not to mention deluded and doomed. Dennis set out to be a co-parent; Marie has her own career. If that's not a recipe for disaster I don't know what is. Of course they had sexual difficulties: they didn't know who was supposed to be the woman. I've forked over enough money so that Sonia could raise, clothe, feed, school, and house "our" child without having to fritter away the kid's high-maintenance years in an office, factory, or restaurant. She had the rare opportunity to carry this out according to her own rules, her own proclivities, schedule, disposition, and moods. I gave Sonia the best marriage anyone has ever had, and now she wants to ruin it.

This is how I see it.

Bun told me he would take my number and ask his wife to call me back, although—he added this peripherally, as far as I could tell—this might not be until tomorrow, because they're going to dinner at Marie's tonight, and Stephanie is still at work. He then reminded me, as we were hanging up, that he too is a lawyer. I countered with the on-the-spot stroke-of-genius reply that I thought a female lawyer might be a better advocate in such a case. "Of course," he said sagely, and we parted amicably enough.

Two hours later, she has not returned my call. I am aware of an uneasiness I haven't felt in years. Because I haven't pursued a woman with any intent since Jennifer the college administrator ended our liaison last year and married her erstwhile boyfriend. Lately, I've preferred cornering a postadolescent cashier with limited education, cockeyed opinions, and a chatty personality. It hasn't been entirely satisfactory, to say the least. But is this any better? Awaiting a married woman's phone call like a lovestruck doofus? I need more cigarettes; I've somehow consumed the entire carton I bought several days ago, up in smoke, poof poof poof. But I don't want to leave the house, and so I sit here in the kitchen with one lamp burning—a symbol of my ever-hopeful heart, I suppose. The shade is a little ratty, which is appropriate, and the bulb flickers periodically. Dennis has taken his daughters to the movies. It's a rainy, windy, very dark night. This . . . sitting around waiting for someone to call, this unaccountable desire to hear a specific voice again, to see one particular face, is an unpleasantly disconcerting itch I haven't felt in so long I've conveniently forgotten how distract-

ing it is, how futilely time-frittering and anxious. I remember
now why I've confined my romantic pursuits to unattainable
shopgirls. I prefer the pain in my foot that's been keeping me
awake at night, or in fact any sensation, no matter how un-
comfortable or excruciating, that doesn't require the actions of
someone else to alleviate it, and that isn't caused by another person's actions. Or lack of them.

Meanwhile, I sit at the kitchen table scrawling nonsense. I've
turned into that teenage girl waiting for some socially chal-
lenged ape to telephone with some tedious offer of a bad movie
and lukewarm hamburger so he can fondle her budding breasts.
She waits for her ultimate reward with nothing but the self-
manufactured chatter of Dear Diary to console her.

This is unacceptable. Writing about it only makes me feel
like even more of a sap. If I don't artificially generate some sort
of forward propulsion right this minute, I might as well shoot
myself in the head. I think I'll go on over to Marie's house,
friendly Uncle Hugo greeting with genial affability anyone who
might answer the door. I hope this will remind them that a
masculine presence in a house can be enriching and reassuring,
despite what they may think or feel most of the time. Show a
little fake but convincing brotherly concern.

It hasn't escaped my notice that Stephanie has been invited
there for dinner tonight.

Dennis has recently made a few more of his creepy silent
calls to his wife; I'm sure as a result she's been operating on the
low-level panicky alert of a woman alone in an old drafty house
trying to convince herself that the doors and windows are
locked and the locks will hold, the sole protector of her own
children and a teenage girl. I'm sure as she lies in bed at night
every creak and rattle and moan makes her stare with sizzling
veins into the darkness. I'm sure she gets up to gaze in at her
vulnerable, sleeping, helpless girls, double-checks each door and

window, then stands in the mudroom, staring out at nothing but darkness and her own car in the silent driveway, shivering in her nightgown, exhausted but unable to go back up to bed. I imagine it would take very little at this point to make her scream with movie-heroine coloratura. I further imagine that if there were some way for her to contrive Dennis's return to-morrow without her losing any face, she would leap at it like a thrown rope and hold on to it, a woman in white water ap-proaching the falls.

And I suspect Dennis has plans of his own, and is probably far more conniving and self-interested than I've ever given him credit for being. This is disconcerting. I detest being surprised by people, especially those to whom a certain degree of my identity depends upon feeling superior.

Something strange is happening. I started writing this note-book to escape Dennis and to reclaim my solitude. More and more, as I contemplate my death, it strikes me as vital in some way to hedge my bets. These fragments here . . . I leave them in lieu of a life's work, a series of achievements. "This is my let-ter to the World," as Emily Dickinson wrote. A sorry offering, but I'm a sorry specimen, and I don't say this out of self-pity or false modesty, I say it out of years of self-scrutiny.

November 3—Evie and Isabelle were spending last night at Waverley, so I ambled the truck over to my sister-in-law's house yesterday just after dark, hoping to finagle a means of ambush-ing Stephanie Fox when she arrived for dinner. On my way I stopped at an elderly, beaten-down strip mall consisting of a cluster of sad little businesses that looked as if they had weath-ered several recessions already and were unlikely to survive this new one, with one exception, a dazzlingly bright little haven whose neon sign, "Liquors," was as bright as the North Star must have looked to escaping slaves on the Underground

I tucked one bottle into the glove box and left the other beside me on the seat in its paper bag (bait) and then continued on my scheming, ardent, falsely altruistic way.

I left the little town's business district behind and turned onto a small lane; treetop branches met overhead to form a nearly bare arch filled with falling raindrops illuminated by my headlights. I found this claustrophobia-inducing, as always. Lights flickered through fences and hedges: other people's cozy houses—or "homes," as they're called now—filled with sedentary overfed citizens seething in lonely but overpopulated hells, vapor-locked into a computer or television screen. Less than a mile along this road, I turned up Marie's steep, unlikely driveway and parked innocently in front of their house. Its outline against the night sky showed peaks and gables, a chimney. Windows within were lit.

To my delight, Louisa came to the door when I knocked. She smiled when she saw me, then remembered all at once that our friendship might compromise her standing with her employer. I saw it in her face.

"Hello, Hugo," she said, trying to sound cool. But she's too young still, her heart too warm and healthy, for her to be any good at dissembling political maneuvers.

"Hello, Louisa," I said. "I was in the neighborhood. I thought I'd see how you were. And I brought Marie a bottle of wine. A humble offering, to be sure."

"Wait here," she said breathlessly.

I waited there. A moment later I was face-to-face with my sister-in-law.

"Hugo," said Marie, managing to loom in the doorway, although she is quite small in stature. "What can I do for you?"

She looked ravishing. Her black hair was springy and agleam, her slanted Gallic eyes narrowed with suspicion. She wore a red dress.

"Hello, Marie," I stammered slightly, as if she had caught me off guard with her fierce beauty, as she had obviously intended to do. "I was passing by and thought I'd see if you needed anything. Check up on you. I thought Dennis would appreciate it." To flatter her further, I reached for the doorframe as if I needed to steady myself with a hand against it to regain my composure. Accidentally, or not, I touched her shoulder, which was likewise resting there. She leapt back as if it had burned her. Her skin was very warm through the thin satiny cloth. "And I brought you a bottle of wine I'm fond of. I thought you might appreciate a good St.-Émilion. The blood of your countrymen, so to speak."

"What a disgusting image, but thank you," she said firmly, taking the proffered bottle. "I don't mean to be rude, but I'm expecting a few people in a little while, so we're just getting ready. Thanks for the thought, Hugo."

She began to shut the door.

"Oh, Marie," I said, "do you mind if I come in for a moment and use your bathroom?"

She sighed; clearly she wished she could tell me to go away, but she couldn't because I'm family, in a way, and we have to allow family into our houses—otherwise who will take them in? "Okay," she said, "just for a minute, Hugo, but please don't bug Louisa."

I raised my eyebrows at her to show my complete lack of ambition in that area, then smiled a little, no offense taken. I slunk through the house, sniffing the homey air with shivery half-dreadful pleasure. Some sort of roast was in the oven. Additionally, I thought I detected a whiff of baking gingerbread.

I emerged from the bathroom into the kitchen and, seeing that Marie was busy doing something in the dining room, I inspected all the various pots and baking dishes Marie had going on the stove and in the oven. I lifted lids, inhaled, and peeked into the oven. I found gingerbread, a pan of potatoes, and a large roast in the oven, and a bundle of asparagus waiting in a steamer on the stovetop. In the pantry, a bowl of crisp-looking lettuce and a plate of cheese. On the counter were a bowl of apples and pears and a large loaf of bread on a cutting board.

"All right," said Marie, bustling back into the kitchen, "I'll see you out now, Hugo. My guests will be here soon."

"Who is coming over?" I inquired, picking up an open bottle of wine and looking curiously at the label.

"Hugo," said Marie, "why are you really here? What are you doing?" She was trying very hard to be tough but her face had an expression I was unfamiliar with, a sort of loopy softness. It dawned on me then with a little zing that she was tipsy; the bottle was half empty. So I might have a chance here.

"I came to see how you were," I said. "I've been thinking how hard it must be sometimes for you with Dennis gone. Despite the fact that we've never been close, to put it mildly, I am still your brother-in-law. I thought you could use a brother right now. I apologize for intruding."

"It's all right," she said, clearly debating internally whether she should let herself be taken in by this patent pile of hogwash. As a therapist, she should have seen right through it. Well, she was drunk; I'd give her the benefit of the doubt. "But it wasn't necessary. I'm fine."

"I just wanted to put my mind at ease. I feel partly responsible; I'm not my brother's keeper, but he hasn't been acting very well by you lately."

"He certainly has not."

"Marie," I said with what for me was genuine sincerity, "Dennis misses you. He'll come back if you'll have him."

She shot me a proud and angry look I knew was intended for Dennis, but was conferred upon me as his stand-in.

Even my heart has its soft spots. I smiled at her. My best, san-est, most trustworthy smile. "And I thought we could enjoy a glass of the wine I brought," I added, dangling between two fingers the corkscrew I'd palmed a moment before.

"Oh, all right," she said, and smiled back at me. "Damn it, Hugo. Have a seat."

"I'll leave the minute you push me out the door," I said, then settled into the breakfast nook for a cozy chat with Marie while we waited for our friends to arrive.

Thus did I insinuate myself into the dinner party, and, for the first time ever, my brother's wife's confidence.

I learned that her younger sister, Veronique, was upstairs napping that very minute, having taken the train up from the city for the night, and so Marie had invited Bun and Stephanie Fox to come for dinner. Louisa was going to take the car into town to spend her night off pursuing whatever entertainment she could find in that depressing backwater.

Marie's sister, Marie informed me, was until recently Louisa's French professor; it was Vero who recommended Louisa for this job when she dropped out suddenly at the beginning of this, her sophomore year. Vero would prefer to be teaching medieval French literature at an Ivy League school, but is stuck in a third-rate outer-borough zoo trying to drum the fundamentals of *la grammaire française* into mediocre brains. Marie frankly thinks Kings College is not appreciably worse than any college with a so-called great reputation. A lot of perfectly capable and even great teachers end up at places like Hunter College and City College, and they're lucky to have teaching jobs at all; Ivy League graduates tend to land the plum teaching spots because people take care of their own, it stands to reason. Vero went through the New York City public-school system, then got her B.A. from Hunter College and her postgraduate degrees from SUNY Stony Brook, so what does she expect? And those are good schools, Marie thinks; this Ivy League superiority thing is a big fat myth. But Vero has never got over the fact that their older brother, Didier, the firstborn, graduated from Columbia, and Marie, next in line, went to Wesleyan. By the time it was her turn, the country was in a recession, and their father's import-export business had declined with the economy.

"We're not blue bloods like you and Dennis," Marie added without scorn or resentment. "But Vero is a snob."

"May I smoke in your house?" I asked.

"I don't usually allow it," she replied.

"If I don't smoke I'll likely become agitated and froth at the mouth," I rejoined pleasantly. "I have to smoke. It's my human condition."

"Evie will smell it when she gets home. She won't like it. She'll think it was me, and disapprove."

"Well, you can just tell that puritan child of yours it was that nasty Uncle Hugo. Let me take the rap. It will be my pleasure."

She smiled, sighed, and proffered a dish I took to be a sub-stitute ashtray, which I made use of right away; I felt better without having been aware of feeling worse beforehand.

Vero, it seems, didn't qualify for enough financial aid to go to a "good school" like Swarthmore or Yale because her father looked much richer on paper than he really was. So Vero, ar-guably the best and the brightest of the Dupins, certainly the most intellectually promising, went to Hunter College, where she got straight A's, while Didier took over their father's ailing business and turned it around, and Marie got her degree in so-cial work. Neither of them did a thing with the educations Vero would have given a limb for. Vero still resents this years later, but Marie maintains that her disgruntlement isn't so much about a good education as it is a class issue. Marie herself, or so she claimed to me, has never had any interest in or patience for class issues; it just isn't in her makeup to care about such things, and she isn't someone who feels it incumbent upon herself to try to transcend her makeup. She is who she is.

I caught a certain undertone of boozy defiance in all this.

"Your attitude must not sit very well with Dennis," I offered with sly sympathy.

"No," she said, "it doesn't. His lineage, as he calls it, matters more to him than anything. It galls him that I'm not impressed by it."

"Well, I don't care any more than you do about my lineage. As far as I'm concerned, they were all a bunch of freaks. Hot-house orchids. Everyone has ancestors; what's so special about mine except that they had a lot of money and married other people with a lot of money?"

"Maybe Dennis should have married Vero instead," said Marie. "She would have appreciated all that proud-to-be-a-Whittier crap."

"I understand," I said companionably, settling a little more comfortably into the banquette and lighting myself another cigarette off the dying embers of the first one, "that you have more than once enjoyed referring to me as Quasimodo or a troll under a bridge. Of the two, I frankly prefer the troll, which appeals to my reverse vanity and is funny besides. Quasimodo is completely inappropriate."

Marie was spared having to reply to this by the doorbell, which yielded the fragrant, golden, wryly self-possessed object of my desire and her husband, a bemused and rumpled fellow in a maroon button-down and olive-green trousers. Bun Fox was in possession of a black, shiny, velvety mole on his right cheekbone the size and shape of a small cockroach.

"Hugo Whittier," he said, "the name sounds familiar."

"I called and left a message for your wife earlier today," I said, looking him straight in the eye. "I wanted to consult with her about a legal matter."

"I forgot to pass along the message," said Bun. "I've been addlepated lately, to put it mildly. Stephanie, this guy here called. Call him back. His number is somewhere at home."

"Hello, Hugo," said Stephanie coolly. I shook her hand with no flirtatious pressure or undue significance.

"Hello, Stephanie," I said.

"Wine, everyone?" Marie asked, holding up the bottle.

"Yes indeed," said Bun.

"Here's an interesting trivia question," I said. "Does anyone know how many pounds of meat a day the Roman Emperor Maximus consumed to keep up his strength?"

"Oh, Marie," Stephanie said, "it smells delicious in here, speaking of meat."

"Forty pounds," I said, but Stephanie was looking into the oven. "A day. He must have done nothing but eat all day long. And vomit, being Roman."

"Really," said Bun, who was sticking close by my elbow, looking intently at me. Male solidarity, perhaps. Whatever the reason, it was giving me the willies.

"Greek actors made a point of consuming gross amounts of meat as a sort of entertainment," I added chattily as Marie handed Bun a glass of wine. "One Greek actress could eat ten pounds of meat at a sitting, washed down with six jugs of wine."

"I feel like I could do that right now," said Bun.

"The great banquets of antiquity," I went on loudly, aiming my voice at the seemingly oblivious Stephanie, feeling like a lovestruck buffoon, a fourth-grade grossout showoff, "featured stews made of erotic offal, such as sows' vulvas and nipples, or the testicles of calves. In the French region of Languedoc, where such dishes are still eaten, they call them *frivolités,* frivolities."

"Thanks for that information, Hugo," said Marie. "Unfortunately, all I've got tonight is a humble roast. Sorry to be so unimaginative."

"I'm not entirely disappointed," said Stephanie dryly.

"Shall we go into the dining room? I'll go wake Vero. She's taking a nap. She says she's been sleeping a lot this fall. I don't blame her. It must be unspeakably sad and hard, living down in the city right now."

The Foxes and I took up posts around the long dining-room table while Marie vanished upstairs. We set our wineglasses down with sudden happy clatter, guests together in someone else's house, irresponsible and carefree as children. In the center of the table was a cluster of small plates and bowls of food. Olives, nuts, smoked oysters, crackers and cheese, that sort of thing. I took the chair nearest to this offering and helped myself liberally; I was feeling light-headed, possibly because Stephanie was sitting directly across from me, watching me feed myself, looking amused and completely mysterious. Bun leaned back in his chair, looked up at the ceiling, and sighed.

"This fall," he said, "I haven't slept well, not one single night. This is the tip of the iceberg. This is only the beginning. It's all going to go to hell now."

"Can we please talk about anything else just for one night?" Stephanie asked in an even voice with a glint of anger running through it.

"There is nothing more urgent at the moment to discuss," said Bun.

"I say, the less we talk about it, the less power those animals have," Stephanie said back.

"No," said Bun. "We have to remain on our guard, and remember all of it."

"Remembering," she said, "won't help. Nothing we can do will help, because we did nothing to bring it on ourselves."

"Sure we did; it's the chickens coming home to roost," said Bun. "Right, Hugo?"

I had a few things to say about this, but decided not to say them. There was something about their exchange that seemed marital, personal, fenced off.

"Bun," said Stephanie, each word as hard and deadly as a gunshot, "don't start this here. Not now. You can't just say these things."

"Life is tragic," said Bun. "We never learn from our mistakes."

I said mildly, without import, "Maybe it's tragicomic. Look at us, inflated with our own busy godlike importance, but at the same time we're fools who fuck and fart and scratch, get weak and decrepit when we're old, and die sooner or later. What a joke on us, to leave the two to duke it out in us, god and dog."

"God and dog," Bun repeated bemusedly, shaking his head.

Vero preceded her sister down the stairs. She was a taller, plainer, but somehow more immediately striking version of her elder sister. She had the same slanted eyes, the same lustrous pallor and long slender nose, but on her it all looked less organized and more dramatic. "Hello," she said to all of us in general. She had a low melodious voice with a faintly plummy accent. There was something of the old-fashioned stage actress about her. Her hair was cut into a saucy bob around her long face. She wore a low-cut watered-silk purple dress from which her bare neck and bony shoulders rose with Edwardian starkness. I sensed immediately a high-strung, quivering self-regard that precluded the inclusion of anyone else. She was her own hermetic system.

"Bun, Stephanie, this is my sister, Veronique," said Marie.

"Finally we meet," said Stephanie, reaching sideways to shake her hand. "I was beginning to think you were Marie's imaginary sister."

"I'm Dennis's brother, Hugo," I said to Vero, who had already given me a swift appraising look and sized me up while I did the same to her.

"I see," she said.

Colliding waves of mutual animosity met in the air between our gazes. I disliked her because she appeared to have a far higher self-regard than was strictly warranted; why she disliked me was anyone's guess.

"When I was a kid I had an imaginary friend named Frederick Marshall," said Bun. "He was six foot seven, from Des Moines, an opera singer, and a horse thief. He was absolutely real to me. I was the only child of somewhat elderly parents. Stephanie and I are embroiled in a discussion about whether or not to have children right now. I would like to have at least two, so the first one has someone to talk to besides the likes of Frederick Marshall."

"This is all too typical of Bun," said Stephanie, "to blurt out personal or marital news as if it were no more off limits than what he read in the paper today."

"Marie used to be my therapist," said Bun. "I guess I'm in the habit of speaking frankly around her. I always assume she's interested."

"That's how we met," said Marie, on her way into the kitchen.

"I was suffering from a certain rather delicate physical difficulty," said Bun. "Marie helped me to get to the roots of the problem, which I was astonished to learn was actually my own fear of inadequacy."

"Bun!" said Stephanie.

"It's nothing to be ashamed of," Bun countered. He looked over at me. "Right, Hugo?"

"I wouldn't know," I said, on the surface apologetically. I lit a cigarette and looked at Stephanie, who looked steadily back at me for the first time since she had arrived. My hands shook a little as I held the flame to the tip and breathed in.

"I can't take him anywhere," she said, referring to Bun, I assumed. "He drops these little bombs into conversations and then sits back to enjoy the explosion."

Marie returned with more wine, which she splashed liberally into everyone's near-empty glasses. She set my ashtray before me without a word of complaint. I was apparently increasingly welcome to make myself quite at home here in my brother's house.

"If he gets to smoke," said Vero, eyeing me with disgruntlement, "then I do too."

"Oh, all right," said Marie. "I'll get you an ashtray."

"I want one too," said Stephanie.

"See what you've done," said Marie to me.

"Yes, of course I do," I said. "I've done everyone a favor. You might as well smoke too, Marie."

Vero held a lit match to the end of Stephanie's cigarette, then her own, then Marie's, then mine, then shook the flame out, and finally said, exhaling smoke, "Now, this is more like it."

"Since Dennis and I split up," Marie said once dinner was served and we were all busy with our meat and potatoes, "when I'm not livid at him, I'm starting to feel a little heady with freedom. Let everything go to hell now that everything's gone to hell, you know?"

"I just talked to Dennis today, speaking of Dennis," said Stephanie to the table at large, slathering butter on a piece of bread.

"You did?" I echoed more sharply than I would have liked.

"He called to say hello just before we left to come over here. Maybe he was feeling left out of our dinner."

"But he's at the movies," I barked. "With his children."

"What I'm trying to say," Marie broke in, spreading butter

on her own piece of bread, "is, who's going to fix me up with
someone nice and eligible?"

"Marie," Vero cried with soap-operatic dismay, "his side of
the bed is still warm."

For the first time, I felt an unspoken alliance with the horrible Vero. "She's right," I said. "I'm not sure I want to hear this."

"I know a very nice man," said Stephanie slyly. "Two of
them, in fact."

"Who?" Bun asked curiously, perking up from a reverie he'd
fallen into. "What two nice men do you know? I don't think
we know any."

"Look, Vero," said Marie, "don't get all sanctimonious with
me. You never had anything nice to say about Dennis while we
were together, so it doesn't wash that you're suddenly so loyal
to him now."

"Not loyal to him," said Vero, "loyal to propriety."

"Right," said Marie. "You're the poster girl of propriety; I
forgot."

"Well, I like to think I am," said Vero, holding her forkful of
meat in midair, two spots of color high on her cheeks. "What
on earth do I do that isn't absolutely proper?"

"Anyway, they're probably both present or former clients of
mine, like everyone else around here," said Marie dourly.

"Bun," said Stephanie, "don't you think Jim and Marie
would like each other?"

"Jim might like Marie, but she wouldn't like him," said Bun.

All of the women ignored him.

"We'll have you both over for dinner," Stephanie told Marie.
"You can look him over at your leisure; I promise I won't say
anything to him about you. He lives down in the city, but he
comes up here every so often."

"Maybe I'd like Jim if he lives in the city," said Vero. "Marie
can have the other guy."

"Arnold," said Stephanie.

"I wouldn't want to marry him, though," said Vero. "A husband? What would I do with a husband underfoot all the time? But I'd let the right person visit me every now and then, if I ever met him."

Marie gave her a sidelong glance. "Visit you? Is that a nineteenth-century euphemism, or what?"

Vero was too busy with her fork and knife (which she handled, I noticed, the sophisticated continental way her parents had no doubt taught her, knife remaining in right hand and fork in left with tines facing down, rather than the gauche American switcheroo technique the rest of us were employing) to respond to this.

"So," said Marie, turning to Bun and Stephanie, "who's Arnold? I don't like the name Arnold."

"Bun, how would you describe Arnold?"

"Arnold," said Bun democratically. "Well, he's a decent poker player, and he's reasonably well groomed."

"Come on," said Stephanie, "you can do better than that."

"What do you want me to say? He's a guy," said Bun to Marie. "Men don't describe each other. Right, Hugo? It's not done. We'd have to admit we looked at each other, and we're squeamish about such things. I admit, though, to peeking occasionally at a urinal, but only for comparative purposes."

Again, he looked my way for affirmation. I regarded this curiosity of a man and didn't say anything. Who talked this way? How did a man who talked this way get a woman like Stephanie to marry him? I accepted anew the fact that I'll never understand my fellows no matter how long or closely I'm required to observe them.

"Okay, Bun," said Marie, "but let's say you had to describe Arnold to a jury."

"That I can do. He's shorter than I am but not by much, say five ten, balding but not bald, glasses, beaky nose, sallow skin, slight paunch," said Bun. "A real catch."

"Bun!" said Stephanie. "He does not have a paunch, Marie, he's just solid, and he's balding in a sexy way, and he's Jewish; it's that Mediterranean skin, which is actually more olive than sallow. Anyway, he's a writer, a novelist, and I think you might like him. And, Bun, that beaky-nose comment was just beyond the pale."

"His nose," said Bun, "is beaky. It's an objective fact."

"Bring him on," said Marie. "Beak and all. Why haven't I met these guys before?"

"Because you were married and had no need of them."

"Oh, Stephanie," said Vero. "I'm curious about something: did you and Bun fall prey to the ripple-effect syndrome when Marie and Dennis split up? You know, seismographic trauma in your own marriage caused by your friends' breakup, making you question everything, et cetera?"

"That is quite frankly none of your business, Vero," said Stephanie pleasantly.

"She means yes, we did," said Bun. "We almost split up ourselves. Stephanie got the idea that our whole marriage was a fifteen-year mistake. I had to summon all my rhetorical powers, every lawyer trick I know, to persuade her otherwise. I'm still not entirely sure I succeeded."

"I'm not entirely sure you succeeded either," said Stephanie, smiling coldly at him, "but here we sit, man and wife, at dinner."

"Well," said Vero through an exhaled plume of smoke, "let's discuss Louisa, then. How is she working out?"

"All right, on the whole," said Marie. "She's nice, Vero, but she's a little annoying sometimes. She's so eager to please, it gets on my nerves."

"She is a great girl," said Vero. "Her mind is one of the sharpest I've ever encountered in all my years of teaching. I'm encouraging her to apply to a few good schools during her year off."

"When can we meet her?" asked Stephanie as Bun cleared

his throat and jiggled his knee up and down and looked around distractedly. "Bun, pay attention, you're acting like a three-year-old."

"Twenty-year-old au-pair girls should be of paramount interest to middle-aged men," said Vero. "You should be riveted by this conversation."

"Twenty-year-old au-pair girls are of interest to me primarily when they're taking care of my own children," said Bun. "Which I hope will happen someday soon."

"Be nice to her," said Vero to Marie. "She's had a rough time of it lately."

"I am nice to her," said Marie. "I'm nothing but nice."

"What sort of rough time?" I asked.

"Oh, she's got a couple of dark secrets," said Vero.

"She has?" said Marie.

"Nothing to be ashamed of," said Vero, "but they're secrets all the same. And she doesn't know I know, so I'm certainly not going to tell any of you."

"Well, did she do something wrong?" Marie asked, laughing. "Is she a criminal?"

"I recommended her for a job in my sister's house, taking care of my two little nieces," said Vero. "The children I care about more than anyone else in the world. Would I have done that if I didn't think absolutely highly of her and trust her completely?"

"They're my nieces too," I said pleasantly, offhandedly. They all ignored me.

Stephanie and I washed the dishes together while everyone else sat around the table over cheese and fruit and Armagnac. Since

I'd crashed the party it seemed like the least I could do; also, although I tried not to seem too happy about it, this was my first and only chance to be alone with Stephanie. "He's always like this," she said, handing me the salad bowl. "I think he thinks he's being charming and witty. He thinks this is adult conversation, to discuss his sexual problems and marital conflicts and vaguely anti-Semitic leanings. Well, not anti-Semitic, but he thinks his English master race is superior and doesn't mind if it shows. He thinks these are all things people want to hear about."

I had discussed Bun Fox quite enough for one night. I was thoroughly sick of him.

"When can I take you out to dinner?" I asked, wiping the bowl clean with a paper towel so the wood gleamed with lingering traces of oil.

"How's a week from Monday?" she asked, in such a matter-of-fact way I wanted to leap in the air with something like joy. "The twelfth."

"You're in luck," I said. "I just happen to be free on the twelfth. You choose the time and place; keep in mind that the sky's the limit and I don't mind paying through the nose to eat well, especially when I lose a bet."

"The Turtle Inn, at eight," she said. "In the lounge."

"Done," I said. "So why did Dennis really call you tonight?"

"What do you mean?"

"I mean, what did he want? Besides just hearing the sound of your voice."

"I thought you said . . ."

"What did you think I said?"

"I thought you said he didn't . . ."

I waited for her to give my lie right back to me, but her nerve seemed to fail her, or else she couldn't bear to say aloud that Dennis didn't want her because her heart was broken; either way, I didn't care, because I was the one having dinner with her on Monday week. But I hadn't meant to give her any hope.

"Of course," I said hastily. "But he regards both you and Bun as dear friends; he told me so."

"Actually," she went on after a moment, "he sounded lonely."

"How can he be lonely when he has me?" I said, doing a little jig with the dish towel. Somehow we had switched places, so that she was washing now and I was drying. I wasn't sure suddenly how or when this had happened. Our bodies seemed to know the score a lot better than we did. I had also at some point begun to sport a semi-erection, which was now rubbing against the edge of the counter and threatening to grow into a whole one if I didn't switch on the thing in my brain that controlled it. "Please don't go fixing my sister-in-law up with some goon," I said. "She has a husband already, Stephanie. I'm disappointed that Dennis's so-called friends would collude so easily in the ultimate destruction of his happy marriage."

"He doesn't have a happy marriage!" she said, laughing. "No one does. So what if Marie wants a boyfriend?"

"I smell an ulterior motive," I said agitatedly. "Stephanie, despite what you would no doubt love to believe about this situation, my brother's happiness depends upon his ultimate reconciliation with his wife. I have been doing everything in my power to help him bring this about. What do you think I'm doing here tonight? Do you think I was invited? Marie can't stand the sight of me. Normally I respect this and keep my distance from her. Tonight I dropped in uninvited, without any hope of thanks or appreciation, to encourage her to give him another chance. So I'm pained and even irritated by your attempts to thwart my altruistic scheme with a selfish one of your own."

She laughed. "Are you, now?" she said. Her arms were bare in a black sleeveless shirt with little straps; she had taken off her sweater during dinner. She has very nice arms. They are muscular, but imperfect: there are flaps of skin in the back, virtually the only part of Stephanie that betrays the fact that she is my own age, which is to say, middle-aged. I'm frequently at a loss to do verbal justice to the glorious mysteries and complexities of women's anatomies, but I find those flaps touching and vulnerable imperfections on an otherwise impeccably and even dauntingly muscular and perfect body. Although I'm sure she reviles them and would loathe my mentioning them, they only increase my already overwhelming desire for her. I am delighted that she is imperfect. She won an unwinnable bet, but—aha!—she has arm flaps. However, plunged into the dishwater, gleaming in the soapsuds like a doubloon in a sunken ship, her wedding ring looked silly and vestigial, especially now that I had met her husband.

"How are you feeling lately, Hugo?" she asked then, scrubbing the roast pan. "You're smoking as much as ever, I see, not that it's any of my business."

"Yes," I said. " *'Mais que j'aie fait mes étrennes, honnête mort ne me déplaît.'* You'd like to know what the hell that means. Well, essentially it means that death is my fair due."

"Showoff," she said. "I don't buy that you really feel that way."

" *'Mais où est le preux Charlemagne?'* Which is to say, my own mortality is more immediately in question than most, but we all share it. And according to Montaigne, the most pardonable suicide is one that allows escape from unbearable pain."

"Oh, that's just bravado," she said, staring hard at the caked-on lump of caramelized animal fat she was going at with a bit of steel wool. "You could easily cure yourself, you said so the other night. You just choose not to."

"I'm no different from you or anyone else," I said. "The human race is dying out too. The race could save itself if we all collectively chose to forgo our addictive pleasures, fossil fuels, corporate growth, and ecological despoilment for our own gains, but collectively we choose not to, and so we will certainly perish. As for you, Stephanie Fox the individual, you're doing the same thing I am, only more slowly, and less honestly. You drive a car; you use plastic products; you do whatever the hell you do knowing full well that it's contributing to the end of everyone, and a lot of other animals besides. So don't get all more-life-affirming-than-thou with me, missy, you're on your way out too. In a way, you could see me as the canary down a mine shaft, or maybe synecdoche, the small part representing the whole."

"I know what synecdoche means."

"Of course you do."

"When you're really dying, or even when you really face amputation and immobility, I'll bet you won't sound so macho and devil-may-care about all this. I bet you another dinner that you'll quit smoking long before it gets bad enough to make you kill yourself."

"You're on," I said. "It's a bet. It almost makes me want to lose, just for the pleasure of buying you another meal. How will I collect if I win, though?"

She busied herself then, and didn't answer. Scrub, scrub. At this rate those arm flaps would be gone; she attacked the underside of the pan, which probably hadn't been washed in ten years. My erection, I was interested to note, was gone, poof. I stood there watching her, the wet dish towel folded neatly over my forearm as if I were the maître d' in some down-at-heels bistro. She rinsed the shining, like-new roast pan, set it in the now empty (thanks to my rigor with the dish towel) dish rack, and pulled the plug to drain the now gray water from the sink. It glug-glugged steadily for a while as it ran out into the pipes, then all at once it sucked itself violently away down the drain, and was gone.

"I know I'm right," she said then, stubbornly.

"I love it when someone reads my mind," I said. "It makes me want to sing and dance."

"Of course it does," she said with a smile, turning to look at me. "And when are you going to tell Dennis that you're sick? It's not right that your own brother doesn't know."

"He wouldn't care," I said breezily.

"You have to tell him, Hugo."

"You seem to have a lot of strong opinions about all this," I said, "although you did preface them by reminding both of us that it's my beeswax you're minding here."

I'd had the impression that she had been about to say a lot more, but she let it drop. "Let's go have some dessert," she said. She'd had a brisk sound in her voice, I realized, since this topic had arisen. The topic of my death. Which didn't exactly arise: she brought it up.

We rejoined the others at table. The rest of the night went by, I had some fresh warm gingerbread and coffee, then a snifter of Armagnac and some very good cheddar and a sliced pear, and then I thanked Marie and said good night to everyone else and came home.

Dennis was awake, sitting at the kitchen table with a book, a glass and an opened bottle of wine. Of course the book was *Anna Karenina*. I took my new bottle of whiskey from my coat pocket and set it on the table. Then I got a glass from the cupboard. The glasses had recently, I was interested to see, been arranged as I had requested. I felt an internal click of satisfaction.

I pulled up a chair and poured some whiskey into the glass.

"Where have you been?" Dennis asked. He looked to be in some need of attention.

"Your old house," I said. "For dinner."

"Where?"

"Marie's house," I repeated patiently. Dennis is always a bit thick when you catch him off guard with unexpected information about any goings-on that don't directly involve him. I often suspect that he imagines the world is a dark stage on which he himself is the sole spotlit actor. "She was having a dinner party," I added cruelly. "Bun and Stephanie Fox were there, as well as her awful sister, Vero."

He looked crestfallen. "She invited you over for dinner?"

"I dropped by," I said.

He ran both hands over his face as if he could just erase all this. "And she invited you to stay?"

"Well," I said, "she did. I think she was feeling in need of a stand-in for you somehow. She seemed to recollect all at once that I am her brother after all. She makes the most delicious roast. You never told me."

"You never asked," he said with a grim smile.

"I dropped by," I said, "in order to ascertain her agreeability to your return. I was trying to do you a favor."

"Don't interfere in my marriage, Hugo. It's in enough trouble already."

"Well, if I hadn't interfered tonight, then I wouldn't be able to warn you now that your wife is looking into seeing other men. Not only that, during the course of the dinner party she asked your quote-unquote friends Bun and Stephanie to help her find one."

"What the hell are you talking about?" Again, that startled look, as he realized that some of the other characters in his play had scenes sometimes without him.

I cocked an eye at the ceiling, squinting as if I were trying to decide exactly how much information he could handle, as if I were tiptoeing around him because there was no sense in upsetting him more than necessary. I waited just long enough to give him the impression that there were a few things I had decided not to tell him out of concern for his frail emotional condition.

"Well," I said, drawing the word out skeptically, "Marie sort of announced, I suppose the word is, that she's ready to date again. Your wife, the mother of your children. Stephanie immediately trotted out a couple of likely candidates. Jim and Arnold."

"I don't know," Dennis spat savagely, "any Jim or Arnold."

"And, interestingly," I said, "the only people in the room tonight who seemed to have any interest whatsoever in defending you—or, rather, your marriage—were Vero and me. Blood, it appears, is thicker than water."

"Vero can't stand me."

"That may be."

"And what do you care about my marriage?"

"I care about reuniting you with your wife and small daughters, who are barely out of diapers, and who need to grow up under a father's loving guidance. Isabelle in particular is going to need a lot of protection. Evie I wouldn't worry so much about. She can already take care of herself."

"That's true," he said. "I worry about Isabelle."

"Dad would have wanted you to stay with the woman you married. The way he himself did. That's what Whittier men do, they stay with their wives."

Dennis snorted. "I don't see Sonia anywhere around the house these days." Another of his wildly courageous forays out onto the bright, thin, and treacherous ice of badinage.

I gave an abrupt bark to acknowledge this game attempt at humor, then pulled my trump card from my boot. "Well, you will very soon," I said. "My wife and I are reuniting. I'm putting, as they say, my money where my mouth is. We were not raised to be divorced, Dennis, nor were we raised to allow our children to grow up without a father underfoot. I am not divorced. Neither are you—yet."

"Well, I'm going to be," he said. "Just so you've got it all straight." He took an emphatic swallow of wine.

I took a moment to knock back some whiskey and pour myself some more, then asked slyly, "How's that book you're reading? Ringing any bells?"

He looked at the cover of the novel as if it would tell him the answer. "All the marital goings-on?" he asked. "What? I don't see what you're getting at."

"You mess with legal marriage at your peril."

"Right," he said, although he obviously didn't see at all. "That was a long time ago, in Russia, Hugo. And, frankly, I don't believe Sonia is coming back."

"Well, she is," etc., etc., until I had to go up to my room and produce the letter from my wife and pretend that I had written back encouraging her to return instead of doing everything in my power to keep her far away from me forever as well as our fearsome spawn, etc. By the time my dullard of a brother finally understood that I hadn't forged the letter from Sonia and I wasn't bluffing about all this for my own unworthy purposes, quite a lot of my bottle of whiskey had somehow disappeared, and it was after one in the morning, and my leg was aching to beat whatever band was playing anywhere, mariachi, marching, garage, swing, or brass. Dennis had likewise made impressive inroads on his own bottle of wine.

"So it appears I'll finally meet my niece," he said with half-sloppy sentiment.

"Well," I said, "it does appear that way, yes. But I would bet any amount of money you care to name that she doesn't look anything like me."

"Why is that?"

I raised my eyebrows and waggled them, which made my scalp move over my skull, a slightly creepy and slightly pleasurable sensation I was in no hurry to repeat.

"Maybe you should ask Sonia that question," I said, "because I sure as hell don't know."

It was time for bed, so we turned out the lights and took

ourselves upstairs. I walked with all the normalcy I could muster until Dennis peeled off on the landing for his own (temporary, temporary) room and I could gimp my way to the tower room I've made my lifelong home.

November 4—Tra-la! The lovely Carla is back at her post, brightening my twice-a-day cigarette runs, gracing me with the deliriously warm and fantastically fuzzy delusion that I am not entirely alone in the world, there are others like me, others who have no real business holding down jobs, speaking frankly to strangers, being entrusted with small change or the keys to the till, etc.

"You're back!" I cried.

She handed me my shiny pack of cigarettes with an urchin-like grinning-ear-to-ear expression that is not the most flattering to her face, since it has the unfortunate effect of accentuating the puffiness of her cheeks and squeezing shut her eyes, which are her best and indeed only really good feature, being clear, blue, sparkling, and filled with a certain impish light. But I didn't mind; that smile told me all I needed to know about the requitedness of my feelings for her. I envisioned her at once on the old Whittier iceboat with me in the wintertime, riding along the ice beside me, clutching a package of Lorna Doones to her large-breasted parka'ed chest, the icy wind in her hair.

"Hi, Hugo," she said in her husky voice tinged with the local accent, the real voice of my youth, no matter what I may have told Louisa about her own husky voice. "How ya been?"

"I been just swell," I replied, settling in to my old perch, out of the way of the flow of customers, leaning on the counter at the end, where no one would jostle me.

Oh, how we chatted. There seemed to be a great deal for us to say to each other. First there was the matter of the utter lack of developments in the government's so-called efforts to capture this autumn's national villains, the anthrax mailer and the former would-be playboy and rich oil brat Osama. In Carla's opinion, the government is falling down on the job and she doesn't care who hears her say it, she's as patriotic as the next person but this administration is just totally unworthy of leading the greatest nation on earth. While she talked, I noticed, as I always do, the heaving swell of her enchantingly oversized bosom beneath her olive-green smock, her name tag riding the crest of her left breast like a surfer hanging a glorious ten upon a majestic wave. Those are womanly breasts on a slight and girlish frame, the milk-rich bags of a madonna intended for serious childbearing, meant to have a toddler still nursing at one while the new baby clutches experimentally at the other and all around her the supplanted postinfants clamor for their old feeding stations . . . and yet her limbs are lanky, and her full, round, oversized head teeters on the frail stalk of her neck. These juxtapositions of paucity and surfeit I find exceedingly, aesthetically erotic.

I think I must have slipped into a bit of a reverie, fixated upon the Kubla Khan I saw before me, in need of no opiates as long as Carla was in front of my dreaming eyes, as real as anything else I know of, when suddenly I came to with the instant, dismaying awareness that her male relative, my old friend, had entered the store and was fixing me in his sights.

"Well," I said, "hello. I'm beside myself with joy to see that you've allowed your lovely niece another whack at the cash register."

Carla looked at me, startled, then a grin spread sneakily across her face, a grin I was flummoxed by. This wasn't, probably, the most tactful remark I could have made. There were a few other customers in the store, within earshot and seemingly with nothing better to do than eavesdrop. This remark had the

triple effect of alerting the customers to that funny business between Carla and the cash register, and her uncle to another
brand entirely of funny business in my professed joy at her return, and Carla to the fact that I knew about her criminal behavior. It was time to go, I could see that as well as anyone else
in that family-run Stewart's franchise.

I went out to my truck clacking my heels together mentally
with elation. Carla is back!

As I drove out of town I saw him again, that man, that
face. . . . I drove right by him, our eyes met, I drove on, he
drove on. He didn't turn his car about and come after me with
a sawed-off anything, he drove on peaceably, like the good citizen he has no doubt become in the interim since he was a
sinister low-level mobster and I was a two-timing kept boy.
Shlomo, his name came back to me. Shlomo Levy, Shlomo
Levy of Brighton Beach, hired by his cousin Tovah to dispatch
me to Hades. I eluded Shlomo Levy then by slipping out of
town. I've eluded him all these years but, I have an uneasy feeling, no more.

He's not looking for me. He's not here to find me. He
can't be.

It was all so long ago, but the icy sensation of recognition
made me realize that, to my corporeal self, it was yesterday. *Les
neiges d'antan* have caught up with me.

The irony is that ostensibly I don't care now if I get iced.
Actually, the real irony is that I don't care, but the other-Hugo
someone who lives alongside me in this wreckage does, some
vestige of that younger self. My mother might call this someone my astral body. Or my etheric body. My mother would
say . . .

Tovah would say I was about to get what I deserved.

I myself would say that Shlomo is not following me and I
don't give a damn any more what he does.

Tovah could be dead by now. For all I know or care.

I was an old hand, an expert, at handling older women, giving them what they wanted, being whoever they craved me to be; I was raised to do just that by the proto-archetype. Tovah needed me, I needed her. Or, rather, I needed the books I read, the clothes I wore, the meals I ate, the bed I slept in. She was forty-two years old and could not get enough of me. She said that she had a hungry, aching feeling all the time, an engorged feeling in her vaginal canal that made her insatiable, that only fucking could assuage, and only momentarily. I myself, being eighteen, with an identical engorgement problem, had an identical hunger and need, at least at first, at least until I met Annika and we began meeting on the sly and I began bestowing all that appetite on a girl my own age, and then, mysteriously, inexplicably, I began to run out of juice sometimes, and guess who figured it out? Tovah was no idiot, her animal native intelligence clued her in to the fact that her plaything, the boy she'd taken in, was now taking her in.

One day in her Fifth Avenue penthouse with Central Park laid out below in shades of glistening green, Shlomo and Tovah plotted my demise, and I only found out about it in time to escape—which I was fairly happy about, because in those days I felt my stupid life was worth preserving. I happened to overhear them. Actually, I was about to go into the salon to bring Tovah her afternoon tea, a ritual she had induced me to observe for the simple reason that she liked being pampered, she liked having me pamper her, and she liked to have afternoon tea brought to her and then to fuck all afternoon long. She must have intended me to overhear her and Shlomo. I have parsed it all out in the ensuing years, having had a great deal of time to consider each plot point from every angle and get it just right in my own head. Tovah must have known I had an assignation later with Annika in that very park below the window at which she sat. I had begun to contrive reasons for leaving Tovah's bed early. I liked very much to fuck Annika in the Rambles with all the homos and drug addicts watching. I liked to lean her up against the wall that bordered Central Park West and go at her from the rear with pedestrians passing by high above, oblivious. A twitchy Negro fellow in a baseball hat often lurked along the path within eyeshot of us, thinking himself unobserved. We called him the Charleyhorse, because Annika sometimes suffered from them in her feet or calves when he was nearby. Not always, but often enough to create a kind of association in her mind.

"There is the Charleyhorse," she would grunt through her teeth, her hands splayed on the brick wall, the light from the leafy trees playing over her freckled, slitty-eyed face. In ecstasy she resembled some sort of slinky little beast.

Anyway, somehow Tovah figured out what we were up to. And apparently she wasn't happy about it.

"I want him taken care of," she was saying in her gravelly voice to someone I couldn't see. "He's playing me. I won't have it. You know what to do."

"Leave it to me," said her cousin Shlomo, whose scary, high, nasal voice I recognized immediately. "Not to worry, it's done."

That was the day I left New York forever.

Tovah had inherited millions from her Brighton Beach carpet-king father. She had pretensions to class, but was unapologetically florid, which is to say obese. She loved food, she loved sex, but she denied that these were anything but the highest intellectual and aesthetic and spiritual passions; she pretended to study the *Kama Sutra,* to pore over Brillat-Savarin, to be an epicure rather than a glutton pure and simple. But no epicure allows her body to balloon, no gourmet shovels food into her mouth many times daily and each time, whether she is hungry or not, grunts in salivating ecstasy over a pastrami sandwich on rye with a dill-pickle spear and potato salad on the side, and, as young as I was, I saw right through her affectations and self-delusions and gave her what she wanted, which was straightforward pastrami sandwich, good and hard, not those spiritual fancy-ass Eastern techniques and poses she affected to know all about and to be "very curious to try." She lay in her billowing, beautiful bedsheets made of the softest cloth—not satin, because satin was tacky, but some sort of dense, very soft cotton, I think it was—she lay there like a mountain I had to climb again and again, a mountain I struggled with, carrying many pounds of food and water through storms and ice and strong winds, up into the heady realms of oxygen deprivation, far, far up into the clouds, real life a tiny dot below, seemingly so far away it didn't exist any more, whatever it was. She was like a geographical formation, Tovah, whereas Annika was a young leopardess, smaller than me, and younger, firm and hot and elastic to the touch; Tovah's flesh was clammy, quivering, pale. Her mouth was a sucking sea creature. Her limbs were vises that clamped my head to her flat beige nipples, between her spongy thighs.

Annika had come to the city from Sweden to study English literature at Columbia. Her mother, somehow, had contrived with Tovah that Annika should live with her because of the ancient connection between them: Tovah had studied as an exchange student in Sweden one year as a teenager and had stayed with Annika's mother's family, and now it was time to return the favor.

After Annika arrived, there was nothing else but for me to seduce her. How otherwise should this plot have developed? Fierce, sexy Annika comes from Sweden and the kept boy is unable to resist the temptation to have her: this was the only possible thing that could have happened.

Instead of understanding my needs—I, whom Tovah professed to adore—instead of sympathizing with the young lust of her wards, instead of appreciating all the favors I performed for her, she tried to have me killed.

I've borne Tovah a grudge all these years for trying to punish me for doing what I had to do according to the laws of the universe. The one thing that has saved me from viciousness where she's concerned is that parallel fact that she arranged it so I would overhear her, giving me just enough time to get out of town under my own steam.

There is much more to the story, of course. Primarily the question of what Shlomo is doing here: here of all places, here in the Hudson River town of my youth.

That day, I walked with my tray right into Tovah's drawing room as if I hadn't heard anything and stared hard at Shlomo. "Hugo, Shlomo just dropped by for tea, could you get us another cup?"

I eyed with some trepidation his overbite, schnozz, arc of paunchy cheeks, snarly rat-faced pallor, eyebrows as see-through as plastic brush bristles. He sported a soul patch and long sideburns that didn't become him. He fancied himself something of a hipster, this Cousin Shlomo. I'd never liked him. He was menacing in an overtly slimy, rather than an elegantly subtle, way. He would have been the obvious choice to be fingered in any lineup anyone put him in. He didn't like me; he considered me a pansy-boy freeloader and would have loved to sock me in the face. The only thing that stopped him was his cousin's cloying affection for me.

"How's it going, Shlomo?" I said nervously.

"Forget the tea," said Shlomo, flicking his glance my way and then retracting it. "I gotta go. Like I said, Tovah, it's done." And off he trundled.

I was headed out of town on a westbound bus two hours later; I never saw Tovah or Annika again. Maybe Shlomo trailed me to Port Authority, saw that I was headed out of town, and considered it a job well done.

November 12—Tonight is my dinner with Stephanie. The pain in my leg is less bearable than usual. Of course I'm compensating for this by smoking more cigarettes than ever, since that's the only thing that calms me down.

Just stopped writing for a while and smoked another one, looked out the window at Erasmus and his feathered cohorts hopping around the branches chattering. They were having a very lively discussion out there just now about something—the shocking goings-on of the birds in the next tree, the location of a few new bird feeders within a ten-mile radius, the likelihood of a storm, whatever it was they were agitated and het up about, interrupting each other, sometimes talking all at once. Now most of them have flown off, apparently in agreement about where they were going and why, but Erasmus is still on his branch. He's either an alpha male who makes everyone else forage for food and bring it back to him, or, more likely, a female, staying behind to mind the hearth. What do I know? I can't tell whether birds are male or female, these average-Joe species without distinctive sexual plumage. This particular species all look alike; the males didn't get any bright coats of many colors like the peacocks' shimmering drapery, the blue jays' iridescence.

The sky is a heavy white. It's three o'clock in the afternoon; the river looks flat and turgid, the trees are tattered, dulled. It's warm today, and still; the day feels as if it's got its breath held. The storm is sitting overhead, pent up and sullen. As for me, I am exploding out of my skull, or wish I could. Erasmus is watching me with sharp black eyes, fat-chested curiosity. I'm watching him right back, although I have no idea what we expect to learn from each other. If I met him in a bar I wouldn't talk to him.

What intelligence resides in the interplay between two be-
ings? None, as far as I can see. When people are in a room together they feel compelled to talk. Marie's dinner party, for
example: people sat around a table eating together, eating well-
prepared food they didn't pay nearly enough attention to because they felt compelled to talk. I speak, therefore I am not.
Talking precludes thought or consideration; most interpersonal
yakking is prompted by the concomitant desires to appear to be
something and to get something, commerce and advertising
masked as "social communion."

Erasmus seems much more at ease in his own feathers, at
home in his tree, now that his pesky compadres have gone off
and left him alone.

These are brave words written by a man who has a date with
a married woman in a few hours. I have stage fright. I suppose
it's only natural to feel a certain degree of nervousness about
this impending evening from start to finish. Regret for having
initiated this entire dalliance. A slight fear of Stephanie, who I
have an uneasy suspicion is not my inferior in any way, and
who moreover has my number, assuming I have a number.
Trepidation . . .

The first time we met, I didn't know her and expected nothing. Now I know her and want her again. Vulnerability has set
in, self-doubt, all the things I remember from my youth and
mistakenly thought I had jettisoned in middle age.

Would I rather not see her at all?

Well, no. I would rather see her than not.

Lately I'm finding myself increasingly embedded in other
peoples' lives, which nauseates me and fills me with fear.

SECOND NOTEBOOK

November 16—I met Stephanie at the bar of the Turtle Inn, the Black Orchid Lounge, as agreed. We never made it to our table, because neither of us was hungry, and evidently we both had our own reasons for wanting to get as drunk as possible. We stayed in the bar and drank three martinis each, during the second of which Stephanie had an odd confessional meltdown.

That was four nights ago, by my count.

And now I'm back from Atlantic City, where Stephanie insisted we go, straight from the Black Orchid Lounge. We drove in her car and stayed for three days at Resorts, in a room high above the Atlantic Ocean, which glinted in the hard morning sunlight with a sinister invitation, mocking us where we stood, trapped like flies behind suicide-proof glass. At night, all we saw in the window were our own pale naked reflections, engaged in a number of interesting contortions.

I'm getting ahead of myself.

"I made Bun go to Marie all those years ago because he never wanted to have sex with me," she told me at the Black Orchid Lounge, during our third round of martinis.

I gave her a look intended to discourage any further revelations about her marriage.

But she went on. "He still doesn't, and the only difference in the situation is that I've given up and accepted this stalemate. He's dangling the prospect of conceiving a baby like some carrot in front of my nose with a paternal twinkle in his eye, Hugo, and you cannot imagine how dismaying it is to be confronted with that at bedtime."

"I do not care," I said.

"Want to know what his problem is?"

"I do not care," I repeated.

"I'll tell you: he's a pedophile."

I stared at her for a moment, debating internally with myself: whether to pursue this objectively interesting topic, or to continue trying to keep at bay any further revelations which might prevent me from getting Stephanie into bed again, on the theory that women who talked to other men about their marriages weren't likely to sleep with them afterward.

Curiosity won out. "What do you mean he's a pedophile?"

"He's got the hots for children," she said impatiently. "Isn't that pretty much the standard definition, Hugo?"

"How do you know? Why are you still married to him?"

"Well, I found out—a while ago, when I was so angry at him and he never wanted to touch me."

"That's funny," I said. "Peculiar, I mean. Dennis told me Marie kicked him out because he never wanted to fuck her. I thought it was supposed to be the other way around in marriages—I thought wives were supposed to withhold sex and husbands were supposed to complain."

"Who told you that?" she asked, surprised. "Not about marriage, about Dennis and Marie?"

"Dennis did," I repeated.

"Well, if you ask Marie, you get a completely different story," she said.

"What story?" I asked, hoping it didn't involve anything about Dennis's attraction to Stephanie herself, and hoping to steer her away from the subject of her own marriage now that I'd imprudently allowed it to rear its head.

She took a deep breath; the infusion of oxygen to her brain must have caused her to change her mind about telling me whatever she had been about to reveal about Marie. "Anyway," she said. "About Bun. This is serious, and I'm really sort of at my wits' end about it now. I found what I guess would be called soft-core child pornography under his side of the bed in a manila folder about two years ago; I guess I was supposed to think the folder held a law brief or something, and leave it alone, but I came across it when I was looking for something else to do with a case we were handling together. Ironic. I was horrified, beside myself, I'm sure you can imagine. Kiddie porn. I mean, not anything really bad, it was sort of tasteful and seemingly innocent, if you can imagine tastefully innocent kiddie porn, but I know porn when I see it, like the guy said. I tried to tell myself it had to do with a case; I thought maybe it was for his research; I tried to think it was anything but what it was. But when I confronted him about it, he blurted out that he was attracted to children. It was almost a relief for him to say it, I could tell. He said he had no desire to have sex with a child, it wasn't that, but he was attracted to them sexually. He said it was different. And he was struggling; he wanted to change, he couldn't stand feeling this way, it seemed hard-wired and he couldn't stop it. He said he had been about to get help." I was going to ask a question, but she forestalled me. "Why did he tell me? He tells me everything. He is incapable of keeping anything a secret. He likes to shock people, anyway." She forestalled my next question just as deftly; I could see her in court. "Sex has nothing whatsoever to do with it; not any more. I'm still married to him because I like him, we understand each other, and we're in the same business." She laughed shortly. "Actually, I used to like him. Lately he's been driving me insane. Maybe that's what I'm doing here with you."

"Does he like boys or girls?" I asked, despite my innate aversion to talking about Bun. I had been wondering.

"Little girls," she said, rolling her eyes.

"Has anyone ever brought charges against him?"

"No, because he's never really molested anyone. Never even come close."

"Well, then, I have to ask: what's the problem?"

She gave me a dark and scornful look. "It could erupt at any time," she said. "He swears it won't. That only makes me more suspicious. Repression is a dangerous thing where sexuality is concerned."

"Resulting in adultery?" I said. "Well, I suppose that's another story."

She didn't seem to hear me. "He never even told me he had this quote-unquote problem until I began confronting him about our pathetic and frustrating, for me at least, lack of a sex life, and then one night it came out. Although he spent two years in therapy with Marie, I'm not convinced she entirely cured him of it. How can you be cured of what you are? But according to the didacticism of current parlance, no one is just plain crazy. No, it's a disease. Well, some diseases are incurable. It's all so fucking tedious, frankly," she added distractedly, lighting another one of my cigarettes. "And it compounds my desire not to have children."

"So," I said, "just so I have this straight: Bun has pedophile-like urges but has been through therapy to control and cure them, and has never once acted on them."

"Right," she said. "That's exactly it."

"Well, I have strong urges to disembowel my brother and fondle the cashier at Stewart's and ram my truck so hard into the rear ends of slow drivers they get whiplash, and those urges don't seem to be curable either. Far be it from me to try to defend your husband, but honestly, in a spirit of intellectual inquiry, let's look at the facts: he married an adult woman; he hasn't molested anyone; and, Stephanie, you surely must agree that the potential to commit heinous acts exists in all of us. That's where ethics and morals come in, if they come in, which they often don't."

"Forget it," she said, smiling in spite of herself and waving her hand in front of her face as if the smoke were suddenly bothering her. "I should have known you'd be on his side."

"I'm not on his side."

"Let's change the subject," she said. "Let's talk about nothing at all."

"With pleasure," I said.

The tension between us dissolved immediately: it had no history or heat behind it. It's a strange phenomenon, talking and drinking. You talk and talk and talk, and drink and drink and drink, and it all vanishes into air, into hot air, and memory retains only a flavor of the undercurrent that usually runs unnoticed beneath all social commerce, and is most present during these often confessional, feverish, impassioned, heartfelt, rambling, almost unconscious conversations. I was quite aware of Stephanie's arm on the table, its blond hairs brushing those of my left arm, skin not touching, feeling as if a nest of ants were gently wandering over my forearm. It was not at all unpleasant, but this no doubt had everything to do with the fact that I knew it was caused by the proximity of Stephanie's arm hairs rather than a tribe of pismires. And I recall the changing shape of her mouth as she talked, listened, smoked, laughed, grimaced, drank, stared off into space.

A couple of hours later, we were in her car on our way to Atlantic City for some reason having entirely to do with the volatile but not unhappy combination of her desire to go and my desire for her. I left my truck in the parking lot attached to her office building; she promised it wouldn't be ticketed or towed. She asked me to drive. The windshield was besieged with a constant spatter of rain. We listened to the skritch-skritch of the wipers and smoked cigarettes. Air blew in the cracked-open windows smelling of diesel and wet asphalt. I drove just fine on animal reflex and muscle memory. Stephanie was restless from all the vodka. She quivered with a coiled, rebellious, unhinged defiance, an attitude that never failed to provoke untrammeled lust in me when I encountered it in girls in high school, and little had changed in the meantime; in fact, I had become a puppet for her to do with as she liked. Her packed suitcase turned out to be stowed in the trunk; she was supposed to be going there for a conference, she said, which she had no intention of attending now, even though she'd paid and was registered. It had started that afternoon, and Bun thought she'd already left, but she'd missed a day of it to make our date. She had planned to drive there tonight, alone, after our date. Dragging me along as her escort, I was meant to infer from this, was a spur-of-the-moment decision. But I inferred no such thing: I had the strong feeling that she had planned all along to bring me with her.

We got into Atlantic City in the middle of the night, technically early Tuesday morning. We checked into our aerie and flopped fully clothed onto the hard synthetic bedspread with its no-doubt unspeakable bacteria count; we fell into twin comas. When we woke up it was noon, and I had all sorts of things raging on my body, a headache, thirst, an erection. I opened my eyes to find Stephanie's eyes staring directly into mine. I looked back at her for a minute or two while our brains ticked in unison, then, wordlessly, vehemently, with deadpan calm, we fucked ourselves into puddles of melted butter. Then we showered and brushed our teeth with the toiletries provided by the thoughtful hotel staff, made our somewhat unsteady way down to the hotel restaurant for coffee and scrambled eggs and Bloody Marys, then walked along and squinted at the glittering ocean, strolling slowly as geriatrics on the sunny, chilly, gusty boardwalk, that windy wasteland of a strip that separates the wide, flat beach and ocean from Casino Land, rows of false fronts, an artificial movie set. We left the corporate casinos and conference centers, turned inland to walk through the run-down old resort town, or what's left of it, seedy bar-and-grills, pawnshops trolling for gold, falling-down row houses, bleak and shabby behind all the ersatz glitz.

Time started to pass, and we went right along with it. We drank free casino vodka at the roulette tables, where Stephanie won a considerable amount of money. We slept, intermittently, or at least she did. I watched her sleep, or stared at the ceiling, or read the room-service menu, and then, when she woke up, we relieved our sexual predilections and urges on each other without much premeditation, thought, or shame, like a couple of orangutans. There was a certain amount of affection between us; how could there not be? In public we stayed a chaste six inches apart, as if we were mere acquaintances—at the roulette tables, walking along the boardwalk, in restaurants. We didn't talk much. I have rarely if ever felt more closely allied with another person.

The casinos are a series of hells that ring with a high, eternal sound of slot machines being fed quarters one after another, handles being jacked, wheels whirring inside. Under the higher ringing of wheels turning is the occasional exciting clamor of quarters spewing out. The high ringing sound becomes inaudible after an hour or two in a casino. When you leave, you hear a sudden silence as deafening as a wind tunnel. There's nothing natural there. I should have loved it all.

Stephanie played roulette, and I stood behind her with a series of vodkas on ice in plastic cups brought around free by a nice ample-breasted lady in a tailless bunny suit. The croupiers wore black pants, white shirts, and patterned vests that contrasted interestingly with the casino's already contrasting decor. Their expressions were identical, although they themselves varied widely—size-husky bull dyke, size-zero ex-geisha, soft ruddy chubstein with mustache, reed-thin black gentleman with close-cropped 'fro—a distant smirk that occasionally ignited into a half-smile when someone won and tipped them a chip. This look was directed at Stephanie more often than anyone else, all night long.

Stephanie gambles with casual but focused brio. She puts down chips here, there, stacks of dollar chips, sometimes as many as ten on one number. She hit twice in a row on the same number; then came a long dry spell, which she waited out; then she hit again. As a boy gigolo I used to gamble with my keepers' monies, but I never played roulette, it was always baccarat, blackjack, or craps. Roulette is a woman's game. It involves "intuition" (plain luck, really) and stamina. I stood drinking behind her because I had no desire to go off on my own. My gambling days are over, long gone. This was her idea, and her game, and her trip. I was along to keep her company. Watching her was all the pleasure I cared to pursue, to put it mildly. I watched her with admiration, and her fellow gamblers with the usual loathing and disdain I feel whenever I'm surrounded by strangers, misshapen, fat, stupid, boring hordes with their outfits and hairdos and quirks and hangups, all certain they're original, essential to everything, the center of the universe, all equally grasping, gluttonous, wasteful, misguided, pointless, and disgusting. Stephanie, alone of us all in the casino, struck me as a necessary thing.

Being drunk didn't seem to affect her betting any more than it had affected my driving. The muscles have a memory of their own. My foot was hurting badly, but I didn't whine or make a fuss, I stood there stalwartly, pierced through by the sharp trident of pain, desire, and misanthropy, while she hit three times in a row, let her chips stay on the number, and pocketed half her winnings. There was something about watching Stephanie gamble that galvanized some long-dormant part of me. She seemed completely alive to the game—the numbers, chips, and wheels; the other people at the table. Her back was alive to me. No part of her was abstracted. She's the same way in sex too. It's that whole faggy hippified Zen-of-whatever theory I've never subscribed to any part of, but it does explain Stephanie. She wore a pair of black jeans and a little black tank-top affair, maybe the same one she wore to Marie's dinner party. The most flattering clothes ever worn, by any woman, ever. I sound besotted, I know, and I don't care.

Yesterday morning we awoke early, ready to leave our temporary haven and return to our real lives and separate existences, her marriage and job and house, my whatever you want to call it. Situation. Not that there's no room for her in it. On the contrary. Anyway, the day was windy, cold, and so sunny that the light hit my eyeballs in shards that made them stream with water. We ate breakfast before driving home this morning at the grimy old Poseidon Grill, across from the grimy old newsstand where we bought our papers. Stephanie bought them: I prefer to have breakfast unmolested by the news of unstoppable catastrophe. "Nothing I can do about it all," I said to her when she threatened to read parts of it aloud to me over our breakfast. "And no amount of palliative, in the form of treacly human-interest stories or impassioned editorials plying solutions to this mess, can sugarcoat that. I'd rather eat my breakfast without having to hear about any of it. Anyway, the other night you told Bun not to talk about these things."

"I just didn't want to hear him talk about them," she said back.

Stephanie ordered us beer with tomato juice, assuring me that this vile combination would cure the most pernicious hangover. It did nothing for mine. Then she read aloud to me from the newspaper. I tried to tune her out, and tried to choke down my red-eye, or whatever the horrible concoction was called.

I came home last night to find my estranged wife and purported daughter ensconced in the suite of rooms my parents once occupied.

To my complete astonishment, moments after I'd returned I encountered Sonia in the second-story bathroom. I walked in without knocking to take a badly needed pent-up piss, and there she was all splayed on the throne, reading a book and soaking her feet in my dish tub, her hair in a sesame-seed-colored bun.

She was still beautiful in her pale, malnourished way. The shock of the unexpected sight of her sent a wave of some ancient emotion splashing against my sternum. As it receded I half-consciously identified it as the sort of pleasure derived from roller coasters, horror movies, and near brushes with death or great danger. Pleasure! I was glad to see her again, in other words, or part of me was, in spite of or even because of the horror, danger, etc.

"What are you doing here?" I hissed, light-headed and trembling.

"Hello, Hugo," she riposted in her throaty growl, looking up from her book to flick a glance my way. "I'm back, as you can see. As I said in my letter."

"I told you not to come," I said.

"Our daughter is asleep," she informed me stoically, "and I'm not going to wake her, so you can wait and meet her tomorrow."

"I don't want you here," I said urgently. "Sonia, please go away, go back to New York tomorrow."

"Your brother was so hospitable," she said. "He came to get us at the train. He thought I'd be staying in your room, but I told him that this is a reunion after a long separation, and I don't want to rush anything. He gave Bellatrix and me your parents' rooms. Where have you been, Hugo? I was very hurt that you missed my homecoming."

"Out of town," I said. "I went out of town, nothing to do with you. I wasn't avoiding you. I wish I'd met your train, so I could have put you on the next one going in the opposite direction. Dennis is a meddlesome prat."

"A meddlesome prat," she repeated with a flash of her old world-weary scorn for my linguistic anachronisms.

I leaned against the doorway to the bathroom and ran my hand over my eyes. It had been a long drive home with Stephanie, who'd slept most of the way in the passenger seat, then I'd had to collect my truck and drive alone back to my own side of the river. I was sorry to be separated from Stephanie, deflated by the end of our adventure together. After the initial animal shock of pleasure at seeing Sonia, I felt only dread and the memory of great pain.

"I wish you hadn't come back," I said.

"Your daughter wants to meet you," she rejoined impassively. "It is for her I came."

"She is not," I said, "my daughter. I have to go to bed now. I'm exhausted."

"You look exhausted," she said flatly, without sympathy or concern.

I stalked up to my room, bladder bursting, in a complete lather. I pissed a lively, lengthy stream into the antique water pitcher on the shelf in my closet, then poured it out the window and felt slightly better, or at least well enough to get myself to bed and lie there, seething and howling inwardly with pain, until the first gray glimmer of dawn matched my gray and wrung-out self, and then I fell into a sandy-eyed sleep for a few hours and awoke in a sweat.

"They called two days ago," Dennis told me this morning, as if he thought I must be nothing but glad to find them here. "I told them you were expecting them. Where the hell were you? They arrived two nights ago, and I picked them up at the train. I gave them Mother and Dad's rooms. Finally, after all these years, I get to meet my one and only niece. She's not what I expected, frankly. But Sonia seems exactly the same as ever. She hasn't aged, or changed, has she?"

"Sonia," I replied, "has evidently made a pact with Satan concerning some rudimentary soul she may have once possessed and given up in exchange for eternal youth long before I ever met her. Or maybe she's just been preserved in her own brine, like a sardine."

At that moment, a medium-sized girl ran into the kitchen. "Uncle Dennis!" she said with some excitement. Then she saw me, and stared at me for an instant. "Are you my father?" she asked, I thought with some skepticism, but I might have been imagining this.

I stared back at her. If I had ever harbored any doubts about

Sonia's child's patriarchal lineage, the sight of Bellatrix dispelled them forever.

"This is your dad!" said Dennis with foolish emotion. "Hugo."

"Hi," she said shyly. With a dull, blankly dutiful expression she advanced toward me, flung an arm around my neck, and kissed my cheek with lips that were warm and moist.

"Hello, Bellatrix," I said, and drowned my unspeakable consternation in a gulp of coffee. My cheek had a damp spot on it, one I wanted to wipe away, though I maturely forestalled myself from doing so. I realized that I had been holding out all those years for some sort of proof that she really was mine after all, despite my darkest suspicions.

Well, I don't have to think too hard about it, given her general character and appearance. She must be, as I have somehow known all these years, the spawn of some village gas-station attendant, or Carla's uncle at Stewart's. She's a soft potato of a child, with no spark or density of character. Her hair is as blond as her mother's, but lank and thin where Sonia's is thick and silky. Her face is a blue-eyed vacuity, a pink-cheeked wasteland. She looks Polish, the worst of the Polish character, the superstitious, mind-numbingly provincial ignorance that enabled an entire nation, as one, to turn a blind eye to the mass murder of any and all of their friends and neighbors who were too dark, too intelligent, too bookish, too deviant, too different from them, and then go to confession and tuck into a hearty meal of overcooked meat and boiled lardy eight-pound dumplings afterward in a stupor of self-forgiving Catholic ignorance.

Sitting here writing all this down, I can't rid myself of this monstrous teenage idiot's erection. Now, instead of being the lovelorn girl, I've been transformed by Stephanie's body into her ape of a boyfriend. I seem to be unable to stay my hand from writing the clichés I know I'm about to write, very much in the style of that teenage lovelorn diarist. Stephanie . . . her hair is a gold, fragrant nimbus, her body a preternaturally sensitive organism, her belly the perfect canvas for my deposits of splooge (she uses an oral contraceptive, but refuses to accept any stuff inside her, according to some crackpot theory that it contributes to cervical cancer; I refuse to wear a condom; we are both clean, nice people, and so I deposit it where she tells me, with joy). My appetite for her, rather than being sated during our debauchathon, is now essentially out of control. Holding the pen to write in this new notebook, running my hands on the new white sheet of paper, reminds me of touching her. Even the act of writing, pressing and moving pen on paper— or, for that matter, driving my truck: the gearshift, my foot on the pedal. Everything I touch that is not myself reminds me of touching her.

Her mouth, her eyes, her hands. She holds nothing back, not at gambling, not at fucking. Throughout the most lost-in-space moments with her, when our eyes are wild, our breath is raspy, our lips are chafed raw on each other, when we're wholly given over to our plundering instincts and all our animal cells are plumped with satiation likewise, such preternatural, hotheaded, adamantine intelligence gleams from every radiant, heedless glance of hers, every follicle of her hair crackles as my hand runs through it, each cell of her responds fully, electrically, to every cell of me; I suspect, with no false humility and every ounce of admiration I possess and am capable of marshaling, that this is none of my own doing, and all of hers. There must be such a thing as sexual genius, as musical genius is said to exist, or scientific, or literary, etc. Stephanie is a fucking genius. I have never known one before, but that doesn't matter; I know it when I see it.

It goes without saying, despite the fact that I evidently am compelled to say it anyway, that I would never have chosen voluntarily to become sexually enslaved to someone so inscrutably superior to me. It makes me feel as if I have no skin. I would prefer to be in Carla's thrall, or Louisa's. With either of them I would at least feel that I had the upper hand.

My mind—fickle, untrained beast that it is—keeps straying as I write about the glorious Stephanie (no doubt out of old habit and inclination) to sneaky, essentially unwanted thoughts of the vile bitch Sonia. The body betrays the heart and mind at every turn.

November 21—Now that I've met Bellatrix, now that she lurks downstairs this morning along with my brother and my wife—as if they were all gathering for my funeral, I think in my more mordant moments—I can only be thankful that she's certainly not of my genes.

Do I feel dislike for my purported daughter? Not dislike, no, but grave indifference, and even distaste.

The only compliments I'm able to muster in her direction are the following: her violin playing is surprisingly good, and she knows better than to try to make me love her. She has a particular and admirable talent for rendering Bach in a crisply fluid, soulful style that I find impressive, especially in someone under the age of eleven. Which is to say, she plays well, better than I had any right to expect, and she doesn't seek me out with irritating questions—which is to say, she avoids me.

Sonia is also staying out of my way. Both my wife and her

daughter are, to my dubious relief, seeking out instead the company of my brother, who seems to have made a manful and heroic first impression on both by rescuing them from the train station when I was away.

Which leads me to suspect that there is a tinge of resentment in their cold-shouldering me. How dare they? They weren't invited to come live here, they invited themselves, and then didn't bother to give me any warning. The uppity cheek of it all. As if I should have read Sonia's mind as to their arrival time and then made myself agreeably available to fetch them from the station.

I've begun spending the whole day here in my room, reading, and then at around six, I get into my truck and make a stop at Stewart's to replenish my supply of cigarettes and incidentally talk to Carla. Then I go and have a solitary dinner at the Turtle Inn. I always hover at the entrance to the Black Orchid Lounge; I can't pretend I'm not hoping to run into Stephanie there. I can't call her. I can't do anything. It's all up to her: she's got me. My pride won't let me chase her, won't let me be a supplicant of any kind, or a noodge. She has to come to me, or we'll never come together. This rule, self-imposed, feels harsh and cruel. Still, I can't break it.

Afterward, when I've enjoyed an after-dinner smoke and *digestif* in the Black Orchid, I drive home and park as always on the lawn in front of the house. On my way through the foyer and up the first flight of stairs, I can smell the remnants of their supper, and hear them all laughing together in the kitchen, the clack of dominoes or the first part of the Bach Double Violin Concerto, nicely played, or the radio tuned to a classical-music station, or the crack of a brand-new deck of cards being shuffled. They've become quite the cozy little threesome, my brother, wife, and "daughter." I don't know how late they stay up, because once I close my door behind me I can't hear a thing except for the wind soughing through Erasmus's tree and my own breathing, the turning of a page of a book, the rustling of sheets and blankets.

My leg is worse. The pain is less bearable than ever. This is the most tedious subject in the world. But when I'm in the grip of this night pain, there's no other subject I can think about. No matter how I try to focus on an essay or a poem, to dwell on certain recent and pleasurable erotic memories, I can't—my brain is in the thrall of pain more than anything else. But in the morning, when the pain ebbs, I can hardly remember it. It seems to recede without leaving a mark.

November 23—Dennis asked me yesterday morning, as we sat on the porch with our cups of coffee—I having gone out there to be alone and he having followed to interrogate me— where I was during my three-day absence.

"Atlantic City," I said innocently.

"Alone?" he asked.

"No," I answered, and thought that was the end of it.

However, he had evidently just learned from Bun Fox that Stephanie attended a three-day legal conference in Atlantic City during the exact same time as my own absence.

"Did you go there with Stephanie?" he asked me after a loaded silence.

"Stephanie."

"Stephanie Fox."

"Oh," I said. "That Stephanie. Of course not."

But the jig is up; I played dumb, he tried to catch me out in my lie, I denied everything, but he knows, I know he knows, and he knows I know he knows, and so forth into the endlessly reflecting hall of mirrors.

"Who did you go with, then?" he asked.

"None of your business," I answered pleasantly.

"It's my business if you went to Atlantic City for three days with my best friend's wife."

"Well, I didn't," I said.

"Well, you better not have."

"Why do you care so much anyway?"

We locked eyes. He knows I know he's hot for Stephanie. He knows I know he wants to kill me for getting to fuck her for three days straight. I know he knows I'll never admit to any such thing.

"Well," was all he said, or could say, "you're lying, and you know it."

A little while later, he came up to my room and entered without knocking. As a matter of fact, I had been indulging in a daydream about Stephanie and Atlantic City, and my erection had reached the point at which I wanted very much to take it out of my pants and relieve it of itself. Luckily, I held a book open on my lap, and nothing was under way. Still, I started as guiltily as a prepubescent kid caught with a bootlegged copy of *Portnoy's Complaint* or his sister's soiled underdrawers.

"You were definitely in Atlantic City with Stephanie Fox," my brother said with a pained expression, accusing me of a capital crime he would give anything to have me be innocent of.

"Dennis," I said wearily, "please get out of my room."

"Admit it," he said.

"If you choose not to believe me, that's your own affair, and I can't help you any further."

"Why are you ignoring your wife and daughter?"

"Because I don't want them here," I answered.

"That's not what you told me a few weeks ago."

"Well, it was in my momentary best interests to pretend this little family reunion was my own idea," I said. "It was Sonia's idea; I tried to keep her away, but she insisted on coming anyway. That little corncob down there is no child of mine. I'm waiting until they go away. If you want to entertain them, that's all very well, but don't expect me to thank you for it, because the sooner they leave the better."

He sighed and sagged a little against my doorframe.

"I'm way ahead of you," I said, "brother mine. Don't even try to keep up with my machinations. It's all way over your head."

" 'Brother mine,' " he repeated ruefully. "Where do you get these expressions?"

I picked up my book and began to read with beatific concentration.

"All I want," he resumed, desperately picking at the nit in his brain, "is to know whether you and Stephanie slept together."

"My sex life," I responded without looking up from my book, "is of interest to me and possibly, although I don't assume it, to whatever woman or women I'm fortunate enough to have it with, and no one else. But how about this: the moment I have any interest in having another person know anything about it, I promise I will unburden myself of this fascinating information to you before anyone else. Hot fresh poop, newly minted, all yours, exclusive story, you and only you. Have we got a deal?"

He went away then without another word. He didn't slam the door, although I could tell he was itching to. Dennis isn't a violent man and never will be. He imagines himself capable of grand gestures but is manifestly not.

I got up, closed and locked my door, and got back to my busy morning.

I'm reading a book called *Consider the Oyster,* which my foodie soulmate Mary Frances Kennedy Fisher wrote while her husband, my late ancestor Timmy Parrish, was suffering from his protracted bout of Buerger's disease. I suppose I'm reading it for clues, for bits of breadcrumbs dropped along the trail ahead of me. She found it important enough to note, during a time when Timmy was screaming with pain all night long, and when both husband and wife greeted each bright new California day wracked with sadness and exhaustion, that Louis XI obliged his courtiers to eat a huge heap of oysters every day because they contained a lot of phosphorus, which was supposed to make one more mentally acute. Oysters were considered brain food, in other words; this goes far back, apparently all the way to Cicero, who ate oysters to make himself more eloquent.

This led me to consult Maguelonne Toussaint-Smart's *History of Food,* translated from the original French by the no-doubt lovely and brilliant and gustatorily sophisticated Anthea Bell. I learned there, on page 389, that Henri IV ate so many oysters he got indigestion, which is somewhat less fascinating than Mary Frances's anecdote about Louis. But then, reading not very much further, I was rewarded by this pearl: someone named Marshal Junot, whom I've never heard of but who is invoked here as if he were a universally famous personage, was the champion oyster-eater of the early nineteenth century. He ate, according to this source, three hundred of them every morning (interestingly, the chapter I'd just finished reading in Mary Frances's book is called "Take 300 Oysters . . ."—further proof that the universe, the one I live in at least, is ruled by Loki the trickster god). Marshal Junot died of insanity. Were the two facts connected? The (voluptuous, scholarly, and highly sexed, I hope) Maguelonne speculates that they may have been, but no one seems to know for sure.

November 24—I'm in that ole-devil-garum mood again. I'm steeping in my own bile, festering violently in the harsh sunlight of crowded quarters, and if I don't actually reek in a literal sense, I am inwardly foul with bad humor.

Dennis has begun a day-care center. As I drank my coffee

this morning, his daughters and Sonia's spawn were embroiled in the old ballroom, shrieking noisily and finding it necessary to jump up and down as much as possible. Sonia was meanwhile sitting in the oddly warm sun on the lawn beneath my window, precisely in the spot where my urine landed the night I returned from Atlantic City, or so I hoped, singing along to a battery-powered tape player on which she was playing one of the trashy 1970s pop songs of her Soviet Warsaw youth.

I was trapped in my own house, and meanwhile the dishes were upside down in the cabinets, the refrigerator was a shambles, and someone had drunk a good deal of my whiskey. I hoped this was Bellatrix but strongly suspected it was Sonia, who feels herself entitled to half my worldly goods.

Sitting in my chair in a funk of irritation, it occurred to me that I have the means to go somewhere else; I could take myself to a remote island somewhere, a cabin, a hotel, a stateroom, a chalet. I have neither seen nor heard from Stephanie since she dropped me off at my truck. What is keeping me here, then? I'm not sure.

And so, in search of reprieve from the twin hells of the downstairs nursery school and my estranged wife's impromptu concert, I hied myself to Stewart's for a lengthy chat with my favorite cashier, and then I had lunch at the old diner (lurking, I confess, from doorway to doorway like a film-noir shamus, in case my old hit-man nemesis should choose that moment to pass by in his car), then spent the afternoon at the town theater watching a pair of movies starring the legendarily winsome, smart-mouthed Barbara Stanwyck. I was in luck: they were showing *Baby Face* and *Ball of Fire*. I reveled in her wised-up, loose-limbed, smart-mouthed splendor for a few hours, watched her sleep her way to the top and do whatever the hell else she wanted, and left the theater in an itchy mood to stir up a little trouble.

So, to punish my brother for I know not what, and feeling unaccountably uninspired by the thought of the usually appealing menu at the Turtle Inn, I bought a sack of groceries and drove to my sister-in-law's house, which I knew to be child-free tonight, and possibly friendlier now than it had ever been before.

Marie and Louisa were at home, I saw immediately when I drove up the driveway and came into view of the house. It was an unseasonably warm evening; they were in chairs on the lawn, a picturesque tableau in the gloaming. The treetops overhead were black, and nighttime had fallen on the ground, but the sky was still light, the birds still sang. When I got out of my truck, the air smelled of woodsmoke. Anticipation came over me at the sight of my sister-in-law and her au-pair girl there on the lawn, a particular kind of social anticipation I didn't know I could still feel. I dismounted from my cab and hiked over to where they sat, hauling the bag of foodstuffs.

"Hello," I called.

Once again, the young and fresh-faced Louisa tried and failed to hide her frank, instinctive friendliness toward me. The primary difference this time around was that Marie, rather than looking horrified, had a neutral, if wary, expression.

"Anyone in the mood for a little Shrimp Newburg?" I asked jovially. "It's one of those mid-twentieth-century butter-heavy dishes whose names list the main ingredient first and the name second. Clams Casino, Oysters Rockefeller—along those lines. It's easy to make, and looks unprepossessing in the extreme, but it's very good."

"Hugo," said Marie with a smile so faint it might have been a mirage. "This is a surprise."

"My own lodgings are overrun with tedious interlopers. I also brought some wine I thought you'd enjoy and a few other tidbits."

Rather than waste time awaiting an answer, permission, invitation, or assent, I left them sitting there (I thought I heard them chuckling in my wake, but this may have been my imagination) and bustled through the house to the kitchen, where I stowed the food, opened a bottle of chilled Pinot Grigio I particularly like, and brought the bottle and three glasses out to the lawn. I sat on the grass beside their chairs, and we drank it while the sky darkened still further.

The mood was so convivial I felt I'd wandered into a European movie, one set in the bucolic but civilized countryside of southern France or Sweden, in which people choose to sit in the grass and drink wine. Louisa is doing very well up here, away from the industrial factories, waste-transfer stations, and toxic-waste storage facilities of her native Greenpoint. Her eyes have lost their shadowy, repressed shyness. And Marie seems to be thriving without her husband, I have to admit. Although naturally this isn't at all what I want to see happen, I can't blame her for being happier in his absence. I would feel exactly the same way, and I envy her. She didn't tell me and I didn't ask, but I had the strong intuitive sense that she, like me, has recently experienced an erotic renaissance of sorts. She looked satiated and calm, all the static electricity discharged. Was it urban-dweller Jim or Mediterranean novelist Arnold? Maybe both.

"Do you find it in any way strange," I asked Marie, ostensibly out of some wild blue yonder, "to be friends with Bun Fox after he was your client?"

"Sometimes," she admitted. "But I'm usually fairly good at compartmentalizing the things he told me back when he was my client, before we were friends."

I leaned back on my elbows. If there'd been a stalk of wheat nearby to chew, I would've plucked and chewed it: Hugo at ease, making pleasant chitchat. "Did you cure him of whatever he came to see you for?"

"Cure him?" She laughed. "Well, yes, I think so. We agreed

to terminate the therapy after a couple of years, when we felt we'd done all we could together."

"So with Bun," I pursued, a little brusquely but not, I hoped, unduly so, "for example, was there one specific issue he came to you about, or a complex stew of neuroses, or a specific problem caused by many forces, both ex- and internal?"

"Good question," she said.

I preened inwardly at my glib and chummy way with psychobabble.

"All I'll say," she went on in her cagey therapist's manner, "is that we accomplished the work we set out for ourselves."

I wanted to ask whether her confidence in her work with him would extend to allowing Bun to take her younger daughter on an overnight camping trip, but of course I couldn't without revealing how much I knew, and how I knew it, and although I might have done this once, lately, now that I had so much at stake (in particular, the prospect of getting to fuck Stephanie again, which wouldn't happen if she somehow found out that I'd blabbed to Marie about what she'd told me in confidence about her husband), I had been learning a little bit of social self-control.

"I wonder," I said instead, "what the effect will be on your daughters if you and Dennis don't reconcile."

Marie looked shocked. "Hugo!" she said. "Don't try to guilt-trip me into taking your brother back. Is that why you're here? Did he send you?"

"I was just wondering," I said, "what your professional opinion of this matter is. After the tragic incidents of September the Eleventh—"

"I can't believe you're referring to this unspeakable human tragedy in a sneering voice."

"I wasn't using a sneering voice."

"You were, Hugo. Wasn't he, Louisa?"

"Maybe not sneering," said Louisa, "but he sounded sort of like he was making fun."

"I'm not making fun," I said. "I'm trying to perform a mitzvah here."

"What are you," Louisa huffed, "like, Jewish now?"

"Trying to get on your good side by speaking your tongue," I said.

"Well, you're trying to talk me out of a job, that's all I know," she rejoined.

"Listen, I'll be blunt: Marie, what were you thinking, throwing my brother out when you did? I understand the urge to get rid of him; I feel it every day, more strongly than I can begin to say. What I'm asking is, did the terrorist attacks cause you to question everything and determine that your life with Dennis was a waste of time?"

"A waste of time," said Marie slowly, in a kind of negative wonderment. "This is completely none of your business. I can't believe you're suggesting I didn't think of my children in asking Dennis to leave. You, of all people, Hugo, you who want nothing to do with your own wife and daughter."

"That's different," I said. "Sonia left me. I have supported her and Bellatrix all these years. I have never not done my duty as a husband and a father."

"You know nothing whatsoever about marriage," said Marie with a small laugh, as if my opinion mattered so little to her it wasn't worth her while to be offended by anything I said.

"That's true," I admitted.

"I worry about Isabelle and Evie every time Dennis takes them. I hope he's watching after them as well as he should be. That's what upsets me most in this sorry situation. Having Louisa to help me, and being the undisputed head of the household, coming home from work to find dinner on the table and my children excited to see me, their homework done, is a far greater source of freedom and pleasure to me than I ever dared dream of when Dennis lived here. I can depend on Louisa to do what I need her to do without any fuss, whereas having him around was like having a third, half-grown child who demanded sex as well as every other form of attention. It was the least convenient arrangement imaginable. You can tell him I said so."

"I hope I won't have to," I said meekly, smiling in spite of myself. "I'll make dinner now."

I got up, brushed off my trousers, and went inside. In the kitchen I found what I needed and got down to work. While the green beans steamed, the Boston lettuce drained, and the rice boiled, I made a roux with butter and a handful of flour, a dash of salt, and a cup and a half of milk. When it thickened, I stirred in sherry, paprika, ketchup, and Worcestershire sauce, then opened two cans of shrimp and drained them and added them to the mixture. This was Shrimp Newburg, and I defy anyone to make it correctly and not want to devour every single gooey orange bite.

I served this simple but very satisfying meal in the dining room with the second bottle of Pinot Grigio I'd brought.

"It's important to use canned shrimp," I said. "Just as when making spinach dip the only acceptable variety of spinach is frozen. It just tastes better. I've tried making this with fresh shrimp and it just isn't the same. It wasn't out of cheapness or laziness, I assure you, just reverse-snobbery gourmet know-how."

"Thank you, Hugo," said Marie. "It's good, but I have to admit, you never struck me as the culinary type."

I was tempted to reply flirtatiously that there happen to be a few other things about me she might be surprised to learn, but as I said, I'm learning about self-control, forestalling a momentarily, pleasurably incendiary remark to achieve a higher end. More to the point, I'm not in the business of making overtures to my brother's wife; it would suggest an underlying incestuous urge the very notion of which I am utterly repulsed by. Marie is very appealing; what keeps my interests firmly elsewhere is that my overt pursuit of her would imply, however faintly, that I was incapable of lighting my own fires and so must warm myself at my older brother's, which we all know isn't the case.

So I said instead, "I'm glad you like it," and left it at that.

However, clearly my off-limits rule where Marie is concerned applies not at all to her au-pair girl.

After we enjoyed blushingly ripe Bosc pears with robust Stilton and the surprisingly potent and palatable Calvados I'd found at the town's dusty little liquor store, Marie cleared the table and began to wash the dishes, leaving Louisa and me alone in the candlelight, able to talk under cover of the noise of the washing up. Louisa, whose night off it was, surprised but didn't disappoint me when she agreed to my suggestion that we take a stroll down to the nearby lake.

Stephanie is naturally completely in control of any situation we could possibly find ourselves in together. Louisa, although she controls by virtue of her sex certain aspects of the outcome, has been entirely in my thrall from the moment I first met her. Or so I flattered myself then with thinking. The memory of my pressing her undies to my face playfully yet with intent was foremost, uppermost, in my brain as we went out into the gusty evening and strolled along the road down to the lake, which is more a brackish pond than anything so stately and expansive as a lake proper, but no matter.

"It's nice out," she said when we had gone about halfway.

We were walking not close together but not far apart; not like lovers but not like strangers either.

"Are you nervous?" I asked her.

Out of the corner of my eye I caught the sidelong gleam of a quick glance in my direction. "A little."

"Why?"

"Well, it's like, how well do I really know you?"

"You don't," I said, "not technically, but in one way you do."

"Which way is that?"

"We're a lot alike."

I let this sink in and stumped along by her side in comfortable silence. I allowed us to drift slightly closer together. Louisa has a pleasant smell. She smells yeasty; I know this carries intimations of vaginal infections and whatnot, but I don't mean that. Stephanie has a faint astringent scent, clean and crisp. Louisa smells like bread, Stephanie like lemons. Louisa is comforting and familiar; Stephanie is neither of those things. Also, Louisa is slightly less than half Stephanie's age, not to mention my own.

"I meant to say," I said, "that in some ways we're alike, but I'm sure we're also very different. I didn't mean to offend you. Naturally I meant it as a compliment, having a high opinion, not of myself, but of you anyway. Have you read any Rabelais?"

"Yeah," she said. "I read some last year in Vero's class. Professor Dupin. What's it called, *Gargantua et Pantagruel.*" Her French accent sounded like something stuck in her throat. She laughed self-consciously.

"Well, then, you know what the term 'Rabelaisian' means."

"Oh my God," she cried. "It means fat, right?"

"No," I said, laughing, "it means full of brio. And that's a good thing."

"Yeah, right," she said shortly.

We came to the glimmering path that led through a small copse to the pond. Without hesitation, she plunged from the road onto the path and disappeared into the dark stand of bare trees.

"Can I ask you something?" she said. "So what is it really like to have your wife back?"

"Irritating beyond my powers of description. We finished

with each other long ago. My daughter is a great disappointment to me. Not to mention quite likely not really my daughter at all."

She ignored this last bit of information for reasons I couldn't
guess at. "What do you mean, she's a disappointment?"

"I mean, she's not my daughter. This was a mistake on
Sonia's part, coming back. She should have known better, but
it's all too typical of her that she didn't."

"Does she hope you'll fall in love with her again?"

"What kind of question is that? Have you heard a word I've
told you about her?"

"Well, what do I know, I've never been married and I don't
have a kid, obviously. But I think you should give them a
chance."

"Do you think Marie should take Dennis back?"

Louisa turned suddenly to face me. "What?"

"I didn't think so."

"No," she said, turning to resume her progress down to the
"lake." We came out of the woods onto a small, sandy beach
that glowed white. I could smell the water and hear it lapping
against a dock.

"Here," said Louisa, "you lie on this table and I'll lie on the
one next to it."

"I'd rather lie on your table, next to you," I said in a
wheedling but charming tone.

"I'm sure you would," she said, and plumped herself onto
her own private tabletop, leaving no room for anyone else.
"So," she said, "I recently checked a book of the constellations
out of the library. I've been studying the stars. This is the first
time in my life I've lived somewhere where I can see them."

"What have you learned?" I asked politely.

"For one thing," she said, "Bellatrix is a star in Orion, also
known as the Amazon Star."

"My estranged wife," I lied, "used to be something of a stargazer herself."

"She chose the name?"

"Not exactly," I confessed.

"Orion," Louisa went on in an eager, scholarly tone I didn't much care for but was faintly amused by because I could easily see her as a bright-eyed, bushy-tailed student, although she clearly is more naturally suited to a light, humorous knowing-ness, an aspect of her personality that will have an increasing dominance in her as she gets older and her family ceases to dic-tate her self-image, "was a hunter Artemis fell in love with, then her twin brother got jealous and stuck him up in the sky. The most famous stars in Orion are Betelgeuse and Rigel."

"Tell me about Sylvester," I said, perching obediently on the edge of the table she'd assigned me.

"What?"

"Sylvester," I repeated. "The reason you had to leave town."

"How do you know about him?"

"You mentioned him when we went out for ice cream. Very mysteriously, then you said you'd tell me about him someday. That's why you agreed to come down here with me, of course, not for chitchat about the infinite wonders of the universe. You need to tell someone, and I'm the obvious choice. It's very lonely for you to keep it all inside, and if you were completely honest you'd acknowledge that there's a swaggering element to the story that you're anxious to enjoy. So let's have it. How did you two get involved, what happened, and why did you run away?"

"You don't have to be snide, first of all," she said, "and sec-ond [she pronounced it "suckint," to my inward delight], you're wrong about why I wanted to come down here. It's hard to see the stars from Marie's yard, 'cause the neighbors have a bright garage light. I always want to come down here, but I'm scared of rapists and perverts."

"I'm resisting the temptation to make the obvious joke that, instead of leaving it up to fate to make you run into a strange rapist and pervert, you've brought your own along with you."

"Huh," she snorted. "You're such a wack job."

"Although you have a powerful crush on me," I pointed out.

"I do not."

We bantered playfully in this vein for what to me was an unnecessary length of time before she felt at ease enough with me to confess the things I'd been brought here to learn.

Sylvester, it turns out, was the middle-aged Negro janitor at Kings College with whom Louisa began an affair last spring in a spirit of derring-do, the fear that if she didn't do something bold and rebellious and ill-advisedly reckless then, she would never have the nerve. She allowed him to seduce her and relieve her of her virginity, late one night at the school library, improbably behind a carrel where anyone could have seen them. Which reminds me of my assignations with Annika in Central Park: the risk of getting caught confers a dollop of erotic suspense that heightens everything. Sylvester is fifty, married, a self-taught political activist, and the father of three daughters, all of whom are older than Louisa. He entertains delusions that if he hadn't been kept down all his life by the white establishment he would be a professor instead of a lowly toilet-scrubber. He is boiling with rage at the university. He hates all the professors; he despises the students. He himself is a high-school dropout.

"Like me," I said.

"Get out of here!" she said back.

"No," I said. "I got kicked out of many schools, then narrowly escaped being banished to fester and rot in military school by sneaking off into the night and never looking back. But that's another story, and not germane to this one."

"Well, for a high-school dropout," said Louisa, "Sylvester seemed pretty smart to me. He's a Marxist, he reads a lot. He told me that he knows more about sociology and political science than any professor, because he lives in the real world and they live in the ivory tower or whatever. Like, he knows from experience what they only read about."

"Really," I said, feigning impressed curiosity. "And does he think the new sixties are about to happen, and he's going to be the new Malcolm X, only Malcolm X didn't go far enough, so the power structures didn't change? So he plans to bring it about with his followers, his movement, which until recently consisted only of you?"

"Something like that," she admitted. I heard wariness in her voice.

"Did it not occur to him that the student body is racially mixed, as I'm sure the faculty is too? No, wait, let me guess. According to him they're all slaves of propaganda, they're kowtowing to the power elite. Like Uncle Toms, they buy into a racist system for their own protection. But for any real change to come about, that old system has to be completely dismantled."

"How do you know all this?" she asked, still wary.

"I can well imagine," I said pleasantly, "the rambling, paranoid, nostril-flaring, adamant hectoring he inflicted on you, his young white freshman mistress."

"Is that what you think I was?"

"For the purposes of this story," I said.

"So anyway," she said, "then, at the beginning of this semester, he told me he was plotting to blow up the library."

"Why?" I asked.

"To make a statement and put them all on alert. He called it 'the book prison.' He asked me to help him. He said if I loved him I would be faithful to his cause."

"Makes perfect sense," I said. "Don't you think?"

"He's so full of himself," she burst out. "I can't believe I was so fucking stupid. After the World Trade Center thing I realized that was what he was talking about, sort of. I mean, it's, like, almost the same thing only smaller. I'd been buying all this bogus crap he was feeding me. I sent a letter to the administration but I didn't sign my name. I think he probably lost his job or worse. I'm sure he knows it was me. He's probably really pissed. So I came up here."

"Louisa," I said, "you did the right thing."

"I learned one thing from Sylvester: I don't need any shit from anyone. That's something, at least."

"Why don't you come over here to my table if you won't let me come to yours?"

"I tell you this story and you hit on me?" she asked, her voice cracking with scorn and disappointment.

Since this was precisely what had happened, I found I had no comeback, snappy or otherwise. "Well," I said, "yes, in fact."

Then she let me have it. What made me think I could treat her like she was some easy prey? What, did she wear a sign that said, "I'm desperate"? Well, she wasn't desperate. She could read me as clearly as if it was written on my face: I thought she was too young and naïve to get that she was being played. I was just like Sylvester, we both hit on teenage girls because we thought they couldn't tell what total sleazebags we were, but I was wrong about that too.

"Really?" I asked, perching on the edge of my chaste picnic table. "It's also possible that you're making assumptions about me, rather than the other way around."

At this patently ridiculous suggestion, she snorted.

"And, then again, maybe not," I conceded. "In any case, I feel I owe you an apology. I apologize. What you did, turning Sylvester in, was very brave and admirable. It made me want to kiss and probably fondle you, but this is due to my own cynical impurity. I promise not to attempt to sully you again."

She was silent.

"Listen," I said. "I can't help issuing a warning to you about heroes. Hero-worship of any kind is bound to cause you disappointment and disillusionment. Heroes at the personal level are almost universally egomaniacal tyrants who cheat on their wives and treat their loyal followers abysmally. Maybe some people are meant to be and are most fully themselves as public heroes who lead and comfort and inspire the masses in times of crisis although they're really horrible up close, sometimes even cynical bastards who fool a lot of the populace into thinking they're compassionate, caring guys, say, for instance, the current mayor of your hometown—oh, and by all reports Martin Luther King, Jr., was no sweetheart to the people closest to him either. Maybe Jesus was a jerk to the apostles. Maybe it's impossible to be both a nice guy and a leader."

"What are you talking about?" she asked.

"I'm babbling," I said. "Would you like to go back?"

I sensed her hesitation. "Maybe so," she said, but she sounded reluctant to me.

"Louisa," I said sternly, "you can't have it both ways, accompany a lonesome old bachelor down here to stargaze with you, a lovely young girl, on an unseasonably warm evening in a secluded romantic spot, then both establish a precedent for such assignations and win my sympathies with the moving tale of your busted-up love affair, the emotional, racial, and political overtones of which only serve to heighten my desire for you—and then light into me for presuming. And then, when I offer to take you home—"

"Why are you so impossible?" she snapped. "You're rewriting history. You're mixing up everything."

"All I'm asking, Louisa," I said, "is whether you'd like to go home now. It's entirely up to you; as for myself, I would be thrilled to enjoy your company for a while longer."

"Let's go, then," she said, and stomped up the path to the woods.

On the way back to Marie's house, I allowed Louisa to walk several feet ahead of me. She seemed to derive a certain amount of comfort from this, judging by her utter lack of interest in waiting for me to catch up with her. As we mounted the steep driveway, she said stiffly to me over her shoulder, "So now you know you can't just take advantage of me."

"I certainly do," I said. Something welled in me. I don't know even now what prompted the following outburst, but I do know that I am still too dismayed by my sudden paternal rant to transcribe it word for word. I believe I said, in a full-throated voice I have never or rarely used before in my entire life, that she should never worry about my intentions toward her again, that I respected and liked her very much, and that I found her to be entertaining, intelligent, and wise beyond her years. She had been through something very difficult, had handled it admirably and all alone, and she could trust me not to betray her confidence.

The very thought of what I told her next causes me to grimace and slap the side of my head.

I said I could see the woman she was going to turn into— Louisa at, say, thirty-five or forty, permanently free of the constraints she's had imposed on her all her life to date by virtue of birth order, physique, and class. No more younger-sister drudgery, no more synagogue with her basset-hound father, no more enslavement to her mother's drooping shoulders, no more cringing obeisance to her tyrant of a sister: she will be highly educated, well married, sexy and knowing and funny, well liked amongst her colleagues and friends, and fulfilled in her work.

I assured her that she doesn't project any degree of neediness, and that I had flirted with her solely out of admiration.

I said a few more things. I don't remember what.

Her eyes were boggling slightly by the time I finished, or possibly well before—I hadn't noticed because I was too busy singing my little aria.

"Um," she said. She couldn't quite meet my eyes. "Okay, whatever, good night, thanks for the dinner."

And she went in, leaving me standing by my truck. I got in and drove home to Waverley with a kind of twisty, curdled feeling I recognized from long ago but haven't felt in many years.

When I got home, I parked on the lawn and skulked up the stairs to my aerie, where I sit now, steeping, as I said, in my own garum.

November 27—Was interrupted then by Sonia, of all people, who rapped on my door. She wore a black and slinky dress, and her straw-colored hair was sleek from a recent washing and much brushing.

I asked what I could do for her in as frosty and uninviting a tone as possible; I knew exactly what I could do for her, and how.

"I have chosen to forgive you," she said, "for your long silence and then your unfriendly letter. I am ready to resume our relations."

"You've chosen to forgive me," I said. "That's rich irony. I thought that might be the case, given your garb and demeanor."

"My garb and demeanor," she repeated in the familiar withering tone that for Sonia is direct flirtation. "Garb and demeanor, Hugo, really."

I wasn't tempted so much as overcome with garum; I was in no position to withstand her. Sex is one of the only recourses in this mood, the only solution or distraction, and here it was, being served in a shiny black dress I shucked off my wife posthaste. Underneath she was white and smooth as an oyster

out of its shell, quivering with briny juices and piquantly yield-
ing to the teeth.

Speaking of oysters, M.F.K. Fisher's *Consider the Oyster* has
enthralled me. I read and reread whole passages lately. One of
these concerns the American regional varieties of oysters and
Mary Frances's opinions of them. The chapter entitled "A Lusty
Bit of Nourishment" is concrete lyricism, a *cri d'estomac*. I don't
trust my adoration of Mary Frances, of course; she's too smug,
too sure of herself, to fully merit such slavish admiration. For
example, let's take the following: "I have thought seriously
about this, while incendiary bombs fell and people I knew were
maimed and hungry. . . ." After this introduction she then has
the breathtaking audacity to maintain, in her consistently light
and reasonable tone, that a reinstatement of brown bread in
restaurants served alongside raw oysters would make nostalgia
seem like a lusty bit of nourishment, rather than a perver-
sion. . . . Meanwhile, her beloved husband was dying of
Buerger's disease, and wouldn't, the same way I won't, quit
smoking. No matter what her own personal tragedy may have
been in those days, only a preternaturally, even unreasonably
confident woman would calmly discuss the essentialness of
brown bread with oysters in the same breath as starvation,
maiming, and bombs. She must have been angered beyond reason by his stubbornness, but in the diaries she wrote while he
was dying, she is nothing but supportive, loving, admiring,
claiming that Timmy can't be expected to live without cigarettes because that wouldn't be a whole man's life, it would be
some kind of sissified loserdom, a concession to mama's-boy
Goody Two-Shoes crybaby scaredy-cat pansyhood.

Well, of course I agree.

As for her final thought about nostalgia's being a form of per-
version usually, I don't know exactly what she means and am far
too slothful to parse it out, and I have my own strong ideas

about nostalgia, but nonetheless this passage makes me yearn passionately for a buttered slab of pumpernickel sprinkled with fresh lemon juice, a plate of ice-cold smallish oysters in their briny liquor-filled shells, and, served alongside, Mary Frances's commendable battery—horseradish, Tabasco, cocktail sauce, vinegar with chopped onion, French dressing.

I was rough with Sonia, to be sure, and had little to say to her before, during, or after. I loved her once, and that was enough for me in my engorged, self-loathing, semi-tipsy, restless state. Her body is smaller and weaker than Stephanie's. She makes a hell of a lot more noise, and scratches me, and stares at me with demented, fixed eyes while riding me up and down, and generally behaves like a starving civet cat. She mewls, turns over to raise her little rump in the air for me to do with as I please, and elongates her spine and licks her chops when I ram my sausage into her puckered little bunghole. It's a strangely pathetic, adolescent performance that's not altogether unappetizing.

I tossed her around, and as I did so, I informed her that she was a filthy whore, a vile bitch, a yellow nag, a stinking harridan, a fishwife. This is a brand of ill treatment she still enjoys. I found the things I was saying to her so hilarious it was all I could do not to laugh aloud. But I knew she was in dead earnest about the pleasure she gets from this degradation, and if I had laughed, she would have yowled and scratched my cheek, then disengaged herself from my piston before it had shot its engine grease. And so I kept a poker face and rode my little hobbyhorse into the night.

Afterward she asked me in her same old ragged postcoital voice to cook her a midnight supper, as I used to do in the old days. I had already cooked for two women that day, and now I found myself cooking for another one.

I have thought seriously about this, while my leg rotted out from under me and my house fell down around my ears and a handful of desperadoes destroyed an ugly but symbolic part of the city that used to be the seat of my most cherished and treasured nostalgia, and I believe that all self-respecting American kitchens should be organized in such a way that any cook, at any time of day or night, can quickly make a satisfying meal from staples in cupboard and refrigerator. I've always prided myself on keeping on hand a permanent selection of ingredients—a jug of olive oil, bottles of hot sauce, cooking wine, and Worcestershire sauce, beef and chicken broth (usually I make my own, but in a pinch I'll use the best commercial brands available), jars of olives, pine nuts, and capers, cans of clams, shrimp, and tuna, boxes of noodles and cornmeal, onions, shallots, and garlic, frozen peas, lima beans, and spinach, hunks of Parmesan and Gruyère, cans of tomato purée, chickpeas, and white beans—ingredients that will yield, in various combinations and permutations, in roughly the time it takes noodles or polenta to cook, something that satisfies that particular late-night itch for savory comfort.

I didn't make anything as special as Seafood Newburg for Sonia, of course. While the elbow macaroni cooked, I sautéed minced shallots and garlic in oil, then added white cooking wine and a little chicken broth, black pepper, drained rinsed white beans, a can of tuna, and some frozen peas. I sprinkled the simmering stew with red-pepper flakes and fresh black pepper, and when the noodles were done I tossed the whole mess together and dished it up with grated cheese and a small dish of capers. I availed myself of the pine nuts but didn't offer her any, out of a perverse wish to have a better supper than she was getting. In retrospect, I'm even gladder about this now than I was in that moment, if such a thing is possible.

Sonia ate as she always has eaten, shoveling the food from plate to lowered face with rapid fork. I ate as I have always eaten, painstakingly, savoring every bite with a prearranged order and design.

We ate it all up, and wiped our plates with pieces of bread. I lit a cigarette when both our plates were gleaming and empty. It was after midnight, and the house was quiet. Dennis was asleep, or at least elsewhere.

"You're not well," Sonia said; she has never been able to let a comfortable silence get too comfortable. "Not healthy. I can tell. It's the cigarettes, isn't it. You're in pain a lot too, and you walk with a limp."

I stared at her. She looked back at me with her skewed indigo eyes.

A certain knowledge descended on me like an avalanche.

"You can't tell anything," I said, and laughed. The calmness of my voice, if she but knew it, might have been, if I were a different man, the one slender thread that sheltered her from certain death by evisceration and disemboweling with a butcher's knife, her exposed insides then to be sprinkled liberally with salt and lemon juice. If the line between sex and food is fine, the one between cooking and murder is finer still.

"What are you talking about?" she asked. "I can tell."

"I know how you know that, Sonia, and you can't lie. You read my notebook. You went snooping up to my private room when you first got here, with no right whatsoever to be there, and you found my notebook and read it, and now you have the gall to refer to what you read as if you had dreamed it up yourself. Frankly, I'm amazed and disappointed that you're still alive and no one has run you through with a dull blade yet. Of course, you've read my notebook, so you know what I think about the past and how I feel about you, and why. You knew I didn't want you here when we first saw each other, but you stayed anyway."

She had the grace to look unnerved. "Hugo," she said in a

wheedling breathy whine I know all too well, "you're still so paranoid, Hugo, always. Why? You have nothing to fear from me, I'm here for our daughter, Hugo, and to see you again. You were my great love. A woman knows when her husband isn't feeling well."

She says my name repeatedly when she's lying, in order to flatter, lull, hypnotize me so I'll forget what I'm angry about.

"Sonia," I said, fighting fire with fire, "Sonia. Sonia. You don't fool me now and you never did."

"Hugo," she snapped, "I know you, don't forget. You haven't changed at all, over these years. You still pretend you don't care about yourself. I know you're sick because you don't look well; I haven't seen you in all these years, and you've changed. Someone who saw you every day might not be able to tell. I can because I knew you so well in those days."

"People don't change," I said. "No one does. Why should I be any different?"

"Do you know what it means, to die? Have you thought about what this will do to our daughter, who's just met you?"

"She's no daughter of mine," I said, laughing.

Sonia gasped as if I'd slapped her. This made me feel zingy and terrific.

"How can you say that?" she said, her mouth hanging open like a thirsty weasel's.

"If she were my daughter," I said reasonably, or so I flattered myself I sounded, "I would know it. She's nothing like me at all. Her father was obviously one of the other men you strung along, you heinous slut, you porn rat, you dishwater skank. Was it old Albert the caretaker? He's dead now, by the way, so if he's her father she'll have to cope with that somehow. Was it your holistic therapist?"

"He was a homosexual!"

"So you said."

"He was!"

"So you said."

She had begun to hyperventilate, an old trick she's always used during fights to throw me off. "You," she said with venom, "should behave like a father instead of pretending she's nothing to do with you. If you're determined to kill yourself, at least grow up a little before you go."

I rolled my eyes. "Actually," I said, "none of this surprises me at all. You're still as vicious and scheming as you ever were."

"I am not what you think," she said hotly. "You never knew me, and you never will now."

"Did you let Dennis read it too? Did you tell him about Stephanie?"

Unconvincingly, true to form, she denied everything. Perspicaciously, and equally true to form, I saw through it. I knew she was lying, she knew I knew, and so forth. If I took myself or my life or anything else seriously I might have killed her, or at least sought some means of retaliation, but as far as I can see, the rest of my life should be dedicated to pure enjoyment. What else is there? Life is but a dream.

I went up to bed and lay awake, sweating, steeling myself against a particularly relentless onslaught on my nerve endings, until dawn.

I got up shortly after the sun came up and went downstairs to forage for some toast and coffee. I walked in on Dennis on the phone in the dining room with his back to me. He had it pressed to his ear while I stood and watched him, and then he abruptly hit the disconnect button and clonked the phone onto the table.

As if he sensed me standing there, he whirled around. "Oh," he said enthusiastically, "you're up early."

"I certainly am," I said. "Making crank calls?"

He looked puzzled. "Want some coffee? It's freshly made."

"In a minute," I said. "Who were you calling?"

"None of your business."

"Yes," I said, "that may be true, but you and I have no history of respecting each other's privacy, so I'll reiterate: Who were you calling just now? Your wife?"

"Like I said, coffee's made. I'm taking my cup out to the porch."

He walked past me, out of the room, toward the porch. If that was really where he was going.

I picked up the phone and hit redial. It rang a few times, and then an answering machine clicked on. As I expected, I heard Marie's recorded voice saying the usual things, out or unable to come to the phone, leave a message, etc.

I went out to the porch with my own cup of coffee and said to my brother, "Why do you call your own family and hang up without leaving a message or talking to anyone?"

He took a sip of coffee with an expression of innocent absorption, as if he were the protagonist of a novel about an intelligent, sensitive, handsome man beleaguered by the combined forces of fate, change, time, and the inferiority of everyone around him. "I'm thinking of moving back to the city," he said. "Get myself a loft in TriBeCa, be closer to the gallery."

This took me so aback I had to sit down immediately in the chair nearest to his. The willows at the foot of the lawn looked exhausted this morning, like the unwashed hair of overworked waitresses; the river had that glum, pissy look it gets sometimes, as if it were just sick of running along in the same old goddamned riverbed, century in, century out. Since the end of its golden era, the attentions and celebrations of the Hudson River School of painters, the river must have been in something of a snit. Getting to end its eternal run straddled by George Washington and shooting its wad into New York Harbor can't possibly be adequate recompense.

"Why are you moving to New York?" I asked.

"Part of it," said Dennis piously, "is that I'm beginning to feel ready to get back into the life down there now that I'm single again. The girls can come down and visit; it would be more fun for them than coming here. Anyway, your family is back now, so it makes sense that you'd like me to clear out so you can all be alone together. I feel a bit like a third wheel, actually."

I filed this surprising knowledge away for later use. "Even though my family and I have nothing to do with each other?"

"Oh, I think that's because I'm here," he said.

I examined his face closely for any glimmering of irony or self-knowledge but as usual found none whatsoever. "Really?" I said, raising my eyebrows over the rim of my coffee cup.

"Of course," he said. "Sonia and I have always had a very friendly connection, and because I have daughters, it's only natural that Bella" (I almost snorted at this hilariously unlikely nickname, but forbore, so as not to shake him from his topic and disrupt this revealing conversation) "should gravitate to me. I'm used to little girls, I'm good with them; you've never been a father before, you've never really taken to my own daughters. And from living with Marie all these years, I'm used to women too. I really do feel, though, that, with me out of your hair and a bit of time, you'll get the hang of it. I was always so ambitious, so domineering, so focused, it must have been difficult to be my younger brother. The fact that I have a successful career, I've raised children, bought my own house . . ." He didn't finish the sentence, just let it trail off into a marsh of implications.

I nodded as if in complete agreement.

"Why do you think I had to disappear for all those years when we were young?" I asked with a hangdog expression.

"I can imagine why," he said. "I can also completely understand why you've been so paralyzed all these years, why your

marriage failed so quickly. I told Sonia I thought it was courageous of her to come back and give it another shot with you."

I had an immediate image of Dennis and Sonia, late at night
around the kitchen table, hunkered elbow to elbow with my
bottle of whiskey between them while Sonia played Dennis like
a violin, more specifically like the violin of a certain someone
who was at that moment sleeping in my mother's former bed.

"Did you," I said.

"She said she had never stopped loving you, all these years,
and she just couldn't give up on you."

"Ah," I said. "You still haven't answered my question."

"Which question?"

"About your crank calls to Marie."

"Crank calls? Me, to Marie? What the hell are you talking
about?"

"I hit redial just now and got her machine, which you had
just hung up on. I might add that it wasn't the first time this has
happened."

"I'm under surveillance?"

"Are you trying to scare Marie into taking you back?"

He shook his head in mock disgust. I'd struck a nerve.

"That strikes me as semi-dirty pool," I said mildly, "not that
I'm above dirty pool myself, but you at least pretend to be."

His nose twitched as if he'd suddenly smelled something off-
putting and foul. "Why are you suddenly Marie's champion?
And why are you suddenly going over to that house for
dinner?"

"Someone's got to keep her company since you spend all
your evenings in cozy chummy little tête-à-têtes with Sonia."

There followed the usual rounds eight, nine, ten, all a draw;
I'm used to it now. No one owns up to a thing at Waverley, my-
self included; no doubt there's something in the air or water.
Well, he knows I know. That's all we can hope for around here.

Then I went into the kitchen and made my annual batch of mincemeat out of finely chopped cooked beef hearts and livers, plenty of lard, nuts, dried fruit, and brandy, and packed it into sealed jars to fester in the pantry like garum until Christmas. I don't know who will eat it this year; I don't know where I'll be.

Dennis's moving to New York provokes in me, in addition to relief and delight, a torrent of nostalgia. This nostalgia is somewhat bogus, or at least it's someone else's. If I had chosen to have the kind of life in which I behaved as if I were some sort of protagonist of a novel the way Dennis does, which I manifestly have not, I would have settled in New York City. All self-styled protagonists of novels seem to migrate there self-consciously, to seek their own kind—all the other former drama nerds, bookish eggheads, debate-club champs, chess prodigies, and school-orchestra dweebs, anyone too loud, egotistical, big for his britches, blatantly hungry, alienated, and overweening to make a big splash in the high-school yearbook, marry another low-brow popular sort who likewise peaked at sixteen—anyone too much of a misfit to remain contentedly in the provinces. Not to mention all those hundreds of thousands of other, Dominican and Puerto Rican immigrants, that abrasive sect of Jews in medieval garb, the hordes of Negroes and Orientals. A recipe for disaster: take this stomach-turning Otherness, the maddening fact that the city proper is not like anywhere else despite the current mayor's determination to turn it into another Akron, not to mention what's generally agreed upon by natives and tourists from the hinterlands alike to be its incandescent, unquenchable allure and thrum, and you get a bubbling, messy stew of emotions in various outsiders, among them fundamentalist terrorists and myopic schlubs who would never be able to cut the mustard in New York themselves. I hasten to add, I am not one of these; I think I most likely could have cut the mustard there if I'd had any sort of hot dog I wanted to put it on.

December 2—It has been many days since my last confession. Ha ha. That's because I managed to get the hell away from Waverley for Thanksgiving. I took my own advice to go somewhere secluded. I didn't go far, just holed up in the motel where Stephanie and I once spent such entertaining hours. But I'm not so pathetically far-gone in my crush that I stayed in the same room; no, I took a different one, although the room we spent our delirious time in was available, which I knew because I was the only guest in the place that first night of my stay. Others came and went the second and third nights, but on that first night I was alone in the place except for the obese proprietor, whose sex I was tantalizingly unable to ascertain: deep voice, mustache, big meaty hands, but breasts! And it wore a shapeless sacklike garment I thought might have been intended by its designer to be worn by some species of female. Its age was a less compelling but equally opaque mystery: no wrinkles on its hammy cheeks or near its beady eyes, but a few of the coarse hairs on its upper lip were a wiry gray.

I took all my meals in my room, thanks to deliveries, and spent a lot of time watching TV, in an inexplicable attempt to gain a passing familiarity with its more popular personalities and characters. TV is exactly as I expected it to be. In addition to eating construction-paper–like pizza and watching manifestly unfunny sitcoms, I drank whiskey, whacked off, watched more TV, slept, writhed in pain, took many showers, etc. It was a pleasant interlude, overall. I was alone, and that was the idea. Appropriately, during the darkest hours of the night, when the pain wouldn't let me sleep, I worked on my own translation of Montaigne's essay "On Solitude." Montaigne was someone I would have happily drunk and eaten with anywhere, in any rough-hewn country inn or swank city establishment. He liked to eat and drink as much as I do. His views concerning solitude are comfortably close to my own (except for his unfathomable admiration of religious nuts). He was levelheaded and not stupid. He appreciated and even celebrated both the solitary life and the willed death, and respected those who embraced either, or both.

During those sleepless hours after my powers of concentration failed me and I was on the edge of pain-blunted sleep, I leafed through *The Dictionary of Difficult Words,* which I'd found at an otherwise sad and tawdry Catholic-church rummage sale across the street from my motel. I learned that the rather clumsily constructed word "homoousia" means "sameness of substance," the unpronounceable word "athymy" means "melancholy," and "pergameneous," a word that's just asking to be kicked in the ass, means "resembling parchment." Many of the other words, to my intense disappointment, I found as familiar as clothes I'd seen on someone else. However, along with the interesting challenge of translating Montaigne without a Larousse, it got me through a night during which the athymy of my soul and the pergameneous sheet of my bed were homoousiatic in that both were crackling, tissuelike, yet durable.

Solitude needs no journalistic expunging. But now, now that I'm back at Waverley, the need to write has resurged for the usual reason, that being the need to pop the swollen memory of conversations like fat boils and wipe their effluvia on this paper; I've felt the renewed pull of this notebook after my encounter with Bellatrix an hour ago on the stairs.

Bellatrix, during her stay here under the ancestral roof, has not appreciably come to resemble me or any other Whittier any more than she did when she first arrived. No Whittier ever had such a dumpy build, such a rabbity nose. No Whittier ever had that fragile blond transparency either; Bellatrix is fairer and more stolid than anyone else I've ostensibly shared a bloodline with. We've always been a dark, wiry line, possessing a kind of psychological opaqueness, an unwillingness to be cracked open too easily. Bellatrix has the foreign (to me) tendency toward splotches on her cheeks, a quaver of her voice, contracting of the pupils, frank intake of breath. She's a brute, feeling, flat-footedly simple animal of a nature repellent to someone who has always prized and honored any evidence of murky motives in himself and anyone else.

"Well," I said upon catching sight of the little potato one landing below me, stumping upward as I gimped my way down. "If it isn't the Amazon Star." This, unfortunately, is the sort of pleasantry I blurt when I'm taken unawares and haven't spoken to anyone in a while. I regretted it instantly: it marked me as something of a git.

"Hello, Dad," she rejoined in her colorlessly adenoidal voice, her pudgy knees flashing bare with each step.

Dad. The word detonated with a spiky ferocity in my sternum; the shards lodged there and stuck as I made my way down and she trundled up. Then we were face-to-face. There was nothing for it but to say something else; I couldn't just keep going as if she were a stranger. Well, she was, but I'd already given her an advantage with my ill-advised greeting; no sense letting her have the moral upper hand as well.

"You're not a bad violinist," I told her skeptically, the implication in my tone being, I realized just after I'd said it, that she was a tragic failure at everything else. Well, that was all right. No harm in being honest.

"Thanks," she said implacably.

I met the frank empty blue of her gaze.

"Do you ever play anything by Vivaldi?" I asked in all innocence.

"I hate Vivaldi," she said. "He reminds me of shopping malls. I like Bach better if I have to play something baroque."

"They don't play Bach in shopping malls?" I asked, impressed in spite of myself by her discernment.

"They do," she said, "but it's not the same thing. He sounds totally out of place there, because his music has nothing to do with malls, and Vivaldi sounds like elevator music."

"How many shopping malls have you been to?"

"Mama takes me sometimes. She likes the one in Paramus, New Jersey, and also the one in Nyack. She thinks they're fun."

"And you?"

"They're okay," she said insincerely, the loyal immigrant's child. "Mama likes food courts and shoe stores and those places where they sell a lot of accessories like belts and earrings."

"Food courts," I said. "That makes perfect sense."

"Excuse me," she said then. "I have to go to the bathroom really badly." And continued up the stairs.

I went down to the kitchen and helped myself to an apple, and now I'm back up in my room staring at a page of French, the denuded apple core at my elbow. Let's see what we've got here. . . .

"And it is not the prescription for one solitary sickness; death is the prescription for all our troubles. Death is a promised haven, never to be feared, often to be sought. It amounts to the same result if a man puts an end to himself or passively accepts it; whether he hastens to his final day or simply waits for it; wherever death comes from, it is always his death; no matter where the thread breaks, the whole thread is broken; no life remains on the spindle.

"The most beautiful death is the one that is most willed. Our lives depend on the will of others; our death depends on our own."

I wish old Michel could meet me tonight at the Turtle Inn and the two of us could converse over plates of vulvic oysters with brown bread, bowls of vagina-aromatic bouillabaisse, rare steaks au poivre as tenderly pink as the inner walls of labia, and a bottle or two of menstrual-blood-red wine.

I could write forever about food and women, the connection between them, eating and fucking, etc., etc., but I find myself distracted by the memory of my recent little chat with that child who bears my name: she is not the sort of starchy, dense, earthbound person I first assumed she was. This gives me something to chew on, but nothing much to write.

December 4—I have spent an hour or so this morning with my pen held impotently over the paper, brooding in some distress over Stephanie's failure to make our assignation. I am not accustomed to being stood up, to put it mildly.

When I telephoned her office yesterday, she answered, to my relief. I didn't want to have to speak to any officious secretary-type employee or leave a message with my name on it, and have her call me back, and have Dennis answer . . . only my craving for her, which now rivals my hunger for cigarettes, allowed me to breach my aversion to interrupting someone else's solitude or peace of mind. We chatted somewhat superficially for a few minutes before she agreed to meet me for a drink that night when she finished work. We arranged to meet at Rex's, the same disreputable roadside tavern where we first drank together. She sounded friendly, but distant and distracted, as if she could hardly remember who I was, as if I were some cousin she'd forgotten about.

When it was finally time to get into my truck and go, after counting the minutes all afternoon while I pretended I was otherwise occupied, I drove fast through a lowering dusk that threatened rain, arrived right on time, then proceeded to sit at the bar. Over the course of an hour and a half, I drank several whiskeys; then I returned home, slowly, moodily, through a rainstorm. I came into the house, and there was my wife lurking like an alley cat in the humid hallway, looking trashy and hungry and mean.

"Hello," she said as if she were yowling on a fence with her back humped and her front legs stretched provocatively out in front of her. "Hugo," she added after a brief pause, as if to show that, despite my avoidance of her and recent absence, she still remembered my name.

I gave her a look and informed her that she could come to my room that night. "Maybe not," she said; "you smell of whiskey." But of course she came, and I abused her in every way I could think of. After it was over, we went down to the kitchen, hungry. She sat at the table in her robe while I made our supper. I melted a "lump of butter," as Mary Frances calls it (the phrase conjures for me that nostalgia-world of lipsticked women with cigarette holders, men in hats and trench coats drinking rye on the rocks), until it foamed in a hot cast-iron griddle, turned the heat very low, then slipped four beaten eggs into the hot fat. Meanwhile, I boiled a handful of frozen corn for a couple of minutes, drained it, and sprinkled it onto the omelet along with some smoked kippers I happened to have on hand, roughly chopped, and a heaping spoonful of small, salty capers.

I served the omelet with a bottle of chilled white wine and a plate of buttered toast. It was delicious. At least, I thought so. I didn't care what Sonia thought.

"You're still smoking too much," she said. "Please stop, Hugo. You'll die if you don't."

"That's my decision, I do believe."

We were silent for a moment, and I was about to go up to bed alone when she inhaled in a way I recognized: she was poised like a deadly little snake about to strike.

"I am having a Christmas dinner," she announced. "Here at Waverley. Dennis will invite his friends the Foxes, and I am trying to convince him to invite Marie also, and that girl who takes care of the children, and Marie's sister, who will be visiting."

The Foxes.

"Christmas," I said. "Here? Are you out of your mind?"

"Please," she said with a cold smile. "Hugo, don't be difficult about this. I don't know how to cook, and Dennis says he does, but you and I both know you're the only one who can do it."

"Actually, what I know," I said, "is that you could have it catered if you wanted, or hire a cook. But you would rather have me serve forth platters of festival meats while you lounge at the table and order me around. In your fantasy of this Christmas, you probably even have me in an apron."

She snorted. I suddenly recalled those times, long ago, when I managed to coax a laugh out of her, a dark and bitter laugh, of course, reluctant, hard-won, but somehow worth the effort it took to wrest it from her.

"Will you do it or won't you?" she asked, tapping her nails against the tabletop.

"Unfortunately, I have plans to be far away on Christmas," I said, munching unconcernedly on my last buttery corner of toast. "So the answer is no. No, I won't do it. No, I won't be here."

She reared back and spat, "You are not going away again. You can't. This is an important family holiday, and your daughter would like to spend it with both her parents for the first time in her life."

"If this tantrum were about your birthday, I could understand your concern," I said, "since it's largely self-interest that's making you perform this little charade, but Christmas isn't up your alley, Sonia, it never was. It celebrates the birth of Christ, who spawned an evil religion that made you afraid to masturbate. Catholicism is the nuclear meltdown of Judaism, remember?"

"I have since changed my opinion," she said. "I've come to understand the deeper meaning of Christmas. It's a nice holiday, and it's more about family and food than any glorification of Catholic hypocrisies, and, most of all, Christmas is very important to Bellatrix. She's a little girl. Children love Christmas."

I stared at her. My ruination by financial security of the old passionate, opinionated, artistic Sonia, I saw, had been a great success.

"Some might," I said crisply back at her. "I never did. Good night," and stalked up to my room.

Since these notebooks could be viewed as one long, extended suicide note, it seems fitting that I record my latest decision concerning my untimely, inevitable end. I would prefer to eliminate myself with a minimum of fuss and bother: no illegal prescriptions, no bloodshed, a minimal possibility of failure. I'm casting about for a method: cheap, legal, and of a cleanly toxic nature that won't cause me to bespatter my innards and humors about the room, which would be horrible for whatever relative or hired hand has to mop me up. Poison of some kind, but what?

Montaigne . . . "The end of our race is death; it is the necessary object of our aim; if it scares us how can we go forward without a fit of ague? The remedy of the vulgar is not to think of it, but from what brutish stupidity can proceed so gross a blindness? We must bridle the ass by the tail."

I like this image: the ass in full bray held by its shit-and-fly-specked tail, bowlegs splayed, back swayed. I can see it. But I don't understand the metaphor, exactly: Is the ass death? Are we the ones holding it by the tail? Why the tail? Why an ass and not a lion or a shark?

Maybe the ass is ourselves; maybe he means to imply that we

bumble blindly through life like animals, with no thought of death. Or maybe I was right the first time: the ass is death. That must be it.

"Premeditation of death is premeditation of freedom. He who has learned to die has unlearned to be a slave."

I find this sentiment strikingly interesting. I don't believe any of that afterlife garbage invented and sustained by those too chickenshit just to live with the fact of their own deaths without going out of their trees. As for me, I see no compelling reason not to believe my own death will be a perfect nullity, nonbeing, a full stop.

"There is no evil for him who has rightly understood that the privation of life is no evil"—yes, and what's so admirable about trying to prolong your life? I never saw the point of it.

It appears I'm also rethinking my position concerning painkillers. . . . I know what's coming as soon as I put down my pen and get into bed and turn off the light and lie in the darkness with nothing to distract me from the Anschluss, as the krauts like to say: I don't look forward to the night ahead, or any night, for that matter, for the rest of my life. Morphine is starting to look pretty good to me as a secondary addiction, or tertiary if you count whiskey, which I don't, because it's a crutch but I can limp along without it if I have to, whereas cigarettes are like another limb.

December 5—I heard a knock on my door at seven o'clock this morning. I was already up and dressed and sitting in my chair, watching Erasmus and his cohorts enjoy the life of birds in a tree. The sky was pinkening in the east, and the birds were waking to their fresh new day. The few leaves left on the tree shuddered in the dawn wind. Inside, all was snug and warm. I rejoiced in the comforts of humanity, rejoiced not to have been born a dumb animal incapable of sitting in a chair enjoying a cigarette, the anticipation of breakfast, which I had almost decided would be, today, a bowl of creamy oatmeal with brown sugar and a cut-up pear, the luxury, upscale version of my vile childhood muesli.

"Come in," I barked, fancying myself a four-star general in a bivouac, a snowy-headed, intimidating old gimp who'd been decorated and wounded more times than anyone else in the army, and whose underlings' passionate devotion was satisfyingly tinged with abject fear.

Bellatrix stuck her big, pasty head around the door; then a cup of coffee followed, proffered by her pudgy little hand. "Mama told me to bring you this," she said, her eyes wide.

"Did she," I snarled. "Well, it's not because she's nice, you know, it's because she wants me to do something I don't want to do. A lot of things. So you go downstairs," I said, taking the cup, which she handed me without betraying the least bit of passionate devotion, but with some other feeling tinged satisfyingly with abject fear, "and tell her I can't be bought. You might want to add that you won't be used as a pawn, but that's entirely your affair."

"You don't like her," she said. Her forehead was wrinkled. She seemed about to sneeze. "You don't want us to be here."

"That's right," I said, not unkindly.

"Why not?"

"Because I prefer to live alone. I wish Dennis would get the hell out of here too, and he's my very own brother."

She looked around my room, then back at me. "Can I sit down?"

"No, you can't sit down." I drank some coffee. It wasn't strong enough. Sonia, even back when we were proper sweethearts, has always refused to understand how to make a pot of coffee, no matter how many times or how clearly and patiently I've tried to explain it to her. She's a blindered, blockheaded mule. An ass who won't be held by the tail.

I thrust my coffee cup at Bellatrix. To her credit, she managed to take it without falling backward.

"Listen," I said. "Take this back downstairs, and tell your mother that if she's going to try to bribe me with coffee she could at the very least try to make it the way I like it."

"How do you like it?" she asked coolly.

"Very strong," I said. "Not like mud, but like mud with water added. She knows, she just won't do it."

"Why not?"

"And tell her, while you're at it, to send a messenger who doesn't ask questions. Go."

Off she went. I limped over to my bed and lay down and propped my back up with a big heap of pillows. I waggled my foot, which was aching, for a few minutes, then gave it a vengeful thump with my fist. This made my leg feel worse, but it made me feel better. I was about to go down to the kitchen to get myself some breakfast when there was another knock on my door.

"Enter," I barked, the crusty old general in his bivouac.

"I'm not going to ask any questions this time," said Bellatrix with firm resolve as she bustled over to me, bearing a cup again. "I was just trying to be polite before. I don't really care. I thought I should act like I cared, but I don't."

"You don't care about your father?"

She looked bleakly at me.

I tasted this new cup. "Finally!" I said. "Finally, that mother of yours has given in and made it right. I never thought I would live to see—"

"I made it," said Bellatrix.

What a strange child she is.

"Oh," I said. "Well, you made it just right."

"Goodbye," she said, and made her way over to the door.

She would have gone through it if I hadn't said suddenly, "You don't want to be here either, do you?"

She turned and said flatly, not meeting my eyes, a flush rising in her pergameneous skin, "I wanted to stay in New York. I like it there. I don't see why we had to come up here. It's boring, and anyway I don't believe you're my father. If you were, you would act differently."

I looked at her as a light dawned suddenly in me. "Frankly," I said, laughing, "I don't believe I'm your father either."

"You don't?"

"What I think is that your mother prowled around behind my unsuspecting back with some rawboned blond proletarian fellow, and pretended I was the one all along because it was in her best interests to do so. I assume this other fellow was a butcher or a mailman or someone equally unable to provide the things she wants and seems to require. What I also think is that she was raised a Catholic and therefore had a head full of voodoo propaganda, despite all her efforts to rid herself of it like a sow trying to chase off a horsefly; she felt too guilty to stay here, so she made me drive her away. Why she brought you back here to live I have no idea."

What she made of any of this was hard to tell; I wasn't in the habit of addressing children, and had decided that the best approach was to talk to them as if they were adults in waiting, capable of shelving anything they didn't understand until later, when it would come in handy.

"She talked about you all the time," said Bellatrix.

I blinked. "She did?"

"All the time. Your father, blah blah, your father. Anyway, all the things she told me about you made me expect someone . . . really great."

The general gave his crusty bark of a laugh. "What did she tell you about me?"

Bellatrix took a deep breath and said in a singsong, reciting from memory, slightly mocking, "She said you were smart, you were handsome, you made her laugh like no one else ever did, you lived in a mansion, you took her to Europe. You sang songs to her under the balcony of your hotel in Venice, you took her to a place in the Alps where there was the best view and then you had a picnic. You brought her strawberries you'd picked in the dawn in the south of France and woke her up by putting them in her mouth."

"And they were wet with dew," I added in the same mocking singsong. I cocked an eye at her. "And you believed all that?"

"I used to, till I met you."

"Those," I said, "were your bedtime fairy tales."

She cocked an eye back at me. "So you never did those things?"

"Let's just say," I said cautiously, "that a different man did them."

Our eyes were still cocked at each other.

"She told me you did all those things," she said staunchly.

"And do you believe her?"

"No! I used to, though."

"Bellatrix," I said, "if you must know, she was the only woman I ever sang to. But I had no idea, blind and foolish and trusting as I was, what she was up to."

"What was she up to?"

"She was fooling around behind my back."

Bellatrix is not even eleven yet; I wasn't sure she'd grasp the implications. But she is a New York child who's watched enough TV to augment the knowledge gleaned from street and subway and fellow New York children.

"So you're not my father," she said after a moment.

I felt like yelling, "Bingo." "No, I'm not," I said. "So let's just stop this lovey-dovey father-daughter charade. Why don't you go find your real father? He might be the man who runs the local convenience store."

"What lovey-dovey charade?"

"I was being ironic," I said. "If you were my real daughter you would understand."

"Well," she said, "your real daughter might not know how to make coffee right, so there."

"Did you know what your mother wants me to do, why she tried to bribe me?"

"Love her again?"

"Well, there is that," I said. "Yes, that's certainly on her agenda. She also wants me to quit smoking and make Christmas dinner for everyone in the nearby universe, although she knows full well that it's highly unpleasant for me to see anyone at all, much less everyone all at once in my own house."

"I love Christmas. It's my favorite day of the year. And smoking sucks. It kills you."

"What's wrong with deciding you'd rather die than quit smoking?"

She shook her head at me as if she couldn't believe what she was hearing. "That's just stupid," she said. "So should I bring more coffee?"

"Yes, please," I said, and she was gone.

December 6—I woke up this morning with a sense of having misplaced something irreplaceable. Without too much unnecessary cogitation, but with a certain amount of dismay, it dawned on me that this supposedly precious item was my younger self. Further inquiry pinpointed which younger self it was: it was that decade-plus younger self revealed to me by Bellatrix. She gave me a flash of memory of his now entirely foreign inner workings in her recounting of Sonia's romantic embroidery—I saw him again, that starry-eyed cuckold, trapped inside my decrepit older self, waking up with me this morning after a long sleep. He's groggy and blinking, but he wants to get out, and when he wakes up fully I'll be in trouble.

I would like to kill him, but can't think how to do it without offing myself, which I'm not entirely ready to do yet—the thought of getting to fuck Stephanie again is still too compelling for me to quit the stage, and there are a few new dishes I'd like to make before I go. These tenuous, temporary, but unbreakable threads bind me to my life like a wriggling, trussed-up fly, not dead yet, trapped in a crooked web made by a spider on acid.

This young chump of a Hugo—the serenading, strawberry-picking, hormonally charged moron who thought he had won the greatest prize the planet had to offer—ten years after the dissolution of that never-to-be-broken bond . . .

The cliché of a tree adding rings is tiresome to me, not unuseful, but overused, and therefore like the elastic of my boxer shorts that has no stretch left in it. I am still that young Hugo, the way a withered apple is its fresher self as well as its rotted self, both at once. Midlife is like standing on a high peak looking down at the plains, temporal and spatial simultaneity; it's a congruence of life and death, ashes that you came from and the ones you're heading toward becoming. Fresh-faced Newlywed Hugo wakes and sings within my sagging, soon-to-be decomposing chest; innocent, wakeful Hugo embraces his bride, while bitter old Hugo wakes, smokes, contemplates his end, and that same wife, now loathed and despised, sleeps elsewhere. Meanwhile, the Childe Hugo sits downstairs, kicking silently at the rung of his chair as he chokes miserably on his putrid muesli, his equally miserable brother across the table doing likewise, their ever-watchful mother eagle-eyed, admonishing them if they flag even for an instant in the dispatching of their hated and punishing breakfast. And Dead Hugo, delivered at last, lies behind me on the bed, still and white. And Rotted Hugo grins cheekless underground, somewhere nearby.

Forty, the time of reckoning with unwanted memories, when

old and buried sap rises hot and sturdy again, and of death waiting ahead of me, fully in sight now, while behind me I can clearly see everything that's brought me here, and none of it is good, none of it brings me joy, it all hastens me along toward Old Scratch, who waits with wheelbarrow and pitchfork and stony face. His expression says it's rude to keep him waiting, impolite to take more time when I've already had so much and there are others coming up behind me who need the air and water more than I do. Well, they're welcome to it all, soon enough. What a relief, no longer to care, no longer to be burdened by the future, as I was when I was younger.

Recalling the urgency I felt about my Work as a young sprat makes me laugh inwardly, a long, low, mocking guffaw that would curdle the blood of anyone who heard it. My Work! I still have it all somewhere, all the reprehensibly impish doggerel, the self-serious philosophical grandiosities. The arrogance of youth—those poems I wrote stank like soiled diapers in the sun, the essays were so snot-nosed they might as well have been written with colored chalk on a sidewalk in a hopscotch pattern. Back then I had intimations of grandeur every bit as fulsomely swashbuckling as Dennis's apparently still are. I cringe to think of the way I used to whisper aloud my own name, Hugo Whittier, the smarmy thrill I would feel at my breathless intimations, soon-to-be renowned. . . . As I recall, I intended that it would be shortened, in seminars and conferences, to a crisp "Whittier," as telescoped and important as "Montaigne," or (the happy young Hugo inside me whispers urgently) "Shakespeare."

Being forced to recall it this way, on this particular morning, seems unnecessarily cruel. I need no prompting or reminders to fuel my self-loathing: ongoing present circumstances serve to keep it blazing and alight.

This is always the case with writing, and there are plenty of handy ways to refer, either obliquely or head-on, to the gap running between what I might be writing in a perfect world and the constant falling-short of the words I manage to get onto the page.

The subway train doesn't match up exactly to the platform, mind the gap. It runs out of the station. . . . This calls to mind one of the "profounder" insights I recall from Early Hugo: successful metaphors cause us to look up abruptly from the page to catch them as they fly, and bad ones cause us to shift uneasily in our chairs as if in the grip of a bad smell, rubbing the page in hopes of erasing it. A bad metaphor makes the world seem dim and creaky; a good one shines a light into the gap for a brief instant.

This proves if nothing else that he was right about bad metaphors.

Early Hugo. Here he is, all shiny-cheeked and bustling, resplendent in his vigorous earnestness, the type of young man I now want to run over with my truck whenever I have the misfortune to come across one. I always recognize the loathsome species by his unabashedly creative facial hair, his attention-attracting haircut (my hair is now maintained by the town barber to resemble my father's hair in the 1960s as much as possible, and my cheeks are shaved blisteringly clean every morning, right up to my hairline), and, worst of all, his idiosyncratically up-to-the-minute clothing (I wear my father's old trousers, cotton twill in summer, wool or corduroy in winter, all of which are in good shape still and fit me fine, and button-down shirts that are slightly too large, but what do I care?)—never do I not want to smash this boy to a pulp, no matter where he is or what I'm doing when he catches my eye. That I respond to him so violently hints to me, despite my strong preference not to know this, that Early Hugo has possibly never been asleep in the sense of a dreaming, restorative slumber—he's been in a coma, most likely because I've bashed him in the head repeatedly through the years. I'd do it again right now if I hadn't lost the wherewithal.

I went into town yesterday to get my mail and gently harass my beloved Carla, not to mention replenish my stock of whiskey and late-night-supper ingredients. I found Carla sullen and withdrawn, not her usual chatty self, so, with businesslike consideration, I made my usual purchase and continued on my unmerry way to the post office. In my box was a brief note from Stephanie, written hastily in black ballpoint pen on an index card, enclosed in a plain envelope with no return address. It said in its entirety, "Dear Hugo, Sorry I missed you the other night; something came up and it was too late to let you know. I just realized I could have called the bar, but for some reason it didn't occur to me then. I apologize. Stephanie."

She apologized. Fat lot of good that does me. I don't believe she wants to see me again, and I don't believe she, a lawyer, didn't think of calling Rex's at the time to let me know she wasn't coming. She did it on purpose, and then sent me an apology that means nothing at all. It's the opposite of a recipe, but similar in the way of opposites, of the same nature: A recipe pretends to provide exact instructions for re-creating a dish whose essential nature is, like that of all alchemical processes (including sex, prayer, smoking, dreams), unique, inimitable, completely different every time. An apology pretends to cancel out whatever action, or in this case nonaction, caused injury or offense, but it doesn't carry the same significance or weight as the action or nonaction itself, not even close. An index card in an envelope doesn't mend the gap between sitting alone at a bar feeling itchily dissatisfied and the anticipated pleasure of getting to fuck Stephanie again, any more than a recipe for Seafood Newburg in any way allows one to re-create the experience of sitting at Marie's dining-room table on that Euro-cinematic evening.

December 7—I was given a prescription yesterday for pain relievers and sleeping pills when I went to see ancient Dr. Schuyler, who looked me over and pronounced me worse. The amputation of a toe or two is an imminent possibility. More distressing, some degree of erectile dysfunction or even full-out impotence is not out of the question. "It's all part of the same thing," he said sternly, unhappily. It pains him, as a doctor, to watch me, a (to him) youngish man he delivered as a newborn and vaccinated as a tot and helped as much as my crazy mother would allow through all the childhood ailments, now willfully condemn himself to certain death, and all he can do is stand by and watch and predict all the unhappy results of my untoward, incurable passion for cigarettes.

He gave me the predictable injunctions against smoking—it's what he was trained to do, preserve life at all costs—and, when I asked him for it, he wrote me a prescription. I went along to the pharmacy and got my knockout pills and pseudo-morphine. I already feel much better—merely having them is a nice insurance. Not taking pain relievers has until now been my bulwark of cognitive-dissonance bravado against what I intellectually but maybe not entirely viscerally accepted as my imminent death. Now that I've got them, the floodgates have opened.

After I filled the scrip, I went off to the woods and sat on a fallen log in the cold gray wind and smoked an entire pack of cigarettes, one cigarette after another, perversely, feeling as I did another Young Hugo turning gently in his casements, said casements being my present-day self, his prison and his guard both. When the pack was empty and the last butt stubbed out, I vomited in a patch of bare underbrush, then drove back to Waverley and joined Sonia, Bellatrix, and Dennis in a game of Monopoly, a disgusting game of avarice and blunt-headed acquisition. It was strangely painful to me because of the memories it evoked for me of Atlantic City, which may well be the happy finale to my life, barring any other, unforeseen happy occasions that may surprise me on my now inevitable passage to my end. Thanks to a series of unlucky rolls of the dice, my metal hat cooled its heels in the two-inch-square jail far more than was its natural due; I shared my whiskey with two of my opponents, and somehow, despite my incarcerations, handily beat all three of them. Outside, a storm came and went, and the electric lights flickered on and off a few times. Dennis hauled out and lit the old hurricane lamps, and built a fire in the fireplace. After my stunning victory, he said with half-drunk surprise and brotherly condescension, "You could have been a mogul, Hugo," at which time I thought I should scuttle up to bed. I stumped upstairs and for the first time in months slept long and deeply, knowing those pills were there if I needed them.

I woke this morning to a heavy, gray, disastrously moody day. That note from Stephanie is rising in my gorge. I'd ripped it to shreds and burned it during my woodsy smokeout, but not before I'd memorized every word for all eternity. How irritating memory is. I can no longer play a stupid game of Monopoly without cringing at the words "Ventnor Avenue." This sharp, piercing nostalgia for a recent time is nothing like that other nostalgia, that longing for nonexistent, imaginary eras. One is cruelly heartbreaking, the other pleasantly so. How can they be described by the same word?

Everything is a matter of degrees, I guess.

Today Waverley feels like a big ship beached here on this sloping lawn, ablaze with lights and filled with sea-drunk madmen. Bellatrix is sawing away at her violin, first a bit of Dvořák, an odd piece she's been learning lately, full of spiky incidentals, shiveringly passionate asides, and now she's playing Bach, which is allowing me the only shred of focus I've had all day. I like her playing; I am thrilled to find something to like today, and by the fact that her well-played Bach is a pellucid bath of light that's enabling me to see clearly enough to write here. For the first time it occurs to me to wonder why she's not in school. Shouldn't Sonia have enrolled her in the local barracks by now?

As Bellatrix plays, Sonia is, I fear, down in the kitchen baking some doughy things that will no doubt taste like baking powder, like all her attempts of that nature. And the kitchen itself will be in a shambles of dislocation when I next go down to forage for sustenance, as usual at a time that enables me to avoid eating en famille.

And as for Dennis, judging by the rhythmic banging sounds coming from the depths below my aerie, he's still deeply involved in the renovation of the second-floor bathroom. Apparently, the walls by the old claw-footed tub have rotted through the years—bathers have come and gone, but the steam has lingered on. The other day, in a fit of all-too-characteristic derring-do, he took a crowbar and God knows what other destructive implements and worked out some of his angst and artistic inner turmoil by bashing out huge swaths of plaster. He disappeared in his Dart off in the direction of the hardware store in the strip mall on the way to town, then returned with all manner of things tied to his roof and poking out of his passenger window. He parked on the lawn, even closer to the house than my truck, something he usually considers a sacrilege (he has repeatedly begged me to park in the driveway; I have repeatedly assured him that I will do so when I find the kitchen arranged the way it ought to be arranged and as the gods intended it to be arranged, and if and when this happens in my lifetime I will hold up my own end of the bargain); then he came huffing and puffing up the stairs, bearing an unwieldy slab of green Sheetrock. I watched, smoking, from the rear landing as he fought it into the hallway and along to the bathroom. I stubbed out my cigarette in the ashtray I held and did not offer to help him, and of course he refused to ask me, for reasons I give not one flying fuck about. Let him do it all by himself if it's so important to him. I have better things to do than patch up this leaky, scabrous old vessel. But Dennis, ever the optimistic aristocrat, soldiers on alone, muscling the house into the future with him single-handedly. Well, I wish him luck with all of it, smooth sailing, the rest. Why wouldn't I? I don't care what happens after I'm gone.

I won't think about Stephanie any more. I will abuse Sonia all I please in the usual ways, and maybe wholly new ones I may devise in the near future, and I'll likewise allow her to believe that I'm fully capable of offing myself at any moment, which I am. Why does she pretend to care? She will inherit whatever is mine, all the money held in trust in my name—the exact amount of which remains a mystery to me, except that there always seems to be enough there for as many cigarettes and bottles of whiskey as I could want. I have a vague idea how much I'm worth, of course, but the actual dollar amount fluctuates with the stock market, rises and falls with the national mood. Whatever it is now (eight hundred thousand? nine hundred? surely it can't be a whole million dollars, or I'd feel much richer than I do), they'll inherit it all, Sonia and that bastard chick of Carla's uncle. I don't care what happens to it, it came to me from someone else who got it from someone else and so on back into the dawn of financial time. Anyway, they've already been issued so much of it, through the years; they may as well get the rest. In a sense, I consider it my charitable contribution to the advancement of music, in that it will allow Bellatrix to go to Juilliard, which she claims is "her dream."

This stands as the last will and testament of Hugo Whittier, on this 7th day of December, 2001, being at the moment in soundish mind and hopelessly fucked-up body. They'll inherit all I've got no matter what, but whoever reads this will know I wasn't duped, I willed it this way.

December 9—I recalled with a lovestruck pang, as I was cleaning out the refrigerator yesterday morning, something that Stephanie told me as we lay postcoitally alight and bathed in sweat in that Atlantic City bed: she said that, on hot summer evenings when she gets home from the office and Bun is still gone, she likes to sit on their screened-in porch and have, for her supper, one cored and sliced red bell pepper still cold from the refrigerator dipped bite by bite into a jar of very hot salsa, washed down with a large, icy dry martini, and then, for dessert, a lightly boiled and salted ear of corn.

I knew then that I could and might possibly already be in love with her. . . .

Apropos of something I can't put my finger on, Mary Frances Kennedy Fisher uses the word "plenty" much the way Hemingway uses the word "good," to conjure up a sense of generous warmth in lean, uncertain times. Sometimes I whisper to myself now, the way I used to whisper my own soon-to-be-famous name as a simpering idiot of a young man, "Serve with plenty of hot buttered toast." This is one of my favorite directives of all time. It never fails to give me a glimpse of Mary Frances herself in her belted dress, her dark hair falling glamorously, the way it did, over her cheek, her round, sexy Irish face a little puckered, a little abstracted, since she was far too sensual and intelligent to be sunny. Her "plenty" is a mannered, self-conscious thing, of course, but its repetition, sometimes even stilted overuse, offers a vicarious sense of good American overabundance, stout comfort to those in alien lands and heartsick fugue states alike. "Serve with plenty of hot buttered toast" gives the disaffected and ill-at-ease—me, for example—a momentary welling of joy.

After I cleaned the refrigerator and had that sudden hankering for a red pepper dipped in hot salsa, despite the fact that winter is nigh, I got in my truck and drove to the supermarket, and was standing in line with my little arm basket of goodies when what to my wondering eye should appear but Shlomo the hit man, carrying his own basket of goodies, which I couldn't help noticing consisted entirely of packaged, nitrate-heavy, artificially flavored dreck.

He saw me; I saw him. Too late for either of us to backtrack: recognition was full-blown in my expression and had just begun to dawn in his squinty eyes.

"Shlomo," I said, placing my purchases on the conveyor belt with feigned relaxation. "Amazing coincidence to see you again after all these years."

"Hold on," he said. "Wait till I buy all this crap, I want to talk to you out in the parking lot."

"Yeah," I rejoined, "I bet you do."

We carried our single bachelor plastic sacks through the pneumatic door, out into the cold wind. I hunched into my coat; he did likewise.

"Why exactly am I not dead?" I asked.

"Shut up," he said without heat. "I don't give a fuck; I got out of the business and relocated. If anyone knows I'm here I'll be the one who's dead. They didn't move me very fucking far away from all the trouble."

"Surprised you recognized me," I said, "after all these decades."

"You're a million years older and uglier now, but you look like the same jerkoff you were back then. I wish I woulda whacked you."

"Me too," I said.

"I'm serious; it woulda been better for everyone, especially me right now."

"Your secret," I said solemnly, "is safe with me. If you want to whack me now, it's fine with me. Back then I had reason to care; now I don't. Let's go get a drink and talk it over."

"Let's go get a drink and not talk over a fucking thing," he said. There was no heat behind his words. He seemed almost glad to see a familiar face. Judging by the contents of his grocery basket, there was no dumpy little missus cooking his supper at home, wherever that home may have been; I pictured a rented upstairs room in an old row house in some depressed river town. He had that look we all get when we've gone too long without a woman, the pinched shlumpiness of the unfucked middle-aged man. "I don't want to hear any grousing from you. You got away, be glad you're alive—same way I'm glad I got away without concrete ankles. You and me, we were both caught in the same fucked-up shit."

"Well," I said, "but I was innocent."

"Sure you were," he said, "fucking around on my fat, pathetic cousin, dipping your little pecker where you shouldn'ta."

"Those were the days," I sighed.

"I tried to have a poke at that Swede cupcake myself," Shlomo said with equal wistfulness. "She shut me good."

"Why, I oughta," I said without any heat myself.

A matched pair of defanged old snakes, we went, as fate would have it, to Rex's, where the drooling retard of a bartender set us up with shots and beers after scratching his head puzzling out the logic of it all: Four glasses, two customers? It didn't add up, is what it didn't. But he managed to pull it all together while my new best pal Shlomo visibly cast about for topics that didn't include organized crime, witness protection, or the question of why I wasn't dead.

"So how long after you were supposed to kill me did you get out of the mob and into the witness-protection program?" I asked pleasantly as he took his first nip of whiskey.

He coughed, as I had intended him to do. "Shut the fuck up," he said with some of his old malevolence.

"Just wondering," I said with a chuckle.

We settled in the way you do at a bar, our elbows rocking a little on the bartop to find the best angle for resting, our butts gently, gradually coming to a comfortable stop that balanced us on the butterfly wingtips of our pelvic bones. Neither of us has much of a rump, so this was a delicate, precise, but largely unconscious process.

"A hit man," I said musingly. "What a thing to be."

"What do you do?" he asked wearily.

"Not much," I said. "Nothing at all. I find myself deeply engrossed in this and that, but not in any lucrative or sustained way."

"No job?" he asked, peering at me.

"No job," I said back.

"At least I had a calling," he said.

"But don't you feel them all flocking around you in the middle of the night, looking at you accusingly with their empty eye sockets?"

"Who?"

I stared at him as if I were one of them so he'd get the picture.

"Oh, them," he said. He looked around the bar. The bartender was wiping beer glasses at the other end. At the various tables sat a faintly transparent crowd of no-goodnik kikes and sinister guidos, affectless slitty-eyed thugs, invented by me out of noir-film whole cloth.

"None of your fucking business, of course," said Shlomo. "But, no, they don't. There's no ghosts in my life at all."

"There might be ghosts in your life and you choose to ignore them, or there might be no ghosts at all because ghosts don't exist. I ask only out of curiosity about how you live with being a serial murderer after the fact. What I'm asking is, are you haunted by conscience—you got away with it, sure, but you know you're somehow still guilty?"

"Listen," he said. "There's different ways to die. The long, slow, sad death, from cancer or whatever, someone's beloved wife, their dear old mother, their brother-in-law who fixed the roof, their bowling buddy—that's the kind where you get ghosts. When there are people who want you to stick around, you linger after you croak because the living are keeping you alive. Trust me on this, a gun to the head, bullet goes in, shithead don't even know what hit him—that's different."

I threw back my whiskey and said, "Oh, barkeep."

The bartender ignored me: the word "barkeep" was not in his vocabulary, and, like many a youth raised in these parts, he had learned that he was best off ignoring whatever he didn't understand; otherwise it might bite him.

"Hey, you," I barked. "Another whiskey, please."

"Make that two," said Shlomo, and threw back his own shot. "So, anyway, the thing is, let's say we're sitting here, you and me. And that dumbfuck bartender comes over and shoots you in the head. Boom. First, there's no pain receptors in the brain. Dying that way don't hurt a bit, and since you don't even know what's coming, there's no fear or sadness or nothing, it's just over, kaput, just like that. Best way to go in the universe. I figure I was doing them a favor. Most of these guys were real lowlife pieces of shit, you know what I'm saying?"

"You were meant to kill me, you may recall," I said. "And I was many things, but I wasn't old enough yet to be a lowlife or a piece of shit. I was just a gigolo, as the song goes, trying to keep my head above water."

He looked me over. "Yeah, well, you were clearly a piece-of-shit-to-be. No, you weren't my usual clientele, it's true, but that was a favor to my cousin, and she and I went way back, and our parents went way back, and our grandparents before that, et cetera, back to Noah, most likely. Jesus, was she pissed off. Pissed. She wanted you blown to bits so bad she was smoking out of her ears."

"She was a very fat and strange woman," I said. "She was altogether too attached to me."

"You were a fucking sponge. Poor Tovah. She peed herself

up on the bima at her bat mitzvah. Thirteen years old and she wets herself. No one could tell, but afterward she told me, that's how close we were. I felt like someone had to take care of her, and it had to be me, because she had no brothers and our fathers were brothers who came through the camps together."

It strikes me as somewhat interesting that Shlomo, whether discussing murder, his tragically unattractive and obese cousin, concentration camps, or his interest in another whiskey, uses the same nasal monotone, has the same flat expression, as if there were nothing whatsoever behind his words, as if in fact he had become his groceries and his brain had turned into Swiss Miss pudding, his heart into a lump of some sort of dense, unappetizing luncheon meat, like olive loaf. He talks like a man who's merely biding time in his own psyche and physique until the time comes to vacate them. He wears himself very loosely, as if he didn't care one way or another when that time might be. We have a thing or two in common.

"Answer me this," I said suddenly, shifting gears to obliterate the image just forced upon me of my erstwhile keeper and mistress at thirteen, plump and terrified and pissing herself, which was causing my stomach to convulse. "Would you say dying in the camps was worse than being bumped off by a hit man?"

"What kind of question is that?" he whined in his monotone.

"Surely you've thought about it."

"Dying in the camps," he shot back as if he'd just been waiting for his cue, "dying in the camps is worse, I would have to say, than getting bumped off as you walk freely down the street with your head in the clouds or sit stuffing your face at your uncle's restaurant. You jackass. You ignoramus dipshit goy. Dying in the camps means being in the camps. Know what I'm saying? That's the difference."

I thought it wiser not to say anything. I waited for him to go on.

And he did. "Listen, I never thought killing was wrong per se. To me it depends. I'm raised Orthodox, I know what the Torah and Talmud say, yadda yadda, the commandment, thou shalt not. But some people are asking for it. Those scumbag shitwads. It's like mountain climbing, those putzes who go up Everest. You choose that way of life, odds are pretty good you're gonna bite it at some point. And it's a living—I wouldn't say I got rich, but I was comfortable for a time. I just brought about the inevitable. I brought them to their natural end."

"That's a nice story to tell yourself at bedtime," I said. "But according to your sources, killing a human being is wrong, no matter what, end of argument, although you can flap on and on about varying degrees and shitwads and anything else you want all night—I'm not going anywhere that I know of, and I can hold a lot more whiskey than this. By the way, I happen to think the only person you're allowed to kill is yourself."

"Not according to the Talmud," said Shlomo with a faint gleam of relief that he wasn't the only reprobate here.

"I'm not Jewish," I pointed out without inflection. "And although you could say that certain aspects of Jewish Law would also apply to me insofar as I was a Christian, I'm not a Christian, so that's moot. I see nothing wrong with suicide, and I don't care about what anyone else thinks, even God. I don't believe in God, by which I mean I don't think about God."

"Everyone thinks about God," said Shlomo flatly.

"I don't," I said, and had a nice pull on my beer glass.

"You can't not think about God. God is like air or water or sleep or beer . . . or maybe the point is, not thinking about God is a negative action, like fasting, holding your breath, going on the wagon. You still gotta have air and food and beer even so."

"I'm not," I said, wiping my upper lip on the back of my hand, "going to listen to a theology lecture from a hit man."

"I'm not a hit man any more," he pointed out. "And I was raised Orthodox, I believe I mentioned."

"Two more whiskeys, barkeep," I trumpeted.

Barkeep now recognized his appellation on its second repetition, nodded, sucked up some drool, and got busy.

"Let's just say, for the sake of argument, that I was planning, for reasons of my own, to kill myself," I said. "And then you come along with your cockeyed idea about how it's better to whack someone than kill yourself."

"Not so cockeyed," he said. "Taking your own life is a sin. Taking the life of a scumbag who's asking for it is just social hygiene."

"Right, you go ahead and keep telling yourself that, that's very comforting, I'm sure. Now, here's my question. Would you then stop me from killing myself by whacking me with a bullet to the head?"

"Why?" said Shlomo. "What the fuck do I care? Who are you to me? No one. Go ahead and rot in hell, I don't care. Unless," he added with a crafty little crocodile expression, "I was hired to whack you. Then everything would come into focus."

"That's a form of suicide, it seems to me."

"Not if you hire me by pretending to be someone else. Then I don't know what I'm doing, I just know I'm hired to whack a guy and some other guy is paying me."

I rolled my eyes around to look at him without turning my head. "I thought you weren't a hit man any more."

"I'm not," he said, sitting up a little straighter.

As the evening wore on, we eventually fell into a half-drunk blue-tinged silence. I stared at the double image in the plate-glass window to the right of the bar: reflections of two pale, morose sad sacks, shoulder to shoulder, slumped at the bar, superimposed over the brightly lit stream rushing by below on its eternal, busy way to somewhere else.

"Hackneyed," I said aloud. "Yet symbolic."

Shlomo said, "It's fucking moronic, is what it is." He got up, put on his coat, and clapped me on the shoulder. "See ya round, fuckface."

And my new best friend mooched his way out of Rex's Roadhouse and went home to heat up a can of ravioli on his hot plate.

As for me, I headed back to Waverley. It was almost nine o'clock, and I was just drunk enough to feel that I was an exceptionally brilliant driver. At my advanced age I have learned that in the grip of such alcohol-fueled delusions it's probably good to be especially careful, but I threw caution to the winds and took the elderly, crooked, narrow highway at a dizzying forty miles per hour, flying along, screeching around the bends. I made it home in one piece, more or less, parked at a jaunty angle on the lawn by the house, and heaved myself out of the truck. Then, for some reason, I stood there in the chill wind and for a moment stared up at the dark, hulking curiosity of a house I lived in, blinking in consternation: why did the place have to be so big? Had it sprouted new gables and turrets since the last time I'd seen it? It looked gothically deformed, way out of proportion to the rest of the world, like a freakish mutant house in some hypothetical horror movie that grew and grew until it either collapsed from its own weight or took over the planet. I stumbled up to the porch and into the maw of this frightening apparition and sloped along to the kitchen, where my beloved, closely knit family were sitting cozily around the table, playing cards in the lamplight, the remnants of some sort of supper permeating the air and cluttering the counters and stove. Hamburgers, white rice, and boiled peas, from the uninspiring looks of things. It had Sonia written all over it.

"Hello, my chickadees," I called in a warbling falsetto; for reasons unknown to me, I was impersonating a robin-breasted society matron from a *New Yorker* cartoon, circa 1953, with a lorgnette and little lapdog. Bellatrix flashed me a shy smile and ducked her head. Sonia scowled at my obvious inebriation, clearly not approving in any way, and Dennis ignored me, since it was evidently his turn to discard, and he takes his gin rummy very seriously, the way he takes everything.

I poured myself some more whiskey and straddled an empty chair backward and glared at my brother, glass raised with inquiring accusation. "Have you been adding more gables and eaves to the house?" I asked him.

Dennis laid the two of spades on the table and said with a little furrow in his brow, "Why would I do that?"

"I don't know why you would do it. Why do you do anything you do? All I want to know is whether you did, and the answer is yes, judging by the looks of things out there."

"You see extra gables and eaves on the house, do you?" said Dennis.

"It looks terrible. The proportions of the house were bad enough before, but now it's monstrous. What did you do?"

"Well, today I finished the bathroom wall," he said, glancing at me with honest concern. "I raked leaves and straightened the tool shed so in the spring it'll be easier to figure out what to do about the yard."

"Hugo," mewed Bellatrix.

"What happened to 'Dad'?" I asked. "I found it enchantingly ironic to be called 'Dad.' "

"I don't want to call you that any more," she said. "Because of what we said. Anyway, can you play my hand for a second? I have to go to the bathroom." She handed over a grubby fan of cards.

I took it and peered suspiciously at it. "You've got them organized wrong," I muttered, moving cards around with impatient little snaps of my wrist.

She didn't hear me; she had scampered off to the loo.

"Hugo," said Sonia, finally deigning to speak, in a low,

sonorous voice that was evidently intended to convey her dis-appointment in me. "Hugo, it's bad for your daughter to see you like this."

"It's all right," I said. "She knows she's not my daughter. Now nothing I do can affect her in any way."

Sonia slammed her hand against the table. "Don't joke about this!"

"It's no joke, Sonia," I said with the unfortunate little laugh I produce when startled.

"You think this is funny?"

"Hugo," said Dennis, "are you crazy?"

I flicked a chilly eye at him. "What the fuck business is it of yours, you cocksucking asshole?" It felt good to say; I could see what Shlomo was up to.

This rocked him back on his figurative heels a little, although he was sitting down. He inhaled sharply, suddenly all flushed. "Well, Hugo, it's the same sort of business my wife's life apparently is of yours. You yourself seem to have nothing better to do than interfere in other people's private lives. Why don't you do something around here instead of drinking and smoking and living off Dad's money while the house falls down?"

"Good question," I said, "and thank you for the fraternal concern."

I put Bellatrix's cards facedown on the table, stalked over to the counter, and began to rustle busily in my small bag of groceries. I was ravenous, despite the unappetizing detritus from the dinner Sonia had made. Raw red pepper just wasn't going to cut it. That had been for a different man. I needed real food; I needed food that didn't remind me of Stephanie, or my love-sick funk of the past week or two. Luckily, I had planned ahead and thought to add to my basket a nice big slab of aged porter-house, two baking potatoes, and a rubber-banded swath of bitter-smelling broccoli rabe.

"Seriously," said Dennis obtusely, "why don't you? Why did you end up like this?"

"He used to be a writer," Sonia interjected. "He was working on two books. His work was rough and juvenile, but had a certain originality."

"Actually," I said, "I wrote two books. In that I completed them."

Dennis looked at me with concern, of all things. "I never knew that," he said.

"It never crossed my mind to tell you," I said wearily. "And by the way, another thing you probably didn't know is that Sonia used to be an actress. Actually, she was a con artist pretending to be a performance artist who aspired to be an actress. But that all ended the minute she got onto my payroll. You could say, of the two of us, she's the greater success at her chosen vocation."

"Pah," Sonia spat. What else could she say? She couldn't deny it. I allowed my shoulders to shake with silent laughter, taking cold comfort in amusement at others' expense wherever I could, as was my God-given right.

Dennis wasn't listening. "You know what your problem is?" he asked.

"I know all too well what my problem is," I said.

Out of the corner of my eye I saw Bellatrix lurking in the doorway, out of sight of Dennis and Sonia, hovering there as if she knew exactly what bombs had been detonating in the kitchen in her absence and knew better than to walk into a catastrophe. I caught her eye and winked at her. She frowned and shook her head. Apparently she was in on this collective dressing-down of Hugo. And here I'd thought we were beginning to be allies. Just went to show, you could never trust anyone, which I'd never actually forgotten.

"All right," Sonia burst out; she had been fulminating after my crack about her acting, and now she had her answering salvo ready to go. "She's your daughter, Hugo. If you think she's not, then why don't you get a DNA test and prove it?"

I flicked an eye over to the subject of this conversation, but she didn't look back at me. She stared raptly into the middle distance, as if she were listening with all her ears.

"That's a bluff," I said. As I talked I patted the steak with a paper towel, then rubbed it with a little oil and salt and put it in a broiling pan and set it aside for the nonce. "You know I'd never subject us all to that. Frankly, I like her fine, she's a talented musician and an upstanding citizen, but I'm not her father. No tragedy there for her."

"He is lying," she said to Dennis.

"I believe you," he said foolishly. Clearly my own self-imposed restrictions against attractions to women my brother had a claim on didn't cut both ways.

Sonia gave him a soulful look that verged on the bovine.

"I know it's none of my actual business, but why isn't she in school?" I asked. "She's almost eleven, am I correct? Shouldn't she be spending her days in some classroom somewhere?"

Sonia stared at me. "You big idiot," she said. "She goes to school five days a week. I enrolled her right after we got here."

At this, I caught a faint smile from the upstanding citizen hiding in the shadows.

"Well," I said, "good. Because that's the law of the land." I scrubbed the potatoes at the sink, poked a few holes in them—perhaps stabbing them a little more vehemently than was strictly necessary—then rubbed them in oil and stuck them in the toaster oven on the counter to bake at 450 degrees.

Standing in the center of my kingdom, I surveyed its progress: family in a bit of a shambles, meat ready to go, potatoes under way, broccoli rabe to wash, chop coarsely, then put to steam in chicken broth and chopped garlic. More whiskey, certainly. I topped off my glass and set about chopping garlic heads. Sonia and Dennis and Bellatrix, from her outpost, all watched me silently, each no doubt thinking admiring and complimentary things about my cooking skills, which weren't being taxed in any way by this simple exercise.

"You were going to tell me what my problem is," I prompted Dennis.

"Your problem," said Dennis, "is that you have lost all hope. Hope is not something you sit around and wait to have hit you in the side of the head. Hope is something you cultivate and develop through action—it's a skill." He paused. "It's a moral necessity," he added then, firmly.

"What I hope," I said, "is that when you all go away again my solitary meditations will be that much richer, that much more fruitful, for having been violated during this brief interlude."

"Do you ever engage with anything sincerely?" Dennis asked sincerely.

"Why, whatever do you mean?" I asked.

"You know what I mean," he replied.

I laughed.

In the ensuing silence, I scraped the chopped garlic into a nice-sized heavy copper pan, then poured a little chicken broth into it.

"What has happened to you, Hugo?" said Sonia. "Something went wrong in your head before Bellatrix was born. I thought maybe, after all this time . . . I don't know why I was stupid enough to hope you would have recovered from it by now. Why should you have done that?"

I snapped the rubber band off the rabe and plunged it under the stream of cold water in the sink. I shook it gently, rolled it all around a little, so the water distributed itself evenly on the thick stalks of leaf and bud, and shook it again.

"Poor Hugo," Sonia said in her "concerned" voice. "Dennis, I told you he's dying. We cannot stand by and let this happen."

Bellatrix chose that moment to rejoin us. She slid into her

chair and took up her cards coolly, as if she'd heard none of the foregoing.

"Actually," Dennis said, "the way I see it, he's choosing to kill himself this way. He's a big boy."

For the first time in about twenty-five years, I almost liked him.

"I cannot believe," Sonia said to him in the nineteenth-century manner, as if her heart were swollen with a distress so intense she could hardly speak, "that you are on his side."

"I'm not at all," said Dennis. "But he's got nothing to live for. He's not even any kind of father to his own daughter. To a man like me, with my strong paternal urges and sense of responsibility, that's the worst wrong you can commit. Might as well die if that's how you're going to play your hand."

"I'm not on his side," said Bellatrix softly, looking through her eyelashes at her mother. "I think it's stupid to smoke."

Sonia stroked Bellatrix's wan locks with an absent, listless hand.

I burst out laughing at the sight of that fake limp white hand, but after one exhalation of laughter I realized it sounded insane, because there was obviously nothing to laugh at, so I forced myself to stop. In immediate playback, I realized that the whole thing had sounded as if I had barked like a dog out of nowhere, at nothing. Barking mad.

"Dad died before you really knew him," said Dennis. "You couldn't have learned what I learned from him."

"Dennis," I said, "what can you possibly be trying to say?"

"Look at yourself," said Dennis.

I looked down at my shirt, which was clean.

"Your wife left you ten years ago," he went on. "You've been alone ever since, doing nothing."

"This line of inquiry is so tedious I can't even—"

"He went crazy on me, Dennis," Sonia burst out, clutching Bellatrix's hand. Not for the first time, I had the feeling that she

would have happily played all our parts if we had let her, like a
one-woman melodrama with an accordian-folded piece of paper pinched in the middle that doubled as the heroic Dennis's
bow tie and the villainous Hugo's mustache. Instead, she had to
content herself with bringing to her portrayal of Sonia all her
black and sparkling intensity. "That's why I left. I was afraid of
him. Every time I went to the grocery store and stayed away
five minutes too long because of a line at the checkout, or traffic, I would come home and find him in a rage, ready to stab
me through the heart. Then, when I got pregnant . . ." Her
voice caught with the precious memory of this pregnancy, during which she was a hormonally raving madwoman, in almost
constant agony from morning sickness and backaches. ". . . he
lost it, he went crazy."

"I brought you bowls of ice cream at three in the morning,"
I reminded her. "I massaged your feet, I stroked your head. I
felt like I was living with my mother again, in fact. And I never
complained. I was devoted to you, you bitch."

"The things you call me in front of our child," she said, suddenly haggard with pain. The air in here was so thick I could
hardly breathe, and it wasn't the cigarette smoke.

"You like them well enough when it's just the two of us," I
pointed out.

"Hugo," said Dennis warningly, "don't say these things in
front of Bellatrix. This is her mother you're talking about."

He was right—I do happen to know when I'm out of line—
but I was inflamed, I was a bloodhound on the trail of a weasel,
and I couldn't stop to protect the young and tender heart of an
innocent bystander.

"You wonder why this marriage failed?" I asked Dennis.
"Ask Sonia. Given the turn of affairs, so to speak, in what I had
viewed as a lifelong marriage, I could have sent her off without
a sou, but my sense of responsibility, instilled in me by the same
father who gave you yours, forbade me. Bellatrix," I added with

sincere apology, "I'm sorry. She's your mother and the only one you have, and I don't actually know who your father is, because I could never catch her. . . ."

"Catch her what?" Bellatrix asked, as well she should have.

At this rate my dinner would never get done. Couldn't they genetically engineer quick-baking potatoes on the same principle as fast-rising yeast? I poured myself some more whiskey.

"You," said Sonia to me, "are so fucking insane."

"Such language in front of the child," I said.

"You didn't catch me," said Sonia, "because there was nothing to catch. Never, Hugo, not even once."

She gave Dennis a trembling, saccharine smile; he was obviously the intended audience for this little display. Dennis made a move from across the table as if he were about to leap to his feet and embrace her, but thought better of it and managed to restrain himself.

"Well, once was all it would have taken," I said back. " 'Not even once'? Once would have been a bullet in my head. But it was a lot more. How many women do you think I've ever loved enough to marry? Let's take a head count."

"Oh, Hugo," she moaned "piteously," as Dickens might have called it. "You never used to be so bitter. You became so paranoid. But in the early days of our love, you were such a prince, Hugo, such a romantic and tender husband. We were so happy together. Why did you have to change? You broke my heart!" Her voice broke.

"Did you cheat on him, Mama?" asked Bellatrix.

Sonia covered her eyes with her hands, apparently too overcome to answer.

Bellatrix looked straight at me. I looked back at her. Then she turned and tapped her mother on the shoulder. "Did you, Mama? Tell me."

"I cannot believe you are asking me such a question," Sonia said in a hard voice, her face pressed to her hands.

"Look at me and answer," Bellatrix persisted. "I want to know."

"Bellatrix," Sonia said, "don't listen to him, he is really crazy."

"Mama, look at me." Bellatrix put her hand on her mother's cheek and tried to lift it to her own eye level.

Sonia resisted, sinking her face even lower in her hands. Bellatrix looked up at me with a bewildered, compassionate stare.

"There's your answer, Bellatrix, and it might be the only one you ever get," I said with equal compassion, and turned to prod the potatoes to hurry them along.

"Oh my God," said Dennis, staring at Sonia, looking very pale.

December 10—Finally, a break in the weather. Today is sunny, and I slept through the night with the help of my new drugs. I have nothing to say, because I didn't talk to a soul yesterday. Everyone kept a healthy distance from me, and I from everybody, and the day passed without incident, and now my mind, insulated by this one clear, clean, solitary day from the tangled mess of the day before it, is comfortable once more, soothed by the brief respite from my fellow humans.

A respite that just ended with a phone call from Fag Uncle Tommy. I just hung up the phone a few minutes ago. No one else is home.

It can't be. Or else it's part of a cosmic joke on me, one or the other, but I don't believe I'm important enough to have a cosmic joke of any degree played on me, even by my patron saint, Loki. Therefore, this isn't happening.

My father's elder brother, Tom, no doubt dying of AIDS at over seventy years old after a happy lifetime of sticking his pecker up other men's rectums in bathhouses, gay bars, Fire Island shares, bus-station men's rooms, and countless other creepy homo fucky-fucky hotspots, has announced that he is coming back to his childhood house, I assume to die; I further assume that the drugs are no longer working for him, and that, although he must have managed to stave off the full-blown disease for a number of years with a combination of the new AIDS medications, his number is now up.

He asked that his childhood bedroom in the tower be made available to him—which is to say, my room; which is to say a little more vehemently, the room I've been living in since my mother's funeral and have made my sanctuary and in which I myself want to die. The thing is, he has more of a right to be here than either Dennis or I: he is my father's only brother and owns half the house, whereas Dennis and I each own a quarter. Fag Uncle Tommy's got *droit de seigneur*, in a manner of speaking. Plus, he's dying more legitimately than I am: he's got something that could have been prevented by abstaining from his own particular addiction, or at least by doing it a little differently, but can't be cured by stopping, whereas the thing I've got . . . Well, this might be Talmudic nit-picking. He's old and dying, I'm young and dying, so his death trumps mine.

Tommy is a very nice man, a trifle querulous at times, and not overly intelligent, but a nice, kind, gentle man about whom nothing worse can be said than that he always seemed like a limp-wristed pansy to me, with his high, fluted voice and his dandyish clothes and his taste in Broadway musicals and certain Verdi arias sung by other pansy-sounding fluted-voiced men or big ball-crushing divas. Well, he's a fag, what did I expect him to be like? He said just now, "I have no one else to go to, nowhere else to go." Our father would come down from heaven and knock Dennis's and my heads together hard enough to cause brain damage if we didn't do everything in our power to make the end of his beloved only brother Tommy's life as warm, easy, comfortable, and carefree as humanly possible. There is no doubt plenty of money still in Tommy's coffers to hire round-the-clock care for himself, but nonetheless I thought it the thing to do—the beau geste, in other words—to reassure him in return that Waverley currently offers quite a few people to provide a family for a lonely, sick old man, all with plenty of time to cater to any of his needs—turning over his Bette Midler records, fluffing up his pillows, playing cards with him, and fetching him another gin cocktail, for example, for all of which, I craftily thought, Bellatrix will certainly come in handy.

I am going to go out of my exploding fucking skull—I want to wring Fag Uncle Tommy's chicken neck and throw him down every flight of stairs in the house, or at least physically force him, doddering old weakling that he is, to sleep in any other bedroom but mine. I want to leave squashed-up dead shrimp in the floorboards of my room, once I vacate it, to render it uninhabitable to any semihuman nose. In short, I seem to be reacting to this turn of affairs with all the maturity of a five-year-old monster.

And then, to make matters worse, after I wrote the foregoing, the phone rang again. It was Stephanie.

"Dennis," she said.

"No," I said, and my heart pounded, annoyingly. "This is Hugo. Hello, Stephanie."

"Hugo," she said, slightly more coolly. "Hello. Is Dennis around?"

"No, he's not," I said. "You stood me up the other night."

"This isn't a good time to have this conversation," she said crisply.

"All right," I said. "When would be a better time?"

"Please tell Dennis to give me a call," she said. "It's urgent."

"I will, if you'll agree to have this conversation with me another time."

"Hugo," said Stephanie, "I'm hanging up now."

And she did. And then I stared at the receiver for a while. It seems I have, unless I'm mistaken, just been roundly, unceremoniously dumped. Rudely too. By someone I thought I was in love with, completely unexpectedly, just as I thought our affair was reaching some sort of critical mass.

Maybe she rejected me because she feels guilty about her betrayal of her husband. Or is it that she can't bear to get too close to a man she knows she'll lose? Since she won't tell me, I'm left fearing the worst: I wrecked it somehow, I fucked it up, and it's highly likely I'll never know what I did or could have done differently.

I could go mad, I realize as I parse this thing out to its furthest implications. There is nothing more disquieting than loving someone who does not love you back and won't tell you why, or give you any sort of glimmering of understanding. The insanity of heartbreak lies in the unfathomable mystery of another's heart—how can she not feel exactly the way I do? In other, more plaintive and pathetic words, how can she not feel joyous and enthralled about our time together, and yearn for more of it? How can she seem to feel so indifferent to me, so coldly uninterested? I had thought we were experiencing something together, and now it appears I've been a fool. There are no words to describe how humiliating and disappointing this is.

Well, of course there are words, I feel some heading down my arm into the pen now. Sonia disappointed me all those years ago; I thought I had learned my lesson, which was to stay away from anyone who might make me vulnerable and trusting and therefore ripe for betrayal. In other words, to flirt with the Stewart's cashier, although, for all I know, if our affair ever got off the ground, she might smash my frail heart to bits of hamburger meat and squoosh them into the dirt with her sneaker heel. Stephanie was a bit of revenge on my brother, as I recall; the genesis of my interest in her lay in my urge to thwart his own. A spot of fun, I thought I'd have, at Dennis's expense, with a woman I didn't care about at all; she was a healthy specimen and clearly in need of a good fucking.

Which means I poached my brother's game, sort of. Which is another thing I've always sworn I wouldn't do.

There were moments between us in Atlantic City, disconnected, anxious, which I may have overlooked because of the idiot swoon that had overtaken me, but which are occurring to me now, for the first time, with a little clarity and some perspective, not to mention a healthy reason to examine them closely.

Now that she has maltreated the heart I proffered her without reservation, a certain expression of blandly snooty preoccupation, which at the time I chalked up to her superiority to all other mortals and her understandable impatience with us all, returns to my mind's eye with a different interpretation: I suspect she may simply be just that, blandly snooty and preoccupied. She certainly sounded snootily preoccupied just now on the telephone, and her voice was bland. Worse—she sounded disdainful and brusque. Rude! My love is like a red, red rose with thorns.

She sings horribly, embarrassingly, speaking of that poem. On our way to Atlantic City she sang along with a song on the radio, one I in fact deplore, which was popular when Stephanie and I were seventeen or so, by a group called Heart. "Oh, this song!" she cried approvingly when the opening chords issued forth from her truck radio, sounding even more tinnily cheap for the tinny cheapness of her speakers. And then her voice chimed in with the singers', surprisingly nasal, tuneless, and as bad as her taste in music. I thought it charming, back when I believed she was equally charmed by me.

And occasionally there would fall between us an odd silence, although I felt, as I recall, that I had no end of things to tell and ask her. I thought it indicated, once more, her superior depth of character to mine, her thoughtfulness and inscrutability, and respected her desire for silence, proud of my ability to understand her complex and subtle inner workings so early on in what I assumed would be an ongoing liaison. This silence was, I realize now, strained and without mercy, brought about by her lack of interest in me and her self-absorption.

And then there was the matter of that hangover remedy, the beer with tomato juice. "I don't want one," I said firmly as we sat at the Poseidon Grill's booth, the one in the bar, nearest the door, because I didn't much care for the looks of the meaty-forearmed, beer-bellied, tattooed Hell's Angels types in the back room, and thought I might need to beat a hasty retreat if they happened to feel the same way about me when they got a gander at me.

"No," she said, "you have to have one, Hugo. Trust me, you'll love it. They're really good, I promise."

Like a sap I let her order me one, and like an even sappier sap I choked the damn thing down, sip by revolting sip. I got myself through it without gagging because I was focusing on Stephanie, who was reading me bits of the newspaper, which I also told her I didn't want.

"I don't like to hear any news over breakfast," I said. "Or ever, really."

"Oh, Hugo," she said with a smile that wrenched my heart,

"don't be such an ostrich. We have to know what's going on in the world."

"Why is that, exactly?"

"Because otherwise we'll just live our myopic lives of luxury and ease, thinking the whole world has it this good. Knowing about famine and war and torture of political prisoners at least allows us the illusion that we're compassionate and aware. It alleviates some of the guilt from our happy little lives."

"I don't have a happy little life," I said. "I have plenty of my own misery, and don't want to know about anyone else's. I don't feel any guilt anyway. What I feel is a hangover, and I would appreciate being left to it."

I wasn't joking, but she laughed heartily and began to read aloud from the front page.

And, sap that I was, I sipped my medicine and kept my piehole shut. My headache was like . . . a headache. No more metaphors after that visit from Young Hugo.

I watched this woman I had just fucked for three days straight reading aloud things that hurt my brain, and choked down a noxious concoction she had forced upon me, and I was so gaga I didn't put it all together: She had no interest in what I might or might not have wanted, anything I myself might have thought would be a good idea to drink or not to drink. She wanted me to be her puppet, and I obliged.

What a fool I was. That's exactly what happened with Sonia, and Sonia betrayed me in the worst imaginable way.

But although I may still be as much of a sap as ever, at least now I can recognize the signs early enough to quit the whole unfortunate cycle before it runs me over. I will not call Stephanie, nor will I be friendly to her if and when we next meet. I am made of stone, ice, glass. I am an island, a mountain, a—oh, metaphors will creep in, no matter what fences I try to build to keep them out, like raccoons—a hermit, and therefore people don't matter to me, even unspeakably beautiful ones who melt in my hands in a way that drives me to delirium. It's only delirium, and I know it. The fever has broken.

THIRD NOTEBOOK

December 21—I'm reluctant to start this new notebook; it implies a hold on life I feel less and less every day. And meanwhile the landscape has almost died. Outside, branches are bare and knobby under lowering skies, shaking in the strong wind. There's a spitting, nasty rain, the kind that goes down the back of your collar and seeps into your spine. The surface of the Hudson is a churning brown chaos. Today is the first day of winter, the shortest day of the year.

Despite these conditions, I feel an odd giddiness. This may have to do with the decision I've reached concerning my end. I sit and smoke in my armchair, and enjoy it all the more knowing I won't be doing it for much longer.

———

Many hours have gone by since I wrote that last sentence, during which I was required by unforeseen circumstance to have social commerce with a number of people, which made me chafe and itch.

First Bellatrix came up to my room with a cup of coffee and found me sitting, staring into space, and exhaling smoke. She was spruce and clean. She carried her violin case and wore a backpack affair with an unattractive, big-cheeked female cartoon character on it. It looked ridiculous on such a serious child.

"I need a ride to school today," she said. "Mama says she's sick and she can't take me, and Dennis said to ask you."

I felt highly disinclined to get into my truck at such an absurdly early hour.

"Why are you going to school on a Saturday?"

"It's Friday."

"What's wrong with Sonia?"

"She doesn't feel well," said Bellatrix obtusely.

"Maybe she's just got a hangover."

"You maybe shouldn't say things like that about my mother in front of me."

"Well, Uncle Dennis would certainly agree."

"I'm not saying that because he said it, I'm saying it because nobody ever likes to hear bad things about their mothers."

"You can say whatever you want about mine," I retorted darkly. "She was much worse than yours."

She shifted from foot to foot, eyeing me tentatively, as if gauging her chances. "So will you drive me to school?" she asked.

"Maybe you should stay home," I said. "Kids like to stay home from school—at least normal kids."

"I have to go," she said without wheedling, stating a fact. "It's the last day before winter vacation. We have a test."

I noticed then that her hair was up in a sort of droopy, anemic waterfall-like ponytail high on her head.

"What did you do to your hair?" I asked her.

"Why do you care?" she asked matter-of-factly.

"Because I'm not your father," I said, nodding. "I see your point. Well, it looks nice."

"No it doesn't," she said. "I had to do it myself because Mama's sick, and I know it looks stupid, but we have gym today and I don't want it flopping in my face."

"All right, Bellatrix, let's go," I said. "You've won my sympathy, but I honestly have no idea how. Wait for me in the truck; I need another cup of coffee."

We drove along the river and crossed the bridge. Bellatrix directed me along the roads, and otherwise we didn't talk. The truck smelled old and musty today. I was conscious of this because children didn't often ride in it, and I have always suspected that children have acute senses of smell, like dogs, that get wrecked through the years by pollutants, cigarettes, the blunting effects of time, and the general ongoing decay of all the bodily senses and vital organs.

"My school is right here," she said finally. "Turn in the parking lot and I'll get out by that fence over there."

I did as she told me; I had no real reason not to, although something I couldn't put my finger on made me want to drive right into the side of the nearest building. Something about the adults I saw as we pulled into the parking lot. The kids all looked normal enough in their bright jackets and backpacks, but every adult I saw, and there were a lot of them milling about herding children, gave me the willies of one kind or another.

"Bellatrix!" brayed a tall, broad-shouldered frau in a frumpy dirndl of a skirt and a baggy purple sweater. She had shoulder-length white hair, a pale moon face—oddly wrinkle-free, like those of witches in fairy tales—and an unnaturally high, loud, German-accented voice.

"Mrs. Appelbaum!" called Bellatrix, waving madly. "My teacher," she announced to me, flushed with a suspicious kind of manic energy she'd never shown the slightest hint of around me before. "Thanks, Hugo, see you at three o'clock," she said in a rush, and flung herself out of the truck and onto the ground.

Mrs. Appelbaum was staring curiously at me in the manner of a small-town busybody, so I gave her a jaunty little fuck-you wave that was actually the universal go-away gesture. Smiling with something that was meant to appear to be warm friendliness, she gave a big wave back at me and then headed toward me, Bellatrix flapping at her heels as if to forestall her at all costs.

I rolled down my window to see what the hell she wanted.

"So you're Bellatrix's father," said Mrs. Appelbaum with a didactically eager smile that hinted at black, simmering, repressed puritanical anger somewhere not too far below the surface. Behind her bright, clenched smile, her round blue eyes bored into mine with an intensity that reminded me of hatred. Up close, she smelled like lavender. I was afraid for Bellatrix, having to spend every day with this woman. I wanted to drive away as fast as I could and if at all possible spray gravel on her dull, gray woolen skirt as I did so, but I stayed put: Bellatrix was waiting for me to answer the question.

"Actually . . . ," I said with a smarmy little grin. From behind her teacher, Bellatrix looked beseechingly at me. I added in a false tone, "I've been meaning to come and see her school for quite some time."

"Well, do come in, then!" cried Mrs. A. "Come and see our classroom!"

She led me through a before-school, milling assemblage of children of varying ages and sizes being marshaled by a willowy young man in a sweater-vest with a bobbing Adam's apple and medieval haircut; another middle-aged Teutonic Brunnhilde, with iron-gray braids and the same scary blue drilling gaze as Mrs. A.'s, who likewise reeked of lavender; and an ungainly but preternaturally perky young woman in a flowing purple scarf and long, shapeless blue corduroy jumper-dress. All these people wore Birkenstock sandals over thick woolen ankle socks, as if this were the prescribed faculty footwear, which it may well have been.

The sixth-grade classroom smelled of beeswax and Christmas. The reason for this became obvious: stumpy brown candles were arrayed on one scratched oak table in a far corner, and pine boughs were draped all along the upper moldings of two walls. A small table against the far wall under the windows was covered in a purple cloth, on top of which, it appeared, reposed relics from the natural kingdom: shells, primarily, with the occasional smattering of colored stones and pine cones. The gleaming wooden shelf above it was neatly lined with twenty or so recorders, those shrill wooden flutes my mother played so irritatingly so many years ago. My mother would, in fact, have loved everything about this creepily wholesome room and Mrs. Appelbaum, who went back out to the playground to oversee her charges, and left Bellatrix to give me the grand tour.

"This is my desk," said Bellatrix, bustling over to a wooden desk with a hinged top like all the others in the room, and opened it to show me the contents: paper, pens, colored pencils, etc. All very neat and tidy, and right in the front row, which had always struck me as a crazy place to choose to sit; I myself preferred to lounge, doodling and heckling under my breath, near the back. The kids who sat up there were invariably the ones who gaped pacifistically from the sidelines at recess while the rest of us beat the hell out of a tetherball or smashed the foursquare ball into each other's quadrants with intent to kill. The front-row sitters were the ones who volunteered whenever anything needed doing, seemingly suicidally, as if to cement their life-threatening unpopularity: blackboard cleaner, hall monitor, taunted in-charge flunky during the few minutes the teacher was called out of the room.

"And this is my painting," she added, pointing. I peered obligingly at a wall of identical quasi-abstract watercolorish renderings of the same two fuzzy shapes, one yellow, one green, with swaths of blue and red surrounding it all. "St. George and the dragon," she prompted. "Mine is the second from the left."

"Very nice," I said insincerely, and was rewarded by a skeptical glance from the artist.

"St. George," she said, "fought with the dragon and killed it."

"Why did he do that?" I asked, yawning.

"Because he had to."

"Why did he have to?"

"Because the dragon was bad," she answered.

"What are they teaching you in this school?" I asked, laughing jovially (possibly not jovially; possibly with some hostility). "That doesn't sound very ecoconscious to me, to kill a rare animal because it's considered bad. By whose standards was the dragon bad? According to the dragon? I doubt that."

"I can't believe you don't know about this," she said with scorn. "Didn't you learn it in school too?"

"I didn't go to a religious school," I said.

"This isn't a religious school," she said back.

"Well, St. George is a saint, and I bet you eighty bucks that dragon is some medieval stand-in for Satan."

"Satan?" she said, laughing.

"Anyway," I said, "this is a fascinating subject, Bellatrix, and

I'd like to take it up again, but now I have to go home and smoke my morning cigarettes."

She made a strangled sound of disgust, the closest written approximation of which might be "ugh."

I made my way from the classroom; she bustled behind me. I felt her hand on my elbow, and turned.

"Don't go yet," she said. "Please. Let me just introduce you to some friends, really fast. I'll just say you're my dad, okay? They always ask who my dad is."

A dragon would have been swayed.

"Friends!" I said. "I never pass up a chance to make new friends."

"Not your friends," she said, beaming, "mine." And so I was trotted round the schoolyard, posing as a kindly, dadlike personage, to smile and nod to various schoolchildren with names straight out of a play about elves and village maidens: Saskia, Cornelia, Sabina, Rosemarie, that sort of thing. Rosemarie, it appeared, had her own father in tow, a tall, upright fellow. His eyes twinkled at me. He wore corduroy trousers and a home-knit pullover. I assumed my best man-to-man expression as he shook my hand.

"Otto Froelich," he said, I surmised by way of introduction, in a deep German-accented voice.

"Hugo Whittier," I offered in return. It developed that we were going to take a little fatherly get-to-know-you stroll together, along toward the back of the school, down a gravel path. I pulled out my cigarettes and offered him one, then lit us both up.

"Bellatrix has been to our house," he announced without inflection. "She's a good girl. A good musician. Very impressive. You are musical as well?"

"Listen, Froelich," I said briskly.

"Otto, please."

"Otto, then. I can't help wondering what this place is about. This school, I mean. Everyone seems a little . . . enthusiastic, for so early in the morning. A little bubble-headed, frankly. As if they were all under some sort of mind control."

He said with furrowed brow, "Actually, it's a very sound method of education; however, I do think sometimes, to people unfamiliar with the methods and philosophy, it might seem a little . . ."

"Fruity," I offered.

There was a brief pause.

"Why, then, did you send Bellatrix to a Waldorf school?" he asked with calm good manners.

"Her mother sent her," I said.

"You're not familiar with Rudolf Steiner's views on education." It was not a question.

"Rudolf Steiner," I repeated with foreboding. "Oh, for God's sake. Don't tell me he's behind all this. My mother was under his sway when I was a kid. We almost died of malnutrition and lack of medical attention, my brother and I, thanks to his mumbo-jumbo, him and Madame Blavatsky and a couple other mystical fruitcakes. And what is this George-and-the-dragon business? What the hell? It's a Christian fable of some kind, a didactic fairy tale, as I recall. The dragon was a stand-in for Satan, or man's baser nature, and George was light, good, truth, that sort of dichotomy, am I right?"

"St. George," he said. "Yes, it is considered a Christian story, but it reverberates much more deeply than that, and many ancient cultures have a story that's similar in some way. The story goes that a dragon was attracted to a village by the smell of its hoarded gold and silver. The village is said to be Uffington, in England; there's a shrine to St. George there. The dragon lived above the village on a hillside, breathing terrible fire that stank of brimstone and sulfur, and demanded live sacrifices every

night. It consumed all the livestock, night after night, as the vil-
lagers offered first their chickens, then their sheep, then their
cows, until none were left. Then they drew straws amongst
themselves every day to see which of them would have to go
to the dragon's lair that night and offer himself up as a sacrifice."

"Women and children too?"

He cast a look at me. "Yes," he said. We shared a puzzled
look about this. "At any rate, the king's daughter drew the straw
one night, and there was a lot of fuss and terrible grieving
throughout the land."

"Weren't the peasants secretly glad? The princess having to
take her turn along with everyone else?"

"No," he said. "She was beautiful."

"Of course she was."

"A symbol of purity and goodness for a terrorized people.
They didn't want to lose her."

"I see," I said. "The ray of hope. So off she goes to be swal-
lowed by that fire-breathing beast, and then along comes George
at the eleventh hour on his white horse to kill the mighty fearsome beast and win her hand? He smote the dragon with his
sword, and after a great battle he slew it? When the dragon was
finally dead there was much rejoicing?"

"Exactly. Some versions of the story end with the village's
conversion to Christianity, their enlightenment and salvation.
St. George is the patron saint of England, and of soldiers, and
some diseases. Historically, he lived in the third century A.D.
and was a tribune in the Roman imperial army. It is also said he
was beheaded by Diocletian for protesting the persecution of
Christians. However, there is absolutely no historical proof one
way or another."

"At the moment," I said, "my sympathies lie squarely with
the dragon. There didn't seem to be any other dragons around.
He was without others of his kind, crouching outside the vil-

lage on a wet hillside, frightening and alienating everyone with his fiery breath and insatiable appetites. And if they hadn't hoarded so much gold and silver, they wouldn't have been in such a predicament, it seems obvious to me. The moral of that story seems to be, Spend your money right away, don't hide it under your bed, where the dragon will smell it."

We paused on a wooden bridge over a small, endearing brook. Dead leaves bobbed and floated on the surface of the water and snagged against rocks. The water smelled fresh, wintry.

"You are familiar with the Book of Revelation?" Otto asked, smiling. "The Archangel Michael with his sword and scale?"

He pronounced it "Mee-ka-el," which made me suddenly queasily suspicious that he was going to try to convert me. I lit another cigarette off the butt of my old one, then offered him another, which he declined. The butt of my old one found its way into my trousers pocket; I was tempted to toss it off the bridge into the water, but didn't want to litter in front of Otto, who exuded rectitude from every pore, and whose butt had found its way into his own pocket. Even though there is nothing that I know of in the Judeo-Christian tradition that prohibits littering, polluting, or befouling the natural landscape in any way, this was arguably school property, and there were no doubt grave proscriptions against besmirching those.

"The Archangel Michael," I repeated, pronouncing it the normal way. "He killed a dragon too, didn't he? Gee, so many dragon slayers. Sts. George and Michael, of course, and then you have Sigmund, Beowulf, Sigurd, Arthur, Tristan—it's a wonder there were enough dragons to go around. Apollo, Cadmus, Perseus. It's all coming back now. Interesting, isn't it, how dragon slayers and dragons seem to coexist in a perfect one-to-one ratio. The minute a dragon appears, it seems, on any landscape throughout human history, there's a hero to kill it—and you don't hear of any dragons who got away, or would-be dragon slayers who can't seem to find a dragon. Why do you suppose this is? The dragon might be an interesting symbol, really, if you were given to interesting symbols."

"The sword and the scale," said Otto, "are also interesting symbols. I could tell you about them, but it all depends on how deeply into this you want to go."

"Let's start with not very," I said breezily. "I've got a lot on my plate today. The sword, we know where we're going with that, we're going to stick it into the dragon's heart and kill it dead. The scale . . . was to weigh the heart?"

"Was to weigh men's souls," said Otto darkly. "According to one interpretation. But the legend of St. George is, on another level, concerned with human incarnation, the cycles of the immortal soul on earth. The lower self, the dragon, is destroyed by the higher self, St. George. Ahrimanic forces must be balanced with Luciferic on the scale that Steiner called the Christ Impulse. The scale is a sort of inner sun that guides us on our true path of freedom between the Luciferic illusions in our thinking and living and Ahrimanic enticement into a shaping of things that satisfies our ego, but isn't rightly meant to be ours in our present epoch. Michael's sword is the outer, literal sun; the rays of the sun contain iron, like his sword, that permeates our blood and wages war there on anxiety, fear, and hate. The iron, raying in, drives these unwanted beasts, the dragons of our time, from the blood. We pick our way through the maze of Luciferic-Ahrimanic snares by keeping the Michael-Christ impulse before us always like a compass, looking outwardly at Michael, inwardly at Christ. Only then can we both attain our spiritual evolution and become fully human, and free."

Suddenly, in the midst of this jibber-jabber, most of which I have forgotten and failed to record here at any length, a shooting pain attacked my foot, so fierce it made my knee buckle. I broke out into a clammy sweat and clamped my jaw shut against the scream I felt ripping up through my throat.

"Ah," I said when it had abated enough for me to speak normally. "Well, did you know that medieval Japanese warlords ate the tongues of komodo dragons? They most highly prized swallowing whole a tongue from a live komodo. They believed it conferred power and glory to the man who ate it. Dragon's tongue. Can you imagine the taste? The texture? I imagine a cross between liver and leather. I wonder whether it was already cooked from the fiery breath. I wonder whether there was a whole silent, suffering tribe of tongueless komodos roaming the land."

"I doubt that," said Otto, clearly skeptical, as well he should have been, since I'd made it all up on the spur of the moment to counteract his talk of souls.

"Can I offer you," I said as we headed back toward the school, "another cigarette?"

"I'm only allowed three per day," he said with a rueful, slightly impish shake of the head that caused me to imagine a wife tut-tutting in the background. "I'd better not. Don't want to use up my rations before lunch!"

I drove out of the school parking lot feeling as if I needed a long hot shower and a profound, skin-tingling exfoliation with a spanking-new loofah. The image of sunlight raying iron particles through my blood, infinitesimal swords wiping out invisible dragons of fear, anxiety, and whatever that third thing had been, irked me greatly, as did the idea of the compass-scale holding in balance, not good and evil, but those two. . . . Damn it all to hell. My mother's ghost hovered just above me. I felt her breath on the back of my neck, smelled her lavender perfume in my mind's nose. Why did all the teachers in Bellatrix's school smell of lavender? Yet another mystery I'll never unravel. Luckily, the pain in my foot had abated enough to make driving possible, so I aimed the truck toward town to find out whether any mail had piled up in my box since the last time I'd checked. Also, I was hankering for a greasy diner breakfast with plenty of ketchup to drive away this succubus threatening to devour me in my own truck's cab. My mother couldn't abide the smell of bacon fat.

Well, at least Bellatrix seems happy in that place. They aren't hypnotizing her, to all outward appearances, or turning her into a zombie; and she seems to have a lot of friends. So that's all right, insofar as anything ever is. If I were her father, I suppose I would be delighted with her progress, her situation.

(Here I can't avoid confessing my horrid, treacly, hypocritical pleasure at being introduced to those schoolgirls by Bellatrix as "my dad," so prosaic and humble a word, so false and sentimental too. What was this pleasure? What was my brief but significant flash of envy when I imagined Otto's wife, so plump and fond? What was that? And why is my mother still hovering over me and causing me such horror now, so many years after her death, even still now, when I'm middle-aged and theoretically in full possession of my identity and powers?)

These thoughts will stay right there, safely contained, quarantined in those parentheses, while I return to a forcible account of my day to blot out the imminent arrival of Fag Uncle Tommy, which is gnawing at me like a rat.

Mail, there was none. Breakfast, there was in spades. I ate for several healthy men. My genetic predisposition toward a wiry physique allowed me to consume without a qualm a short stack of buttermilk pancakes with syrup and butter, a plate of eggs and bacon with potatoes, then a piece of blueberry pie, all gummy filling and Crisco crust. Five cups of coffee to wash it all down. My favorite waitress, with her quivering buttocks, was in fine fettle, refilling coffee cups with her soft dimpled hand, bestowing saucy glances everyone's way. It appears she's found herself a feller, by her attitude, by the swing of her hips. Her face looked abraded by kisses, the rough getting-to-know-you kind, not the perfunctory married kind. It only made me want her more, of course, to see the traces of some other man's having already been there.

(I wanted her, but to what end? What did I want, for that matter, with Stephanie? What game have I been playing with that child Louisa, and that other child Carla? I certainly don't want to be coupled. I certainly don't want some woman underfoot day and night; when is Sonia going to clear out? My own proclivities aside, I'm a bad prospect, given my life expectancy. To fuck, perchance to live—is that it? Where am I going with all this, and why am I asking these questions now, when I've doubted nothing in so many years?)

. . . those parentheses again, barricades . . . against what? Dams to hold what water back? Who am I trying to fool, or impress? No one ever. That is the point.

Apropos of nothing except that it occurs to me to write this, Hamlet always struck me as a neurasthenic little nancy-boy, stamping his foot with self-pitying outrage, a desire for vengeance that feels formal, manufactured, empty of blood-lust or love for his murdered father. I read his soliloquies with impatient boredom. No matter how beautiful the language is, there's no force behind it. He doesn't have the weight of experience to support such a terrible dilemma. I want to cuff him on the ear: Just kill yourself if you want to, and get on with it. Who cares? Just another rich kid with a distant father and a controlling mother.

It's really almost about that time.

As I sat in my diner booth alone before the wreckage of my breakfast, I beheld, as I seem to lately at this particular diner, someone I recognized going by outside the window, someone I didn't want to see. Today it was Marie's sister with her haughty airs and pretentious clothing. Today she wore a tailored black leather coat with a spray of lace spilling out around the collar and a shapeless crushed-velvet sort of hat. Her hair looked more ridiculous even than it did the night I crashed Marie's little dinner party. Her bangs slanted down over her eyes, and a small swath stuck out unbecomingly between the stupid hat and silly lace collar. I was irritated immediately just by the sight of her, and then became more so when, as I was about to look away and pretend I hadn't seen her, she caught my eye.

I nodded coolly, then looked away from her to gesture to the waitress, assuming Vero would keep going to wherever her destination might have been.

The waitress was, of course, not looking in my direction, and it took some doing before she finally acknowledged me. As she did so, the diner door opened and in barged Vero. She made a beeline for my booth. She wasn't smiling, and she didn't look glad to see me. She flung herself into the banquette across from me just as the waitress placed my check down on the table in front of me. The check fluttered a little in the air Vero displaced, but it didn't blow away.

"Hugo," she said straight away, "there's something I need to discuss with you."

"With me?" I said. "Aren't you supposed to be down at Kings College administering final exams right now?"

"That's all over," she said. "I'm up here for the holiday. And what did I just learn last night over dinner with Marie? My sister is seeing two men at once. The same two men Stephanie Fox essentially offered her at that dinner last month. Jim and Arnold. Anyway, Marie seems to think this is all just fine."

I raised my eyebrows, trying not to laugh. "And meanwhile you're not seeing any men at all, because she's hogging them."

"Please," she said wearily. "I'm in no mood. Not only is she throwing a perfectly good marriage down the toilet, she's setting an execrable example to my nieces and jeopardizing her chances at getting custody, if it comes to that."

"Our nieces."

"I beg your pardon."

"I didn't know anyone besides me ever used the word 'execrable' in the course of casual conversation."

"This is not casual conversation."

"Anyway," I said, "you're the one who's jeopardizing Marie's chances of getting custody, it seems to me, by telling her husband's brother about her affairs."

"But you want to help them preserve their marriage too," she said adamantly. "I could tell, at that dinner. You have to do something."

"What exactly do you imagine I can do? What sort of influence do you think I wield? And since when do Marie and Dennis have a perfectly good marriage?"

She nodded. "He's an insufferable fool, anyone with half a brain can see that, but he's the girls' father, and they deserve an unbroken home. When people get married they ought to stay married. It's an opportunity to work on themselves, but instead people just quit and go make the same mistakes again with other people. Life is not fun. God, Americans are such children."

I was struck again by how strangely and disconcertingly Vero resembles Marie. Her face is what Marie's might look like if a sculptor tugged all its features this way and that to render them less conventionally beautiful and more exaggerated. She's like the cartoon version of her sister. Where Marie is compact, rounded, femininely proportioned, Vero is long and a little gawky, her hands slightly too big, her shoulders broader than the rest of her narrow frame. I couldn't help thinking, with my always-on-the-lookout horndog appraisal, that if Vero let her hair grow out and wore something flattering she might be passably sexy, to someone else, of course, but at least I wouldn't wonder what her husband saw in her, if she ever got one.

"And you of course are not American," I said with some amusement.

"Not by temperament. And from the look on your face, you're probably thinking there's a reason why I'm not married, and you're right, but it's not what you're thinking."

"I wasn't thinking anything, necessarily."

"There's no man I've ever met that I could put up with for a minute, let alone all those years. Men are worse than women, and women are bad enough. Men are good for one thing only. I'm not a lesbian either. I just can't bear to have someone around me all the time."

"Neither can I," I said. "I see your point."

The look she gave me implied that I was a dung beetle not worth half a dram of the invective she might have crushed me with had she been so inclined. "This is horrible, what's going on with my sister, and now Dennis is apparently carrying on with someone, Marie says he told her, but he won't say with whom, only that he's in love with her and wants a divorce."

The earth opened up for a moment and sucked me down into some pit of hell, but then, after a split second, it spat me out again, and I was able to say calmly, "Their sex lives are none of our business, Veronique." I pronounced her name with as broad, nasal, flat, and American an accent as I could muster. "We're not their keepers. What do you care, anyway, about Marie's marriage? I don't believe you do."

"I'm not concerned about them," she said. "Those children are all that matter here."

Stephanie and Dennis! The whole idea hit me with the force of a nuclear aftershock. Not that I hadn't suspected.

"I don't buy that either," I said. "I think you're angry at your sister for . . . sisterly reasons. Far be it from me to discourage a reconciliation between her and Dennis, which I very much want for my own good, not theirs or their children's. At least I'm honest about that."

I handed the waitress some money, and she took it over to

the cash register, an old-fashioned silver, curlicued thing with keys as big and round as gumdrops that whirred and jingled as she put it through its paces. The cash drawer shot open with a brisk ding. My adversary and I were momentarily distracted by the fascination of it, but once the waitress had headed back with my change, Vero said crabbily, "I need a cigarette. I should have known it was useless to try to talk to you."

I wanted to ask her why she could ever have thought it would have been otherwise, but something forestalled me from pointing out the obvious—or, rather, deflecting someone with the usual self-loathing obfuscation. Instead I said, "I have plenty of cigarettes. Let's go outside."

Outside, windy, brisk weather had begun to prevail over the morning's calm. We ducked into a shadowy entryway and lit up, furtive-looking as we cupped our hands around the ends of our cigarettes to block the wind.

"I don't really smoke," she said.

This was a bald-faced lie. I know her kind: Vero belongs to that species of smoker who can't admit it but is a smoker all the same. The kind who never buys them, only cadges them, as if it didn't count to smoke someone else's.

"So," I said as we strolled along the sad, depressed old Main Street, past lawyers' offices and antique-store windows full of old lamps and antimacassars with yellowed price tags dangling from them, "Dennis is having an affair. I can't even imagine how he thinks he has any right to say a word to me about my own marriage and behavior. It boggles the mind."

"God, Marie irritates me so much sometimes," Vero burst out. "She's so self-righteous. Everything she does, she just does. She doesn't question herself. She judges me, but it never occurs to her to wonder whether or not I'm judging her, and why."

"Substitute Dennis for Marie and I know exactly what you mean."

"Since birth, she's been this way. Looking down at me and pointing a finger."

"They're born that way, the older ones. With a chip in their brains that blocks out self-questioning and new information. They're the guardians of the parents' trust. But they seem to think it gives them license to act in any way they want."

"We're expected to fall in, the minute we're born. No wonder we rebel."

"Is that what we do?" I turned to look her in the eye.

She laughed, a genuine laugh of amusement. "Hugo. Look at us. How old are you? I'm thirty-five."

"Forty," I muttered.

"Ha ha," she laughed.

"I don't see what's so funny," I said.

"Well, we are, really. The joke's on us. What have we done since we were born? Watched them, reacted to them. Listen," she added seriously, shifting gears as though her emotional workings had been recently oiled, "I do care about Evie and Isabelle, you're wrong. They're good bright sensitive little girls, and this is beyond upsetting for them. Isabelle has started to wet the bed again, and she's doing inappropriate sexual things in public."

"Like what?"

"Meanwhile, Evie is taking out a lot of aggression on Isabelle, punching her and tearing up her drawings and calling her names. Marie is a therapist, for God's sake, but she doesn't seem to make the connection. She thinks it's because of what those terrorists did. I think it's that, of course it's that, kids all over the country are reacting to that, but it is severely compounded for Evie and Isabelle by the fact that no sooner did madmen attack our country than their father moved out and their mother started acting like a slut."

"Their father makes crank calls to their mother to scare her."

"He does what?"

"He calls his old number and breathes into the phone when Marie answers and doesn't say anything, and then he hangs up. Or he gets the machine and doesn't leave a message."

"I always knew Dennis was a creep."

"He wasn't always a creep," I said. "Something happened to him."

"He's acting like a twelve-year-old!" said Vero. "Crank calls to his wife?"

"I've caught him doing it. And he denies it. He may not even know that's what he's doing. But it implies to me that he wants to go back but doesn't know how to ask. I'm sure Marie is fed up with him, though. Last time I was there, she said she was much happier without him, and she really seemed it."

"Well, whatever you may think about my motives here, I don't buy it for a second. It's only sex, and it won't last, because sex never does. I know Marie: she'll wish he'd come back soon enough. I know, easy for the childless to judge, but they should do whatever soul-searching and soul-baring is required to present a genuinely united front and discipline these girls strongly and appropriately, so they feel safe and loved and protected."

I had nothing to say to this. I was thinking that Vero was impossibly earnest and tiresome and I was glad she wasn't my sister. I felt glimmerings of empathy for Marie but kept them, wisely, to myself.

"I know I'm an 'eccentric childless academic spinster with cats,'" Vero went on in her earnestly tiresome way, "and I say this in quotation marks to put words into my sister's mouth, because that's exactly what she thinks I am, although she would never say it aloud of course, but even I can see what the problem is. I have tried telling Marie, but she looks at me as if I'm speaking Martian. She's not used to taking child-rearing advice from me, to put it mildly. I'm glad I sent Louisa up here to take care of them, but she's just a girl herself; she can't give them their father, and he's the one they want, incomprehensible as that may seem to us. Listen, I need another cigarette."

We ducked into another entryway and lit up again. Then we walked (she paced; I hobbled) up and down Main Street, smoking and talking, all hostilities suspended in the interest of our common goal, as if we were setting an example to our sister and brother of how this could be done.

"Why are you walking like that?" she asked me.

"Because I have Buerger's disease," I answered.

"I see," she said, not seeing a thing; people like Vero only need answers. They can't admit they don't understand when they don't, so they take all answers at face value and go charging ahead.

Without too much trouble, we came up with an agreement that this Christmas dinner would be brought about. Vero presented the idea to me, arguing that it might be most effective for general morale if the food were edible. Dennis and Marie would benefit from an evening in the same room together with their children in a congenial, warm, familiar setting, a setting that smacked of home, tradition, family history. She said this in a persuasive, velvety way that almost made me believe Waverley could be such a place if I squinched my eyes shut hard enough. So I agreed to cook the damn dinner, in part because I'd already decided to do it. It's my fitting final gesture, Hugo's last supper. Of course they don't need me to cook it; any one of them can do it. What they want is for everyone to gather, even the horrible Hugo, and they think they can get me to show up by playing on my vanity and pretending no one but me can stick a turkey or a ham in an oven and pull it out when it's done. This overwhelming urge to gather the whole club together in a huddle without any members missing to eat a large meal en masse is one of the many social instincts I've never understood.

"I'll help you cook," Vero added, almost as an afterthought.

"You can set the table. I don't need any help. Besides, do you even know how to peel a potato?"

"I know how to cook," she said. "Fuck you for assuming I can't just because I'm not married."

"Wait a minute," I said. "That's not why."

"I'm a fantastic cook."

"I'm sure you are."

"I am!"

"I have no doubt," I said.

Soon afterward, negotiations broke down and we went our separate ways. I went home and finished packing my "personal effects." For obvious reasons, I moved them all into the room in the "new wing" where Great-Aunt Charlotte hanged herself in 1928. Packing and moving took most of the early afternoon, but I finished sweeping out my old room and making the bed with fresh linen for Fag Uncle Tommy well before three o'clock. I was getting into my truck when a voice from the porch, Sonia's of course, said, "You don't have to pick her up, if that's where you're going, Hugo."

I looked up to see my wife standing on the porch, leaning against the railing, wrapped in a blanket, looking red-nosed and forlorn.

"Sonia!" I cried. "I see you've survived the bubonic plague. I don't mind, I'm on my way there now."

"No," she said. "Don't bother. Stephanie Fox said Bun would get her; she said he was planning to be over that way anyway."

"What do you mean, Bun Fox is picking her up? She doesn't even know him."

"She knows him."

"Well, I took her this morning, and she asked me to fetch her home again, and that's what I'm doing. If she's properly brought up, she'll know better than to get into a stranger's car."

"She knows him," Sonia repeated obtusely. "She's met him a couple of times."

Off I trundled as fast as my little wheels would go along the roads we'd traveled this morning; I was glad I'd paid enough attention to remember where the place was. I got there in twenty minutes flat, spurted into the parking lot, and careened to a stop. Children were trickling from the school building, and a couple of them were hanging around the school steps. However, there was no general melee and hullabaloo, as there had been this morning, which made me suspect I'd missed her. I scanned the crowd for a pale, pasty little dumpling and saw several, but none of them was mine.

I breathed some air and reminded myself that Bun has never actually molested anyone, according to Stephanie. Also, Bellatrix is not the kind of little girl who might easily be scared into keeping her mouth shut. She can't hide much, for one thing, and though she may seem like a cream puff, she's no cream puff. If he tried something on her, she would scream and bite.

In a moment, I decided, I would drive back along the road to Waverley as fast as I could, in hopes of overtaking them. Unless he'd already driven her into some wooded wilderness . . .

My heart beating unnaturally fast, I approached the kids on the steps. "Has Bellatrix Whittier gone yet?" I asked.

"She's still in the classroom," said one of them, a dark little girl I recognized from our introductions this morning. My eyes closed momentarily with relief. "Bella, your dad's here," another kid screeched as she raced into the school. Everyone else regarded me with idle curiosity. I smirked at them all. Score one for the Special Forces. Humbert was going to be very put out. I'd outfoxed him. I'd scooped his crumpet.

Just then, out came "Bella," carrying her violin case and wearing her goofy backpack. "Hi," she said to me. "Have a good vacation," she said to her classmates, beaming a little, try-

ing to seem casual, but obviously beside herself with relief that
her cynical scalliwag of a nonfather had come not only on time
but early, so she wouldn't have to wait unclaimed on the steps
like a loser. I shepherded her to my truck, one hand firmly on
her back, in case Bun drove up and tried to take her by force.

"Let's just sit here a minute," I said. "Bun Fox thinks he's
picking you up, so when he gets here we'll just tell him I came
instead. But I don't want him to think you were kidnapped and
raise a false alarm."

"Okay," she said blandly, then clambered up into my truck
cab and put on her seat belt. Little front-row sitter. I never
wore a seat belt as a kid, and I fought my mother every time
she tried to force me to wear one. It made me feel like I was in
a straitjacket, which I probably needed, come to think of it.

"Why is his name Bun?"

I got into the driver's seat, turned on the engine, put the heat
on, and found a radio station that was playing some Dixieland
jazz. "I think it's short for some other silly name," I said.

"Like what?"

"Bunting? Bartholomew? Bunderella?"

"Bungee cord," she said, laughing, her nose wrinkled.

"Bungee cord," I said approvingly.

"So aren't you going to ask me how school was today?"

"How was school today?" I asked with a sideways look of apprehension; I've never, to my knowledge, asked anyone that
before.

"Okay," she said. "I made two baskets in gym and played my
cadenza really well in orchestra and I aced my test."

"I'm sure you ace all your tests," I said.

"Yup," she said. "Sort of."

A few minutes later, the eager-beaver Bun Fox drove into
the parking lot in search of fresh prey in his sporty red child-
molester's car. I thought I saw that soft, black, shiny child-

molester's mole on his cheekbone gleaming through his windshield.

"Bungee cord," said Bellatrix softly.

I haven't bothered to hate anyone for a while. Dennis is my older brother, so the hatred I bear him is tinged with familiarity and some sort of nebulous but unbreakable blood bond. My feelings for Bun Fox are, for reasons I can't entirely articulate or name, pure. I hate him. Maybe because I fucked his wife and thought I loved her and she dumped me to fuck my brother instead, all seemingly unbeknownst to Bun, who is meanwhile still married to her. Maybe because I suspect he wants to molest Bellatrix, or any other little girl, and would if given the chance. And although she's not my daughter, I consider myself her—what's the word they used to use in the olden days?—protector? caretaker? My memory is failing me now too, along with everything else. But if not Bellatrix, he'll eventually molest someone else. If he ever has a daughter, chances are that he'll be unable not to molest her. Maybe he'll molest a series of little girls through the years, until he dies, or someone kills him. He's a potential creep of the highest order, a villain waiting to happen.

And I'm Bellatrix's . . . Interesting, that this should be the word my brain would snag on. Let's play a little game of jog-the-memory. It has something to do with custody but isn't "custodian," something to do with caretaking but isn't "caretaker," it's that legal thing when someone bears financial and often moral responsibility for a child. . . . I am her . . . guardian, that's it. I am her guardian.

So there I was, guarding her.

Bun maneuvered his car around and pulled up alongside my truck when he saw I wasn't going to get out to talk to him. We both rolled down our windows; then he said in a friendly and falsely innocent tone, "Hello, Hugo, apparently there's been a mix-up. I thought I was supposed to get your daughter from school today."

"There's no need, but thanks all the same," I said.

We locked eyes. In mine he may well have seen hatred, since I made no attempt to hide it. In his I saw frustration. I wasn't imagining it; I saw the shadow of it go over his face as if a cloud had momentarily hidden a moon somewhere.

"In the future," I said, "if I were you, I wouldn't offer to pick up any more little girls from school. Ever. Am I making sense to you?"

"What do you mean?" he asked, seemingly bewildered. "I didn't offer, I was asked."

"Well, don't get yourself asked any more."

"Hugo," said Bellatrix, annoyed, "quit being so weird. That's Uncle Dennis's friend."

"Bun's not his friend," I hissed at her out of the corner of my mouth, and rolled up my window and drove off with Bellatrix safe and sound next to me, although apparently not grateful for my interference.

"Hugo, why did you talk to him like that?" she asked, looking behind us at Bun's car, which was idling impotently in the parking lot. Maybe he was trolling for another passenger, maybe he was just a little shocked by what I'd said and was getting his bearings, maybe both.

I was filled with hatred. My whole torso was ballooning with it.

"It's a grown-up reason," I said.

"Since when do you care about not telling me things just because of that?"

"Just do me a favor and don't ever get into his car or in any situation where you're alone with him. Do you promise me?"

"How can I promise when I don't know why I'm promising?"

Although this was the kind of logic I would have used myself as a kid, I was now the adult, so I didn't have to take it. "Do as I say," I said. "I pay all your bills, including your violin lessons and school tuition. You're a kid, you take orders." I thought this was a good answer, but then a long, probing, clear-eyed stare from Bellatrix prompted me to blurt out impatiently, "He's a child molester. Okay? You're a child. There, now you know. You happy I told you?"

That shut her up.

In the course of the long ensuing silence, during which I have no idea what she felt because she didn't say, we passed the small ugly church on the main drag in Briardale. Dressed-up locals were spilling out onto the street, clogging up the traffic flow.

"Look," I said innocently, "a wedding." I was feeling a little mean and low for having told her flat-out that way, and I was trying to cajole her out of her funk. Girls liked weddings, as far as I knew, even prepubescent ones. It had something to do with imagining the far-off, dreamy day when they themselves would be got up like virgin snow-queen cupcakes and handed over to some undeserving lout. "Unusual, isn't it, to see a wedding on a Friday afternoon."

"Oh yeah," said Bellatrix.

I parked the truck across the street from the church and said, "Listen, Bellatrix, I'm sorry I said that about Bun Fox."

"Well, is it true?"

"Do you even know what a child molester is?"

"Yes. Is he really?"

"Well," I said uneasily, "from what I understand, he's trying hard not to be, but there's no sense in testing him, is there."

"You mean being alone with him in the car?"

"Right," I said carefully. How the bejeezus was I supposed to handle this conversation? I didn't want to have to say all this to a kid on her way home from school, but at the same time I couldn't not say it. "He might not, but he'd probably want to, so is it really worth taking the chance? Good lord, it's Carla. Carla's getting married. Look. She never told me."

"Who's Carla?" asked Bellatrix.

Carla was coming down the steps of the church in a white dress, on the arm of some thick-necked local lad in a tux, squinting becomingly in a hail of rice and confetti as several flashbulbs popped. Her hair was up, her face was alight. She looked as beautiful as any freshly married bride ever has looked, I would have wagered, in human history. I envied the groom in a completely impersonal but direct way. I didn't really want to be him. I didn't want to marry Carla. But . . . her face was illuminated with a kind of electric, radiant joy that's rarely evident on a dismal small-town street in the late afternoon on a winter weekday. And this young square-headed lad, a plumber in training by the looks of him, was its source, its keeper, its . . . guardian.

"She never told me," I repeated stupidly, to what avail I had no idea. Why should Carla have thought to mention that she was getting married? I was her customer, the crackpot who harangued her instead of going about his business, because he had no business to go about.

But what girl doesn't tell the whole world she's getting married? Her hairdresser, neighbor, bus driver, airplane seatmate, karate instructor, Bible-study teacher, mechanic, coffee purveyor, shoe salesman . . .

And so I now know that, despite the fact of our ongoing frequent conversations with only a counter separating us, cigarettes the ostensible link between us, I am no part of that "whole world" of Carla's.

I set out to detach myself from all of human interaction, to live apart and to be alone. It appears I've succeeded at my life's work; I have accomplished this, if nothing else. It has by no means been as easy as it first seemed it would be, or as simple.

December 22—Dennis hauled in a chopped-down pine tree and set it up in the living room, in the corner between the double doors into the dining room and the fireplace. With the three girls and a stepladder to aid him, he hung a multitude of glittering things on its boughs, enough to drive a flock of magpies mad. 'Tis the season.

Fag Uncle Tommy has come home to the roost. He arrived today in all his faded glory, like a bedraggled peacock who has lost neither his voice nor his self-satisfaction, just a few feathers, in Dennis's old sedan, fresh from the train and the city, riding with his head out the passenger-side window like a prissy floppy-eared purebred dog, an Afghan or a tall poodle. His longish white hair was blowing back in the breeze; his eyes were beatifically closed. Dennis and I carried his luggage (two old-fashioned steamer trunks, filled, no doubt, with crimson cravats, vintage maracas, and marabou mules) up to my old room while he swished behind us, thanking us, praising our strong backs, reveling in the old smells of home. "You have no idea," he said halfway up the stairs, "how wonderful it feels to be back again."

He does not look especially ill or weak to me, just old and lonesome and long past his nancy-boy prime.

"Lovely, my boys," he said to Dennis and me when we'd set his trunks down in his old room. He gazed rapturously around at my chair, my bed, my windows, my tree, then appraised us both with frank appreciation that raised my hackles. "And aren't you both handsome? You turned out rather well. As children you were a little peaky, both of you."

"That's because Mig starved us when we were sick, which was all the time," I said. "Dennis here would have died if Vivian hadn't taken pity on him and given him bootleg sandwiches."

"Hugo," said Dennis, "we don't need to bring up all this old history, come on."

"He was afraid she'd see the evidence in the toilet and know he'd been fed, and kill him. And when we weren't sick, things were not a whole lot better. We got food, but it was hardly edible."

"It wasn't that bad," said Dennis, master of denial.

"My brother's wife, Mig, was quite the little lunatic," said Fag Uncle Tommy with a gleam in his eye. "I always thought so. I never understood why he didn't strangle her in her sleep. She was pretty. But what a boyhood you two survived with her. Positively Dickensian . . ." He inhaled the room's peculiar, clean fragrance, an atticlike smell of dry plaster, old wood, and fresh air seeping in from outside. "I wonder how much time I have left." He cast another fond look at Dennis and me, standing there like a couple of numskulls with nothing to do or say, and added, "You are both remarkably handsome men, just like your father. I won't add myself, out of modesty."

"Welcome home," I muttered, and went away to my new, too-big, barely heated barracks in a garum funk. The ghost of my mother seems to be ever-present lately, hovering somewhere over my shoulder, just out of sight, but I know she's there. I understand that most men love their mothers with primal, unthinking loyalty and would defend them to the death. What I recall of mine makes me want to stab her ghost with an icepick: her hot breath on my cheek, the glazed migraine stare she fixated me with, her moans as I (so bored, so fucking, fucking bored) rubbed her neck until she fell asleep, sated and spent, the unspeakably horrific stains in her underwear I was required to remove instead of running around outside getting into neighborhood brawls like the other lads my age, the thin, watery Buchenwald soup, unsalted damp bread that stuck to the roof of my mouth. . . . She was creepy, my mother. Will I never be free of her?

Well, yes. Unless she's waiting for me in the underworld— Mig with a migraine in desperate, permanent need of me.

December 24—Still here. Not for long. I'm feeling bizarrely buoyant at the thought of leaving all this behind. In fact, I haven't felt this cheery in months.

Today I went in search of my erstwhile hit man for the first and last time in our lives. I drove to a former fine family home on a seedily empty street in Bayersville, down by the river, near a defunct train station. His landlady answered the door. She looks like a former stripper who invested her minor-league savings in an SRO and is living out her days renting single rooms to the kind of men who used to shove dollar bills into her sweaty cleavage. She opened the door in a tight sweatshirt and black stretch pants that showed her sagging abundance, her blond hair tied back in a leopard-print scarf, cheekbones high, eyes catlike, skin pouched, makeup festive.

"Hello," she both purred and growled, like a cat-dog hybrid.

"Mrs. Brewster?" I hazarded from the name by the doorbell.

"That's me," she said, arching her baggy throat and slitting her eyes. I half expected her to run her foot up the back of my calf. "It's 'Miss,' though. But you can call me Rochelle."

"I'm looking for a tenant of yours, Rochelle, if he still lives here," I said. "He goes by the name of Pete Stravinsky."

"Second floor, third room on the right. Go on up."

She shoved the door aside with her sneakered foot and allowed me to venture into the gloom of the front hallway, where I saw a plugged-in upright vacuum cleaner.

I went up the stairs as the vacuum cleaner roared to life. The stairwell smelled of mildew. I knocked on Shlomo's door, and he answered it immediately, as if he'd seen me drive up and heard the exchange downstairs. He wore an undershirt and pajama bottoms and had a white towel around his neck. He smelled of a vaguely froggy-went-a-courtin' kind of aftershave. His basketball of a stomach sat beneath his narrow chest and on his narrow frame as if it had been taken from the body of a larger man and surgically stitched onto him. He was smoking a cigar; his eyes were hooded under their transparent eyebrows.

"What the fuck do you want?" he said, gesturing me in. "I was about to take a dump."

"Don't let me stop you," I said hastily, backing out of the room.

"Just joking," he said, unsmiling. "Get the fuck inside so I can shut the door. I don't want that cat in heat coming in here and seeing me half naked. No telling what ideas she'd get."

"I think she's cute," I said jovially.

"All right." He scowled. "What's your purpose here?"

"Is this place bugged?"

He snorted and waved his hand limply, which I took to mean that I should sit down in the armchair he had gestured toward and speak without fear of unwanted listeners.

"I have a business proposition for you," I said, getting comfortable, or trying to. I waggled my foot, which was causing me some discomfort, to put it mildly, and concentrated on not screaming with pain. I fished my pill bottle from my coat pocket, found a pill, and was about to swallow it dry when Shlomo handed me a fifth of something without a word. I unscrewed the cap without looking to see what it was and washed the painkiller down with a big swallow that warmed my chest and made me cough a little. "Thanks," I said.

"By business I take it you're referring to my preretirement occupation," he said tonelessly.

"I want to discuss a couple of hypotheticals," I said. I coughed again, this time to cover a flutter of uneasiness at what I was about to do.

"Hypotheticals," said Shlomo. "I don't like hypotheticals. Never did. They don't smell right."

When he sat down in the chair across from me, a small puff of dust rose up around his head.

"You should let her in here to clean at least," I said.

"Hypotheticals," he repeated with distaste. "Of what nature?"

"First, a hypothetical sum of money."

He inclined his head with a gleam of monetary interest.

"Ten thousand dollars," I said. It was the amount I'd withdrawn in cash from my bank that very morning. During the transaction, to deflect any possible suspicion, I'd made pleasant chitchat with the bank officer, Merry Pratt, whom I'd known as a kid in grade school. We'd never had much to do with each other back then, so we had no reason not to be friendly and polite to each other. She counted out the enormous sum I'd requested without a flicker of suspicion, probably because I had mentioned offhandedly in the process that I planned to use it to buy a secondhand pickup truck with a plow in order to shovel the snow from Waverley's driveway. This fact clearly bored her so much she could hardly wait to be done with me. "A truck with a plow," she repeated dully, her eyes glazing over. "My husband always talks about getting one of those." The bank closed for the holiday at noon; she was clearly longing to get the hell out of there.

"That's a nice round hypothetical sum," said Shlomo with dubious approbation.

"Coincidentally or not, the amount Tovah offered you twenty-two years ago."

"And who do I gotta whack for all this bounty," he shot back on a careless exhale.

I told him briefly what I know about Bun Fox, how he hasn't harmed anyone yet, for all I know, but might.

"And how do you know he might if he hasn't yet?"

I explained about Stephanie, what she'd told me about her husband, and the look on Bun's face in the school parking lot. As I did this, I questioned to myself . . . not the rightness, morality, or probity, but the appropriateness of what I was doing. I disapprove of murder, first of all. Second, I don't care about anyone besides myself; I am an island, etc. Going against my deeply held convictions in order to prevent a possible wrong against people who are not myself is not at all in my line of behavior. However, death sharpens things. I didn't realize this until now. The knowledge that I am about to die makes everything look foreshortened, both less and more urgent, less and more ludicrous.

"So what's all this to you?" Shlomo asked, as if he were following both my spoken and my internal ratiocinations.

"He's a child molester, Shlomo. At some point in his long and scummy life, he's going to molest a child. At least one. That's not enough of a reason?"

"What child in particular, is what I'm wondering. My hunch is this is personal for you. You aren't the type who condones killing for any reason, you said that last time. Is this because he's married to the broad who dumped you to fuck your brother? Whatever, what do I know. Or give a fuck about, for that matter. This is just idle curiosity here."

"I hate child molesters," I said. "The particular kid's name is Bellatrix Whittier, but he could molest anyone."

"Same last name as you," he pointed out offhandedly.

"Not my daughter, technically," I said. "Listen, you can move into the gatehouse on my property. It's empty at the moment, but it would be easy enough to make it habitable. I'll charge you whatever rent you're paying to live with Maggie the Cat at the Shady Rest here."

"Why?" he asked. "Why offer me a house? What's in it for you?"

"I just thought you might prefer to live elsewhere."

"Altruism don't exist anywhere in the animal kingdom. What do you want out of letting me live there?"

"Maybe you'll keep an eye on Bellatrix. From a distance."

"Where will you be while my so-called eye is on the kid?"

"I might have to go away for a while."

He puffed at his cigar for a moment.

"This is very messy and not my usual thing," he said when his head was enveloped in smoke. "I don't like it. A hypothetical scumbag."

"Well, I think it's more expedient not to wait until he molests someone. Afterward, of course, you should stay right where you are and deflect all inquiries. Have an alibi, that sort of thing."

"I know how to do my fuckin' job," he said.

"All the information you need is in this envelope," I said. "Once you agree, I'll give it to you. Memorize what the paper says, then burn it."

"I know how to do my fuckin' job," he repeated.

There was a silence. I watched his face as he sorted it all out. He cleared his throat. "You have only his wife's word, though," he said. "Your sister-in-law the therapist never confirmed this, and no one else seems to know either. And his wife is now sleeping with your brother, not with you, if I got this all straight."

"Right," I said. "You're right, of course. But I know what I know. And I want him dead because I absolutely believe he's going to wreck at least one little girl's life, whether or not it happens to be Bellatrix."

I was a little taken aback by the urgency that overwhelmed me as I said this.

"That wife of his coulda made up the whole thing to make him look bad for her own reasons," said Shlomo. "She sounds like the kind of fucked-up bitch who would. Sounds like she needs whacking herself."

"Don't whack Stephanie, please," I said.

"Well, sounds like she needs it."

"Don't."

"Don't worry. No payee, no whackee, that's my motto." He made a blunt fricative sound intended as laughter and sucked on his cigar for a moment. "So they're divorce lawyers. They're lower than hit men. Lower than Rochelle down there. Foxes in the henhouse."

"Well, divorce is only part of what they do," I said. "But if he were to be, for example, shot in the back of the head in broad daylight in his office, one of his former clients might very well be suspected."

Shlomo and I exchanged a level look. He tapped the wet end of his cigar against the arm of his chair. "This is all very iffy. This is not even something I would have taken on back in the day. I don't like it. He hasn't done a fuckin' thing."

"What do you care what he has and hasn't done? Since when do you require concrete proof of slimebag behavior? And why are your sensibilities so delicate all of a sudden? Were you always this squeamish? Maybe that's why you were mediocre."

"Whaddya mean, I was mediocre? I was one of the best."

"You didn't kill me, did you?"

He sighed so hard I felt a gust of cigar-laden air against my face. "I let you go, you retard. I thought you deserved a medal for shtupping my fat cousin, not a bullet in the head for preferring that other girl. I let you go. You're alive because I had qualms. I had qualms about you same as I have qualms about this pal of yours right now."

"What were your qualms about me? I was guilty of what Tovah said I was guilty of."

"You were a wet-eared pup, and I never sent an innocent babe to the deep."

"What happened after I disappeared?" I asked. "I've always wondered."

"I told Tovah what she needed to hear. I was gonna make you a deal when you made it for yourself and got outta town. I watched you go. I saw how scared you were. But I didn't accept payment, 'cause I didn't deserve it. I told Tovah it was on the house, I couldn't touch her money."

"You let me go," I said. "Sure, you keep telling yourself that if it makes you feel less mediocre."

"I could get you right now, though," he said. "Now you're a proper scumbag."

"Don't do me any favors. Listen, are you in or not?"

He looked at some arbitrary point outside his window. "This is murder of an innocent human being you're talking about," he said.

I sighed, yawned, waggled my foot, shifted in the armchair, trying not to stir up any dust. Shlomo was not jumping eagerly at my offer, as I'd envisioned. These objections he was raising were tiresome and immaterial, and I had a lot to do and limited time left.

"Here's an opportunity for you to rid the world of one last scumbag, which you once told me you saw as your duty and calling, provided the money was right," I said.

"I believe I mentioned I'm retired," he said.

"You mentioned it," I said.

"Well," he said, "I'm retired."

"So you say," I said.

"I have a tidy sum in the bank as well."

"But ten grand more can't hurt."

"Ten grand more," he said with a slight sneer, "is not gonna make or break me, believe me."

"Ten grand is a lot of money," I said. "You don't fool me. I think you see exactly what I'm saying."

"What I see is that you want me to come out of retirement to whack an innocent man when I don't need the money."

"I saw it in his eyes," I said flatly. "You have one day to give me your answer." I got up to go.

"Not sure about the gatehouse offer," he said. "In terms of being linked to you. They might put two and two together . . . defeats the whole purpose. I ain't in this to get caught."

"This is not a negotiation we're engaged in; I'm hiring you for a specific job. I want you nearby, keeping an eye on Bellatrix. If you're as good at your job as you say you are, then you'll erase your tracks, you'll have an alibi, you'll do whatever hit men do so they don't get caught. Or maybe you can't do it. Maybe you're not as good as you think you are."

Shlomo brushed this remark away in midair as if it were a mosquito. "And maybe you're a shithead," he said.

"If this is too much of a stretch for your abilities, just say so and I'll ask another hit-man acquaintance. Someone a little more up to the task."

Shlomo stared fixedly at a spot above my head, his face twitching with rodent cunning.

"Living near you," he said, "I don't like it. I don't wanna be running into you all the time, having to make small talk, yadda yadda, nice fuckin' day, lovely fuckin' sunset. Fuck that."

"I believe I mentioned I'll be going away," I reminded him, inwardly clacking my heels together with glee. Victory was mine. "You will never see me again except once more, because you're coming for Christmas dinner tomorrow to meet the family, so they know who you are." Let him see for himself the high ceilings, intact plaster moldings, and fireplaces in airy rooms, the view down the lawn to the river, the ivy-covered brick-walled little garden in back. He'll be a hog in heaven there, live out his days in cozy splendor instead of in this dump.

I handed him the envelope I'd brought.

He opened it and glanced at the sheet of paper on which I'd written some information about Bun and the lease I'd drawn up for the gatehouse from a blank form I'd bought at a stationery store. He folded them and put them back, then counted the money that was there.

"Doesn't seem like such a negligible amount when you actually have it in your hands, does it?" I said.

"You couldn't jack up the price a little for inflation?" he wheedled.

"Take it or leave it," I repeated. "Here's the key; it's up to you to fix it up. I've done my part, now you do yours. I trust you, Shlomo. I don't know why."

"I don't know why either," he said. He boggled his eyes at me, and we shook hands.

I went out the way I had come in, without encountering the bewitching Rochelle, who was vacuuming the house's nether regions by the sound of things. Outside, it was already dark night, even though it wasn't four-thirty yet. This time of year, it always seems to be dark. Next order of business was to drive over to Marie's and borrow her roasting pan. The roasting pan at Waverley had been used as a sled thirty years ago by little Hugo and left outside to rust. No one roasted anything when I was a boy except beets and turnips, and those didn't require a pan big enough for the largest game birds and cuts of beef and lamb. And I saw no point in buying a new roasting pan when Marie had a perfectly good one I could borrow. Also, as it happened, I had a thing or two that I wanted to say to Louisa.

To my surprise, since things rarely go as I want them to, she was there alone; Marie was out somewhere with the girls. "Last-minute shopping at the mall," said Louisa, looking a little put out. She had beads of sweat on her creamy brow, and her red locks were blowsy around her face, curling like a medieval cherub's. "I said I wanted to go too, but she told me someone had to stay here to be here when the UPS guy comes with some package from her parents."

"Can't he just leave it inside the door?" I asked sympathetically, bustling behind her into the house.

"I know!" she cried as I followed her into the kitchen. "That's what I was thinking. But she said she doesn't trust them to leave it." While she futzed with something on the stove, a pot whose contents didn't smell entirely promising (a cross between pea soup and some species of curry), I looked curiously around. Shlomo's hooch had wetted my thirst.

Louisa added darkly, "She's being controlling, as usual."

"Trouble in paradise?" I clucked with avuncular dismay.

"Oh, you don't know the half of it. I'm sending out applications to schools right now and she won't give me any time to work on my personal essay."

"What's it about?" I asked, cheerful suddenly, having come across a bottle of fine vodka in the freezer. I splashed some into a glass with casual grace. "Your moment as a heroic antiterrorist whistle-blower? That's what I'd write about if I were you, especially in this current climate. There's not a school in the country that wouldn't give you a full scholarship, with a convertible and all the champagne you could drink for four years."

"Ha ha," she said bitterly. "Actually, it's sort of about that, I guess. The theme is the individual's personal responsibility in everyday politics. I've decided to major in political science. Who needs French literature? What does it have to do with anything?"

"Vero might have an interesting answer to that question," I said, "but I'm sure you and I would both disagree with it, each for our own reasons."

"But," she went on forcefully, not listening to me, "do you know, every day I wonder whether I did the right thing. Not in turning him in, I don't mean that. But running away. What am I doing up here? He might not have done anything to me.

Anyway, he's probably in jail by now. Meanwhile, my sister is driving my mother crazy and my father is working himself to death." She looked close to tears.

"Run out of town on a rail," I said. "I know the feeling."

"Think you'll ever go back?"

"It's too late for me," I said. "You can go back, though."

For some reason, she burst into tears at this. I did the only possible gentlemanly thing: I set my glass down, stepped forward, and took the distraught maiden into my strong manly arms. She sobbed moistly against my shoulder, stepped back, blew her nose into a hankie she whisked from inside her sweater sleeve, and smiled at me.

"Ecch, sorry," she said. "I might be premenstrual or something. I'm not always like this. Something you said just got to me."

"Listen," I said, "I'm here to borrow the roasting pan. This is the official reason for my visit. But there's another reason. I want to make myself very clear, because we'll never talk about this again, and neither one of us will ever say anything to anyone about what I'm about to tell you, do you understand?"

"I hope this isn't about something like blowing up the library," she said, rolling her eyes, which were still wet. "Because I can't promise not to tell on you, you know that."

"I promise, it's nothing like that. I have something to tell you, and you have to hear me out and not say anything until I've finished, and not get shocked or fly off the handle before you've heard the entire case I'm about to present; otherwise I'm not going to tell you any of it. All or nothing. Do we have a deal?"

"Deal," she said without hesitation (that's my girl!), so I told her about what I knew about Bun Fox. I told her only the things she strictly needed to know. I did not implicate Stephanie or reveal that I had fucked her or that she had told me about Bun's proclivities, just that I knew what they were and had no doubt whatsoever. I told her I had to tell her because I wasn't going to be around to protect the girls.

I could tell that she was shocked, but as I had expected, she was weighing the implications instead of reacting emotionally.

"Bun Fox loves Evie and Isabelle," she said when I had finished.

"Loves them?" I asked coldly.

"Well, he's really good with them. When the Foxes are here he reads to them and tells them stories."

"Don't ever let him in a room alone with either of them again. I mean it. If he goes off with one or both of them, you go too, I don't care what kind of excuse you have to make or what else you're supposed to be doing."

"I'm not going to be here forever either, you know—I'm eventually going back to school," she said. "You should tell Marie all this."

"She knows. She cured him. Or, at least, she thinks she did. She treated him."

"Marie was his therapist?"

"Yes," I said. "And so she already knows, but she thinks she worked her hoodoo and he won't hurt her daughters, or anyone's daughter. But I think she's wrong. However, I can't prove that, so there's nothing I can say to Marie at all. Hence, I'm telling you."

"Why not turn him in? You know, like, have him arrested?"

"Ah, Louisa, you are still so young and innocent," I said. "Because, if he hasn't done anything, there's nothing to arrest him for."

"Shut up," she said. "I'm not as innocent as you think. If he hasn't done anything, then how do you know he will?"

"I hope he doesn't," I said.

We stared intently at each other.

"I don't quite see what you want me to do," she said finally.

"All I want is to know that you know and that you'll keep

your eyes out for those kids. Bellatrix too. Otherwise I won't be able to go."

"I never even see Bellatrix," she pointed out. "Where are you going, anyway?"

"Away," I said.

She rested her forehead in her hand and tapped her foot briskly against the leg of the table. "I know what you're doing," she said.

"What am I doing?"

"Killing yourself," she said with a weird smile.

"Bingo," I said cheerlessly.

The weird smile turned into a grimace, a shaking of her lower lip, and I realized she was on the verge of tears again. "Oh my God," she said. "Why?"

"I'm dying anyway. I have a terminal disease. I made a deal with myself that when the pain got too bad I would put myself out of my misery."

"What does your doctor say?"

"That it's only a matter of time either way. Meanwhile, I'm taking synthetic opiates now for the pain; I don't want to be addicted to them for long." I held up my glass and took a good slug. "I've been planning this for a while. It's nothing sudden or hasty, believe me."

We both mulled a few things over for a moment. I could see that once again she was struggling to be objective and not react emotionally. For a woman with hormonal problems, this was truly heroic, and I wanted to kiss her with gratitude but didn't, because we'd been through this already.

"Now," I said when it seemed she'd had enough time to absorb what I'd told her sufficiently to return to the topic at hand, "listen, Louisa. Please don't quit your job and go away just yet. Please stay here a little longer. Dennis is a spineless shmuck, and he's the only other man they've got."

"And I'm supposed to do what, fight them all off with my

light saber?" Louisa asked sardonically. "I'm ready to pack up and hitchhike to the train station and go home where I belong right this second. What's stopping me?"

The doorbell rang.

"I have an answer for you when you come back," I said.

She went away and came back bearing a large cardboard box, which she set on the floor by the refrigerator with a heavy thunk. "Okay," she said. "What's your answer?"

"My answer," I said slowly, because I didn't really have one and hadn't come up with one while she was gone because I'd been too busy refilling my drink, "is this: you can't go home right now because you took this job and you're not finished with it yet. You have to honor your promise. This isn't a game. You already prevented a library from being blown up, now prevent something else bad from happening."

"Why me," she sighed with mock distress.

"That's my girl," I said.

"How long are you suggesting I have to stay here?"

"Just until the summer," I said. "Please."

"But after that, then what?"

"I can't ask you to give up your education just to watch over my nieces," I said, "but I can beg you to finish out the year you signed on for. Okay?"

She gave me a canny smile. "You're not so bad, you know," she said. "No matter how you try to come off."

"Yes I am."

"I mean it," she said. "Shut up. I would stop you, if I could, from doing what you're going to do. I don't know why, but stopping people from doing things seems to be, like, my specialty or something. But, you know, I can tell you've made up your mind."

"It is, and I have," I said. "I think you're an exceptional young woman, and I'm sorry I won't be around to know you. See you tomorrow, anyway." I kissed her on the forehead and rinsed my empty glass, left it upside down in the drain, and took my leave.

It occurs to me now that I've implicated Shlomo by writing down all the details of our arrangement here. So before I go I'll have to remember to rip out the offending pages, anything to do with him at all. Actually, I think I'll bury all these notebooks where they won't be found.

On my way home I stopped at Stewart's, where I asked Carla for a pack of a different brand of cigarettes just to prove the point I'd realized when I saw her getting married—namely, that I don't figure into her life at all, and she doesn't really remember me from one meeting to the next, let alone the brand of cigarettes I always buy.

She handed me the unfamiliar brand I'd asked for with a faintly perturbed expression on her moonlike face. "Since when?" she said.

"Actually," I said, inflating with joy, "just kidding, I'll take the usual. By the way, I'm quitting soon."

"Quitting smoking?"

"That's right," I said, and almost added "and everything else" but managed to hold my tongue. I don't want to go around dropping ominous hints, or someone will surely try to stop me—not Carla necessarily, but I don't want to get into the habit. Louisa I can trust not to try to stop me, because she's got a rare, tough-minded sense of tragicomedy. But in general it's the human way to try to corral everyone else to join into whatever activity or group you yourself are stuck in, whether it's a religion, parenthood, or life itself. I leaned on the counter and looked Carla in the eye. She blinked but held my gaze.

"Congratulations, by the way," I said. "If you were still single, I was going to get up my nerve to ask you out on my iceboat this winter, one lovely sunny day, but now I guess that's out of the question. Have you ever been on an iceboat? They're extremely invigorating. You would have loved it. We would have flown over the ice together; afterward we could have had cocoa and Lorna Doones. You could have worn a bright-red scarf, and I might have tried to hold your hand."

She stared at me, her mouth slightly open, quite lovely in her milky way.

"Well," I said briskly, "anyway, I hope he's worthy of you."

At this, I choked on something in my throat. It struck me that I was a little distraught. All the time I'd wasted mooning over a married divorce lawyer with unnaturally taut thighs, I'd thought I was impervious to feeling anything for this stolid local girl. Now I'd lost her to another, more perspicacious, if thick-necked and uneducated man.

"Anyway," I said, "best of luck to you, and much happiness, assuming there is such a thing."

"Um," she said, "I think you're talking about my sister. She just got married. When did you see her? Did you go to the wedding? We're twins, that's why the mistake."

"I drove by the wedding," I said. Her twin sister. "You were coming down the steps in your bridal gown. I thought it was you. You didn't get married? Really not?"

"Um," she said, twisting her finger, the one where a wedding ring would have been and where, I now saw, there was none. "No, not yet, I mean I don't even have a . . ." She flicked a sidelong glance at me. "Anyway, the guy's really nice, Lee, the guy Darla married. You didn't see me? I was there."

Another customer was awaiting her with a gallon of milk, several boxes of sugary breakfast cereals, and a package of mass-produced cupcakes with a cellophane window that flaunted their lurid pink-and-yellow frosting. Carla turned and rang it all up with her usual attention. Not overly quick, my girl, but careful, intent, deliberate, almost Zen-like in her apparent lack of frustration or impatience.

"Darla is your sister," I said with dizzy apprehension when the customer had tootled off with her bag.

"That's right."

"Carla and Darla," I said teasingly, almost tenderly for me (where was this coming from? why now?). "My heart was broken. Now I have hope again."

She twisted around to look inexplicably up at the video monitors. I sensed that I had upset her equilibrium in a way I found I liked, after all these months—or years, has it been? After all this time.

"Will you come out on the iceboat with me sometime this winter?" I asked her.

"Okay," she said skeptically.

"I'd like to take you to dinner afterward, if you'd like to go. An afternoon when the river is frozen, if it ever freezes again, given all the so-called climate changes."

"Okay."

"And you won't marry anyone else in the meantime?"

She looked at me and laughed. "You've got a lot of nerve, making me promise that. What if a millionaire comes in here and offers to take me away from all this crap? I might just say yes. I can't promise I won't. Can you blame me?"

Technically, I'm almost a millionaire and could easily take her away from all that crap, but I refrained from pointing this out, self-protectively: no sense in awakening her no-doubt latent gold-digging faculties with the news that I'm a catch, theoretically, or would be if I weren't already married, and if I had plans to stay alive and live a fruitful life, two nonselling points I was likewise not revealing just now.

"I see your point," I said, trying to seem crestfallen. "I can only hope and pray that the river freezes soon."

"Are you really quitting cigarettes?"

"Why?"

"I can't kiss a smoker," she said, smiling right at me.

At this, an erotic charge went off in my lower belly. "Boy Scouts' honor."

She gave me a look.

"And you're a Girl Scout?" I shot back. "Didn't you steal from the cash register and lose your job for a while?"

"Who the hell told you that?"

"Your uncle."

"He's a big liar," she said. "He told you that?"

"I asked where you were," I said, sorry I'd brought it up. "I missed you."

"You missed me?" She twinkled at this and then remembered. "I never stole. I did take money, but it was mine. He tried to shyster me out of fifty bucks in my pay, because he claimed I owed him for time he says I took off. He fucked with the time sheets from back a month ago and tried to make it look like my fault. He lost some money on the horses and thought he could just take it from dumb little me."

"He tried to cheat you."

"That's right," she said. "And when I fought him on it he suspended me without pay. But the trouble is, I'm not dumb. The trouble for him, anyway. So I told my father, that's his brother, and he had to threaten to kick the shit out of Uncle Evan if he didn't reinstate me with full pay and a bonus, even though I didn't even want the fucking job any more. But I came back. It's the principle. My father said, give it a few more

months and then I can quit and come work for him at the lum-
beryard doing accounts when Maud retires."

"Listen, you can try to change the subject all you want," I
said solemnly. "We have a date. Don't forget."

"I might," she said, "if you don't remind me. I got a lot going on."

"Of course you do," I said. Reading the tabloids! Listening
to talk radio! Teaching Sunday school! Restocking the baked-
goods section! Coming up with complicated theories to try to
explain the craziness of the world at large! If only I were the
kind of man who could court this girl with the proper degree
of passion and sincerity. She is a gem.

I went out to my truck with some of Dennis's recent swagger showing in my gimp and drove off lost in reveries of those
heavy breasts against my bony plate-armored chest. Maybe in
the afterlife, if there is a heaven, I'll spend eternity sailing over
the frozen Hudson with Carla, lying on our stomachs on the
small cushioned platform a foot off the frozen river with the
wind rushing into our faces, hearing the soft slicing of the three
blades against the ice, ducking our heads as the boom swings
across, the sail filling again as we tack downriver; heightening
the pleasure would be the anticipation of hot chocolate and
cookies, and then dinner at the Turtle Inn and of course sex afterward, but still hours of daylight away. . . . That is my idea of
heaven, I suppose, at least one of them, the one I'm most taken
with at the moment. What would sex with Carla be like? How
old is she, anyway? Her twin sister is evidently of a marriage-
able age, which around here could be sixteen, but now I'm
thinking she's twenty, or even older. Old enough for me—
which is to say, old enough for my end-of-life fantasies. I imagine her reclining luxuriantly, taking all the pleasure I give her
with the same divine, mute, womanly composure she brings to
her cash register, with flashes of her crackpot wit and opinion-

ated theorizing surfacing in the clutch of her hands in the small of my back as she positions herself just so under my pubic bone.

Later—I am now back from shopping for that damn Christmas dinner. The impossible Vero insists with humorless academic doggedness on making lists, accompanying me to butcher, snooty yuppie organic overpriced upscale farmers' market, bakery, supermarket, etc., giving unsolicited advice and opinions and directions all the while, which I ignore, and therefore she and I are embroiled in a passive-aggressive mutual disapproval that must make everyone think we're husband and wife. Indeed, we're an unintentionally hilarious parody of a married couple. Meanwhile, my actual wife has taken Bellatrix Christmas shopping somewhere, and Dennis is spending Christmas Eve with his wife and their children while his mistress is off somewhere with her husband, so we're all parodies of ourselves today. The illusion of family harmony reigns supreme, while upstairs in my old room Fag Uncle Tommy sits in my old chair in his tatty silk bathrobe with his hair carefully combed and his teeth in, and communes, I imagine, with the echoing afterimage of my old friend Erasmus, that either dead or departed-for-sunnier-climes maladjusted obsessive-compulsive bird.

Because the pack I bought earlier today was already gone and I was hankering for a chat with Carla, I stopped in again at Stewart's, leaving Vero to guard the groceries in the truck. Carla wasn't there, so I had to buy them off her villainous blockhead of an Uncle Evan. I wanted to box his ears, as they used to say in olden times, but didn't care to get involved in the family melee, not in that way. I am now consumed with a physical hunger for Carla's long gawky limbs, those delectable teats, her enormous head on its funny, erotic stalk of neck. . . .

When we got home I realized that I had left something in my old room, something important.

I left Vero unpacking grocery bags and went back to my old room and knocked on the door.

"Come in, door's unlocked," Fag Uncle Tommy called in a garbled voice.

"Uncle Tommy," I said with businesslike casualness, "I forgot to take a few things when I moved out of your room. Is it all right if I get them now?"

"Come in, dear boy," he said. He was sitting up in bed with a book propped open on his bony knees. He looked delighted at the interruption, a little human contact for a lonely old soul. I perched on the edge of my former favorite chair while he fluttered to make himself presentable. "How are things downstairs?" he asked.

"Chaotic and distressing," I said dourly. "You're not missing a thing. Where are all your male nurses? Why don't you have any?"

"Male nurses? I can still make my way to the lavatory and keep myself tidy, and I can still feed myself. I'm not ninety-three yet."

"But I thought your disease . . ." I began, then all at once I realized I had never actually been told that he was dying of AIDS, I'd simply assumed it because in my ignorance I thought that's what all homos died of. "Never mind," I added. "I lived in this room for many years. It's the nicest one in the house, and you're lucky to have it."

"Of course," he said absently. "What do you mean, my disease?"

"Well," I said, "on the phone I thought you said you were sick."

"Sick?" he chirped with a puckish twitch of his lips. "You mean AIDS? No, I'm just old and homesick, and the city isn't so easy when you're over a certain age." He pressed both hands to his sunken cheeks and chuckled. "You assumed, because I'm gay, of course. You are such a homophobe, Hugo. Aren't you cute. You almost belong to a different era; you remind me of those pugnaciously hetero blue-blooded boys running around Greenwich Village when they still called it that. Actually, now that I think of it, you remind me of my uncle Sebastian."

"Sebastian," I said churlishly. "Didn't he live in a tree house in California and chant all day?"

"Oh, but that was later, in the sixties, all that ecological mysticism. No, he was a real boys' boy when he was younger, like you. And like your father, also."

"You said you always wondered why he married my mother," I said. "Why?"

"I can't pretend to know why men choose any women, obviously," he answered shrewdly. "And your mother never liked me either."

"Just tell me, Uncle Tom. I didn't like her either."

"Well, first of all, there's a natural antipathy that exists, almost universally, between a coupled person and his or her partner or spouse's siblings, and vice versa. What do you think of your brother's wife?"

"I like her fine now that he left her," I said. "And he seems to like my wife more than is strictly brotherly."

"Well, you boys never did conform," he said. "But as for your father and me . . . I was the older, gay misfit, and Bim was the younger, golden boy who married the French beauty who turned into a beast. She was sweet enough at first, just a little flighty and demanding, until he got blown to pieces and she went off the deep end. I always suspected you boys suffered at her hands, but what could I do? She rarely let me anywhere near you lest I corrupt you, or something to that effect. I went off the deep end a little too when Bim died. I adored my brother madly. He was the shining star, really the sun, of my existence. From the moment he was born I knew myself to be eclipsed, but, unlike many boys like me, I didn't mind. I never had any hunger for the limelight, any wish to be other than what I was and am. He grew up to be everything a man should be, which neatly offset my own character, which has always tended to the secretive, shallow, and debauched. He was brave and strong and bright and proud and true. I should have died, not him, and I do mean that. I would have traded my life for his. It would have been the one noble gesture of an otherwise fatuous life. My goodness, you smoke a lot."

"Like a cigarette?"

"Oh, I haven't smoked in years," he said, wagging his head. "But why not. You make it look so pleasurable."

"It's not, trust me," I said, finding myself warming to this odd duck of an uncle of mine despite my admitted homophobia and strong native distaste for my own relatives. "Anyway," I said, handing over a cigarette and lighting it for him, then settling back into my chair a little more comfortably, "my mother."

"Mig," he said, and chuckled as he exhaled a stream of smoke. "Mig the Twig. Poor little thing, all alone in this big house with Vivian, who was a good person but quite out of her tree as well, and two little boys. You know, don't you, that Vivian was in love with your mother. Mig was very needy physically, very clingy and demonstrative. Apparently, on several occasions she asked Vivian to sleep in her bed, and although nothing overtly sexual transpired, Vivian blew this up into a love affair in her own mind. Of course, she knew it was all in her own mind, but that only made it more intense; you know how that works, I'm sure."

"How do you know all this if you weren't allowed anywhere near us?"

"After your mother died, Vivian and I met at the funeral. She sat next to me, and we began talking, as two old homos will, and when I asked her her plans for the future she told me she had not a clue what to do next. So, in an uncharacteristically generous mood, maybe because I pitied her for having had to live with Mig all those years, I offered to help her. And then, without too much trouble, I found her a job taking care of a bedridden friend of a friend, and a rent-controlled sublet in the Village, right near my place—the lease belonged to a friend of another friend who'd relocated permanently to Morocco, and she lived there forever. That was back when you could still hope to find a place to live down there. She never forgot my kindness to her. She and I had lunch together once a month for years until she died, and she always picked up the check. She was a great old gal, that Vivian, when you got used to her."

"I hope she didn't cook for your bedridden friend of a friend," I said. "And you don't have to tell me that my mother was physically needy. She practically molested me for years."

"Molested?"

"Well, she didn't pull my little wiener or anything, but she might as well have," I said tersely.

"I am not," he said compassionately, "altogether surprised. I always suspected she was particularly demanding of you, much more so than your brother. You were a sweet, charming little boy. I'm sure she took advantage. What a terribly fraught situation. I'm amazed you chose to come back and live here after such a childhood."

"With her gone," I said, "it's a nice enough place."

He chuckled knowingly. "And you've had the run of it for years. That must have been lovely. If you're not scared of ghosts. But you're not, are you?"

"No such thing," I said.

"Oh, please, they're everywhere here, the place is crawling with them. Well, luckily, they're all relatives, so I don't mind. Except for that creepy dead governess who was stabbed by the Swedish butler in my grandfather's day. Eliza someone. She's the only one I'm afraid of. But she stays over in the new wing, where you're sleeping. Along with poor Aunt Charlotte—poor Charlotte, who got knocked up by the dairyman, at least according to my mother. She was only fifteen; she couldn't face it. She hanged herself, you know."

"I'll collect my things now," I said, "if it's all right."

"Oh," he said, waving his hands magisterially, "by all means, go right ahead."

I stuck my head into the closet, waggled my hand around the shelf to the back, touched the wall, but couldn't find the packet I was looking for.

"Where did it go?" I said.

"You're looking for your bag of pills?"

"You have it?"

"I found it when I was unpacking," he said, reaching over to his nightstand, trying to disguise his disappointment. He handed over the bag. "This is an odd thing to accidentally leave behind."

"Well, it's my reserve supply," I said, as innocently as I could. "I thought it was in my Dopp's kit with the others, but then I remembered I had squirreled it away for when I needed it. I hope you didn't take any."

"I might have helped myself to one or two to ascertain their identity, but the rest of them are all here. My goodness, you have quite a supply. Hillbilly heroin, if I'm not mistaken, and I rarely am. Very potent, very nice indeed. Of course, you have to sniff it, once it's powdered."

"It's a legitimate painkiller prescribed by Dr. Schuyler," I said.

"For what?" he asked, concerned.

"For pain," I said tersely. "I have a foot condition. I'm not a drug user."

"Well, you are, but in fact you're using them in the way

they're intended to be used rather than abusing them wantonly like me—let's get our terms straight here. I'm sorry about your foot. But are you sure you can't spare a couple for a lonely old man in a tower?"

I laughed grimly and shook my head. "Unfortunately, Uncle Tom, I need them all," I said. "But alcohol is cheap, available, legal, and stimulating as well as relaxing."

"It's nowhere near as exciting as that stuff in the bag," he pouted. "Not by a very long shot."

"Well, maybe you can get your own prescription," I said, but not without affection, and a little while later I went away to manage my pain.

It's become so bad I'm using more and more pills now in daytime, which raises my resistance to them and makes me slightly fuzzy-headed despite their time-release properties, a double whammy of ill effects, and I need all my faculties because there's much to oversee in the kitchen. I'm sure Vero is putting things where they don't belong and causing no end of chaos I'll have to undo before I can think straight enough to cook. Have tried on numerous occasions to get rid of her and send her to her sister's, but she sticks to me like a burr. If I had any ego left I'd suspect her of harboring a crush on me, but the fact that writing these words makes me laugh indicates this is every bit as ludicrous as it appears. No, there's something else going on. The family has appointed her to make sure I really go through with the damn dinner? Maybe.

Time to go and restore whatever she's disarranged.

On my way downstairs I ran into none other than my horse's ass of a brother, who was up on a ladder in the stairwell replacing a light bulb.

"Hugo," he said importunately as I attempted to sidle by, "could you hand me that bulb there?"

I knew full well what bulb he meant, since there was only one that I could see, but didn't want to make it too easy for him. "What bulb?"

He pointed, I affected to look, picked it up, and handed it to him, he got back to work, I attempted once again to sidle by.

"How's dinner coming along?" he asked.

I looked up at him. "We haven't started cooking yet," I said patiently.

"Well, I know that," he responded with good cheer. "I just mean, how is it working out with Vero?"

"Who assigned her to me, anyway?"

"What do you mean?"

More back and forth until he realized I wasn't backing down.

"Marie thought you could use a hand," he said.

So Dennis and Marie were getting along well enough to conspire. This was interesting news.

"Are we being set up?"

"Of course not," he said. "Neither of us would wish either of you on each other."

"You know she talked me into cooking this dinner," I said, "when I 'happened' to run into her the other day. Was that a setup too?"

"There is no setup," he grunted, and tossed down the burnt-out bulb. I caught it in spite of my determination not to. "Well, except apparently in the other direction. Marie said you and Vero are trying to save our marriage. She said Vero told her you agreed to cook and host this dinner for the good of our daughters. You should save your energy in that case. We've pretty much decided it's over."

I sputtered ineffectually for a moment, genuinely embarrassed. In that moment I felt exactly like Dennis, transparently caught in the act. "Listen," I said, "she's the one who came at me like a chattering squirrel when I was just sitting there minding my own business and trying to finish my lunch. All I agreed to do was cook a meal. She's all fired up about the good of Evie and Isabelle. You know how she gets."

"All I know is, for a while I thought there was a chance for reconciliation, but we've both moved on, and we're with other people now, and this is the way it ought to be. So now you know, and you can continue to mind your own business from now on."

He climbed slowly down from the ladder with his left hand on his lower back, grimacing.

"Looks like your acrobatic sex life is taking its toll," I said, in spite of my determination not to bring up anything to do with Stephanie.

He didn't respond to this. Instead, he folded up the ladder and tucked it under his arm and began to carry it downstairs.

"How did you like the ending of the book?" I asked his receding back.

He barked over his shoulder, "Which book?"

"Anna Karenina," I said.

"I couldn't finish it."

"Why not?"

I followed him the rest of the way down to the first floor, waited while he stowed the ladder in the closet under the stairs and mopped his brow, and then followed him into the kitchen, where Vero was scrubbing the floor on her hands and knees, her hair up in a babushka-style head scarf that did nothing to flatter her angular face.

"Why couldn't you finish it?" I asked again.

"Well," said Dennis, at the sink with a glass, filling it from the tap, "although it's an undeniably great and immortal novel, one of the greatest ever, I can't stomach it when I sense that an artist knows how a work will end from the outset, whether it be a novel, a movie, a piece of music, or a painting. I require a sense of mystery, discovery, and surprise; by which I mean to say, the artist himself—or herself, of course—"

"Gee, thanks," Vero called up from the floor.

"—should not show his or her hand. I need to feel a sense of collaboration—as an artist, maybe—nonartists may not feel this way when they read or watch or see a work of art. But for me, knowing that Tolstoy sees Anna's death from the very first sentence causes me to lose interest."

"What if," I said, "I told you he'd changed the whole work over the course of many years? Revised it from top to bottom? He intended Anna to be a blowsy, coarse, voluptuous adulteress, but in spite of his best intentions she came to life under his hands. She was transformed from that rude fishwife of her creator's intent into the sophisticated, beautiful woman we all know and love, in our way, although she also has certain shallow qualities, that carapace of obliviousness that makes her more complex than if she were a heroine pure and simple."

"Well, judging from what I've read," said Dennis, "Tolstoy seems to be didactically killing off his heroine because he doesn't approve of adultery. Punishing her. Meanwhile, who can blame her for choosing Vronsky? Not me. Do you? Why should she die because she makes that choice?"

"Don't take it so personally," I said.

Dennis drank the glass of water in several manly gulps while Vero ignored both of us.

"Vero," I said, turning to her, "what the hell are you doing?" She ignored me.

"She's scrubbing our kitchen floor," said Dennis.

"But it's clean," I said. "She's scrubbing the floor as if no one had washed it in seventy-five years. I myself mopped it two days ago. Vero, this isn't necessary. In fact, it's intrusive. And what is that thing on your head?"

"I don't mind doing this," she said obtusely. "It'll be much easier to cook this meal if the kitchen is spotless."

"It's spotless already." I gave her an exasperated look. As I said, things had not gone smoothly earlier, in the markets. I consider myself the boss of this meal, but apparently Vero thinks otherwise. She seems to assume that she knows better than I which vegetables are freshest. Then there was the gravy squabble. I told her, in the appropriate aisle, having added several packets of turkey-gravy mix to the cart, that I make it from this mix, to which I add defatted drippings. Packets of mix make better gravy than from scratch with flour and fat. Vero refused to allow this as a possibility. What followed was a strained argument too tedious to reproduce here in this journal.

"It can't hurt to wash the floor again, can it?" she said now.

"If you want to waste your time," I said.

Dennis refilled his glass and slunk off in the direction of the back porch. I gave Vero one more grim look and followed Dennis; our conversation, now that I thought about it, was not over yet.

He stood on the crowded little kitchen porch and pretended to study the defunct kitchen garden, which in the decades since Vivian's departure has settled into a sort of democratic free-for-all; it looks completely wild, but in fact over the years I've sneakily cultivated certain of the weeds and routed out others. Occasionally I pull many gloved handfuls of nettles and make an excellent soup out of them; the dandelion and mustard greens are all right in salads, and the wild onions will do in a pinch instead of store-bought, although they're very sharp-tasting, so they have to be cooked longer. Nasturtiums, violets, and roses grow along the borders; a smattering of their petals is just right in these wild salads. Every year I stick a few carrot, parsnip, and turnip seeds into the soil so there are homegrown roots to add to soups in early winter. The idea, I suppose, is that there's always something to eat around the place. Never mind that these are exactly the same vegetables I was force-fed as a boy by we-all-know-who. When I cook them, they behave entirely differently, and it's entirely possible that I cook them because of this, as yet another form of exorcism.

Nettle soup . . . so simple, so bizarrely delicious. A big basket of the tender heads of nettles (not too many flowers) gathered from a clean garden with well-gloved hands, washed clean of grit and bug piss, set aside in a colander. Sauté minced onion and diced peeled potatoes in olive oil. Add the nettles, stir, and cook for a few minutes. Add enough chicken broth to cover plus two inches, boil lightly till the potatoes are soft, purée, then add salt and pepper, nutmeg, cream. I always have a slight, amazed contraction of the palate at the first spoonful of nettle soup, as my eyes roll back in a culinary swoon. . . . Nettle soup tastes like a concentration of powerful green. Nettles, which raw are terrible to touch, are rendered superbly edible by boiling, so tender they melt on the tongue with a rich, faintly fishy, multidimensional flavor. Maybe it's the Waverley soil; maybe they aren't as good elsewhere. I'll never know.

It was very cold out there. I hunched in my shirtsleeves and said to Dennis, "By the way, I rented out the gatehouse. I may have neglected to mention to you that I was doing so. It's much too nice a place to stand vacant. I was planning to move down there myself, but this seems to be a more elegant solution since you say you're moving to the city eventually. And he said he'd make it habitable again."

"Who said he'd make it habitable again?" Dennis asked testily.

"Oh," I said, "our new tenant. He signed a lease today. Pete Stravinsky."

"Pete Stravinsky? Who the hell is Pete Stravinsky? Since

when are we renting out the gatehouse to strangers? It's not as if we need the money. Why did you do this without talking to me or Uncle Tommy first about it?"

"Look," I said, "down there. Is someone breaking into the tool shed?"

"That's Bellatrix," he said. "As you well know. I sent her down to get some hooks so I can hang the wreaths and pine boughs."

"Well, it might have been an intruder. And the more eyes we have around the property, the better. Since when do you give orders to my kid?"

"Since when is Bellatrix your kid? I thought you disavowed all blood ties."

"She's not related to me," I said, "but she's my ward, and I'm her guardian, not you."

A strong wind came up from the river and ruffled the sparse, paltry rows of weeds in the garden, and continued up to the porch to lift Dennis's and my hair from our brows. We Whittier men do not go bald. Lack of testosterone, I would say, except that we both seem to have an unhealthy surfeit of it.

"The last time there was a Christmas tree at Waverley," I said, "was 1977."

"Wrong," said Dennis. "It was 1978. You were gone, but we had one anyway. The world didn't grind to a halt around here just because you ran away from home, you know."

"Just you and Mother, alone at Christmas together? How cozy."

"And Vivian, and a couple of friends of mine from school. Where the hell were you, anyway?"

"New York," I said airily. "Then I went elsewhere. I worked my way around the world in the gigolo and drug-running trades, you could say."

"Right," said Dennis, obviously not believing me. "Someday, Hugo, maybe you'll learn how to answer a question directly, like a grown-up."

"Gosh," I said, "do you really think so?"

"No," he said shortly.

Bellatrix came running up the lawn in her blue puffy down coat, her legs knock-kneed and ungainly, her expression earnestly intent on not dropping whatever was in her hand. She trampled through the sodden garden and tracked wet earth up the steps to the porch. "Look," she said to me once she was within easy earshot, "I found this in the shed."

She opened her hand and showed me, ignoring Dennis.

"Well, look at that," I said.

Dennis and Bellatrix and I peered together at the stoppered test tube in which, one winter day when I was about Bellatrix's age, I'd preserved the dead litter of mice I'd come across. They were still there in a cozy row, their tiny pinkish-gray snouts and paws pressed against the glass, their fur as crisp and fuzzy as if they'd just been licked clean by their mother.

"Oh, for God's sake, I thought I made you get rid of that," said Dennis, and went back into the house with his empty water glass.

"He didn't think much of that back then either," I said. "That's why I had to hide it."

"What is it?" she asked.

"Dead baby mice in a stoppered test tube."

"Chuh," she said in a singsong, evidently some contemporary expression of childish scorn. "I mean, why did you make this and hide it in the shed?"

"How did you know it was me? I mean, rather than Dennis, or someone else who grew up here?"

She gave me the glance equivalent of "chuh."

"Well," I said, "I had test tubes in my chemistry set, which every kid had back then. We all got them for Christmas. They came with chemicals, real ones, glass test tubes and beakers, and Bunsen burners. Back then, you know, no one wore bike helmets either, or knee pads. Nowadays there's nothing like that, it's all safe and fire-retardant and shatterproof, I imagine because of lawsuits and child-safety laws and everything else. We could make horrible smells with those chemicals, mix them and cook them and cause explosions and messes. That's all a chemistry set was really good for; I don't think anyone actually learned anything about chemistry. Anyway, I found these mice one day, dead, in the ballroom fireplace, and thought I'd see how long they'd last if I kept them like that."

"How long have they lasted?"

"About thirty years," I said. "It's amazing how fresh they look. You found them on the shelf where all the nails and screws are, right?"

"Yup."

"So no one found them all those years."

"Maybe someone did, but they were so grossed out they didn't want to touch it. There's all kinds of weird stuff in that shed. I hate going in there."

"Did you get Dennis his hooks?"

She gave me another look. "I forgot. Can I keep this? Or just bring it to school to show my friends? I promise I'll take care of it."

"Don't let anyone steal it," I said.

"I swear I won't."

"Guard it carefully."

"I will."

"You can have it."

"Do I have to go back down there and get those hooks for Uncle Dennis? There's all these spiders."

"You're scared of spiders but not this test tube full of dead baby mice?"

In the end we went down to the shed together, I found the

hooks, and then she scampered off with her prize to deliver the little box to my brother. And I went alone up to my room to write, which I am now almost finished doing. I've been contemplating all along as I've written, like a nagging itch, a phantom pain, the fact that Vero, that awful woman, is mucking about in the kitchen downstairs. Well, I gave up the test tube, the talisman from childhood; but I have to acknowledge now that I've decided to relinquish everything: my kitchen and its arcane, inscrutable, essential order, its cupboards stocked with late-night supper ingredients, its garden, tended for so long, and these notebooks (I'll burn them, I think, or bury them under the floorboards in my room), and my own body, which will likewise be either burned or buried, I don't much care which.

December 26—This will be my last entry, and then my life is done. Or, rather, undone, by me. *Et Dieu sauve le remenant!* Christmas dinner is over; it's two in the morning of the day after, Boxing Day, the last day of my life, or, rather, the last night. I won't live to see the dawn. (There's an odd pleasure in writing that—I realize I've always wanted to say it.) I've lined up all my ducks in a row, the dinner has gone off, and the dishes are, for the last time, all washed, dried, and put away where the will of God dictates (to me, and apparently only me) that they belong.

On Christmas Eve, after all the traditional present-opening-by-the-tree-in-the-firelight shenanigans were completed (during which I stayed writing in my room; I neither give nor receive gifts and made this clear to one and all) and the rest of the household had gone to bed, I went to Sonia's room, knowing this would be my last crack at a pastime that has afforded me some of the greatest pleasure I've known in my life.

If I stay alive longer and keep smoking, I will very likely lose my ability. . . . Unthinkable.

I took all the pleasure from her I could and allowed her to

have some too, and afterward she lay in my arms, breathing into my neck without talking on and on, something she has never done.

Then she fidgeted, sat up, and began to yammer at me. It was time to shut her up with food. I escorted her downstairs, lit candles in the silent kitchen, and opened a bottle of a robust, spicy Spanish wine I'd been saving for a special occasion. To make onion soup properly takes time, so I took time. I found in the root bin four good—not moldy or sprouted; the skins have to be papery, dry, and blemish-free—medium yellow onions, cut them in halves, and sliced them thin, then sautéed them in butter and olive oil for nearly an hour, with a little sugar and salt sprinkled on them, until they caramelized and turned slightly brown. "Consider the onion," I said as the onions sizzled in the pot. "A perfect white globe of many tightly packed layers wrapped in parchment paper and secured at either end. It's a perfect world unto itself, pearly white and beautiful to hold and look at, cool to the touch, firm, and unscented until you cut into it—then it releases its sulfur, and makes grown men cry."

"I do not cry when I cut onions," said Sonia.

"Well, you, of course not," I said. "It's a paradoxical root, the onion. Did you know that, thousands of years ago, the Egyptians buried their pharaohs in their tombs with small onions in their eye sockets? They were a sacred symbol of eternity."

Sonia leaned her head on her hand and watched me, evidently having become used to these little food lectures of mine, so she no longer tries to redirect and reclaim my attention with her narcissistic wiles and tactics.

"They were also the subject of sacred art: Egyptian painters painted onions on the insides of pyramids. There was a small sect of Egyptian priests who were forbidden to eat onions, no one is exactly sure why."

"Priests," said Sonia, "do all sorts of things and no one understands why."

"In Pompeii, onion sellers had to form their own guild, because the other fruit-and-vegetable sellers rejected them. But in Pompeiian brothels, the onion was highly valued, down in the places where the underworld could meet the elite, as the song goes, where the snobs and the onion eaters intermingled. Archaeologists found a basket of overcooked onions in the ruins of one of the most popular whorehouses in Pompeii."

"Speaking of overcooked," said Sonia. "You'd better stir the pot; I think I smell burning."

"Alexander the Great fed his troops onions to make them strong, on the theory that strong food made strong soldiers."

"Strong food," said Sonia, "makes strong breath."

"Onions were considered peasant food until the Middle Ages, disdained by the rich, possibly because the peasants ate them raw with bread and beer as a staple diet, so the rich considered them rough and insulting to the nose and suitable only for those who didn't care what they smelled like, but in the Middle Ages onions became worth their weight in gold. Charlemagne ordered them to be planted in the royal garden, and they were accepted as payment for land. And of course they had many other uses. The superstitious used strings of garlic and onions to ward off vampires."

"My mother hung garlic to ward off vampires," Sonia said, sniffing with the special brand of disdain she reserved for her backward family. "And her mother, and so on all the way back to the medieval ancestors who knew nothing. They still know nothing."

"And did you know that, in a certain small town in Texas whose name escapes me, it remains to this day against the law for young women to eat raw onions after six o'clock in the evening? Cooked onions, no problem, but one nibble at a raw Vidalia will send any *chiquita* to the slammer for the night."

"Isn't that interesting," she said absently, still caught up in all-encompassing scorn for her native land.

"In ancient India they used onions as a diuretic, and to benefit the heart and other organs, even as the Brahmins turned up their noses at them. And people now believe certain compounds in this cheap common little root fight cancer. Meanwhile, there's a religious group in Paris with a few thousand followers who call themselves the Worshippers of the Onion. Mystical, curative, legislative, aesthetic, culinary . . . it's a powerful little orb. A sulfur-breathing dragon packed into a pearl that becomes sweeter and softer the longer you cook it, the longer you expose it to the heat of the fire."

"Very poetic, Hugo."

"Thank you. I think so too."

I poured a half-cup of dry red wine over the caramelized onions and brought the whole thing up to a boil, then down to a whispering simmer; when the fumes had burned off, I dumped in a thawed quart of beef stock from the stock I made and froze a few months ago. I added several shots of Worcestershire sauce, salted the broth to taste, and let it simmer undisturbed while I toasted slices of firm, crusty French bakery bread, so different from the cheap supermarket sponge tubes that are half air. I ladled the finished soup into sturdy bowls, laid two slices of toast on top of each, smothered them with thick slices of pungently nutty Gruyère, and ran the bowls under the broiler for about five minutes, until the cheese was bubbling and brown, and the toast had soaked up a little of the savory, oniony, buttery broth.

We sat across from each other at the kitchen table and opened our napkins. I lifted my wineglass and looked at Sonia through the candlelight and gazed long and hard at her, sitting there in her robe with her hair loose and her face naked and rosy, and said, "To a long and successful marriage."

"We never saw each other through most of it," she protested.

"That's why it's been so successful," I said. "And long."

She laughed as we clinked glasses. It was possibly only the fifth time I've ever heard Sonia laugh.

As we ate—or, rather, as Sonia gobbled her soup like a starving dog the moment it was cool enough, and I took judicious, appreciative bites of cheese and toasted broth-soaked bread interspersed with spoonfuls of slippery, savory onions—I found myself saying with untoward calm, "Sonia, now that it's over, we've been through it, and here we are, tell me: who is Bellatrix's father? Doesn't she have a right to know?"

She stopped eating and looked squarely at me. "Let it go," she said. "Just let it go. You are my husband and she is the child I gave birth to during our marriage, and so you are her father, Hugo, and you should forget this whole question of who, who, who. Does it matter, really? Does it? That was very cruel of you to say all that in front of her. She might be scarred by it forever."

"Bellatrix," I said, "does not scar easily. And blood is thick. Someday, when she's older, I hope you'll tell her who he is. She has a right to know. If I were her I would want to know."

"If I were her I would want my parents to get along, and for my father to acknowledge me as his child."

"The truth," I said. "That's what matters."

"The welfare of a little girl is what matters," she countered.

"And the two are not at all mutually exclusive," I said. "Just remember, someday, that I wanted her to know, all right?"

"How can I ever forget if you're always reminding me?"

"I'll stop now," I said. "I promise, this is the last you'll hear of it, if you promise to tell her someday."

"Hugo," she said wearily.

I knew from long experience that this was the best I was going to get out of her in terms of a promise, and any more cajoling on my part would only backfire, so I subsided.

After we had drunk the wine and eaten the soup, we went

up the stairs together. She paused before we parted ways and looked at me. "Come and sleep with me," she said. "Just to sleep."

"I can't," I said.

"Why not."

"Because I'm crazy as a coot," I said.

She didn't laugh at this, but she smiled slightly, and so I parted from my wife with some warmth, and more understanding than I ever expected from her.

This night is very quiet. The house has a sort of warm and postfestivity smell of roast meat and flowers and perfume and extinguished candles. Loud in my head are lines from a poem by a teenage girl who had no idea what she was talking about but got it right anyway: "I feel no haste and no reluctance to depart; I taste merely with thoughtful mien, an unknown draught, that in a little while I shall have quaffed." I see I've dropped, for the first time in so many years, my stance of self-protective mockery. What would be the use of it now? There's no one any more to keep at bay and no thoughts I don't want to confront, no feelings too large for my formerly small but suddenly enlarged canvas. The inside of my head is very quiet. Montaigne is with me, as I knew he would be, at the very end.

These words of his resound as if he'd said them aloud to me, maybe because I translated them myself in my clumsy way, maybe because I believe them and have taken them to heart: "The most beautiful death is the one that is most willed. Our lives depend on the will of others; our death depends on our own."

I strove, above all else, to make my life independent of the will of others. Looking back, I see that in a sense it consisted of little else. . . . Well, it could be posited that my years of solitude were lived in reaction to the will of others, which is to be together. The will of others is the flour that binds the gravy.

Hugo waxes philosophical one last, excruciating time.

I have never, in my entire life, experienced Martin Buber's much-vaunted I-Thou relationship with any form of God. There's no Maker I'm going to meet. My inhabitance of this body and this mind was an ever fluid and shifting trance, but I was always aware of some core, inviolable thing in the pit of my stomach, the thing that I most trust and rely on but which I can't keep, and which isn't mine or me, again a contradiction, a wordless but constant knowing. . . . There's a theory that there's a brain in our intestines. My godlike intestinal brain has informed me all my life of the things I had to do. I never questioned it, and it served me well. I took responsibility for myself at every turn, never laid claim to more than my lawful and natural due, took pains not to inflict my self-loathing on others except as strictly necessary, or for their own good. This finer point was likewise determined by my intestinal brain; I've never knowingly caused harm to another person. Telling Bellatrix I'm not her father doesn't count because I'm not her father, and if I were, I wouldn't feel so free to take myself out like this. The sooner we all were clear about the truth in this matter, the better.

I am glad I lived alone. Human bonds and bondages tear at the fragile fabric of each self: betrayal, misunderstanding, heartbreak, loss, anger, grief. We can't be both true to ourselves and in some sort of relationship to each other, and in almost every instance, minute and overarching, one or the other has to give. I chose what I chose; other people choose otherwise.

Vero turned out to be, to my surprise, an effective sous-chef. Cooking an enormous holiday meal is not difficult or complicated, but it does require a certain lightness of touch and finesse with timing and proportions. Vero has neither, but she can follow orders when she suspends her know-it-all arrogance and simply does what she's told. Of course, I had to beat her about the head with a pair of wooden spoons—no, actually a few sharp words did the trick. Some women are full of hot air but the minute a red-blooded man barks an order they turn as meekly submissive as any geisha, as if that was what they secretly, really, truly wanted, and all the rest was just bluster. . . . Vero is one of those. She arrived promptly at two on Christmas Day. "Cut these," I said to her, and she cut them. "Smaller," I said, and she cut them smaller. Meanwhile, I moved efficiently from counter to sink to refrigerator to cupboard to pantry to oven. . . . I made a ham with holiday sauce and Cornish game hens. Throughout the afternoon of cooking, we spoke little and kept our own counsel. Just before everyone arrived, when the ham was baking, the potatoes were ready to boil and mash, and the rest of the side dishes had been taken as far into their preparation as possible, we had a little chat.

"*Allez houp*," said Vero, drying her hands on a clean dish towel after washing all the cooking dishes. She looked a little battle-scarred, and ready for a drink. I opened us a bottle of wine and poured some out. Not too much for her: Vero strikes me as the type who has half a glass of something and becomes morbid, weepy, garrulous, confessional, giggly, or all of them at once. She is both pent up and determinedly unconventional—a combination that begs to be made woozy and pliable, and I was in no mood to bring about any such thing.

"Christmas was never much fun when I was little," she announced after two sips: so she was of the garrulous and confessional variety. "We had to sing for all the relatives."

"Was Christmas really fun for anyone? Was childhood?"

She laughed, her eyes sparkling. So! A girlish crush on Hugo.

"Do you know with whom Dennis is having his extramarital affair?" I asked.

She looked startled at the change of topic but went right with it and my impeccable grammar. "No," she said avidly. "Do you?"

"Stephanie Fox," I snarled. "Your sister's purported best friend."

"Oh," Vero said, obviously shocked. "That's heinous. Are you sure? How do you know?"

"She confessed to me once that she was in love with my brother, who had already made it clear to me that he was hot on her trail. Then, recently, he started strutting around like Chanticleer on steroids."

"Chanticleer on steroids," she repeated slowly, parsing it out. "What an unpleasant image. But do you know for sure? Has he told you? Has she?"

"No one," I said, "has told me. I have a way of knowing things without being told. But you might want to mention it to your sister, or maybe not. I'll leave that entirely to your discretion; it all depends on how much trouble you feel like causing. In any case, Dennis has made it clear that he has no interest in reconciling with Marie."

"And she has made it clear to me that she will never let him move back in with her. So apparently this is all for nothing."

I raised my glass to hers. "Well, we might as well enjoy ourselves, then," I said.

The thing I am about to do, leaving my corpse for others to dispose of, struck me then and strikes me now as not the most festive, Christmassy thing to do. I've thought of drowning myself in my truck in the river, driving straight in and removing myself that way, making it look as though I had driven off in the night and vanished again . . . but this seems unnecessarily cruel in another way. People like to know what happened.

People don't like an unexplained rift in the social fabric. A dead body is at least a finite answer. And in my will I've specified that I want no fuss: I want my remains put into a plain pine box and stuck into the ground with the rest of the dead relatives, Mother included, and what was left of Dad. It is an odd way to go out, I admit; but I can't think of a better way, which is to say a way that is both more expedient for me and less unpleasant for those left behind. My only consolation is that people apparently can get over just about anything, thanks to the smoothing-over effects of forgetfulness and time.

I added, "Maybe it's better if they get divorced. Apparently children do survive such ruptures."

"According to whom?" she asked, and held out her glass for more wine.

"Good question," I said, and we laughed. It gave me an odd pleasure to laugh with someone who irked me. We worked our way through the whole bottle, and finished it just before Dennis's car, filled with the three girls, Fag Uncle Tommy, and Sonia, pulled in and discharged its cargo. They all came streaming into the kitchen, shedding coats and mufflers, talking and laughing, taking handfuls of pistachios, tangerines, crackers, olives, and figs from the bowls I'd set out.

"I'm starving," said one of the kids, probably Isabelle.

"Marie isn't here yet?" asked Dennis.

"Not yet," I said. "How was the expedition?"

They had been to the Christmas festival on the village green in Briardale, where a tree is put up and decorated every year. Every Christmas afternoon, while the church choir sing carols in their thin, shivering voices, a local Santa in the usual moth-eaten, pillow-stuffed costume hands out cheap trinkets wrapped in cheaper paper, and several mothers dispense cupcakes iced with mint-flavored red-and-white frosting or pour hot cocoa from huge thermoses into Styrofoam cups. Vivian took Dennis and me when we were small boys; our mother had always needed a nap by Christmas afternoon, and this had been a perfect way to rid herself of everyone.

"I invited our new tenant," I announced to no one in particular. "Pete Stravinsky, who's moving into the gatehouse after January first."

"Oh, that's right," said Dennis with as much irritation as he could muster at the moment. "Hugo, seriously, why did you have to do that without asking me first?"

"I lived here alone for so long," I said mildly. "I'm not in the habit of consulting anyone on anything."

"Well, next time . . . ," he said on his way out of the kitchen with a daughter's hand in each of his, which I took as grudging acceptance.

I realize I'm drawing out the events of the day and evening, when in fact I would prefer not to write a word about it, but there's no other way around it. If I'm going to get out of here, I have to purge myself of it all so it doesn't come with me, static-electrically, or however unresolved feelings accompany the dying to the afterworld, whatever the afterworld is. Of course, I don't believe in the afterworld. Still, I hope my thoughts, feelings, memories, hopes, and emotions stay behind with my mortal coil, embedded in these notebooks, soon to be buried beneath the floorboard under the armchair by the window which I've pried up and which is ready to be nailed down again once all is secured beneath it. No one will ever find them.

Marie and Louisa arrived. I heard bursts of hilarity and excitement, most of it in high childish voices, from the ballroom, where the decorated tree is. Vero and I were drifting around the kitchen in an oddly companionable silence; when she heard her sister arrive, she made a beeline for the ballroom and left me alone to smoke and stare into space and inhale the commingled Olde English fragrances of mulling wine and baking ham, mincemeat pies and figgy pudding.

Thus it was that Stephanie found me when she came drifting in about half an hour later, looking for a drink.

I couldn't help it; my heart pounded when I heard her unmistakably athletic tread coming through the passageway from the dining room. She burst into the kitchen looking like a shining and dangerous witch. She wore a red velvet dress with a shimmering gold shawl, and her hair was up in a complicated hairdo from which fetching little wispy curls had been encouraged to float freely around her head and neck in the manner of angels in Renaissance paintings. Her cheeks were flushed; her eyelids had been embossed with gold. She wore a copious amount of soft red lipstick, glittery diamond (or zirconium, of course that's what they were) earrings and bracelets, and spiky shoes perfect for putting out a man's eye or stamping a hole in his groin.

"Well, if it isn't Counselor Fox," I said through the hard knot of venomous desire in my throat.

"Hugo," she said, not meeting my eyes as she kissed my cheek (the scent of her perfume almost undid me—I had smelled it before, of course, in far more intimate circumstances). "Merry Christmas. I hear you've cooked a feast for all of us."

"The feast to end all feasts," I said, and handed her a cup of mulled wine.

"Can I have a teensy splash of something harder in this?" she asked. "It always makes it better."

"Define 'teensy.' "

"Oh, come on."

I brandished the bottle of very good brandy I keep behind the oils in the cupboard. "Like this?"

"Thanks," she said, and held the cup under her chin and inhaled the warm fumes.

I had nothing left to lose. I suspected this moment was the last chance I'd have, and I didn't want to waste it. "How have you been since I last saw you?"

"Very well," she said dreamily. "Are you coming to join us all by the tree, or do you have too much to do?"

"I'm glad to hear that," I said. "Dennis seems to be beside himself with joy lately as well. I'm glad you two have finally found your way into each other's arms. Does Marie know? I told her sister just now; I thought she'd be interested to know that Dennis's mistress is her sister's best friend."

"For God's sake, Hugo," Stephanie said sharply, her blissed-out holiday reverie abruptly gone. "Do you have to meddle in every single fucking pie that comes near your dirty finger? Is it impossible for you just to leave well enough alone?"

"I am capable of not meddling," I said. "However, this particular pie is, so to speak, right on my table. It would be difficult to ignore it. Why haven't you returned my phone calls? Hell hath no vengeful rancor like a man ignored."

"I haven't returned your one phone call," she said, "because I thought we had nothing to say to each other. I'm sorry I stood you up for dinner. That was rude; I should have called the Roadhouse. Listen, okay, Dennis and I are . . . together. Please tell Vero not to tell Marie. It would devastate her to know. And we want to wait until both our divorces are final before we tell anyone. Please, Hugo."

"Your divorce? Does Bun know about this?"

"He and I have just begun to broach the subject of our . . . fundamental incompatibility. Our irreconcilable differences. It's a delicate conversation, one I'd like to keep private and without mentioning third parties. He wants children; I don't. We've reached an amicable agreement to separate."

"I'm curious," I said. "Why didn't you meet me that night? What made you think we had nothing more to say to each other? I liked you and saw no reason to think it wasn't mutual. Granted, you owe me nothing at all. I'm just curious."

"First of all," she said crisply, pitilessly, as if she were presenting a case to a courtroom, "you lied to me about how Dennis felt about me. That alone is unforgivable. He and I have loved each other for a very long time, and you did your self-interested, sneaky, deceptive utmost to keep us apart. I don't know how I got involved with you to begin with. I guess I thought you were as close to him as I'd ever get. Second, there's the minor fact that you're committing slow and deliberate suicide. It feels unsavory, being around you, and when I'm with you I start to smoke too much too, and I cough all the next day and feel sick. Third, you have no inner life, no life of the mind—no life, period. You don't read the paper; you don't work; you have nothing going on whatsoever. And, finally, Dennis told me about the shameful treatment your wife and daughter suffered at your hands."

"What shameful treatment?" I asked. I found, to my immediate interest, that I was no longer attracted to her. I may be a fool, but I'm not an idiot. I have never been attracted to a woman who was not attracted to me. The whole point of attraction to me is that it goes both ways. Suddenly Stephanie's head seemed too big for her body, her face too wide, her nose ludicrously small. And she has a screechy voice. Not constantly screechy, just every now and then, when you're not expecting it, so it sets your teeth on edge, like chalk on a board. "What did I do to them, according to Dennis, that was shameful?"

"He told me you forced them to live apart from you all these years because of your philosophical leanings."

"So I have philosophical leanings but no life of the mind?"

She brushed this aside. "Apparently you sent your wife and infant daughter away because you decided you wanted to live a solitary life. He said your wife came back with your daughter, but you tried to stop her, and since they've come back you hardly talk to either of them."

"My wife and I have been having regular marital relations," I said with half a grin. This conversation was just so preposterous. "And I took Bellatrix to school the other day. Maybe your husband neglected to mention it."

"Bun? What does he have to do with any of this? Listen, I understand not wanting to be a parent in the first place; that's how I feel myself. But once the kid is born, don't you think you owe her anything? Dennis says you refuse to acknowledge her."

"For your information, Sonia cheated on me and then she left me, and Bellatrix is another man's daughter, not mine. Nonetheless, I've supported them all these years, and I didn't ask for a divorce when I easily could have. You're a divorce lawyer, Stephanie. What is the legal likelihood of a woman's being granted a generous amount of alimony or child support if the kid is the product of an affair and she deserts her husband? What does it tell you that I willingly gave it, and have set up a trust for this child who isn't mine? I'm leaving her everything I have and own."

"Whatever," she said, brushing these pesky facts away and returning to the main thrust of what she wanted from me. "Just please tell Vero to keep her mouth shut."

"I will," I said, "but I want something in return from you. First, admit that Dennis might have skewed the facts about me. Maybe, because he was dipping his stick where mine had been, he couldn't bone you unless he destroyed me first. Which would be very male of him."

" 'Bone me,' " she echoed with distaste. She drank deeply from her cup of hot wine and sputtered gently on the brandy. I had put a lot in there, assuming "teensy splash" had really meant "oodles."

"Oh," I said, "sorry. I boned you. Dennis makes *love* to you." She sighed.

"Do we have a deal, or not?"

"I will concede," she said, "that he could have presented the facts slightly erroneously."

"In a way calculated to make me look bad," I prompted.

"Okay," she said, and tapped her foot with bridled, fettered haste to be out of my company. "What else?"

"Two more things. An apology for toying with my affections. And I want to know, really and truly and no kidding around, whether you were telling the truth about Bun. About his proclivities. I assume you know which ones I'm talking about."

"I apologize for toying with your affections," she said bleakly, "although I had no idea you had any to be toyed with."

"That's a bit halfhearted," I said, "as was your first concession, but time is short, so that will have to do. And now I want the last thing."

"Say again what you want me to tell you?"

"Is Bun really attracted to children? Little girls? Or did you make that up to be dramatic?"

"My husband," she said softly, looking over her shoulder to make sure no one was coming into the kitchen or eavesdropping outside, "has an overwhelming instinctive urge to fondle and molest and, no doubt, if he could get away with it, fuck little girls. He can't keep himself from liking them, Hugo, but so far he hasn't done anything wrong. And he went through a lot of therapy to try to—"

"I have zero interest in that therapy," I said. "Just his natural tendencies. Thank you for the information."

The tension between us evaporated, the way it always has and does. There is nothing between us to anchor it or give it roots. This sort of instant evaporation happens either between people who have such a deep, unspoken, ancient intimacy there's no longer any point in sustaining any tension because they've been through everything together and come out the other side and know each other so well there's no need to argue any more, or between people who will never have any degree of intimacy because there is no magnetism or empathy between them to make it in any way worthwhile. Sonia and I could have been the former if she hadn't turned out to be a cold whore, and Stephanie and I are decidedly the latter. I see this now.

"Do you need anything else?" she asked with restrained good humor. The alcohol was taking effect, and she must have remembered that she and Dennis were in love and it was Christmas.

"That's all," I said with some joviality of my own, knowing that I was finished with her forever and that Dennis was welcome to her. "I'll have a word with Vero in a little while and tell her to keep your dirty little secret for now."

"How do I know she'll do what you say?"

"Because she, unlike you, has a big crush on me. Okay, you're free to go now, and I promise I won't trouble you again, not even to give an obnoxiously revealing toast at your eventual wedding to my brother."

"Oh, please, I'll never get married again," she called gaily over her shoulder, drifting out to join everyone else. "It's much too much trouble."

I took a couple more pain pills and poured myself a glass of whiskey, then made the salad. I took pains to establish a certain level of alcohol and drugs in my blood throughout the evening, so the final dose will certainly be fatal. I don't anticipate any trouble pushing my system just that much further. . . . I don't intend to wake up again. I don't intend to vomit either.

Back to my final catharsis. People came and went in the kitchen as I worked, but I wasn't alone with Vero until about half an hour later.

"It's too late," she said in a hard voice when I'd said what Stephanie had asked me to say. "I already told Marie—we took a little stroll in the evening air—and she was shocked, of course, and furious. She's restraining herself right now from ripping out that woman's eyes. Her best friend, or so she thought."

"You told her on Christmas? What the hell is wrong with you?"

"I thought she should know immediately, and she's very grateful I told her, and grateful to you for telling me so I could tell her. She said it's infinitely better for her to know now than go through this evening blind to their treachery and then, afterward, feel like a fool for thinking Stephanie was her friend. She says to tell you she appreciates your loyalty to her. She also promises not to make a scene at Christmas dinner. But when we came back in I could see the look in her eyes. . . . Marie isn't an angry person, but when she's crossed . . . I don't know how Dennis and Stephanie can be unaware of her hatred of them."

I watched her closely as she said this. Her face was open; her voice was nontheatrical and warm with feeling. Her dark French eyes flashed with sparks of wayward light. It struck me that Vero is extremely beautiful when she speaks and acts without considering the effect she's having on her listener. She should do this more often. She might find a husband if she did.

"Shit," I said plainly.

"Anyway, I came to tell you, a strange man is here. He looks like a thug."

"Shlomo," I said.

"Shlomo?"

"I mean Pete," I amended hastily. "He's our new tenant. He's renting the gatehouse indefinitely; I thought he should come and meet everyone, and it turned out he was going to be alone on Christmas. Although he's Jewish. But even Jews need somewhere to go on Christmas."

"Well, he got here a few minutes ago. He was just standing in one corner, not talking to anyone, so Louisa, good girl that she is, went over and introduced herself. Then I offered him a drink and he asked for vodka. Is there any?"

I poured some vodka into a glass and handed it to her. "Tell him I'm in here if he wants to get away from all the merriment and festivity, which I'm sure he does. Although maybe he'd rather talk to Louisa. The Jews probably prefer to stick together on this awful Christian holiday."

"Are you okay?" Vero asked suddenly, with that same warmth and ease. "You look a little pale."

"I'm fine," I said. And I was fine. The drama I'd set in motion was all set to unfold without me now. All I had to do was serve the damn food, and then I would be free to get out. All manner of shit will hit the fan after I'm gone. I'll never know what happens with Shlomo and Bun Fox, with Louisa and her future, with Dennis and Stephanie, with Marie. This is what death is. You don't get to know what happens next. It's like the ending of a novel or a play; you never get to know what happens to any of the characters after the final page or the fall of the curtain, unless the author writes a sequel, which rarely happens. With suicide, you get to choose your own ending. Natural death is messy and ignoble. It has no form, no meaning, no aesthetic satisfaction. "The remedy of the vulgar is not to think of it, but from what brutish stupidity can proceed so gross a blindness?" To anyone who drifts passively along thinking God is the author of his life and death I say, Go ahead, delude yourself, but if I were you I'd bridle the ass by the tail.

I busied myself for a while, and then Shlomo came shuffling back to get a refill.

"Merry Christmas, Pete," I said sarcastically.

"Fuck off," he said. "These people are my worst nightmare. Where's the booze?"

"I hear you met Louisa," I said.

"Fat redheaded Jewish girl who looks like half my cousins," he said dourly.

"She doesn't look like Tovah."

"No, she's gorgeous compared to Tovah." He drank the

vodka he'd poured, then poured himself some more. Shlomo had gussied himself up in honor of the goyim's Messiah's birth. He had squeezed into a shiny brown suit, and his hair was parted on the side and slicked down. "So can I speak freely?"

"No one's here but me," I said. "You see who I'm talking about, right?"

"He's hanging by a thread as we speak," said Shlomo. "I'm telling you, you'd better be sure you really want to make this deal."

"Why?"

"Don't like the look in his eye when the littlest kid goes by. Don't like that, or the tone in his voice when he talks to her."

"Isabelle," I said. "My younger niece."

"Whatever. He's asking for it."

"That's why we struck our deal," I said uneasily. I am uneasy about it still, as I write this. But I know it's the right thing to do, and I won't be around to worry about it.

"You don't look so hot," Shlomo said then. "You're pasty. And you look like if you weren't leaning against that counter you would keel over."

"Since when are you concerned about my health?"

"Since never. I'm concerned about my dinner. You sure it's gonna be edible? I sucked in my gut to get into this goddamn monkey suit and drove all this way in a car with a busted heater, and I don't want to eat burned crap."

"You will not," I said grandly, "be served anything resembling burned crap."

"Well, that's a big relief," he said. "I assume I'm officially on the job now, so I'm going to spend this evening making nice with all the yawns and meanwhile watching like a fuckin' hawk about to take out the rat. As for my alcoholic intake while engaged in my contracted assignment, if you know me at all you know that's not an impediment, it's an occupational requirement."

"Drink all you want," I said.

"I don't need any fuckin' permission," said Shlomo, and off he went to keep an eye on Bun.

I assume Stephanie won't need to trouble herself about the divorce, but I will never know for sure.

Then I began to chop some things, and sauté some others. While handfuls of minced garlic and shallots sautéed in butter, I chopped a rib or two of celery and added those and then some sliced mushrooms and minced fresh rosemary. . . . The smell was pleasant and homey, and I felt completely at ease. My mind is always empty when I cook. The world shrinks down to just my hands, whatever I've got before me, and the pots and pans and spoons and fire and water and whatever other tools I need to bring about the alchemical process that turns base ingredients into a proper dish. Any interaction between me and food invariably gives me as much ease—which is to say, happiness—as I've ever felt. I realized, making this final meal, that all my life I have preferred cooking and eating to almost everything else. Well, smoking. But I don't love smoking, I'm obsessed with it. There's a difference, but I don't know what it is. And maybe I'd rather fuck than cook—the two are inextricably linked. I don't know which I prefer. I prefer to fuck, then cook and eat, then fuck again, then cook and eat again, drinking all the while. Smoking all the while.

I made far too much food for this dinner. And there were far too many components and courses. Cooking for these people on this day was an act of aggression, I suppose. After sending out a plate of several good cheeses, shrimp cocktail, and French bread to the ballroom via Vero, I made a very simple but palatable fresh puréed pea soup, in each bowl of which I floated a dollop of crème fraîche and a sprinkling of fresh thyme. After the soup bowls had been cleared away came the onslaught: ham with dried cherry-and-stout holiday sauce; the little hens filled with Mary Frances Kennedy Fisher's Oyster

Stuffing (plenty of oysters mixed with bread crumbs lightly fried in butter, oyster juice, salt, pepper, celery, salt, and paprika); potatoes mashed with sour cream and garlic; gravy made of half game-hen pan drippings, half instant Durkee packets; butternut squash puréed and mixed with the sautéed minced shallots, celery, mushrooms, rosemary, and pancetta (a dish that never fails to bring me as close to vegetable nirvana as I have ever been); baked yams bursting from their jackets and leaking caramelized sugar; stalwart, neat rows of green beans drenched with lemon juice and butter. After all the diners seemed to have stuffed themselves enough with all this bounty, I bustled out carrying an elegant, faintly snooty winter salad of butter lettuce and endive with sections of oranges, roasted walnut halves, and a simple vinaigrette; and then, when all were groaning and holding their bellies and leaning back looking stunned, I brought forth the pies—filled with the mincemeat I had put up a month ago, baked in the surprisingly expert pie shells I'd inexplicably trusted Vero to make—and the spicy, delectable figgy pudding with hard sauce. A full selection of wines, Calvados, and brandy. Coffee with whipped cream.

I served the desserts to much protest and went back to the kitchen to begin washing the dishes. Vero and Marie tried to help me, but I shooed them away and they went.

All through the afternoon and evening, I had kept away from everyone, staying in the kitchen spinning my web, sending tendrils of tension and drama out into the assembled company like some culinary backstage Loki, the marplot cook. The sound of their voices had wafted to me faintly in the kitchen; in them I imagined I heard anger, disappointment, betrayal, suspicion, passion, lust, all the great products of the human heart, soul, and mind. It seemed fitting that I stay apart all day and night from these gusts of feeling, even as I did my utmost to influence them from my outpost—I had no further business with any of them. I felt I had already said goodbye to them all, except Dennis, but I have no way of saying goodbye to my older brother. There is no resolution or appropriate parting gesture. I can only take my leave knowing he'll never know why I took my leave.

When the dishes were clean, dried, and put away, I poured myself another whiskey and went to sit at the table with everyone for a little while before coming up here . . . a farewell to all these people who've been my companions these past months, and as such have come to matter to me in varying degrees. I can't pretend otherwise.

The table was festooned with pine boughs and red candles and bowls of nuts in their shells and tangerines. Dennis had spiked the chandelier with candles and lit them and built a fire in the enormous stone fireplace; the room was ablaze with firelight, and everyone's eyes shone, reflecting the points of flame. Firelight is flattering to the human face and form: the assembled company gave the impression of being uncommonly attractive, even with Shlomo skulking at the far end of the table and Bun's mole all lit up.

I sat at the table and looked around at them all with a sense of distant curiosity. Sonia presided as hostess, preening and darkly glowing, at the foot of the table, wearing a low-cut yellow dress that flaunted her sculpted clavicle and tiny neck, her blond hair combed straight and shining; Dennis sat at the head, looking like a blockhead in his good suit, too handsome for his own good; at his right was Evie, looking like a smaller female version of her father in an embroidered brown velvet dress, her hair in prim braids. On Sonia's right sat Fag Uncle Tommy in one of his silk cravats, his hair plastered to his skull, clearly besotted with her, the way an old homo is wont to be strickenly enamored of a much younger woman who is obviously out of her mind and nothing but trouble, the kind of woman from whom any sane, eligible straight man would run away with his hands over his ears. I noted approvingly that Bellatrix was seated safely between Louisa and Shlomo, although no one had been able to prevent Bun from wedging himself in next to Isabelle. On Isabelle's other side was Marie, molten with hot righteous anger, in a black velvet dress and the ruby necklace that belonged to Dennis's and my grandmother. I wonder—after Dennis divorces her, will she have to give back our family jewels? That will be a dilemma for him: family tradition and history versus gentlemanly good grace. But none of it mattered. Sitting between Vero and Marie, I felt vaguely detached from them and from everyone else, as if I were already gone. People spoke to me and I to them, Vero sent remarks my way, and Marie smiled at me, but I was encased in a shell, the knowledge that in a few hours I would cease to be.

It's almost time. . . .

"I'd like to propose a toast," said my brother suddenly, standing up and hoisting his wineglass aloft, "to Hugo, for your hospitality, your generosity, and your culinary talents. I know this house is technically as much mine as it is yours, but it's been yours for many years, and only recently mine again. I thank you for welcoming me back to the family homestead. It's been by far the hardest season of my life. I don't know what I would have done if I hadn't had my brother to help me through."

He stopped for a moment and considered what to say next, his glass still in the air. He swayed slightly, and his expression was ponderously grave. He was drunk, I realized then. Well, I'd be drunk too in his shoes, with my suicidal brother and his evil wife and her illegitimate daughter, my furious soon-to-be-ex-wife and her furious sister and our tender, vulnerable daughters, and my new mistress, also my wife's best friend, and her husband, also my best friend, not to mention a hit man, an au-pair girl, and my old homo uncle, all at the same table. Dennis is so entrenched in his complicated and messy life, I could easily imagine how much he needed to be drunk tonight.

"They say," he went on after his moment of thoughtful swaying silence, "home is the place where they can't turn you away, and family is whoever has to take you in. This, then, is my true home, and, Hugo, you're my family. I know our course isn't smooth and never has been, but in my experience, nothing that matters is easy. The relationships that have been the rockiest for me are the ones I treasure most deeply. Here's to you, little brother."

He held his glass up and looked earnestly at me for a moment of general stunned silence. Then Fag Uncle Tommy coughed and said, "Hear, hear," and glasses began clinking up and down the table. What did he mean by all that? I wondered to myself as I smirked and nodded and behaved as appropriately to the occasion as I knew how—which is to say, with as much sincerity as I could muster. Marie was staring at Dennis with a stricken look, I noticed, and Stephanie was looking at the table. Shlomo looked disgusted; Bellatrix was surreptitiously picking her nose.

As if to break the suddenly solemn mood, Bellatrix was prevailed upon, first by Sonia and then by the rest of us, to fetch her violin. With matter-of-fact acquiescence, as if she understood why we would all want to hear her play and accepted that this was her part in the proceedings, she got it out, tuned up, and then, with scarcely a segue between tuning and playing, swept into an unaccompanied Bach cello suite transposed for violin. She played it more fluidly, with more subtlety and range and understanding, than I have ever heard her play anything before. Is it possible that she's a prodigy, a genius? Her violin almost spoke the music, in a clear, supple, restrained, and preternaturally confident voice. After the last note, she lifted the bow from the strings, acknowledged the enthusiastic applause without shyness or apparent vanity, laid her instrument back in its case, and turned back into a fairly ordinary and not especially pretty child.

When the time came for the children to go to bed, Bellatrix followed her "cousins" around the table, kissing everyone good night. As she planted her lips as far from Bun's mole as she could manage, Shlomo glowered and Louisa looked pained. I have done what I can to protect her. I have to believe that she's in good hands. When she came to me, I roused myself and looked her squarely in the eye. She looked back at me with a puzzled expression, most likely because I looked so awful and she couldn't imagine why.

"Sleep well," I said jocularly as she kissed my cheek. "Don't bite the bedbugs."

"Ew," she said, and off she went to kiss Vero, who was next to me.

Our final exchange. I can't help wondering a little what she'll think and feel when she learns I'm dead. I wonder even more whether Sonia will ever tell her who her real father is. I hope, once I'm out of the way, Sonia will feel called upon to drag the offending cheese onstage. I wonder whether he is Carla's uncle. I once hoped so, in my Loki way. Now, for Bellatrix's sake, as sincerely as I can feel anything, I hope her father is someone whom she can love and who will love her.

She'll miss me a little, I suppose, at least at first.

I'm sorry I'll never hear her play again. That, and I'm sorry I'll never smoke another cigarette, cook another meal, eat another meal, fuck another woman. Those are the things I'll miss the most. I'll never go out on the iceboat with Carla. I'll never go back to Gotham City and find it all as it was before, in that shining era of high spirits.

I won't miss this wrecked body with its pain.

All right, there's nothing more to write and nothing more to do. It's time for the Last Cigarette, the one Zeno smoked over and over all his life, but mine really is.

For the last time, I just touched a match to a cigarette. When I've smoked it, I'll end all this. Meanwhile, instead of rhapsodizing tediously about the grand obsession of my life, I'll write out Montaigne's hermit-tower words as a final prayer of sorts—secular last rites:

> *The plague of man is the opinion of knowledge.*
> *I establish nothing. I do not understand. I halt. I examine.*
> *Breath fills a goatskin as opinion fills a hollow head.*
> *Not more this than that—why this and not that? Have you*
> *seen a man that believes himself wise? Hope that he is a fool.*
> *Man, a vase of clay.*
> *I am human, let nothing human be foreign to me.*
> *What inanity is everything!*

Let nothing human be foreign to me. What inanity is everything! And out I go.

Montaigne

FOURTH NOTEBOOK

February 24, 2002—Here I am in the afterlife. It's a place with large windows; outside, a lot of bare trees and a late-winter sky that's usually bleak and lowering; inside, institutional furniture, an efficient staff, and inedible food. The walls are pale beige. The air has a fine, rich, unpleasant moistness and reeks of others' psyches turned inside out, the past exhumed, the stench of rotten pain. I've lost a foot. I no longer smoke, at least not for now. No smoking was allowed in the medical hospital, naturally, and I was there for a while, having my foot amputated, recovering from my addiction to hillbilly heroin. . . . No smoking is allowed here either. It seems I quit cold turkey, involuntarily.

I'm not in pain any more, except for the occasional phantom twitch in the place where my missing foot used to be. They've got me on some sort of meds—antidepressants, I guess they're called—I try not to dwell on the insidious changes they're wreaking in my brain.

Also, it turns out, I'm not dead. The night I tried to kill myself, I've since learned from Dennis himself, my brother went rooting through the hallways and stairwells like a truffle pig until he whiffed the unmistakable black, glossy odor of my imminent end. He "raced" up to my room, where he "unhesitatingly" saved me by dragging me downstairs by the armpits, flinging me into the back seat of the Dart, then racing along small twisty back roads to the hospital "at top speed." He was drunk that night; this could easily have killed us both, but unfortunately it didn't. He "hauled" me into the emergency room, where, as my stomach was pumped and I was hooked up to tubes and monitors and an IV and it was determined that I would live, albeit possibly as a brain-damaged vegetable, he "refused to leave my bedside."

I came out of my coma in the middle of the cold empty white week between Christmas and New Year's to find myself blinking up at the glare of lights, the hovering faces of a nurse and my brother, a white ceiling.

Immediately I was aware of the trouble so many people had gone to, to bring me back to this life I didn't want. . . . It put me in a sheepish, dazed funk that hasn't abated yet and shows no sign of doing so.

According to Dennis, I'd "practically begged him" to "save" me. I had sent out "distress signals" all fall, left my notebooks "lying around" for Sonia to find; he "had a feeling" on Christmas night, he said, that I would "pull something like that." He said a lot of other things as well, but at first I couldn't listen to them, because I wanted to throttle him for dragging me back from wherever I was headed.

Maybe writing again is a bad idea. Once again, my hand is rusty with the pen. . . .

When I had recuperated enough to leave the medical hospital, out of his "grave concern" for me, my brother committed me to the ivy-covered college-campus–like grounds of Jernigan Memorial Psychiatric Hospital, where I have spent the past weeks cooling my one remaining heel in individual therapy, group therapy, physical therapy, and art therapy. These are all dubious and unpleasant pastimes, but it's the last of them that galls me most. Art therapy . . . I shudder to think that anyone might be observing me in there. My old self, maybe, watching through the windows, as Reborn Hugo makes a watercolor depiction of the inside of his head, because if I ever hope to get out of here I've got to convince them I'm "cured." Which is to say, no longer suicidal.

It also turns out that I do know what happened after I "killed myself." Bun is still alive. Why, I don't know. Shlomo isn't living in the gatehouse. Why, I don't know either. Stephanie hasn't left Bun: another mystery. Bellatrix was told only that I got sick and am in the hospital. She and Sonia have gone back to their place in New York. Apparently, commuting to and from Bellatrix's violin lessons in the city became too much of a haul without me at Waverley to provide the necessary reason for staying there. Also, I'm sure the Waverley ghosts were making them nervous.

Vero, to my further mystification, has come on the past three Saturday afternoons in a row from Brooklyn to visit me. Possibly because she'd come all this way and here we were so we might as well talk instead of sitting in silence for the minimum duration of a visit, we found that we had some things to say to each other. We sat on the sun porch, she in her silly Edwardian outfit, I in my customary garb (thanks to Dennis, who brought me my own clothes at my insistence). We passed a not entirely unpleasant afternoon discussing Montaigne and Villon, then other writers and books, then what we think about this and that. On the whole, Vero has more opinions than I have. Since she is a professor, some of these are unnecessarily abstract and analytical, but when I point this out, she laughs at both of us. She threatened to visit me again if I stay here long enough, so we can exchange more opinions. I agreed that she could come if she wanted, and I meant it.

It makes no sense. But there it is. I have no idea why, but I am beginning to tolerate her.

Dennis isn't sure any more whether or not he wants a divorce from Marie, although she's told him there's no way she wants to reconcile after he had an affair with her best friend. I'd bet my foot she takes him back within a month.

This is the only thing I've learned since I "came back" that makes any sense at all to me. It seems I understand very little of anything. It might be the drugs they've got me on. My mind has been foggy and hazy for a while; I'm writing here again only because I hope it might provide some clarity and focus.

February 25—Shortly after I returned to consciousness, I read aloud to Dennis the entirety of Montaigne's "Isle of Cea" from my hospital bed, a lengthy essay that extols the beauty and virtue of suicide. Having brought the book at my request, he listened without complaint or interjection. However, the following passage, at the very beginning, evoked a defensive sigh from him which caused a long interruption, possibly because I read it in an extra-loud and very clear voice, emphasizing almost every word, so he would be sure to get the idea:

"Death can be found everywhere. It is a great favor from God that no man can wrest death from you, though he can take your life; a thousand open roads lead to it."

When he sighed, I stopped and fixed him with a look.

"A great favor from God," I repeated in a steely tone. "You denied me that. How could you do that to me?"

"How could you do that to me?" he asked back in a wet-eyed tone of his own.

"I did nothing to you," I said. "I did it to myself."

"Didn't you imagine it would have an effect on me?" he asked. "You're the only brother I have."

"Why is it so important to have a brother?"

"You're my link to the past. You're part of me."

"I've never been anything but a thumbtack-sticking irritant to you. I would think you'd be nothing but relieved and grateful to be rid of me. But even if you secretly were, it's all too typical of you to drag me against my will back from the edge of where I wanted to go and tell yourself you did the right thing. You tried to get me sent to military school once too. I got away that time—well, I was younger and more agile then."

"That time," he agreed, "you got away and we couldn't find you. This time, I did what I should have done then. I brought you back."

"Dennis," I said wearily, "you have no idea about anything."

"I would say the same to you," he said with a glint of anger.

There ensued a silence during which, because I had nothing else to do, I searched what was left of my soul. Was I relieved, at all, to be alive? Was I grateful, at all, to Dennis?

In fact, no, I wasn't. I see no great advantage in being alive. I meant to die. My carefully laid plan was tampered with. Here I am with my eyes once more open, my brain still ticking. What is the use? Life is arguably not preferable to death. And no one should try to prevent another person from quitting the game. It's not cricket, as they used to say.

However, Dennis thought otherwise, and his will prevailed over mine, if only because at the time he was conscious and I was not, and therefore he was able to enforce it on me without my being able to fight back.

"Dennis," I said then.

He gave a start. He had been woolgathering too. What his own comb held I'll never know; there are still a few things in this world to be glad about.

"Tell me something," I said. "Why exactly is Stephanie still with Bun Fox and not with you, as advertised?"

Dennis winced; I had struck a nerve. "This is the pathological, destructive pattern of their marriage. She hates him, then she loves him, then she hates him again. I can't keep up, and I certainly had no idea how truly and irrevocably she was committed to him when I embarked on my ill-advised affair with her."

"Do they ever have sex?" I asked.

"Hugo!" he said.

"I doubt they ever do," I said. "Did you know that Bun is a child molester?"

"What?" He stared at me.

"You heard me."

"Who told you that?"

"Stephanie told me she found kiddie porn under his side of the bed. He was Marie's client because he wanted to stop being a pedophile; she 'helped' him 'get over it,' but I don't buy it. He's apparently trying hard not to molest anyone, but he'll cave; it's only a matter of time."

"Stephanie was making that up," said Dennis, laughing a little in shock and disbelief. "She was having you on. There's no way in the world that could be true. Bun? No way."

"I saw frustrated desire in his eyes when I thwarted his plan to pick up Bellatrix from school and fondle her in the woods somewhere. Don't leave him alone with your daughters. Guard them with your life."

"Bun is my friend," he sputtered. "And you're . . ."

"Nuts?" I proffered helpfully. "And Bun is your friend, is he? The friend whose wife you fucked."

"That was a mistake."

And so forth, predictably.

He still doesn't believe me, but I've planted the seed.

I finished reading the essay, and he listened, and that was all in the way of recrimination and discussion the two of us will have.

February 26—Instead of relinquishing the parallel burdens of consciousness and corporeality, as I had intended, I am now required to sit in a circle with the other nut jobs every morning after breakfast and subject myself to a tormenting proximity to the pain and suffering of others; as for my own, I'm not much for earnest sharing.

Then I'm required to dip my paintbrush into paint and smear it meaningfully around the paper.

Then it's time I go to see Lance, the thick-necked homo of a physical therapist, to learn how to walk again. This is in its way as humiliating and unpleasant as all my other therapies. I'm currently engaged in an awkward and mutually hostile getting-to-know-you dance with the prosthetic foot they've made me, "they" being unseen and unknown craftsmen far away.

Then comes another sort of dance, my daily verbal gavotte with the formidable, intelligent, sixty-year-old Dr. Emma Jameson, who has trotted around many a dance floor in her day. Seemingly without any idea of what I'm up to, she will lazily and playfully spar with me for a while; then, without warning, she snaps to attention like a lioness I mistakenly thought was asleep in the sun on the quiet savanna and pounces: "Why do you suppose you made that joke, Hugo?"

Apparently I make deflecting "humorous" remarks because I'm afraid of intimacy.

Well, chuh, I want to say.

"Afraid" isn't really the right word, but the subject of my

emotions makes me want to put my head down and go to sleep; I'd prefer to stick to the facts here in this notebook, since apparently I'm not allowed to in my various therapies.

Lately, in these past weeks, poems have been coursing out of me. What this means, I don't care. Whether or not they're any good, I care even less.

Like my notebooks, it's a necessary bloodletting, no more or less.

February 27—Of all the possible disagreeable topics we could have covered, I was encouraged today by Dr. Jameson to discuss my mother. Actually, she once again brought up the fact that I often try to distract her with antics and wisecracks instead of "doing our work," and announced that we were going to explore the reasons for that directly instead of skirting around it, as we'd been doing till then. This led right to my mother, but through no fault of mine; I'm fairly certain Dr. Jameson forced it there. I resisted any discussion of how any attempt of mine to deflect the therapeutic endeavor could possibly relate to Mig, but the good doctor, assuming she is good, would have none of it.

"It might be fruitful for us to explore this, Hugo," she said with the diverting gentleness of a farmer coaxing a cow up the ramp to the guillotine. "Every time we start to get close to your feelings about your mother, you shut down. I'd like to try to get past your defenses and see what's there. Why don't you start by telling me a few things you remember about her."

She leaned forward and peered at me through her bifocals, her full, shapely mouth interrogatory and half amused, her salon-cut shoulder-length gray hair falling just so around her heart-shaped face. She is a very appealing woman, Emma Jameson. If I weren't so wary of her motives, I would make a play for her. But any attempt to flirt with her would only result in a lengthy, utterly uninteresting examination of my feelings toward women in general and my mother in particular, resistance to therapy, and my dissociation from my own feelings. How do I know this? Because I've already tried.

"What is the point," I blustered, "of regurgitating the past? Are you aware of human-interest statistics that suggest that Holocaust survivors who forget the traumas they've suffered are on the whole better adjusted than those who remember? This calls into question the entire premise of so-called talk therapy. Why bring it all up again? I would vastly prefer to forget my entire childhood."

She regarded me with skeptical equilibrium. "Well, for you, this seems to be something of a life-or-death question. You didn't move on and get over it, Hugo. You killed yourself."

"I tried to kill myself," I corrected her. "I would have been perfectly content to have stayed dead."

"Well, you're not dead," she countered reasonably. She double-wrapped one long, thin, black-tight-clad leg around the other in that way only the slenderest women can sit. "Why don't you close your eyes and tell me about your mother," she prompted with steely gentleness.

I sighed and fussed at nothing for a while like an old codger. Damned if I was going to close my eyes. Damned if I was going to blather on and on about Mig's horrible personality.

"There's quite a bit of time left in the session," Jameson pointed out helpfully.

I sucked my gums and jigged my knee up and down and cast trapped glances out the window and at the door. She watched me, bright-eyed, waiting, nobody's fool.

Finally, in a voice that conveyed the strong opinion that this was all very boring for me and she wasn't getting anywhere and we were both wasting our time here, I recited my all-too-familiar laundry list: the barely edible food, the massages I had to give, the migraines and breakdowns and screaming fits, the underwear stains, the crackpot spiritual theories, the time Dennis was so sick and almost died, Vivian's rough ministrations and attempts to care for us boys, how my mother went completely cuckoo after my father died . . .

. . . and what do you know, at the mention of my father's death I was suddenly racked with sobs, me, a grown man. I was blindsided by grief. I can't explain how or why this happened. It must be the lack of booze in this bughouse, it would make anyone cry.

"Boohoo," I blubbered. "Boohoo hoo hoo."

"You were very little when he died," she prompted. "You loved him very much."

I tried to ask her why the bejeezus she felt compelled to point this out; it seemed to me she was trying to make me feel even worse. But I couldn't get the words out.

"I think you're still mourning him, even after all these years," she went on in that diabolically compassionate voice. "You've never let yourself fully grieve for your father. You never really got to know him. You were deprived of the parent you trusted, and left alone with the one who abused you. That must have been so devastating for such a little boy."

I said as forcefully as I could, "But now I'm a grown man, and my parents are finished and over and gone forever; I would happily have joined them in oblivion. The least I can do is let them lie in peace. That's the kindest thing anyone could do for anyone else."

She handed me a Kleenex. "Why is that?" she said. She looked kindly and nonjudgmental, but I saw right through it.

"I'd much rather talk about when I'm going to be sprung out of this hellhole. That, to me, is far more germane."

"They're not leaving you in peace," she said, ignoring this last comment. "That's the crux of the matter, isn't it?"

"The crux of the matter is that no one leaves me in peace,"

I said. "Hey! Dr. Jameson, I have a swell idea! Let's talk about *your* parents for a while. Was your mother warmly self-effacing and mercifully kind? Did your father help you with your algebra and pat you on your head with a kindly twinkle? Did your brothers and sisters flock admiringly round you as you descended toward your date, radiant in your prom dress? I would guess no, no, and no. I can't imagine that anyone else had it any better than I did. Human nature being what it is. Parents being what they are. And my unseemly display of emotion back there is not going to be repeated. I won't be reduced to a large baby by the power of the past. The past only has power if you plug it in, like anything else."

"That's exactly the point. You've tried so hard to avoid being plugged in because of the power the past has."

"I fail to see how this conversation helps either one of us," I said, "unless you've got some issues you'd like to explore here."

Then, of course, it was necessary for us to talk a while longer about why I felt the need to deflect and resist this subject of my mother's "physical and emotional appropriation" of me, my father's "tragic early" death. I did my utmost to continue to deflect this inquiry into my deflections, if only because it's my nature to do so, and Dr. Jameson persisted in trying to "plug me in" (a phrase I now wish I had never introduced into the proceedings; I know it will become her mantra), if only because it's her job to do so, and then our time was up.

As I was about to swing my one-foot-and-a-crutch way out of there, she said out of nowhere, "Hugo, I'm very proud of you. You worked hard today. I didn't think we'd get this far so early in our work together."

"This is early?" I said. "How much longer is this going to go on?"

"Well, that's up to you," she said. "If you keep this up you'll be out of here before too long."

"Keep what up? Blubbering and carrying on?"

"It's a start," she said.

Dennis came in the afternoon. He brought gifts: a box of blood oranges, since fresh fruit is one of the few pleasures permitted me at the moment. He also brought, with typical didacticism, a few current popular-news and highbrow-culture magazines; he evidently hopes I'll acquaint myself with whatever has happened in the world since I "died." I will do no such thing, because I do not care.

And he also brought, to my surprise, Sonia and Bellatrix.

He sent them to explore the grounds first so he and I could have a little chat.

"So," he said, settling himself cozily into the couch next to me where I was reading the big fat glitzy for-women-only bestseller I found on the hospital shelves and have become oddly, nauseatingly engrossed in, "I hope you don't mind I brought them without checking with you first. Sonia called and said she wanted to come with me, and I thought maybe you'd object, and so I just brought them. She said she has something important to tell you."

"What you mean to say is, in your customary fashion, you took it upon yourself to do what you thought would be best for me rather than what you absolutely knew I wanted."

"That's right, Hugo. What you want is usually bad for you. The day I stop trying to save you from yourself is the day I stop being your brother."

"I'm not holding my breath," I said grimly. "I see the kid brought her violin."

"I brought you a letter too," he said. "I was tempted to open it and read it, but I didn't."

"Gee whillikers," I said, "you are a busybody. A letter from whom, pray tell?"

"The guy who came to Christmas dinner, Pete something."

"Stravinsky," I said, suddenly alight with curiosity. "After the composer, no doubt. Why did he move out? Where is he?"

"Search me," said Dennis. "He never moved in."

"Hand it over."

"Listen," he said, giving me Shlomo's letter (a nice thick envelope—it gave me a chill even as it filled me with interest; this is the effect old Shlomo seems to have), "I sent Sonia and Bellatrix off for a little while, because I want to talk to you first about what you plan to do when you leave here. They say you're getting better. In fact, they're all impressed with your progress. Apparently you're extremely cooperative and working very hard in all your therapies."

"Why are they telling you that?" I asked. "I try to thwart them at every turn."

"I wasn't sure they had the right Hugo Whittier, quite frankly. I had to ask if there was more than one. They said no, so all I can think is that you must be fooling them."

"Sure," I said. "So when are they going to spring me?"

"I don't know," he said. "But they advise me that you should have a plan for when you leave, and they encouraged me to discuss this with you. Do you want to go back to Waverley? I'm not sure it's such a good idea, but Uncle Tom would be thrilled. I'm not going to be there forever, because my wife still loves me, she just has to come to her senses and realize it and forgive me . . . and when I leave, he'll be all alone. He misses Sonia, by the way. I think he's got a crush."

"God save us," I said. "Sonia actually flipped an old homo with her black-voodoo trickery. Frankly, I don't know what I'm going to do when I get out of here. I have an idea that I'll take up smoking and living alone in happy idleness right where I left off, and this time no one can stop me."

"I don't believe you," he said neutrally.

"Why not?"

"I don't think you'll take up where you left off," he repeated stubbornly.

"Dennis," I said impatiently, "I know you have an unshakable opinion concerning what I should do—you've never been reticent about spewing your advice any chance you get. Come on. Spit it out, you'll feel ever so much better."

"What about going back to the city?" he said promptly, enthusiastically, without taking a breath. "What about getting a place down there? I think that's what you ought to do, go live in New York and meet people, make a life for yourself. You said you used to be a writer. Maybe get back on that bicycle."

"Empire City," I said in a 1940s movie-actress accent. "The glittering metropole. The honk and bustle of it all. Taxicabs and lumbering buses, hot-dog vendors, messengers mowing me down with their bikes, young women in their summer dresses, young men with their haircuts. Well."

"You asked," he said, nettled, "just so you could mock me."

"I never miss a chance," I said. "Is the river still frozen?"

"It hardly froze at all this year," he said concernedly, probably because he was remembering I'd been unconscious, then foggy-brained, then sequestered behind thick walls for most of the winter. "Brother mine."

"I have an iceboat date with a certain cashier," I said. "And I won my bet with Stephanie; I could collect on that if I really wanted to press my luck, which I'm fairly sure I don't."

"What bet with Stephanie?" he asked with a spark of his old post–Atlantic-City jealousy.

"She bet I wouldn't have the nerve to go through with my death. I won the bet, it seems to me. And against my will, it also seems I'm here to collect on it after all. That's the one upside to being dragged back—I was right and she was wrong. She'll think she has to pay up, because, whatever else she may be, she's no welsher, she's too conceitedly stuck-up to go back on her word. A sail on the iceboat with Carla, a phone call to Counselor Fox with the idle threat of a dinner with me, her treat, so I can listen to her squirm: these are my plans for the future. Shall we join the ladies?"

We went out to find Sonia and Bellatrix and came across them on the glassed-in sun porch talking to one of the crazies from my group therapy.

The four of us strolled off toward a secluded wicker table.

"That lady is weird," Bellatrix whispered up at me as she slipped her hand into mine. I looked down at her. What made her think she was free to express opinions about my fellow inmates? And what gave her the idea that she was welcome to hold my hand with this childish proprietary ease?

"What are you laughing at?" she asked.

"Do you think she's weirder than I am?"

She made a face that expressed a mixture of humor, impatience, and instinctive understanding of what my question meant. She will be an interesting adolescent, I imagine, much too quick for her own good, and consequently a bit of a pain in the ass.

"Now," said Sonia, "it is my turn to talk alone with Hugo. Run along, go and get some tea and cake and bring it back, and we'll have a little party."

"Well, Sonia," I said. "You're looking plump and secretive. I've never seen you this way before. Did my thwarted demise cause you to go on an eating binge?"

She rolled her eyes. "I'm pregnant," she said smugly, triumphantly, "and this time it is yours."

I was rocked back on my heel by this, I confess. I had nothing to say. Literally. My mouth opened and closed. I sucked in some air, but still no words came.

"Oh," I said finally, enraged, blood hot and red behind my eyes. "No wonder you're fatter."

"That's right," she said. "With a little Hugo."

"Or Huguette?" I said nastily.

"Or Huguette."

"Is that why you came back to Waverley? To get implanted with my seed for real this time?"

"No," she said, "but now that it's coming, I want another baby, to give Bella a brother or sister. She is so happy that we will be a larger family. I am here to tell you that you can come and live with us if you would like to."

"I wouldn't like to," I said. "You pulled the oldest trick in the book, Sonia. You tried to trap me."

"How can I trap you if we're already married?" she said. "I didn't plan this, I swear to you, Hugo, I would never try to trick you that way. This is our child, Hugo, about to come into the world, the product of the great love I have for you."

"Anyway, you rank piece of cheesecloth, I want a divorce."

"A divorce?" she repeated, scandalized.

"That's right. That's the deal. Hire Louisa to help you when the brat is born if she's available, or someone else. I never asked for this kid. You're on your own with it. When it's of legal drinking age and can hold its liquor properly, I'll take it on father-child bar outings and we'll get drunk and badmouth you. I won't live with you ever again, Sonia, you drive me mad. Look how mad I went when you came back to Waverley."

"You can't pin that on me," she said. "You were mad always, ever since I met you, and you're mad still, and always will be."

"I assume you haven't introduced Bellatrix to her real father, although you promised me you would," I said.

"I never promised, because I don't know where he is," she confessed reluctantly. "I don't even remember his last name."

"One-night shebang?"

She twisted her mouth and didn't answer.

We talked about this divorce for a while longer. She pretends to be violently opposed to the idea because of some wholly fictional love she claims still to bear for me, but she'll come around, if only because she has no choice. My rage slowly abated until I had returned to my usual simmering mistrust of her. Pregnant or not, she's still a treacherous snake, but unless I'm deluding myself, I know most of her moves by now.

Later on in the visit, Bellatrix played the same Bach suite, at my request, that she'd played after Christmas dinner. . . . While she played I peeled and ate a blood orange. The combination of fruit and music did more than anything else has in a long time to lessen the vise around my head, this maddening life, my ensnarement in this web of people. Dennis, Sonia, Bellatrix, the coming descendant, whoever it may be. What sort of father can I hope to be? I have nothing to offer, paternity-wise, except money. And I can't imagine that any aspect of having Sonia for a mother will offset whatever genetic flaws it inherits from me, except that it will toughen the kid up. Maybe it will make it into adulthood without having to know me too well, and without having to become too much like its mother. I managed to accomplish that much, at least; and so maybe even my poor doomed sod of a kid can too.

My "family" drove off, and I opened Shlomo's letter. It was much shorter than the thickness of the envelope had led me to believe, because he had written it on a slab of thick paper of the sort used to line silverware drawers, probably the only paper he could find when he was moved to write to me. "Dear Hugo," it began, "Surprised I know how to write? I know you're in the nuthouse but I won't embarrass you by sending this there, I'll send it to your house and hope your dickweed brother remembers to bring it next time. Listen fuckface, that gatehouse smelled like cat piss, I couldn't live there, I'm allergic, plus when I heard you tried to off yourself and your dickweed brother saved you I figured the deal was off. I know that scumbag's a child molester, I saw it a mile away, but you don't strike me as the type who can live with the kind of guilt you're gonna feel, being so sensitive and all. What you should really feel guilt for is going against G—d's will. Suicide is just wrong, but I got no time now to quibble on that. Anyway, it's your call, 'boss,' I consider myself on retainer or whatever. Plus I'm back at Rochelle's, so I can always use a distraction. Me and her are shacking up these days, surprise, surprise, I could only hold out against that horny old wildcat for so long. Whatever, don't do me any favors or nothing cause I've got plenty of company, but if they ever let you out of there and you get lonely, you know where to find me. Don't let those voodoo doctors brainwash you. Your pal, Shlomo Levy. p.s. I'm keeping the dough no matter what. You owe me for letting you off all those years ago. You're a rich boy, you can afford it. And you still owe me a drink from that other night a while back. You stiffed me, you didn't think I noticed. p.p.s. When the dough is gone, so's the retainer deal, so think fast."

February 28—Early morning. Woke up and reached for this notebook. Almost reached for my cigarettes until I realized I don't have any at the moment. Peeled one of the blood oranges instead—such an effete and sober substitute, but as long as I'm here it's the best I can come up with besides solitaire, another pathetic old-man solace, soon to be exchanged for something a little spicier and less wholesome, I hope; and if not cigarettes, then what? I have no interest in gambling, booze only gets me so far, and all the harder stuff is more suited for those who are younger and less run-down at the heel than I am.

Well, there's always writing. I hate writing, of course, but can't seem to stop myself from doing it. So I sit, in the quiet hour before breakfast in bedlam, eating my pansy-assed orange and writing whatever comes to mind. Which happens, today, to be nothing at all. Nothing . . . But words will come out of my pen if I hold it over the paper; if I sit here and let the pen do the walking, it walks, and talks. I may write nothing but gibberish for the rest of my life, but if I appear to be busily scribbling away, people might have the tact and courtesy to leave me alone, which goes some way toward solving the conundrum. But of course they won't leave me alone. Here I am again, hounded by the presence of others. And there seems to be some sort of a future in store for me, however long or short it may be. Against all odds, I find I'm curious about this afterlife, whatever time I've been forced against my will to live out. I wonder what will happen next.